The Best
AMERICAN
ESSAYS
2012

GUEST EDITORS OF
THE BEST AMERICAN ESSAYS

1986 ELIZABETH HARDWICK
1987 GAY TALESE
1988 ANNIE DILLARD
1989 GEOFFREY WOLFF
1990 JUSTIN KAPLAN
1991 JOYCE CAROL OATES
1992 SUSAN SONTAG
1993 JOSEPH EPSTEIN
1994 TRACY KIDDER
1995 JAMAICA KINCAID
1996 GEOFFREY C. WARD
1997 IAN FRAZIER
1998 CYNTHIA OZICK
1999 EDWARD HOAGLAND
2000 ALAN LIGHTMAN
2001 KATHLEEN NORRIS
2002 STEPHEN JAY GOULD
2003 ANNE FADIMAN
2004 LOUIS MENAND
2005 SUSAN ORLEAN
2006 LAUREN SLATER
2007 DAVID FOSTER WALLACE
2008 ADAM GOPNIK
2009 MARY OLIVER
2010 CHRISTOPHER HITCHENS
2011 EDWIDGE DANTICAT
2012 DAVID BROOKS

The Best AMERICAN ESSAYS® 2012

Edited and with an Introduction by DAVID BROOKS

Robert Atwan, Series Editor

A MARINER ORIGINAL

HOUGHTON MIFFLIN HARCOURT

BOSTON • NEW YORK   2012

www.hmhbooks.com
ISSN 0888-3742
ISBN 978-0-547-84009-3

Printed in the United States of America
DOC 10 9 8 7 6 5 4 3 2 1

Contents

Foreword: Of Topics

WHENEVER I GET into discussions about the essay with creative writing students, I discover a peculiar notion they have about my favorite genre. They apparently believe that when they write an essay—whether it's required or inspired—they should write about themselves. An essay for many of them is wholly autobiographical, pure and simple. When they start writing, they seem to have only one template in mind: a straightforward personal narrative heavily interspersed with "realistic" dialogue and told in a sincere, casual voice intended to be wholly congruous with their own.

Textured and original description is minimal, as are—if I may use the word—*ideas*. Forget surprising metaphors or memorable observations. Missing, too, is the one literary element that the greatest essays thrive on—reflection. Forgive the redundancy; there is very little meditation, contemplation, deliberation, rumination. It seems as though students want their essays to look like true-to-life short stories that conform to the creative writing manual's central mantra: *Show, Don't Tell.*

Why? I wonder. It wasn't always this way. Essays were traditionally written on topics. In the older writing textbooks students were often presented with a long list of topics that might stimulate essays, though the topics themselves could be quite unstimulating, the schoolteacher's all-time favorite being "What I Did on My Summer Vacation." Yet for the preeminent essayists, the approach to a topic, no matter how commonplace, is part of the genre's artistry. Look, for example, at how E. B. White treats the American summer vacation in his eerie classic "Once More to the Lake."

The inner dynamics of the genre often depended on the essayist's persona leisurely and often unsystematically grappling with or dancing around a topic. It could be Francis Bacon on friendship, Joseph Addison on witches, Samuel Johnson on bashfulness, William Hazlitt on the pleasures of hating, Ralph Waldo Emerson on manners, Agnes Repplier on cats, G. K. Chesterton on sentiment, Virginia Woolf on middlebrow, or Annie Dillard on mirages. Or Jonathan Swift's remarkable contribution to the genre, "A Modest Proposal for Preventing the Children of Poor People in Ireland from Being a Burden to Their Parents or Country, and for Making Them Beneficial to the Public."

Though engaged with topics—some entertaining, others savage—these are still all personal essays, based often on subjective experience and an individual perspective. Emerson was not attempting to be Emily Post, offering the final word on manners, though he could be prescriptive: "The person who screams, or uses the superlative degree, or converses with heat, puts whole drawing-rooms to flight." Imagine Miss Manners advising her audience against using superlatives! All conversation, especially literary and cultural, would come to a halt. Without screams, superlatives, and heated conversation, television talk shows could not exist. Indeed, this series of books, and others like it, are based on a superlative Emerson might find distasteful.

By temperament, the essayist doesn't favor the final word but prefers to remain in an exploratory frame of mind. Essayists like to examine—or, to use an essayist's favorite term, *consider*—topics from various perspectives. To consider is not necessarily to conclude; the essayist delights in a suspension of judgment and even an inconsistency that usually annoys the "so what's your point?" reader. The essayist, by and large, agrees with Robert Frost that thinking and voting are two different acts.

So the essayist's take on a topic is neither conclusive nor exhaustive; nor is it systematic. And at times what appears to be an announced topic turns out to be something else. Such essayistic maneuvers go back to Montaigne, who loved to take a topic through a bewildering maze of associations, so that at one moment he's considering sneezing, the next seasickness, then fear, and that leads to the essay's titular topic, coaches. Essayists had this sort of literary fun with topics for centuries, and their so-called digressions became not a compositional flaw but a virtue, as readers learned to take delight in pursuing links that were not always obvious, as they are in less literary articles.

But by the early twentieth century, the essayist's leisurely, digressive, and impressionistic approach to a topic grew out of fashion, as did the familiar essay in general. In 1951, the essay seemed so obsolete that Joseph Wood Krutch in an essay called "No Essays, Please!" wrote: "The very word 'essay' has fallen into such disfavor that it is avoided with horror, and anything which is not fiction is usually called either an 'article,' a 'story,' or just 'a piece.'" Modern magazine journalism had little use for the traditional essay, and the centuries-old relationship of writer to topic reversed itself, with the writer now becoming subservient to the topic. To be sure, the magazines wanted topics, but they now demanded timely, or "topical," topics, not personal reflections (pejoratively known in the industry as thumb-sucking) about manners, cats, or hating. The nineteenth-century essayist could ruminate on jealousy by citing *Othello* and other relevant literary or historical works and sprinkling personal observations on human behavior into the mix. The modern essayist covering the same topic would be obligated to include findings and research from the latest journals of psychology and psychoanalysis, along with interview quotations from mental health professionals. In "Duh, Bor-ing," Joseph Epstein notices a similar trend in the essay today: "With-it-ness now calls for checking in with what the neuroscientists have to say about your subject, whatever it might be." The traditional essayists didn't hesitate to quote, but they almost always quoted from literature, not scientific studies. They didn't cite or interview experts. This shift, reflecting a change in the expectations of readers, profoundly transformed the genre.

Those wanting to compose traditional essays found themselves caught in a bind. In their demand for more researched and informative essays, the magazines turned increasingly to experts in various fields. The experts didn't always produce eloquent prose, but they provided the new reading public with what it wanted—to be informed and up-to-date on the leading topics of the day. Some splendid essayists could adapt to these demands. Edmund Wilson did his research and his investigations with rigor, although he remained at war with specialists and academics throughout his career. After all, he possessed only a BA (Princeton, 1916) and had the presumption to write about topics that might better have been left in the hands of the experts, such as the Dead Sea Scrolls, literary symbolism, and the federal income tax. Many others adapted but felt the restrictions and requirements of journalism had injured the essay as a literary genre.

What to do? Where to go? Enter the memoir, autobiographical essay, and confessional narrative, which, if I'm correct, now supply today's writing students with their major compositional models. Why try to compete with experts on a topic, to engage in difficult and often tedious research, when one is already an expert on one's own life? It may be that the memoir came into its own because writers were trying to circumvent the demands for professional expertise and factual information. One difficulty with the personal narrative, however, is that it too often invites authors to embellish their life story so that it sounds more novelistic and dramatic than it actually is, especially when it comes to suffering, deprivation, addiction, family dysfunction, and abuse. Writers discovered that editors and publishers, though they may be partial to happy outcomes (addictions and disabilities overcome), rarely seem interested in happy lives. Some writers also learned to their embarrassment that personal misery could be fact-checked as diligently as any other information.

In his introduction to the 2007 volume in this series, David Foster Wallace was especially tough on what he called "abreactive or confessional memoirs." Not because their "popularity" seemed to him "a symptom of something especially sick and narcissistic/ voyeuristic about U.S. culture right now," but because, as he says, "I just don't trust them . . . Not so much their factual truth as their agenda. The sense I get from a lot of contemporary memoirs is that they have an unconscious and unacknowledged project, which is to make the memoirists seem as endlessly fascinating and important to the reader as they are to themselves. I find most of them sad in a way I don't think their authors intend."

Although I have no objections to "abreactive" memoirs or confessional writing (which, when done well, can be as compelling as any literary form), I would, if I were teaching in an MFA program, try to revive interest among students in the topic-oriented essay. From the start, they would need to understand that—as we know from all the great essayists—ruminating on a topic doesn't mean that the writing will be impersonal. The essayist's reflections will be indistinguishable from a particular personality and temperament, as can be seen in this volume in Geoffrey Bent's "Edward Hopper and the Geometry of Despair," where the author, who is not an art historian, offers us his own observations on the great American artist's work. In speaking of Hopper's attraction to architecture, Bent writes, "Hopper loved buildings and found so much character in them they almost function as faces: the spent gentility of a Victorian façade, the spare sufficiency of a clapboard cottage, the redundant thrust of a brick tenement. In his hands, shutters and sills, pilasters and porticos are as individualizing as noses and ears."

Yet why do I find it hard to imagine an essay like Bent's being composed in nonfiction workshops today? Could it be that many students don't know enough, don't have favorite artists, composers, books? Or have no passion for anything outside themselves and their own microculture? Or could it be that today's young writers are afraid to tackle subjects that are presumably for experts? In other words, that they believe that an explication of Hopper's artistic genius could only be set forth by someone with a PhD in American art history? Are students so intimidated by expertise that they've lost confidence in their own powers of observation?

Essayists also traditionally found topics in books and authors. Montaigne's essays are interwoven with references to the classics: Plutarch, Virgil, Horace, Pliny, and countless others. Samuel Johnson wrote brilliant essays on the lives of the English poets, and Virginia Woolf first demonstrated her mastery of the essay form (as well as her love of Montaigne) in *The Common Reader*. That tradition is best seen today in the review essay, a literary form often featured in such prominent periodicals as the *New York Review of Books, Harper's Magazine,* and the *Atlantic*. Note how "In the Bitch Is Back" Sandra Tsing Loh discusses a recent book on the topic of menopause while simultaneously offering readers a lively and unforgettable glimpse into her personal experiences with "the Change."

In my praise of topics, I'm not suggesting that essayists return to a belletristic or genteel mode of detached whimsicality. We live in an altogether different time—as the essays in this collection make abundantly clear—and are engaged with far different issues. But an obsession with oneself and a preoccupation with narrative (why do these seem intertwined?) can be as restrictive as the journalistic standards many literary essayists would like to escape. Deliberation on a topic also returns one to the creative roots of the genre: *essaying*, the trying out of, or fooling around with, ideas and observations, an imaginative activity that the first-person narrative as it's usually written today leaves little room for. Writing students in nonfiction, perhaps, need to back off a little on "showing" and reconsider the art of "telling."

Essays can be lots of things, maybe too many things, but at the core of the genre is an unmistakable receptivity to the ever-shifting processes of our minds and moods. If there is any essential characteristic we can attribute to the essay, it may be this: that the truest examples of the form enact that ever-shifting process, and in that enactment we can find the basis for the essay's qualification to be regarded seriously as imaginative literature and the essayist's claim to be taken seriously as a creative writer.

The Best American Essays features a selection of the year's outstanding essays, essays of literary achievement that show an awareness of craft and forcefulness of thought. Hundreds of essays are gathered annually from a wide assortment of national and regional publications. These essays are then screened, and approximately one hundred are turned over to a distinguished guest editor, who may add a few personal discoveries and who makes the final selections. The list of notable essays appearing in the back of the book is drawn from a final comprehensive list that includes not only all of the essays submitted to the guest editor but also many that were not submitted.

To qualify for the volume, the essay must be a work of respectable literary quality, intended as a fully developed, independent essay on a subject of general interest (not specialized scholarship), originally written in English (or translated by the author) for publication in an American periodical during the calendar year. Today's essay is a highly flexible and shifting form, however, so these criteria are not carved in stone.

Magazine editors who want to be sure their contributors will be considered each year should submit issues or subscriptions to The Best American Essays, Houghton Mifflin Harcourt, 222 Berkeley Street, Boston, MA 02116. Writers and editors are welcome to submit published essays from any American periodical for consideration; unpublished work does not qualify for the series and cannot be reviewed or evaluated. Please note: all submissions must be directly from the publication and not in manuscript or printout format. Editors of online magazines and literary bloggers should not assume that appropriate work will be seen; they are invited to submit printed copies of the essays (with full citations) to the address above.

I'd like to dedicate this volume to Jon Roberts, poet, critic, devoted teacher, and dear friend, who died suddenly at age fifty-one in April. A voracious reader, Jack was a great help to me when I was working on the first book in this series back in 1986, and every year thereafter he generously offered suggestions and recommendations. As always, the Houghton Mifflin Harcourt staff has done everything to bring so many moving parts together in so short a time, and I once again appreciate the efforts of Deanne Urmy, Nicole Angeloro, Barbara Jatkola, Liz Duvall, and Megan Wilson. It was a great pleasure to work with David Brooks. He is one of our outstanding writers and thinkers, and this collection amply displays his wide-ranging concerns and his interest in all aspects of American society.

R.A.

Introduction

WHEN I WAS AN UNDERGRAD at the University of Chicago, I attended classes with a moderate degree of diligence, but my most profitable hours came in the evenings when I'd put off doing my homework by wandering around the stacks of the Regenstein Library.

I'd invariably make my way over to the section where the old periodicals were kept. I was then reading books by the historian Richard Pells, which gave me the impression that between the Progressive era and Woodstock, all of world history was run out of the editorial offices of the *New Republic*. Whatever Walter Lippmann and Malcolm Cowley said went.

I would leaf through the old *New Republics*, then sample, in turn, the *American Mercury*, the *Smart Set*, *Vanity Fair* (the original one), *Partisan Review*, and a bunch of other magazines before ending up with the *New Masses*, which I remember as the most visually striking of them all. At the time my ambition was to be Clifford Odets, an engaged lefty playwright, but if that didn't work out, I thought it would be great to be a cross between Lionel Trilling and Calvin Trillin — writing lofty essays about the state of Our Culture filled with one-liners.

That magazine browsing turned out to be my version of med school — the technical training I would need to do my job. Over the years, I became familiar with some of the classic essayists: Montaigne and Addison and Steele. But the earliest essayist who seemed like a friend — and the job of an essayist *is* to seem like a friend — was Walter Bagehot.

Bagehot, the editor of the *Economist* between 1861 and 1877, lived in an era of high pomposity. But he was a casual, warm, and learned essayist. He wrote on everything from Gibbon to Islam to banking procedures. He could throw off wisdom on the most unlikely subjects: "No real English gentleman, in his secret soul, was ever sorry for the death of a political economist: he is much more likely to be sorry for his life." He could summarize entire policy disputes in one sentence: "Any aid to a present bad bank is the surest mode of preventing the establishment of a future good bank."

He had a modern eye for the counterintuitive. He wrote on the value of stupidity, especially in those who grapple with world affairs. He wrote in praise of dull government. Most important, his writing implied a winning persona. He understood a key fact about essay writing: that essays rarely persuade directly, but they often transform readers obliquely, by holding up a model for how to feel and enjoy. Bagehot believed that essayists persuade most by pleasing most. He wrote:

> Give painful lectures, distribute weary tracts (and perhaps this is as well—you may be able to give an argumentative answer to a few objections, you may diffuse a distinct notion of the dignified dullness of politics); but as far as communicating and establishing your creed are concerned—try a little pleasure. The way to keep up old customs is, to enjoy old customs; the way to be satisfied with the present state of things is, to enjoy the state of things. Over the "Cavalier" mind this world passes with a thrill of delight; there is an exultation in a daily event, zest in the "regular thing," joy at an old feast.

Bagehot edified by having fun.

I didn't read too many nineteenth-century essayists. The Carlyles of the world are just too leaden. I could read through acres of Emerson without having one of his hortatory phrases lodge in my brain. His narcissistic self-reliance shtick is demonstrably bad advice and pseudomacho show.

Before long I was stumbling into what I have come to think of as the golden age of American nonfiction—the thirty years between 1935 and 1965. That was the moment between Victorian pomposity and modern academic professionalism.

There were many great nonfiction writers in those years: Jane Jacobs, Daniel Bell, David Riesman, Digby Baltzell, William Whyte, Irving Howe, Hannah Arendt, Edmund Wilson, Alfred Kazin,

Clement Greenberg, Reinhold Niebuhr, Abraham Joshua Heschel, and on and on. They often wrote for little magazines, but they had wide followings, because the mass middlebrow audience still felt it was important to pay attention to what these people said. Many of these serious writers had bestsellers. *Time* magazine put Riesman on its cover.

The best essays of those years had lost the old pomposity while retaining some grandeur and scope. They were rigorous without being narrow and academic. They were polemical without being partisan. They were countercultural without being sloppy. They were reckless but also learned.

Today, George Orwell is the most revered of the lot. I tell college students to read Orwell (and C. S. Lewis) just so they can mimic their prose styles. Orwell's particular genius was the arresting first sentence. Here are a few:

> From his essay on the Blitz: "As I write, highly civilized human beings are flying overhead, trying to kill me."
>
> From his essay on Gandhi: "Saints should always be judged guilty until they are proved innocent, but the tests that have to be applied to them are not, of course, the same in all cases."
>
> From his memoir of his school days: "Soon after I arrived at Crossgates (not immediately, but after a week or two, just when I seemed to be settling into my routine of school life) I began wetting my bed."

There are few writers who can match first sentences like that, although maybe at their best S. J. Perelman and Robert Benchley can. Here is a typical opening line from Benchley: "It is not generally known that the newt, although one of the smallest of our North American animals, has an extremely happy home life."

Sentences like that mock grandiosity, and many of the mid-century writers did that. Still, they were grand. They took on big, sweeping topics, gave it their best shot, and expected other people to come up with big, sweeping rebuttals.

Along the way they sent out shafts of insight that sound like the bits of wisdom you hear at a good dinner party. Walter Lippmann, who began his career as a member of Harvard's famous class of 1910 but lingered on through the century, noticed an essential truth about American politicians—that while blowhards in public, they are generally smarter and more reasonable in private:

"They flaunt their vices to the public; they shiver and quake at the thought that some indiscreet journalist will expose them to the world as men of virtue and common sense."

Others provided an entire worldview, which could serve as a guide through life. In "Rationalism in Politics," one of the best essays of this period, the British philosopher Michael Oakeshott dissected the rationalist mindset that would lead to such mischief in Vietnam and in the technocratic dreams of twentieth-century social engineers.

The most sweeping and profound essay of them all, in my book, is Isaiah Berlin's "The Hedgehog and the Fox." That essay not only gave us a useful and overused way to describe different sorts of intelligence, but it contains a beautiful description of what you might call tacit wisdom, or canny good sense, or, in Berlin's words, a sense of reality: "Wisdom is the ability to allow for the (at least by us) unalterable medium in which we act . . . It is not scientific knowledge, but a special sensitiveness to the contours of the circumstances in which we happen to be placed; it is a capacity for living without falling foul of some permanent condition or factor which cannot be either altered, or even fully described and calculated; an ability to be guided by rules of thumb—the 'immemorial wisdom.'"

Writers took their work seriously and treated an important essay as a history-altering event. Sometimes they took themselves too seriously. Just before he died, one essayist of the day told me about a frantic call he got after a journal editor had committed suicide by sticking his head in a gas oven. He rushed over to the man's apartment and found the body in the kitchen. Soon other writers rushed over and contemplated the corpse. Pretty soon they broke out his booze. Soon after that a cocktail party had formed, with the writers discussing one another's reviews while the body still lay in the kitchen and the police and coroner went about their business.

Niebuhr wrote a book called *The Nature and Destiny of Man,* which covers a lot of ground. Trilling wrote an essay called "Reality in America," which is also pretty broad in scope. It's a brilliant one, too—an attempt to revive complex emotional depth amid the usual pragmatic forces of liberalism and life.

Writers weren't as specialized then. Irving Kristol could write about everything from Auden to Maimonides to John Foster

Dulles. When these writers wrote about politics, it was with a literary perspective, as if they were doing high criticism, or else they saw it from a distance, as the clash of world historical ideas.

They wrote about pop culture with that sense of loftiness, too. In the highbrow *Partisan Review*, for example, Robert Warshow published a great piece called "The Gangster as Tragic Hero." "The gangster is the man of the city," Warshow wrote,

> with the city's language and knowledge, with its queer and dishonest skills and its terrible daring, carrying his life in his hands like a placard, like a club. For everyone else, there is at least the theoretical possibility of another world—in that happier American culture which the gangster denies, the city does not really exist; it is only a more crowded and brightly lit country—but for the gangster there is only the city; he must inhabit it in order to personify it: not the real city, but that dangerous and sad city of the imagination which is so much more important, which is the modern world.

Back in those days, you couldn't be an educated person unless you knew what they were reading in London, Paris, and Berlin. It was harder to communicate across oceans, but taste was less parochial than it is now. One of the positive byproducts was that British essayists had greater influence over American ones than they do today. My crackpot theory is that British essayists all descend from Samuel Johnson—they are casual, conversational, and a bit loose. American essayists descend from Emerson or Thoreau or Lippmann. We are more earnest, self-absorbed, and stiff. Back then, however, an American reader might have been familiar with Evelyn Waugh's tremendous essay "Well-Informed Circles . . . and How to Move in Them." It's a little guide about how to bluff your way through a dinner conversation filled with poseurs, and how to out-poseur them all. Here's a sample:

> Those who seek admission to this honorable corps [the circle of those with inside knowledge] must have travelled a little in the Near East and, if possible, beyond. They must exhibit an interest in languages—a different and vastly easier thing than a knowledge of them. If, for instance, you are caught out by the menu, say blandly, "I've never been able to pay much attention to the Latin languages," or better still, "the Romance Group"; and to such direct questions as, "Do you speak Magyar?" answer, "Not nearly as well as I ought." It is a good policy to introduce linguistic questions whenever possible;

for instance, if someone says he has spent three weeks in Cairo, instead of asking about the hotels, say, "Tell me, is much demotic Armenian spoken there now?"

Malcolm Muggeridge was another essayist from England who had a wide and positive influence on a thousand wannabes. He wrote a fine essay, for example, called "Down with Sex," about the role sex played in Western culture. Sex was once a mystery, Muggeridge wrote, but one day D. H. Lawrence decided sex's mission "was to fertilize a spent civilization, reanimate the wilting bodies of an unduly cerebral generation of men and generally restore to our mid-twentieth-century lives the joyous fulfillment of happier and more innocent times." This put too much of a burden, Muggeridge wrote, on sex. It was asked to bear more psychological weight than it could handle. "Sex has become the religion of the most civilized portions of the earth. The orgasm has replaced the Cross as the focus of longing and the image of fulfillment . . . Sex is the mysticism of materialism. We are to die in the spirit to be reborn in the flesh, rather than the other way around."

I'm not sure I agree with that, or at least I'm not sure it's true anymore, but it gets you thinking about the role sex plays in modern thought in new ways.

This whole essay culture came crashing down, and oddly it was essays that killed it. Intellectuals decided that this upper-middlebrow form was revolting. Some thought it was revolting because it wasn't sufficiently academic and technical. Others decided it was revolting because it wasn't sufficiently gritty. Dwight Macdonald wrote an essay called "Masscult and Midcult" that savaged the way mass culture sanitized art, music, and ideas.

Irving Howe wrote an essay for *Partisan Review* in which he lamented, "What is most alarming is that the whole idea of the intellectual vocation—the idea of a life dedicated to values that cannot possibly be realized by a commercial civilization—has gradually lost its allure." Howe argued that writers prostitute their talent when they write for general-interest magazines. Writers who contribute to *The New Yorker* become trivial and frozen, he asserted. And yet the commercial pressures compel them to sell out in this way. "Writers today have no choice, often enough, but to write for magazines like the *New Yorker*—and worse, far worse. But what matters is the terms upon which the writer enters into such relationships, his willingness to understand with whom he is dealing, his readiness not to deceive himself that an unpleasant necessity is a desirable virtue."

Howe probably thought that the flight from the upper middle-brow would lead writers to pen bracing essays for *Dissent*. In fact it led them to pen impenetrable, jargon-laden essays for tiny academic journals that only nine people can understand, essays that, if they were written in plain prose, would seem incredibly banal because the ideas underlying them are so unimaginative.

The essay hit a bad patch for a little while. Yet today I think it's coming back. The age of academic jargon is passing. The Internet has paradoxically been a boon to essayists. Yes, there is Twitter and blogging and hysteria on the Internet and all the things Jonathan Franzen says he doesn't like. But the Internet makes far-flung essays so accessible.

Anybody in his or her pajamas can go on websites such as Arts & Letters Daily, the Browser, and Longform.org and read essays from little magazines they have never heard of. These sites have their own ideological axes to grind—the Browser has gone from being perfectly eclectic to predictably left-wing—but they introduce you to things you would never have seen.

More important, the Internet has aroused the energies of hundreds of thousands of intelligent amateurs. There are dumb bloggers, but there are also astonishingly brilliant ones. One of my favorites is Tyler Cowen, who blogs for Marginal Revolution. He is an economist at George Mason University, but he blogs knowledgeably about ethnic foods, chess, the culture of northern Europe (and everywhere else), novels, politics, cognition, and on and on. People like that now have an occasion to vent and realize their skills. They have brought us back to the era of the amateur, the era of the essayist as friend. And they are not just blogging. Periodically, they turn their blog posts into essays.

At the end of every year I give out what I call the Sidney Awards (named after the midcentury philosopher Sidney Hook) for the best magazine essays of the year. Every year it is my impression that the essays are better than the year before.

The same is true, I think, for the essays in this book. Yes, I had to wade through many soporific essays by people who had no truly interesting experience to relate but still wanted to write finely about it. Yes, I had to wade through a lot of essays on what seem to be the primary subjects of our era: Alzheimer's, senior citizen homes, aging, and the death of a parent.

But I still had many jewels to choose from. I tried to pick ones that crystallize an emotion, in the belief that reading them will add to your emotional repertoire. I tried to pick ones with new or daring ideas that will alter how you look at the world. I tried, in short, to pick ones that will be useful to you. That, I'm afraid, is a middlebrow activity. But I plead guilty. I want to be improved by the things I read.

That self-improving ethos was something that was taken for granted in the mid-twentieth century, and now we're fortified by the knowledge that the things that are most lasting and edifying are the things that lodge in the brain most deeply, which means they are emotional, enjoyable, and fun.

DAVID BROOKS

The Best
AMERICAN
ESSAYS
2012

BENJAMIN ANASTAS

The Foul Reign of "Self-Reliance"

FROM *The New York Times Magazine*

MY FIRST EXPOSURE to the high-flown pap of Ralph Waldo Emerson's "Self-Reliance" came in a basement classroom at the private boys' school where I enrolled to learn the secrets of discipline
and because I wanted, at age fourteen, to wear a tie. The class
was early American literature, the textbook an anthology with the
heft of a volume of the Babylonian Talmud; a ribbon for holding
your place between "Rip Van Winkle," by Washington Irving, and
"Young Goodman Brown," by Nathaniel Hawthorne; and a slick
hardcover the same shade of green as the back side of a dollar bill.

Our teacher, let's call him Mr. Sideways, had a windblown air, as
if he had just stepped out of an open coupe, and the impenetrable
self-confidence of someone who is convinced that he is liked. (He
was not.) "Whoso would be a man," he read aloud to a room full of
slouching teenage boys in button-down shirts and ties stained with
sloppy Joes from the dining hall, "must be a nonconformist. He
who would gather immortal palms must not be hindered by the
name of goodness . . . Nothing is at last sacred but the integrity of
your own mind." And then he let loose the real hokum: "Absolve
you to yourself," he read, "and you shall have the suffrage of the
world."

I am sure that Mr. Sideways lectured dutifully on transcenden-
talism and its founding ideas—Emerson's "transparent eyeball"
and its gift of x-ray sight; Thoreau's flight from a life of "quiet

desperation" in society to the stillness of Walden Pond; the starred ceiling of the heavens that Ralph Waldo called the "Over-Soul," uniting us with its magnetic beams—but what I remember most about that English class was the week that Mr. Sideways told us to leave our anthologies at home so that he could lead us in a seminar in how to make a fortune in real estate by tapping the treasure-trove he referred to as "OPM," or Other People's Money. He drew pyramids and pie charts on the blackboard. He gave us handouts.

For years I blamed Mr. Sideways—and the money fever of the 1980s—for this weird episode of hucksterism in English class. But that was being unfair. Our teacher had merely fallen under the spell, like countless others before and after, of the most pernicious piece of literature in the American canon. The whim that inspired him to lead a seminar in house-flipping to a stupefied underage audience was Emerson's handiwork. "All that Adam had," he goads in his essay "Nature," "all that Caesar could, you have and can do." Oh, the deception! The rank insincerity! It's just like the Devil in Muttonchops to promise an orgiastic communion fit for the gods, only to deliver a gospel of "self-conceit so intensely intellectual," as Melville complained, "that at first one hesitates to call it by its right name."

The excessive love of individual liberty that debases our national politics? It found its original poet in Ralph Waldo. The plague of devices that keep us staring into the shallow puddle of our dopamine reactions, caressing our touchscreens for another fix of our own importance? That's right: it all started with Emerson's "Self-Reliance." Our fetish for the authentically homespun and the American affliction of ignoring volumes of evidence in favor of the flashes that meet the eye, the hunches that seize the gut? It's Emerson again, skulking through Harvard Yard in his cravat and greasy undertaker's waistcoat, while in his mind he's trailing silken robes fit for Zoroaster and levitating on the grass.

Before it does another generation's worth of damage to the American psyche, let's put an end to the foul reign of "Self-Reliance" and let the scholars pick over the meaning of its carcass. One question first, though: Is there anything worth salvaging among the spiritualist ramblings, obscure metaphysics, and aphorisms so pandering that Joel Osteen might think twice about delivering them? Is there an essential part of Emerson's signature essay that we've somehow lost sight of?

"There is a time in every man's education," Emerson writes, presuming, with his usual élan, to both personify his young country and issue a decree for its revival, "when he arrives at the conviction that envy is ignorance; that imitation is suicide; that he must take himself for better, for worse, as his portion; that though the wide universe is full of good, no kernel of nourishing corn can come to him but through his toil bestowed on the plot of ground which is given him to till."

As the story in our high school anthology went, the citizenry that the Bard of Concord met on his strolls through the town green in the 1830s were still cowed by the sermons of their Puritan forefathers—we had read Jonathan Edwards's "Sinners in the Hands of an Angry God" to get a taste—prone to awe when it came to the literature of distant foreign empires and too complacent on the biggest moral issues of the day: the institution of slavery and the genocide of the Indians. (At least Emerson saw well enough with his transparent eye to criticize both.) The country had every bit of God-given energy and talent and latent conviction that it needed to produce genius, he believed, but too much kowtowing to society and the approval of elders had tamed his fellows of their natural gifts (the "aboriginal Self," he called it) and sapped them of their courage.

"Most men have bound their eyes with one or another handkerchief," a disenchanted Emerson observed, "and attached themselves to . . . communities of opinion. This conformity makes them not false in a few particulars, but false in all particulars." Society operates like a corporation that requires its shareholders to sacrifice their rights for the comfort of all, Emerson believed. Instead of "realities and creators," it gives men "names and customs."

So what is his cure for the country's ailing soul, his recipe for our deliverance from civilization and its discontents? This is the aim of "Self-Reliance," which Emerson culled from a series of lectures he delivered at the Masonic Temple of Boston—his "Divinity School Address" at Harvard in 1838, denounced by one listener as "an incoherent rhapsody," had already caused an outcry—and published in his collection *Essays: First Series in 1841.* Cornel West has praised Emerson for his "dynamic perspective" and for his "prescription for courageous self-reliance by means of nonconformity and inconsistency." Harold Bloom noted, in an article for the *New York Times,* that by "'self-reliance' Emerson meant the recognition of the God within us, rather than the worship of the Christian godhead." This is the essay's greatest virtue for its original audience: it ordained them with an authority to speak what had been reserved for only the powerful, and bowed to no greater human laws, social customs, or dictates from the pulpit. "Trust thyself: every heart vibrates to that iron string." Or: "No law can be sacred to me but that of my nature." Some of the lines are so ingrained in us that we know them by heart. They feel like natural law.

There is a downside to ordaining the self with divine authority, though. We humans are fickle creatures, and natures—however sacred—can mislead us. That didn't bother Emerson. "Speak what you think now in hard words," Emerson exhorted, "and tomorrow speak what tomorrow thinks in hard words again, though it contradict every thing you said today." (Memo to Mitt Romney: no more apologies for being "as consistent as human beings can be." You're Emersonian!)

The larger problem with the essay, and its more lasting legacy as a cornerstone of the American identity, has been Emerson's tacit endorsement of a radically self-centered worldview. It's a lot like the Ptolemaic model of the planets that preceded Copernicus; the sun, the moon, and the stars revolve around our portable reclining chairs, and whatever contradicts our right to harbor misconceptions—whether it be birtherism, climate science denial, or the conviction that Trader Joe's sells good food—is the prattle of the unenlightened majority and can be dismissed out of hand.

"A man is to carry himself in the presence of all opposition," Emerson advises, "as if every thing were titular and ephemeral but he." If this isn't the official motto of the 112th Congress of the United States, well, it should be. The gridlock, grandstanding, rule manipulating, and inability to compromise aren't symptoms of national decline. We're simply coming into our own as Emerson's republic.

Just recently I was watching the original "Think Different" spot that reversed Apple Computer's fortunes when it was first shown in 1997 and marked the first real triumph for Steve Jobs after returning from the wilderness to the company he helped to found. The echoes of Emerson in the ad are striking, especially in the famous voice-over narration by Richard Dreyfuss, reading a poem now known by historians and Apple's legion of fans as "Here's to the Crazy Ones." The message was already familiar when it first met our ears.

In calling out to all the misfits and the rebels and the troublemakers, the "round pegs in square holes" who "see things differently" and have trouble with the rules, the ad evokes the ideal first created by Emerson of a rough-hewn outsider who changes the world through a combination of courage, tenacity, resourcefulness and that God-given wildcard, genius. While Dreyfuss narrates, archival footage of the "crazy ones" flickers on the screen in black and white: Albert Einstein leads the way, followed by Bob Dylan, the Reverend Martin Luther King Jr., a jubilant Richard Branson shaking a champagne bottle in a flight suit.

This is the problem when the self is endowed with divinity, and it's a weakness that Emerson acknowledged: if the only measure of greatness is how big an iconoclast you are, then there really is no difference between coming up with the theory of relativity, plugging in an electric guitar, leading a civil rights movement, or spending great gobs of your own money to fly a balloon across the Atlantic. In "Self-Reliance," Emerson addresses this potentially fatal flaw in his thinking with a principle he calls "the law of consciousness." (It is not convincing.) Every one of us has two confessionals, he writes. At the first, we clear our actions in the mirror (a recapitulation of the dictum "trust thyself"). At the second, we consider whether we've fulfilled our obligations to our families, neighbors, communities, and—here Emerson can't resist a bit of snark—our cats and dogs. Which confessional is the higher one? To whom do we owe our ultimate allegiance? It's not even a contest.

"I have my own stern claims and perfect circle," Emerson writes. With this one fell swoop, Emerson tips the scales in favor of his own confessional, and any hope he might have raised for creating a balance to the self's divinity is lost. Ever since, we've been misreading him, or at least misapplying him. As a sad result, it has been the swagger of a man's walk that makes his measure, and Americans' right to love ourselves before any other that trumps all.

MARCIA ANGELL

The Crazy State of Psychiatry

FROM *The New York Review of Books*

The Epidemic of Mental Illness: Why?

IT SEEMS THAT AMERICANS are in the midst of a raging epidemic of mental illness, at least as judged by the increase in the numbers treated for it. The tally of those who are so disabled by mental disorders that they qualify for Supplemental Security Income (SSI) or Social Security Disability Insurance (SSDI) increased nearly two and a half times between 1987 and 2007—from 1 in 184 Americans to 1 in 76. For children, the rise is even more startling—a thirty-five-fold increase in the same two decades. Mental illness is now the leading cause of disability in children, well ahead of physical disabilities like cerebral palsy or Down syndrome, for which the federal programs were created.

A large survey of randomly selected adults, sponsored by the National Institute of Mental Health (NIMH) and conducted between 2001 and 2003, found that an astonishing 46 percent met criteria established by the American Psychiatric Association (APA) for having had at least one mental illness within four broad categories at some time in their lives. The categories were "anxiety disorders," including, among other subcategories, phobias and post-traumatic stress disorder (PTSD); "mood disorders," including major depression and bipolar disorders; "impulse-control disorders," including various behavioral problems and attention deficit hyperactivity disorder (ADHD); and "substance use disorders," including alcohol and drug abuse. Most met criteria for more than one diagnosis. Of a subgroup affected within the previous year, a third were under treatment—up from a fifth in a similar survey ten years earlier.

Nowadays treatment by medical doctors nearly always means psychoactive drugs, that is, drugs that affect the mental state. In fact, most psychiatrists treat only with drugs, and refer patients to psychologists or social workers if they believe psychotherapy is also warranted. The shift from "talk therapy" to drugs as the dominant mode of treatment coincides with the emergence over the past four decades of the theory that mental illness is caused primarily by chemical imbalances in the brain that can be corrected by specific drugs. That theory became broadly accepted, by the media and the public as well as by the medical profession, after Prozac came to market in 1987 and was intensively promoted as a corrective for a deficiency of serotonin in the brain. The number of people treated for depression tripled in the following ten years, and about 10 percent of Americans over age six now take antidepressants. The increased use of drugs to treat psychosis is even more dramatic. The new generation of antipsychotics, such as Risperdal, Zyprexa, and Seroquel, have replaced cholesterol-lowering agents as the top-selling class of drugs in the U.S.

What is going on here? Is the prevalence of mental illness really that high and still climbing? Particularly if these disorders are biologically determined and not a result of environmental influences, is it plausible to suppose that such an increase is real? Or are we learning to recognize and diagnose mental disorders that were always there? On the other hand, are we simply expanding the criteria for mental illness so that nearly everyone has one? And what about the drugs that are now the mainstay of treatment? Do they work? If they do, shouldn't we expect the prevalence of mental illness to be declining, not rising?

These are the questions, among others, that concern the authors of the three provocative books under review here. They come at the questions from different backgrounds—Irving Kirsch is a psychologist at the University of Hull in the UK, Robert Whitaker a journalist and previously the author of a history of the treatment of mental illness called *Mad in America* (2001), and Daniel Carlat a psychiatrist who practices in a Boston suburb and publishes a newsletter and blog about his profession.

The authors emphasize different aspects of the epidemic of

mental illness. Kirsch is concerned with whether antidepressants work. Whitaker, who has written an angrier book, takes on the entire spectrum of mental illness and asks whether psychoactive drugs create worse problems than they solve. Carlat, who writes more in sorrow than in anger, looks mainly at how his profession has allied itself with, and is manipulated by, the pharmaceutical industry. But despite their differences, all three are in remarkable agreement on some important matters, and they have documented their views well.

First, they agree on the disturbing extent to which the companies that sell psychoactive drugs—through various forms of marketing, both legal and illegal, and what many people would describe as bribery—have come to determine what constitutes a mental illness and how the disorders should be diagnosed and treated. This is a subject to which I'll return.

Second, none of the three authors subscribes to the popular theory that mental illness is caused by a chemical imbalance in the brain. As Whitaker tells the story, that theory had its genesis shortly after psychoactive drugs were introduced in the 1950s. The first was Thorazine (chlorpromazine), which was launched in 1954 as a "major tranquilizer" and quickly found widespread use in mental hospitals to calm psychotic patients, mainly those with schizophrenia. Thorazine was followed the next year by Miltown (meprobamate), sold as a "minor tranquilizer" to treat anxiety in outpatients. And in 1957, Marsilid (iproniazid) came on the market as a "psychic energizer" to treat depression.

In the space of three short years, then, drugs had become available to treat what at that time were regarded as the three major categories of mental illness—psychosis, anxiety, and depression—and the face of psychiatry was totally transformed. These drugs, however, had not initially been developed to treat mental illness. They had been derived from drugs meant to treat infections, and were found only serendipitously to alter the mental state. At first, no one had any idea how they worked. They simply blunted disturbing mental symptoms. But over the next decade, researchers found that these drugs, and the newer psychoactive drugs that quickly followed, affected the levels of certain chemicals in the brain.

*

Some brief—and necessarily quite simplified—background: The brain contains billions of nerve cells, called neurons, arrayed in immensely complicated networks and communicating with one another constantly. The typical neuron has multiple filamentous extensions, one called an axon and the others called dendrites, through which it sends and receives signals from other neurons. For one neuron to communicate with another, however, the signal must be transmitted across the tiny space separating them, called a synapse. To accomplish that, the axon of the sending neuron releases a chemical, called a neurotransmitter, into the synapse. The neurotransmitter crosses the synapse and attaches to receptors on the second neuron, often a dendrite, thereby activating or inhibiting the receiving cell. Axons have multiple terminals, so each neuron has multiple synapses. Afterward, the neurotransmitter is either reabsorbed by the first neuron or metabolized by enzymes so that the status quo ante is restored. There are exceptions and variations to this story, but that is the usual way neurons communicate with one another.

When it was found that psychoactive drugs affect neurotransmitter levels in the brain, as evidenced mainly by the levels of their breakdown products in the spinal fluid, the theory arose that the cause of mental illness is an abnormality in the brain's concentration of these chemicals that is specifically countered by the appropriate drug. For example, because Thorazine was found to lower dopamine levels in the brain, it was postulated that psychoses like schizophrenia are caused by too much dopamine. Or later, because certain antidepressants increase levels of the neurotransmitter serotonin in the brain, it was postulated that depression is caused by too little serotonin. (These antidepressants, like Prozac or Celexa, are called selective serotonin reuptake inhibitors (SSRIs) because they prevent the reabsorption of serotonin by the neurons that release it, so that more remains in the synapses to activate other neurons.) Thus, instead of developing a drug to treat an abnormality, an abnormality was postulated to fit a drug.

That was a great leap in logic, as all three authors point out. It was entirely possible that drugs that affected neurotransmitter levels could relieve symptoms even if neurotransmitters had nothing to do with the illness in the first place (and even possible that they relieved symptoms through some other mode of action entirely). As Carlat puts it, "By this same logic one could argue that the cause of all pain conditions is a deficiency of opiates, since narcotic pain medications activate opiate receptors in the brain." Or similarly, one could argue that fevers are caused by too little aspirin.

But the main problem with the theory is that after decades of trying to prove it, researchers have still come up empty-handed. All three authors document the failure of scientists to find good evidence in its favor. Neurotransmitter function seems to be normal in people with mental illness before treatment. In Whitaker's words:

> Prior to treatment, patients diagnosed with schizophrenia, depression, and other psychiatric disorders do not suffer from any known "chemical imbalance." However, once a person is put on a psychiatric medication, which, in one manner or another, throws a wrench into the usual mechanics of a neuronal pathway, his or her brain begins to function . . . *abnormally*.

Carlat refers to the chemical imbalance theory as a "myth" (which he calls "convenient" because it destigmatizes mental illness), and Kirsch, whose book focuses on depression, sums up this way: "It now seems beyond question that the traditional account of depression as a chemical imbalance in the brain is simply wrong." Why the theory persists despite the lack of evidence is a subject I'll come to.

Do the drugs work? After all, regardless of the theory, that is the practical question. In his spare, remarkably engrossing book, *The Emperor's New Drugs,* Kirsch describes his fifteen-year scientific quest to answer that question about antidepressants. When he began his work in 1995, his main interest was in the effects of placebos. To study them, he and a colleague reviewed thirty-eight published clinical trials that compared various treatments for depression with placebos, or compared psychotherapy with no treatment. Most such trials last for six to eight weeks, and during that time, patients tend to improve somewhat even without any treatment. But Kirsch found that placebos were three times as effective as no treatment. That didn't particularly surprise him. What did surprise him was the fact that antidepressants were only marginally better than placebos. As judged by scales used to measure depression, placebos were 75 percent as effective as antidepressants. Kirsch then decided to repeat his study by examining a more complete and standardized data set.

The data he used were obtained from the U.S. Food and Drug Administration (FDA) instead of the published literature. When drug companies seek approval from the FDA to market a new drug, they must submit to the agency all clinical trials they have sponsored. The trials are usually double-blind and placebo-controlled, that is, the participating patients are randomly assigned to either drug or placebo, and neither they nor their doctors know which they have been assigned. The patients are told only that they will receive an active drug or a placebo, and they are also told of any side effects they might experience. If two trials show that the drug is more effective than a placebo, the drug is generally approved. But companies may sponsor as many trials as they like, most of which could be negative — that is, fail to show effectiveness. All they need is two positive ones. (The results of trials of the same drug can differ for many reasons, including the way the trial is designed and conducted, its size, and the types of patients studied.)

For obvious reasons, drug companies make very sure that their positive studies are published in medical journals and doctors know about them, while the negative ones often languish unseen within the FDA, which regards them as proprietary and therefore confidential. This practice greatly biases the medical literature, medical education, and treatment decisions.

Kirsch and his colleagues used the Freedom of Information Act to obtain FDA reviews of all placebo-controlled clinical trials, whether positive or negative, submitted for the initial approval of the six most widely used antidepressant drugs approved between 1987 and 1999 — Prozac, Paxil, Zoloft, Celexa, Serzone, and Effexor. This was a better data set than the one used in his previous study, not only because it included negative studies but because the FDA sets uniform quality standards for the trials it reviews and not all of the published research in Kirsch's earlier study had been submitted to the FDA as part of a drug approval application.

Altogether, there were forty-two trials of the six drugs. Most of them were negative. Overall, placebos were 82 percent as effective as the drugs, as measured by the Hamilton Depression Scale (HAM-D), a widely used score of symptoms of depression. The average difference between drug and placebo was only 1.8 points on the HAM-D, a difference that, while statistically significant, was clinically meaningless. The results were much the same for all six drugs: they were all equally unimpressive. Yet because the positive studies were extensively publicized, while the negative ones were hidden, the public and the medical profession came to believe that these drugs were highly effective antidepressants.

Kirsch was also struck by another unexpected finding. In his earlier study and in work by others, he observed that even treatments that were not considered to be antidepressants—such as synthetic thyroid hormone, opiates, sedatives, stimulants, and some herbal remedies—were as effective as antidepressants in alleviating the symptoms of depression. Kirsch writes, "When administered as antidepressants, drugs that increase, decrease or have no effect on serotonin all relieve depression to about the same degree." What all these "effective" drugs had in common was that they produced side effects, which participating patients had been told they might experience.

It is important that clinical trials, particularly those dealing with subjective conditions like depression, remain double-blind, with neither patients nor doctors knowing whether or not they are getting a placebo. That prevents both patients and doctors from imagining improvements that are not there, something that is more likely if they believe the agent being administered is an active drug instead of a placebo. Faced with his findings that nearly any pill with side effects was slightly more effective in treating depression than an inert placebo, Kirsch speculated that the presence of side effects in individuals receiving drugs enabled them to guess correctly that they were getting active treatment—and this was borne out by interviews with patients and doctors—which made them more likely to report improvement. He suggests that the reason antidepressants appear to work better in relieving severe depression than in less severe cases is that patients with severe symptoms are likely to be on higher doses and therefore experience more side effects.

To further investigate whether side effects bias responses, Kirsch looked at some trials that employed "active" placebos instead of inert ones. An active placebo is one that itself produces side effects, such as atropine—a drug that selectively blocks the action of certain types of nerve fibers. Although not an antidepressant, atropine causes, among other things, a noticeably dry mouth. In trials using atropine as the placebo, there was no difference between the antidepressant and the active placebo. Everyone had side effects of one type or another, and everyone reported the same level of improvement. Kirsch reported a number of other odd findings in clinical trials of antidepressants, including the fact that there is no dose-response curve—that is, high doses worked no better than low ones—which is extremely unlikely for truly effective drugs. "Putting all this together," writes Kirsch,

> leads to the conclusion that the relatively small difference between drugs and placebos might not be a real drug effect at all. Instead, it might be an enhanced placebo effect, produced by the fact that some patients have broken [the] blind and have come to realize whether they were given drug or placebo. If this is the case, then there is no real antidepressant drug effect at all. Rather than comparing placebo to drug, we have been comparing "regular" placebos to "extra-strength" placebos.

That is a startling conclusion that flies in the face of widely accepted medical opinion, but Kirsch reaches it in a careful, logical way. Psychiatrists who use antidepressants—and that's most of them—and patients who take them might insist that they know from clinical experience that the drugs work. But anecdotes are known to be a treacherous way to evaluate medical treatments, since they are so subject to bias; they can suggest hypotheses to be studied, but they cannot prove them. That is why the development of the double-blind, randomized, placebo-controlled clinical trial in the middle of the past century was such an important advance in medical science. Anecdotes about leeches or laetrile or megadoses of vitamin C, or any number of other popular treatments, could not stand up to the scrutiny of well-designed trials. Kirsch is a faithful proponent of the scientific method, and his voice therefore brings a welcome objectivity to a subject often swayed by anecdotes, emotions, or, as we will see, self-interest.

Whitaker's book is broader and more polemical. He considers all mental illness, not just depression. Whereas Kirsch concludes that antidepressants are probably no more effective than placebos, Whitaker concludes that they and most of the other psychoactive drugs are not only ineffective but harmful. He begins by observing that even as drug treatment for mental illness has skyrocketed, so has the prevalence of the conditions treated:

> The number of disabled mentally ill has risen dramatically since 1955, and during the past two decades, a period when the prescribing of psychiatric medications has exploded, the number of adults and children disabled by mental illness has risen at a mind-boggling rate. Thus we arrive at an obvious question, even though it is heretical in kind: Could our drug-based paradigm of care, in some unforeseen way, be fueling this modern-day plague?

Moreover, Whitaker contends, the natural history of mental illness has changed. Whereas conditions such as schizophrenia and depression were once mainly self-limited or episodic, with each episode usually lasting no more than six months and interspersed with long periods of normalcy, the conditions are now chronic and lifelong. Whitaker believes that this might be because drugs, even those that relieve symptoms in the short term, cause long-term mental harms that continue after the underlying illness would have naturally resolved.

The evidence he marshals for this theory varies in quality. He doesn't sufficiently acknowledge the difficulty of studying the natural history of any illness over a fifty-some-year time span during which many circumstances have changed, in addition to drug use. It is even more difficult to compare long-term outcomes in treated versus untreated patients, since treatment may be more likely in those with more severe disease at the outset. Nevertheless, Whitaker's evidence is suggestive, if not conclusive.

If psychoactive drugs do cause harm, as Whitaker contends, what is the mechanism? The answer, he believes, lies in their effects on neurotransmitters. It is well understood that psychoactive drugs disturb neurotransmitter function, even if that was not the cause of the illness in the first place. Whitaker describes a chain of effects. When, for example, an SSRI antidepressant like Celexa increases serotonin levels in synapses, it stimulates compensatory changes through a process called negative feedback. In response to the high levels of serotonin, the neurons that secrete it (presynaptic neurons) release less of it, and the postsynaptic neurons become desensitized to it. In effect, the brain is trying to nullify the drug's effects. The same is true for drugs that block neurotransmitters, except in reverse. For example, most antipsychotic drugs block dopamine, but the presynaptic neurons compensate by releasing more of it, and the postsynaptic neurons take it up more avidly. (This explanation is necessarily oversimplified, since many psychoactive drugs affect more than one of the many neurotransmitters.)

With long-term use of psychoactive drugs, the result is, in the words of Steve Hyman, a former director of the NIMH and until recently provost of Harvard University, "substantial and long-lasting alterations in neural function." As quoted by Whitaker, the brain, Hyman wrote, begins to function in a manner "qualitatively as well as quantitatively different from the normal state." After several weeks on psychoactive drugs, the brain's compensatory efforts begin to fail, and side effects emerge that reflect the mechanism of action of the drugs. For example, the SSRIs may cause episodes of mania, because of the excess of serotonin. Antipsychotics cause side effects that resemble Parkinson's disease, because of the depletion of dopamine (which is also depleted in Parkinson's disease). As side effects emerge, they are often treated by other drugs, and many patients end up on a cocktail of psychoactive drugs prescribed for a cocktail of diagnoses. The episodes of mania caused by antidepressants may lead to a new diagnosis of "bipolar disorder" and treatment with a "mood stabilizer," such as Depakote (an anticonvulsant) plus one of the newer antipsychotic drugs. And so on.

Some patients take as many as six psychoactive drugs daily. One well-respected researcher, Nancy Andreasen, and her colleagues published evidence that the use of antipsychotic drugs is associated with shrinkage of the brain, and that the effect is directly related to the dose and duration of treatment. As Andreasen explained to the *New York Times,* "The prefrontal cortex doesn't get the input it needs and is being shut down by drugs. That reduces the psychotic symptoms. It also causes the prefrontal cortex to slowly atrophy."

Getting off the drugs is exceedingly difficult, according to Whitaker, because when they are withdrawn the compensatory mechanisms are left unopposed. When Celexa is withdrawn, serotonin levels fall precipitously because the presynaptic neurons are not releasing normal amounts and the postsynaptic neurons no longer have enough receptors for it. Similarly, when an antipsychotic is withdrawn, dopamine levels may skyrocket. The symptoms produced by withdrawing psychoactive drugs are often confused with relapses of the original disorder, which can lead psychiatrists to resume drug treatment, perhaps at higher doses.

Unlike the cool Kirsch, Whitaker is outraged by what he sees as an iatrogenic (i.e., inadvertent and medically introduced) epidemic of brain dysfunction, particularly that caused by the widespread use of the newer ("atypical") antipsychotics, such as Zyprexa, which cause serious side effects. Here is what he calls his "quick thought experiment":

> Imagine that a virus suddenly appears in our society that makes people sleep twelve, fourteen hours a day. Those infected with it move about somewhat slowly and seem emotionally disengaged. Many gain huge amounts of weight—twenty, forty, sixty, and even one hundred pounds. Often their blood sugar levels soar, and so do their cholesterol levels. A number of those struck by the mysterious illness—including young children and teenagers—become diabetic in fairly short order . . . The federal government gives hundreds of millions of dollars to scientists at the best universities to decipher the inner workings of this virus, and they report that the reason it causes such global dysfunction is that it blocks a multitude of neurotransmitter receptors in the brain—dopaminergic, serotonergic, muscarinic, adrenergic, and histaminergic. All of those neuronal pathways in the brain are compromised. Meanwhile, MRI studies find that over a period of several years, the virus shrinks the cerebral cortex, and this shrinkage is tied to cognitive decline. A terrified public clamors for a cure.
>
> Now such an illness has in fact hit millions of American children and adults. We have just described the effects of Eli Lilly's best-selling antipsychotic, Zyprexa.

If psychoactive drugs are useless, as Kirsch believes about antidepressants, or worse than useless, as Whitaker believes, why are they so widely prescribed by psychiatrists and regarded by the public and the profession as something akin to wonder drugs? Why is the current against which Kirsch and Whitaker and, as we will see, Carlat are swimming so powerful?

The Illusions of Psychiatry

Much of the explanation lies in the American Psychiatric Association's *Diagnostic and Statistical Manual of Mental Disorders* (*DSM*) — often referred to as the bible of psychiatry, and now heading for its fifth edition — and its extraordinary influence within American society. I also examine *Unhinged,* the recent book by Daniel Carlat, a psychiatrist, who provides a disillusioned insider's view of the psychiatric profession. And I discuss the widespread use of psychoactive drugs in children, and the baleful influence of the pharmaceutical industry on the practice of psychiatry.

One of the leaders of modern psychiatry, Leon Eisenberg, a professor at Johns Hopkins and then Harvard Medical School, who was among the first to study the effects of stimulants on attention deficit disorder in children, wrote that American psychiatry in the late twentieth century moved from a state of "brainlessness" to one of "mindlessness." By that he meant that before psychoactive drugs (drugs that affect the mental state) were introduced, the profession had little interest in neurotransmitters or any other aspect of the physical brain. Instead, it subscribed to the Freudian view that mental illness had its roots in unconscious conflicts, usually originating in childhood, that affected the mind as though it were separate from the brain.

But with the introduction of psychoactive drugs in the 1950s, and sharply accelerating in the 1980s, the focus shifted to the brain. Psychiatrists began to refer to themselves as psychopharmacologists, and they had less and less interest in exploring the life stories of their patients. Their main concern was to eliminate or reduce symptoms by treating sufferers with drugs that would alter brain function. An early advocate of this biological model of mental illness, Eisenberg in his later years became an outspoken critic of what he saw as the indiscriminate use of psychoactive drugs, driven largely by the machinations of the pharmaceutical industry.

When psychoactive drugs were first introduced, there was a brief period of optimism in the psychiatric profession, but by the 1970s, optimism gave way to a sense of threat. Serious side effects of the drugs were becoming apparent, and an antipsychiatry movement had taken root, as exemplified by the writings of Thomas Szasz

and the movie *One Flew Over the Cuckoo's Nest*. There was also growing competition for patients from psychologists and social workers. In addition, psychiatrists were plagued by internal divisions:
some embraced the new biological model, some still clung to the
Freudian model, and a few saw mental illness as an essentially sane
response to an insane world. Moreover, within the larger medical
profession, psychiatrists were regarded as something like poor relations; even with their new drugs, they were seen as less scientific
than other specialists, and their income was generally lower.

In the late 1970s, the psychiatric profession struck back—hard. As
Robert Whitaker tells it in *Anatomy of an Epidemic*, the medical director of the American Psychiatric Association (APA), Melvin Sab-
shin, declared in 1977 that "a vigorous effort to remedicalize psychiatry should be strongly supported," and he launched an all-out
media and public relations campaign to do exactly that. Psychiatry
had a powerful weapon that its competitors lacked. Since psychiatrists must qualify as MDs, they have the legal authority to write
prescriptions. By fully embracing the biological model of mental
illness and the use of psychoactive drugs to treat it, psychiatry was
able to relegate other mental health care providers to ancillary
positions and also to identify itself as a scientific discipline along
with the rest of the medical profession. Most important, by emphasizing drug treatment, psychiatry became the darling of the
pharmaceutical industry, which soon made its gratitude tangible.

These efforts to enhance the status of psychiatry were undertaken deliberately. The APA was then working on the third edition
of the *DSM*, which provides diagnostic criteria for all mental disorders. The president of the APA had appointed Robert Spitzer, a
much-admired professor of psychiatry at Columbia University, to
head the task force overseeing the project. The first two editions,
published in 1952 and 1968, reflected the Freudian view of mental illness and were little known outside the profession. Spitzer set
out to make the *DSM-III* something quite different. He promised
that it would be "a defense of the medical model as applied to
psychiatric problems," and the president of the APA in 1977, Jack
Weinberg, said it would "clarify to anyone who may be in doubt
that we regard psychiatry as a specialty of medicine."

When Spitzer's *DSM-III* was published in 1980, it contained 265 diagnoses (up from 182 in the previous edition), and it came into nearly universal use, not only by psychiatrists, but by insurance companies, hospitals, courts, prisons, schools, researchers, government agencies, and the rest of the medical profession. Its main goal was to bring consistency (usually referred to as "reliability") to psychiatric diagnosis, that is, to ensure that psychiatrists who saw the same patient would agree on the diagnosis. To do that, each diagnosis was defined by a list of symptoms, with numerical thresholds. For example, having at least five of nine particular symptoms got you a full-fledged diagnosis of a major depressive episode within the broad category of "mood disorders." But there was another goal—to justify the use of psychoactive drugs. The president of the APA last year, Carol Bernstein, in effect acknowledged that. "It became necessary in the 1970s," she wrote, "to facilitate diagnostic agreement among clinicians, scientists, and regulatory authorities given the need to match patients with newly emerging pharmacologic treatments."

The *DSM-III* was almost certainly more "reliable" than the earlier versions, but reliability is not the same thing as validity. Reliability, as I have noted, is used to mean consistency; validity refers to correctness or soundness. If nearly all physicians agreed that freckles were a sign of cancer, the diagnosis would be "reliable," but not valid. The problem with the *DSM* is that in all of its editions, it has simply reflected the opinions of its writers, and in the case of the *DSM-III* mainly of Spitzer himself, who has been justly called one of the most influential psychiatrists of the twentieth century. In his words, he "picked everybody that [he] was comfortable with" to serve with him on the fifteen-member task force, and there were complaints that he called too few meetings and generally ran the process in a haphazard but highhanded manner. Spitzer said in a 1989 interview, "I could just get my way by sweet talking and whatnot." In a 1984 article entitled "The Disadvantages of *DSM-III* Outweigh Its Advantages," George Vaillant, a professor of psychiatry at Harvard Medical School, wrote that the *DSM-III* represented "a bold series of choices based on guess, taste, prejudice, and hope," which seems to be a fair description.

Not only did the *DSM* become the bible of psychiatry, but like the real Bible, it depended a lot on something akin to revelation. There are no citations of scientific studies to support its decisions.

That is an astonishing omission, because in all medical publications, whether journal articles or textbooks, statements of fact are supposed to be supported by citations of published scientific studies. (There are four separate "sourcebooks" for the current edition of the *DSM* that present the rationale for some decisions, along with references, but that is not the same thing as specific references.) It may be of much interest for a group of experts to get together and offer their opinions, but unless these opinions can be buttressed by evidence, they do not warrant the extraordinary deference shown to the *DSM*. The *DSM-III* was supplanted by the *DSM-III-R* in 1987, the *DSM-IV* in 1994, and the current version, the *DSM-IV-TR* (text revised) in 2000, which contains 365 diagnoses. "With each subsequent edition," writes Daniel Carlat in his absorbing book, "the number of diagnostic categories multiplied, and the books became larger and more expensive. Each became a best seller for the APA, and *DSM* is now one of the major sources of income for the organization." The *DSM-IV* sold over a million copies.

As psychiatry became a drug-intensive specialty, the pharmaceutical industry was quick to see the advantages of forming an alliance with the psychiatric profession. Drug companies began to lavish attention and largesse on psychiatrists, both individually and collectively, directly and indirectly. They showered gifts and free samples on practicing psychiatrists, hired them as consultants and speakers, bought them meals, helped pay for them to attend conferences, and supplied them with "educational" materials. When Minnesota and Vermont implemented "sunshine laws" that require drug companies to report all payments to doctors, psychiatrists were found to receive more money than physicians in any other specialty. The pharmaceutical industry also subsidizes meetings of the APA and other psychiatric conferences. About a fifth of APA funding now comes from drug companies.

Drug companies are particularly eager to win over faculty psychiatrists at prestigious academic medical centers. Called "key opinion leaders" (KOLs) by the industry, these are the people who through their writing and teaching influence how mental illness will be diagnosed and treated. They also publish much of the clinical research on drugs and, most importantly, largely determine the content of the *DSM*. In a sense, they are the best sales force the industry could have, and are worth every cent spent on them. Of the 170 contributors to the current version of the *DSM* (the *DSM-IV-TR*), almost all of whom would be described as KOLs, ninety-five had financial ties to drug companies, including all of the contributors to the sections on mood disorders and schizophrenia.

The drug industry, of course, supports other specialists and professional societies, too, but Carlat asks, "Why do psychiatrists consistently lead the pack of specialties when it comes to taking money from drug companies?" His answer: "Our diagnoses are subjective and expandable, and we have few rational reasons for choosing one treatment over another." Unlike the conditions treated in most other branches of medicine, there are no objective signs or tests for mental illness—no lab data or MRI findings—and the boundaries between normal and abnormal are often unclear. That makes it possible to expand diagnostic boundaries or even create new diagnoses, in ways that would be impossible, say, in a field like cardiology. And drug companies have every interest in inducing psychiatrists to do just that.

In addition to the money spent on the psychiatric profession directly, drug companies heavily support many related patient advocacy groups and educational organizations. Whitaker writes that in the first quarter of 2009 alone,

> Eli Lilly gave $551,000 to NAMI [National Alliance on Mental Illness] and its local chapters, $465,000 to the National Mental Health Association, $130,000 to CHADD (an ADHD [attention deficit hyperactivity disorder] patient-advocacy group), and $69,250 to the American Foundation for Suicide Prevention.

And that's just one company in three months; one can imagine what the yearly total would be from all companies that make psychoactive drugs. These groups ostensibly exist to raise public awareness of psychiatric disorders, but they also have the effect of promoting the use of psychoactive drugs and influencing insurers to cover them. Whitaker summarizes the growth of industry influence after the publication of the *DSM-III* as follows:

> In short, a powerful quartet of voices came together during the 1980's eager to inform the public that mental disorders were brain

diseases. Pharmaceutical companies provided the financial muscle. The APA and psychiatrists at top medical schools conferred intellectual legitimacy upon the enterprise. The NIMH [National Institute of Mental Health] put the government's stamp of approval on the story. NAMI provided a moral authority.

Like most other psychiatrists, Carlat treats his patients only with drugs, not talk therapy, and he is candid about the advantages of doing so. If he sees three patients an hour for psychopharmacology, he calculates, he earns about $180 per hour from insurers. In contrast, he would be able to see only one patient an hour for talk therapy, for which insurers would pay him less than $100. Carlat does not believe that psychopharmacology is particularly complicated, let alone precise, although the public is led to believe that it is:

> Patients often view psychiatrists as wizards of neurotransmitters, who can choose just the right medication for whatever chemical imbalance is at play. This exaggerated conception of our capabilities has been encouraged by drug companies, by psychiatrists ourselves, and by our patients' understandable hopes for cures.

His work consists of asking patients a series of questions about their symptoms to see whether they match up with any of the disorders in the *DSM*. This matching exercise, he writes, provides "the illusion that we understand our patients when all we are doing is assigning them labels." Often patients meet criteria for more than one diagnosis, because there is an overlap in symptoms. For example, difficulty concentrating is a criterion for more than one disorder. One of Carlat's patients ended up with seven separate diagnoses. "We target discrete symptoms with treatments, and other drugs are piled on top to treat side effects." A typical patient, he says, might be taking Celexa for depression, Ativan for anxiety, Ambien for insomnia, Provigil for fatigue (a side effect of Celexa), and Viagra for impotence (another side effect of Celexa).

As for the medications themselves, Carlat writes that "there are only a handful of umbrella categories of psychotropic drugs," within which the drugs are not very different from one another. He doesn't believe there is much basis for choosing among them. "To a remarkable degree, our choice of medications is subjective, even random. Perhaps your psychiatrist is in a Lexapro mood this morning, because he was just visited by an attractive Lexapro drug rep." And he sums up:

> Such is modern psychopharmacology. Guided purely by symptoms, we try different drugs, with no real conception of what we are trying to fix, or of how the drugs are working. I am perpetually astonished that we are so effective for so many patients.

While Carlat believes that psychoactive drugs are sometimes effective, his evidence is anecdotal. What he objects to is their overuse and what he calls the "frenzy of psychiatric diagnoses." As he puts it, "If you ask any psychiatrist in clinical practice, including me, whether antidepressants work for their patients, you will hear an unambiguous 'yes.' We see people getting better all the time." But then he goes on to speculate, like Irving Kirsch in *The Emperor's New Drugs,* that what they are really responding to could be an activated placebo effect. If psychoactive drugs are not all they're cracked up to be—and the evidence is that they're not—what about the diagnoses themselves? As they multiply with each edition of the *DSM,* what are we to make of them?

In 1999, the APA began work on its fifth revision of the *DSM,* which is scheduled to be published in 2013. The twenty-seven-member task force is headed by David Kupfer, a professor of psychiatry at the University of Pittsburgh, assisted by Darrel Regier of the APA's American Psychiatric Institute for Research and Education. As with the earlier editions, the task force is advised by multiple work groups, which now total some 140 members, corresponding to the major diagnostic categories. Ongoing deliberations and proposals have been extensively reported on the APA website (www.DSM5 .org) and in the media, and it appears that the already very large constellation of mental disorders will grow still larger.

In particular, diagnostic boundaries will be broadened to include precursors of disorders, such as "psychosis risk syndrome" and "mild cognitive impairment" (possible early Alzheimer's disease). The term *spectrum* is used to widen categories, for example, "obsessive-compulsive disorder spectrum," "schizophrenia spectrum disorder," and "autism spectrum disorder." And there are proposals for entirely new entries, such as "hypersexual disorder," "restless legs syndrome," and "binge eating."

Even Allen Frances, chairman of the *DSM-IV* task force, is highly critical of the expansion of diagnoses in the *DSM-V.* In the June 26, 2009, issue of *Psychiatric Times,* he wrote that the *DSM-V* will be a "bonanza for the pharmaceutical industry but at a huge cost to the new false positive patients caught in the excessively wide *DSM-V* net." As if to underscore that judgment, Kupfer and Regier wrote in a recent article in the *Journal of the American Medical Association* (*JAMA*), entitled "Why All of Medicine Should Care About *DSM-5*," that "in primary care settings, approximately 30 percent to 50 percent of patients have prominent mental health symptoms or identifiable mental disorders, which have significant adverse consequences if left untreated." It looks as though it will be harder and harder to be normal.

At the end of the article by Kupfer and Regier is a small-print "financial disclosure" that reads in part:

> Prior to being appointed as chair, *DSM-5* Task Force, Dr. Kupfer reports having served on advisory boards for Eli Lilly & Co, Forest Pharmaceuticals Inc, Solvay/Wyeth Pharmaceuticals, and Johnson & Johnson; and consulting for Servier and Lundbeck.

Regier oversees all industry-sponsored research grants for the APA. The *DSM-V* (used interchangeably with *DSM-5*) is the first edition to establish rules to limit financial conflicts of interest in members of the task force and work groups. According to these rules, once members were appointed, which occurred in 2006–2008, they could receive no more than $10,000 per year in aggregate from drug companies or own more than $50,000 in company stock. The website shows their company ties for three years before their appointments, and that is what Kupfer disclosed in the *JAMA* article and what is shown on the APA website, where 56 percent of members of the work groups disclosed significant industry interests.

The pharmaceutical industry influences psychiatrists to prescribe psychoactive drugs even for categories of patients in whom the drugs have not been found safe and effective. What should be of greatest concern for Americans is the astonishing rise in the diagnosis and treatment of mental illness in children, sometimes as young as two years old. These children are often treated with drugs that were never approved by the FDA for use in this age group and have serious side effects. The apparent prevalence of "juvenile bipolar disorder" jumped fortyfold between 1993 and 2004, and that of "autism" increased from one in five hundred children to one in ninety over the same decade. Ten percent of ten-year-old boys now take daily stimulants for ADHD—attention deficit hyperactivity disorder—and 500,000 children take antipsychotic drugs.

There seem to be fashions in childhood psychiatric diagnoses, with one disorder giving way to the next. At first, ADHD, manifested by hyperactivity, inattentiveness, and impulsivity usually in school-age children, was the fastest-growing diagnosis. But in the mid-1990s, two highly influential psychiatrists at the Massachusetts General Hospital proposed that many children with ADHD really had bipolar disorder that could sometimes be diagnosed as early as infancy. They proposed that the manic episodes characteristic of bipolar disorder in adults might be manifested in children as irritability. That gave rise to a flood of diagnoses of juvenile bipolar disorder. Eventually this created something of a backlash, and the *DSM-V* now proposes partly to replace the diagnosis with a brand-new one, called "temper dysregulation disorder with dysphoria," or TDD, which Allen Frances calls "a new monster."

One would be hard-pressed to find a two-year-old who is not sometimes irritable, a boy in fifth grade who is not sometimes inattentive, or a girl in middle school who is not anxious. (Imagine what taking a drug that causes obesity would do to such a girl.) Whether such children are labeled as having a mental disorder and treated with prescription drugs depends a lot on who they are and the pressures their parents face. As low-income families experience growing economic hardship, many are finding that applying for Supplemental Security Income (SSI) payments on the basis of mental disability is the only way to survive. It is more generous than welfare, and it virtually ensures that the family will also qualify for Medicaid. According to MIT economics professor David Autor, "This has become the new welfare." Hospitals and state welfare agencies also have incentives to encourage uninsured families to apply for SSI payments, since hospitals will get paid and states will save money by shifting welfare costs to the federal government.

Growing numbers of for-profit firms specialize in helping poor families apply for SSI benefits. But to qualify nearly always requires that applicants, including children, be taking psychoactive drugs. According to a *New York Times* story, a Rutgers University study found that children from low-income families are four times as likely as privately insured children to receive antipsychotic medicines.

In December 2006 a four-year-old child named Rebecca Riley died in a small town near Boston from a combination of Clonidine and Depakote, which she had been prescribed, along with Seroquel, to treat "ADHD" and "bipolar disorder"—diagnoses she received when she was two years old. Clonidine was approved by the FDA for treating high blood pressure. Depakote was approved for treating epilepsy and acute mania in bipolar disorder. Seroquel was approved for treating schizophrenia and acute mania. None of the three was approved to treat ADHD or for long-term use in bipolar disorder, and none was approved for children Rebecca's age. Rebecca's two older siblings had been given the same diagnoses and were each taking three psychoactive drugs. The parents had obtained SSI benefits for the siblings and for themselves, and were applying for benefits for Rebecca when she died. The family's total income from SSI was about $30,000 per year.

Whether these drugs should ever have been prescribed for Rebecca in the first place is the crucial question. The FDA approves drugs only for specified uses, and it is illegal for companies to market them for any other purpose—that is, "off-label." Nevertheless, physicians are permitted to prescribe drugs for any reason they choose, and one of the most lucrative things drug companies can do is persuade physicians to prescribe drugs off-label, despite the law against it. In just the past four years, five firms have admitted to federal charges of illegally marketing psychoactive drugs. AstraZeneca marketed Seroquel off-label for children and the elderly (another vulnerable population, often administered antipsychotics in nursing homes); Pfizer faced similar charges for Geodon (an antipsychotic); Eli Lilly for Zyprexa (an antipsychotic); Bristol-Myers Squibb for Abilify (another antipsychotic); and Forest Labs for Celexa (an antidepressant).

Despite having to pay hundreds of millions of dollars to settle the charges, the companies have probably come out well ahead. The original purpose of permitting doctors to prescribe drugs off-label was to enable them to treat patients on the basis of early scientific reports, without having to wait for FDA approval. But that sensible rationale has become a marketing tool. Because of the subjective nature of psychiatric diagnosis, the ease with which diagnostic boundaries can be expanded, the seriousness of the side effects of psychoactive drugs, and the pervasive influence of their manufacturers, I believe doctors should be prohibited from prescribing psychoactive drugs off-label, just as companies are prohibited from marketing them off-label.

The books by Irving Kirsch, Robert Whitaker, and Daniel Carlat are powerful indictments of the way psychiatry is now practiced. They document the "frenzy" of diagnosis, the overuse of drugs with sometimes devastating side effects, and widespread conflicts of interest. Critics of these books might argue, as Nancy Andreasen implied in her paper on the loss of brain tissue with long-term antipsychotic treatment, that the side effects are the price that must be paid to relieve the suffering caused by mental illness. If we knew that the benefits of psychoactive drugs outweighed their harms, that would be a strong argument, since there is no doubt that many people suffer grievously from mental illness. But as Kirsch, Whitaker, and Carlat argue convincingly, that expectation may be wrong.

At the very least, we need to stop thinking of psychoactive drugs as the best, and often the only, treatment for mental illness or emotional distress. Both psychotherapy and exercise have been shown to be as effective as drugs for depression, and their effects are longer-lasting, but unfortunately, there is no industry to push these alternatives and Americans have come to believe that pills must be more potent. More research is needed to study alternatives to psychoactive drugs, and the results should be included in medical education.

In particular, we need to rethink the care of troubled children. Here the problem is often troubled families in troubled circumstances. Treatment directed at these environmental conditions—such as one-on-one tutoring to help parents cope or after-school centers for the children—should be studied and compared with drug treatment. In the long run, such alternatives would probably be less expensive. Our reliance on psychoactive drugs, seemingly for all of life's discontents, tends to close off other options. In view of the risks and questionable long-term effectiveness of drugs, we need to do better. Above all, we should remember the time-honored medical dictum: first, do no harm *(primum non nocere)*.

MIAH ARNOLD

You Owe Me

FROM *Michigan Quarterly Review*

THE CHILDREN I WRITE WITH DIE, no matter how much I
love them, no matter how creative they are, no matter how many
poems they have written or how much they want to live. They die
of diseases with unpronounceable names, of rhabdomyosarcoma
or pilocytic astrocytoma, of cancers rarely heard of in the world
at large, of cancers that are often cured once, but then turn up
again somewhere else: in their lungs, their stomachs, their sinuses,
their bones, their brains. While undergoing their own treatments,
my students watch one friend after another lose legs, cough
up blood, and enter a hospital room they never come out of
again.

The MD Anderson Cancer Center in Houston, Texas, where
for over ten years I have taught poetry and prose for Writers in
the Schools, is a world-renowned research institution. I have met
the sickest children in the world there—children who have been
treated already, somewhere else, and who have come for one last
experimental treatment, who have one last chance at survival. In
this capacity, my students often take part in studies. The treatments they receive are often groundbreaking, innovative ones
that, with time, are perfected and standardized. This means their
experiences, whether their disease is successfully eradicated or
not, serve to build treatment protocols that eventually cure children throughout the world. But only a small percentage of the
students I work with in the center's classrooms live. Less than half,
maybe less than a third, and I think less than that: I am just one

of the writers in residence there. The numbers aren't available
to me.

As part of my job I write a yearly reflective journal. In the first one,
I wrote that while I had been an agnostic before working there, my
experiences at MD Anderson made me understand that whether
or not there is a Supreme Being, there is an afterlife. My proof was
an eleven-year-old boy named Gio, who was a thin, shiny-eyed boy
from Mexico. He was simultaneously firmly planted in the world
of the living and the world of the hereafter. Up until the day his
doctors informed him he wouldn't live another two months, he
had behaved like any other little boy: like he was too cooped up,
like he was ready to tear the hospital apart in an adventure game.
Once he received news of his impending death, he changed. He
wasn't afraid of dying and he wasn't angry at the hospital the way
he had seemed to be before. It was as if the news of his cancer's
progression opened something inside of him so that he could
clearly see into another world, another place he was on his way to.
Whatever it was he saw endowed him with an overwhelming generosity of spirit and the most intense humanity I had ever witnessed.
I don't mean he wandered around performing good deeds; it was
something more internal. He was overtaken by something like joy.
Not a giggling and hysterical one, but a calming joy that infected
every room he entered.

Gio's was the first death I witnessed as a writer, as an outsider
who enters into the intimate world of struggling children. I assumed that his death was a template of sorts: this is how the very
young die; they become almost holy. Unlike older people, who
die scared and uncertain, dying children are endowed with grace.
They are able to peek ahead into the world they are about to enter, and so they feel assured it's there. They know it's okay to tran-
scend.

For two years after Gio's death I clung to this vision. But there
wasn't another death like his. He was an exception. Most of the
teens I regularly worked with when I started at the hospital died
within two years of my meeting them: Oso, a big teddy bear of a
boy, a Mexican immigrant who was so sweet it rubbed off on the
edgier teens around him; Kile, an angry teen from Guam who had
watched his two sisters die of the same cancer that was taking his
life; Dolma, a pretty Turkish girl whose family ran out of money to

pay for more treatments and who tried to sell books of her poems to raise the money they needed. None of these kids blossomed sweetly into death the way Gio seemed to: Oso was so scared I could barely breathe looking at him, Kile became too furious to speak, and Dolma died with her family in Turkey, always believing a miracle was possible.

How horrible to be able to catalogue the deaths of children in this way. I don't know what else to do with what I've seen. These former students, these young, beautiful friends of mine were just the ones I met in my first weeks at the hospital, and the truth is that I could name at least a dozen more off the top of my head. After that I could read through my catalogue of student work, which I have saved, and come up with countless more. Names of lives I have forgotten because I didn't teach them first or last.

Working in a classroom whose currency is the eventual death of most of the students runs contrary to the way anybody wants to think about life. People don't mind being reminded that ten-year-olds die so long as they get to hear the story of that child's life, so long as it is a story of resilience, a story about a soul raging on long after the funeral because it touched so many people's lives and changed them for the better. From my current perspective, demanding so much of a dead child is sick. I also understand it is one of the only ways the people left behind have to make sense of these most enormous of losses. However consciously or unconsciously, they want to look in at the life of a young death and say: See, God had pity on these children because in the end, even though this baby died, she knew something we adults don't comprehend. Her death has meaning that changes my life.

More than a decade into my teaching at the hospital, I no longer say I found faith there. I feel stupid for ever having suggested it. I was, like everybody else, trying to make sense of what is nonsensical. What I can say now is that there is something very special about being one of the people in a dying child's life. When you know somebody with less than six months to live and that person agrees to spend any moment of it with you at all, the immensity of that generosity does change you, undeniably.

Some children I know for two weeks, some I know for half a decade. That means that I grow much closer to certain patients than

to others. I grow too close. I say: If Khalil dies, I won't be able
to continue working here. Since I have known him since he was
seven and he's twelve now, his death is the line over which my presence in this institution cannot cross. Khalil is too full of life. He
has written half a stream-of-consciousness novel full of food fights
and basketball games, has written 150 poems. He is too crazy to
die, he is wacko, he is nuts—or, as my coworker Jeff used to say before he left the job and moved to California to be a social worker,
Khalil is crackers, an arrival straight from the cracker factory. Why
would the world endow this young boy with such wackiness, with
the young Johnny Cash's lopsided gait and pool-ball eyes, with the
right amount of kindness to soothe the youngest children in the
room and the right amount of self-assurance not to be intimidated
by the presence of the older children, if he were not meant to
live? I know that Khalil will be famous one day—a rock star, a basketball hero, a politician who will become the first Arab American
president of the United States because he is so beautiful, and he
knows suffering, and he will be cured, and I know for sure: he will
live long enough to enter a presidential election, he will live long
past thirty-five.

The classrooms I work out of, with my coworker Evan, two teachers
from the Houston Independent School District, and sometimes
volunteers, are hospital rooms that have been fitted with a few
computers, textbooks, and a table large enough for about ten people to fit around. There are two classrooms: one for kids younger
than twelve, one for teenagers. Usually Evan and I bring the young
students together with the older—mixing age groups is useful in
writing: the different energies of the different ages of children inspire each other. When we have more than ten students we move
into the Pedi-Dome, a giant indoor playground fitted with a basketball hoop, countless balls, and a dozen or so little fire engines
and cars for the preschoolers to ride around on. Its roof is painted
with stars, there is a yellow brick road painted on the floor, and
an entire wall is made up of windows. Even though the view is terrible—we see the top of the building next door—the windows are
so big that the room is full of sunlight.
      Some kids arrive in class sailing down the hallway on their IV
poles, some in wheelchairs or on crutches. Headscarves and base-

ball caps are the preferred bare-head covering—wigs have been universally proclaimed too itchy and too weird. Some days we have one student, some days we have over a dozen. Writers' class, as they dub it, is filled with poems, stories, blogging, Scrabble or Taboo game playing, arts and puppetry projects, and *This American Life*. We enjoy ourselves in Writers'. Tell Michael you're 3,010 years old, tell Darrian you left your sweet-talking mouth at home so he better get to work, and they'll giggle. They'll start making up jokes of their own. They'll start goading each other.

One of the most meaningful days I had in Writers' was after a particularly raucous class in which I think we laughed uncontrollably for three or four minutes straight at one point. We collectively got the giggles. Afterward, an old woman stopped me on my way to the elevators.

"I stood outside and listened to your class today," she said in the halting English that is common in MD Anderson's corridors. "I just stood outside the door and listened to Umberto laughing, because he doesn't laugh in the hospital room. He never laughs anymore, and I thought I'd never hear him laughing again," she said, and she was crying.

I hadn't realized before then how much the fellowship of kids being around kids changed my students' personalities. Umberto laughed all the time in Writers'; he always looked forward to it. Our classes are usually jolly. Even when there's one student who annoys the others, or when students don't want to work, they all pull together to have a good time. To write, to joke, to be children. But the old woman, Umberto's grandma, made me see how important it is for the children to not just be in Writers', but to be in school. To forget, just for a while, the pain, the nausea, the uncertainty, the boredom of hospital life.

Of course, there are sad days. We can go plowing through months and months with a regular group of about ten children, and then something terrible will happen. Then, unimaginably, after six years of living with a cancer that can only be contained by active chemotherapy, after the doctors tell his parents he will die of the chemotherapy if they don't try a more aggressive treatment, and then, after the doctors fail to successfully remove the almost three hundred tumors in Khalil Al-Almoudi's stomach in an experimental surgery, Khalil dies. Nine students are left in the classroom, students who have known him as long as they have been hospitalized, because nobody has been in and out of the hospital as long as Khalil.

The week after his death, two more children enter the hospital classrooms. Oblivious to reasons behind the sadness the schoolteachers, the writers, and the other children can't shake, they assume those first weeks that there is just a pall in a cancer center's classroom.

Students don't often address their cancer directly, in the day-to-day of the classrooms. They write about thunderstorms, or animals, or when they're being more serious, about family and the homes they left behind. However, conquering insurmountable odds and tricking fate are common themes. When they do write directly about their cancer, they don't write poems, they write essays detailing their experience. Except when a child is about to die. Then they often choose poetry; they often speak directly to God. These poems are angry or they are hopeful. One nine-year-old boy who had spent two years writing whacked-out adventure stories wrote to God in this last poem of his life, which was untitled:

> What thoughts I have of You tonight, God.
> You protect me and You make giant waves
> and wash people away. You owe me.
> You make the tornados that suck
> Up the people and move them to another dimension.
> You lift every rock in the whole wide universe and throw them
> At the people who try to hit me.
>
> God, I see You playing my videogames in my room.
> You're young, with shiny eyes like mine.
> You have a little beard and You play the
> Games without using controls
> Because You can. Because You
> Can fly without wings. You
> Can use magic and make balls of fire and lightning.
> God, You are powerful and I am a cell
> Compared to you.

If you were a teacher, and you loved a boy who died, you might quit because you always knew you couldn't keep going after that death. You could quit any day, knowing his wouldn't be the last death, knowing your employers would understand because really, they have been expecting you'd quit suddenly, one day, all along. It is a hard job you have, after all.

The week before Khalil died, I didn't think he would really die. It had been predicted at least a year beforehand, and I had ignored the prediction. I always knew I couldn't work there any longer if he didn't live.

But a month before Khalil's death, his best friend, Darrian, who was newly cancer-free, lost his mother. His perfectly healthy-seeming, thirty-five-year-old mom just collapsed and died on the floor at home, in front of Darrian and his two younger brothers. Darrian called 911, but it was too late. After moving in with his grandmother, arrangements were made for Darrian to have one more semester in the hospital, in a place with people he loved and was familiar with, instead of starting junior high in the public school as he had been scheduled to do. In Writers' class, Darrian only spoke cryptically about his mom. "You know what's weird," he said, just a month after she died, "My mother's birthday and the day she died have all the same numbers in them. I noticed at the funeral." And then he wouldn't say any more.

When Khalil died I thought, on one level, I can't go back. But in the world of the living the reality is that I can't leave just yet. I can't leave Darrian. Or Amirah. Especially Amirah, because she is eight, a little girl from Egypt who loves the Disney princesses and the color pink, but who is one of the most strange and grave little souls I have ever met. I can't step away from her steady, stoic gaze. And when I imagine my own two-year-old daughter in six years I see Amirah's face, awaiting me haughtily at the end of the hallway every Monday and Thursday. I can't leave the hospital just yet, I say to myself. I say, instead: but if Amirah dies, then I can't come back anymore.

Nicole is the elementary school teacher, and she's worked at the hospital a year longer than I have. In her midforties, she is a silver-haired, pretty, no-nonsense Jewish lesbian who adopted a child from China seven years ago.

"The teacher I took over from said we are supposed to take lessons from all this," she says shaking her head, "Take lessons? If one child has to suffer so that I can learn a lesson, I'll skip it, thank you. Learn a lesson! We're not here to learn; we're here because we can be here, and because the kids need people here with them. We are *here*. End of story."

How it is we all stay at the hospital, or why some people come for a couple months and leave while others of us stay for years I don't know. I wonder about it often, though.

Mr. Nicholas, the secondary school teacher who has only taught a couple of years in the hospital, jokes around with his students the whole day, sneaking in algebra and biology lessons as he goes. After hearing about the death of Darrian's mom, I found Mr. Nicholas, who I know has a particularly close bond with Darrian.

"I feel so sad for Darrian," I said. "I feel so sorry for what he's gone through."

Mr. Nicholas looked me in the eye in a way that told me he wasn't going there, and said, "Who you ought to feel sorry for is me, because Ms. Evie retired and now I have triple the paperwork to get through."

Mr. Nicholas takes night classes to be an undertaker. Sometimes he leaves weird pamphlets around the classroom or he talks about corpses nobody has come to claim. He is a smooth-talking, African American man in his early fifties and one of the best regular teachers I've seen cycling through the system. His love for the children is obvious and unstated. Still, I was shocked by what I considered the callousness of his statement. But only for about six seconds: he was telling me, I knew, that his capacity for discussing his feelings was used up. That he could work among so much sadness, but he wouldn't broach the reality of it right there in the classroom, and then get through to the end of the day. He, like everybody who stays in the hospital, fights hard, every day, to keep coming in the next day.

There is no floor to the sadnesses I have entered into at MD Anderson; there is no dimension that could contain the horrors of watching so many young people suffer and then not survive. I spent a long time, in the first years of my teaching, trying to figure out what makes me able to sustain. At first, it seemed there must be an inherent flaw in the personality of people who can work with dying children without breaking down. I can do it, I thought, because my mother abandoned me as a child, because my sister was sick when I was a teenager, because my father emotionally abandoned me when I was a young adult. I am calloused. I don't let people into my heart, and so these children, whose situations should have broken me long ago, don't affect me the way they should. The way they would if I were a fuller person.

I looked critically at the people working alongside me in the same way: this man likes inflicting pain on himself, this woman doesn't connect to anybody and isn't in danger, this woman is unfeeling, this man is just doing his job, that woman is a ditz. We were fakers, I thought. These children need more intense presence than any other children I have known, and we fake that presence. We fake and we fake, I thought, and the children are too young to know we're not here.

Looking so harshly, judging so cruelly, doesn't get a person very far, and I'm much easier on all of us now than I used to be. Instead of focusing on a flaw inside me that retains me unnaturally, I focus on the pull of the children themselves—because, of course, the reason I have worked so long with children fighting cancer is that they have drawn me in, they have invited me, they have accepted me into their fierce and fragile worlds. I feel proud because they have. For some reason that I realize, finally, doesn't matter much at all, I stagger under the weight of the losses I have encountered with these children, but, miraculously, I haven't fallen. I am a Dixie cup, and these children's lives and needs are hundreds of oceans, and by some incredible grace I have been able to contain them.

Khalil went home to Saudi Arabia the summer before he died, and he came back in the fall. Evan and I went to his room because he didn't come to class the first week he came back. The doctors had told him he didn't have two weeks to live, which I knew, but I still didn't believe.

We poked our heads into his room, where he was watching cartoons on television from his hospital bed. He was skinnier than when we'd seen him in the spring. He was sadder. I told him I'd missed him and he asked what we did in class that day. We had written poems about photographs the students had taken of themselves and then painted over. The art teacher, Jonie, was going to enter it all into Houston's Photofest show. I asked if he was going to make a photograph. Maybe, he said. I didn't know what else to say, and his mother came down the hall. A pretty woman who dresses in Western clothes, unlike most of the other Muslim moth ers in the hospital. She had a baby the same time I had my little girl.

"If you let Jonie take a photograph, I'll come to your room and we can write. Or you can come to the classroom. Or we can write something else. Whatever you want," I said.

He searched his head, and gave his signature crooked nod: "*You'll* be back on Thursday. Mondays and Thursdays."

So simple, the clock of my presence in his life, the presence I could see him measuring alongside the other information he had: you will be here Mondays and Thursdays just the same as always, and I am not expected to live through the weekend.

His mother began asking me about my daughter, and I asked her about her youngest son. Two-year-olds. All over the place. Except, I couldn't help thinking, you have a two-year-old and a twelve-year-old who is dying in the bed in front of us. I couldn't look her in the eyes and I fled, ashamed, full of tears that I didn't let out in front of Evan; I didn't let them out until I was in my car in the parking lot. I was aghast I didn't tell Khalil how much I loved him. I didn't know what to say to the boy I had watched grow from a child into a young man, who died late that next Thursday night while I was out at dinner with friends. I thought if I left without saying more, it would guarantee me a next time to say them.

Some parents ask that nobody tell their fifteen-year-old son about the death of his friend; some parents demand their seven-year-old daughter be present when the social workers sit all the children down and give the news. For this reason, we can't discuss deaths openly in class—because even when the uninformed child secretly knows, or even when their parents break down and admit the death they were hiding, then the parent doesn't want them to discuss the death with anybody but family members. We work in a hospital with divergent cultural beliefs—Christian Scientists, liberal Christians, Muslims, Hindus, and Catholics. Death means dramatically different things to different kids, and we are asked not to tread in that territory unless a child chooses, of her own accord, to enter it in writing.

Only the social workers are allowed into the meetings. After they told the students about Khalil's death, the social worker told Jonie and me how the meeting went: Abdul didn't believe Khalil died, Darrian was too afraid of crying to speak, Bianca, who was new to the school, talked about the many friends she'd lost since being treated for cancer. Amirah left the room when she caught wind of what was about to be discussed, or maybe, she just left because her friend walked by . . . it wasn't clear.

A few weeks after Khalil died, Abdul was scheduled to have a surgery in which his leg might be removed. He had told his parents to do what they thought was right—he trusted them. He referred to the upcoming surgery as "the big day."

"I remember Khalil's big day," Darrian whispered, referring to the unsuccessful tumor removals. Abdul pretended not to hear, and Darrian kept his eyes on the binder in front of him.

Once, I found Khalil himself sifting through the files of the poems we typed on the computer. They were on a password protected computer drive whose codes he had weaseled out of Jeff, years before. He liked having the access because he was the first student who demanded to write his poems on the computer, and he liked saving them into his file by himself. But the day I found him on the computer he wasn't looking at his own poems.

"I found poems by Katie and Michael," he told me. Khalil, Katie, and Michael were all seven when they entered the hospital, in the same school year. But Katie died when she was eight, Michael when he was nine, and Khalil was eleven when he was searching through their poems. He was still certain he was going to beat his cancer. Both his friends had died while he was on a trip home to Saudi Arabia and he'd never gotten to say goodbye.

Michael Hendrix looked like a birdling. He had huge brown eyes, clothes that were always one or two sizes too big for him—and his smile was like that, too, almost falling from his face. He was the first person I worked with whose death I was sure would be an end to my teaching—a tiny, African American boy from Houston, who told wild stories, who was the poster boy for the greeting cards the Children's Art Project sells every year to raise money for children's programs. He loved critiquing poems after a couple months of working with us: *This could have used more details, that poem I didn't really see. You need to be able to feel a poem deep inside for it to be any good.*

Like we thought with Khalil, we believed Michael was cured after a year of treatments. But he didn't make it through a semester of regular school before he was back with us. He was skinnier than ever before, weak, and mourning the loss of Katie, who had died over the summer. He was scared, too: he was going to lose a leg. When he came back to the hospital, he would crawl into my lap at the beginning of every lesson, without asking if he could sit there. He's the only child who has ever done that.

Michael weighed almost nothing; his bones, in my mind, were dried-out honeycombs. His legs were skinny and dry. It scared me when he was on my lap; it scared me to touch him because he was dying and I knew, already, I loved him way too much. But when he sat in my lap, I tried to be the steady warmth he needed from me. We would write out a poem and I knew that what he wanted, what he needed, was the feeling of my shoulders wrapped on either side of his own shoulders. I helped him write—a loose hug that lasted at least the length of a single poem, but often, toward the end of his life, a hug that lasted the entire class. Though there were other kids I should have gone around to help more, I couldn't send Michael from my lap. Like I would feel with Khalil, years later, I believed Michael couldn't die if he were sitting there with me. He felt the same way, I think. He's the boy who wrote that God owed him; he dictated the line to me, and I wrote it down, trembling, because he was right.

The rules of teaching sick children: You don't imagine any of them will die. You are teaching living children with living futures. You notice their missing legs, the tumors on their faces, the poles attached to their chests through IV tubes. You don't avert your eyes, but then you forget that you see all that. The second you look around and begin imagining which five or six out of the ten children in front of you won't make it, you are no good as a teacher.

No teacher I know at the hospital has ever cried over the death of a child, not in front of the others. After Khalil died, I tried to get the teachers and Jonie together over lunch one day, so we could talk. As Mr. Nicholas had made clear before, though, it turned out none of them wanted to say anything. Nicole said she felt him in her room the day he died; Jonie said there is so much sadness, that opening the door to any of it would obliterate her. That was as much as people were able to hear, or willing to share.

A few weeks after that meeting, though, Evan and I were teaching in the secondary classroom. We were expecting Amirah's best friend to arrive from Egypt anytime. Amirah had been looking forward to this moment for weeks; it was all she talked about. There was no way not to be caught up in her excitement.

Since Amirah is usually in the elementary classroom, her mother brought her friend to that room. Nicole was grading there, and as soon as she saw the girl, she grabbed her by the hand and ran across the hall to the room we were in.

"She's here!" she said, breathlessly, dragging the poor child alongside her. "Everybody, this is Amirah's best friend in the whole world," Nicole said, and then she was sobbing. Nicole, who is always so solid and so unflappable, was sobbing so hard from happiness for Amirah she couldn't finish the introductions. The only time I have ever seen a coworker cry.

When people ask me about working at the hospital, no matter where the argument about whether or not I will be able to keep working longer is in my head, I say it is the most important thing I have ever done, it is the one job I cannot quit. That, so far, has proven to be the truth. Few people want to hear much more than this about my job, though. Some people actually scowl when they hear what I do, whether it is because they're upset or don't know what to say, or just feel bad, I don't know.

Once my friend Sarah told a guy named Nathaniel, whom I had gone to college with, about my job at MD Anderson. "Working with dying kids! It's the kind of thing contestants in beauty pageants say they want to do. It is too good to talk about," he told her. "It's not even interesting."

When I worked at a food bank for people with AIDS, as a teenager, friends thought that was cool. It was edgy, the disease was still new, its backstory involved sex, drugs, homosexuality—maybe even adultery. There is a hierarchy of the dying created by the world at large—and people won't talk about stories that don't have apparent moral meaning. Even with AIDS, the patients who got it through transfusions were often the least acknowledged, or at the least, the least memorialized by our culture at large. The tragedy was harder to name.

We prefer to assign morality to death; we prefer a world in which we take risks—we rebel, we resist, we transgress, we love, we

gamble—and sometimes we lose. That makes sense; that is tragedy. One of the reasons I can't stop going to the hospital: the kids
don't avert their eyes when they see each other.

A while back, I walked into the Pedi-Dome and was greeted by
Amirah, her nose, chin, and mouth entirely covered in scabs.
    "Excuse me," I said. I sucked my whole being inside my lungs,
and I walked back out into the hallway where I was nearly bowled
over by my tears. After gathering myself up in the stale, pink hallway, I summoned enough courage to find somebody to tell me
what was going on. It took gaining courage, too: I have worked
with kids with faces blown up twice their normal size, with boys
whose physique resembles young colts and who lose the ability to
move or to speak as I watch, with girls with amputated limbs. These
things I know to expect. But I wasn't ready for Amirah, for my little
Amirah, to begin on a downturn. Not so soon after Khalil's death.
Not ever.
    It was Jonie whom I found a minute or two later. She told me
what I never expect: Amirah had fallen on some steps at the Ke-
mah Boardwalk and skinned her face. Just like any little girl could.

GEOFFREY BENT

Edward Hopper and the
Geometry of Despair

FROM *Boulevard*

BLESSED IS THE ARTIST who finds one small thing that is entirely his own, an individual whose work projects a personality so
distinct he becomes an adjective. Kafkaesque paranoia and Ruben-
esque girth, Rabelaisian humor and Shavian wit, the Caravaggisti's
light and the Pre-Raphaelites' point of departure: these expressions acknowledge an essence so dense it resembles a bouillon
cube. Familiarity to this degree, unfortunately, is largely based
on presumption. As predictable as each of these artists seem, one
can only imitate them in outline; the particulars of their art often
prove surprisingly flexible.

The same dilemma holds true for the American painter Edward Hopper. Everyone thinks they know Hopper because they so
quickly recognize him. How far the figment lies from the fact was
apparent in an exhibition of the artist's work that recently traveled
across the United States. Multiple Hoppers reveal the consistent
concerns he pursued by varying means throughout his career.

With Hopper, context is everything. "Where" defines his people more indelibly than "who." This has led many critics to stress
the national character of the localities he painted, a diminishing
assessment that makes the artist seem like Norman Rockwell's
dour second cousin. Nothing could be further from the truth;
Americana held no interest for this American. Hopper's innate
reticence prompted him to qualify any popular culture references

he included in his work. In *Circle Theater,* for instance, a looming subway exit eclipses most of the theater's marquee; the title alone allows us to interpret the cryptic *C* and *E* that flank the black structure rising before us. The bedraggled flappers who appear in Hopper's work run counter to the popular stereotype; we see them sullenly stirring coffee by themselves in automats or dully chatting together in cheap Chinese restaurants, with nary a hip flask or jazz band in sight. Hopper was attracted to the theater and portrayed it often, but somehow in these scenes it's always intermission. The evening's illusion is kept safely behind a heavy curtain as Hopper studies the audience: the balding men and haggard women who don their boiled shirtfronts and ermine wraps in the hopes of losing themselves for a few hours in an imitation of life. It is the spectators who have become the spectacle.

This indirection is essential to Hopper's temperament as an artist; far from indulging the comfortable myths about his country, the man sought to circumvent them. In *New York Movie,* the titled film appears as an incoherent black-and-white fragment on the extreme left. Hopper focuses instead on the periphery of the main event, where a young woman in an usher's uniform slumps in boredom beneath a dim exit lamp. Administering society's diversions is anything but entertaining. In *Girlie Show,* a nude distinctly past her prime traipses out on a bare stage with a transparent veil trailing behind her. Her audience consists of a few anonymous male heads in the darkness at her feet and the face of a drummer idly awaiting his cue. What makes this painting so unusual is the way Hopper deflates the erotic intent of the scene without resorting to caricature. He doesn't make his stripper ugly; he doesn't need to. Rather than emphasizing the scene's tawdry elements, the artist presents them simply, but at an unresponsive distance. It's the echo of apathy that makes the woman's blighted exhibitionism seem so sad and even a bit heroic.

One only has to compare works like this to the flushed street urchins and slushy urban alleys of Hopper's teacher, Robert Henri, to appreciate how far from the picturesque Hopper resides. The Ashcan school, of which Henri was one of the leading receptacles, use the familiar to establish a camaraderie of experience with their audience. "We know all about this," they signal, and the "we" is fatally presumptuous. Hopper, on the other hand, uses the familiar to breach the visual complacency the familiar engenders. One is most vulnerable to the surprise that comes barging through the front door.

If America isn't the subject of these American scenes, what is? Anyone acquainted with Hopper's entire oeuvre might be tempted to answer: architecture. Hopper loved buildings and found so much character in them they almost function as faces: the spent gentility of a Victorian façade, the spare sufficiency of a clapboard cottage, the redundant thrust of a brick tenement. In his hands, shutters and sills, pilasters and porticos are as individualizing as noses and ears. Part of the appeal lay in the challenge: architecture is an exercise in logic; like a fugue or an algebraic equation, all the elements must resolve themselves symmetrically. One can fudge the perspective of a mountain or a tree, but because it is largely composed of lines, a building's perspective makes any lapse glaringly apparent. The rigor of an architectural design is so relentless it can easily appear repetitive and boring. Hopper disarmed this shortcoming with his use of sunlight, which further complicated the architectural patterns with patterns of its own, privileging certain planes, creating brilliant shafts and vivid diagonals. Hopper's buildings are so alive because they fracture space in such interesting ways. What one has here is cubism without the theoretical baggage.

How Hopper used light to modify the rigid pattern of simple structures is perhaps best illustrated in his *Early Sunday Morning*. An artist interested in local color would have filled the storefront windows with specific merchandise; Hopper doesn't even replicate the signs, using instead uniform smudges of mustard-colored paint to approximate the dulled gilt stencils on the glass. Neither does he populate this commercial stretch of real estate with a swarm of shoppers. It's interesting to note that initially a figure appeared in one of the second-story windows, but Hopper painted it out. A single cough would have violated the deserted character of the scene; only in the absence of people is their essence captured. The tentative crescendo of morning light that approaches from the right becomes the string that threads the beads and keeps the succession of shops from appearing episodic and monotonous. For all the horizontal sweep in the picture, it's important to note how the artist retards this movement near the picture's center with a barber pole, a fire hydrant, and the highlighted folds of a furled awning, delaying the eye long enough to give the scene the serenity of a traditional focal point.

The architectural patterns in Hopper's work do more than give it a compositional elegance; they confine the people that inhabit them. Hopper embeds his figures in a relentless grid of rectangles and squares. Bold vertical and horizontal lines slice away huge chunks of any scene. The artist's men and women seem resigned to their compromised space, but not trapped by it; rather the grid is an outer expression of the attitudes they harbor within. *Room in New York* is a perfect example of this approach. We see a man and a woman in a crowded apartment through the confining frame of a brownstone windowsill. Despite the cramped quarters, the couple remain aloof from each other; there is more than a round table separating these two. The man leans forward, not toward the woman but the newspaper that slants before him. The woman faces away from the man, leaning against an upright piano. The position of her knees and elbow makes it clear she doesn't intend to play the instrument. Instead she picks at the keyboard with a single finger, producing the consolations of sound to fill the conversational void. The rectangular panels of the door repeat those of the three framed pictures on the wall, a repetition that becomes the visual equivalent of dull familiarity. The isolation is so enervating that the people seem to have lost their faces in masks of shadow. In this scene, Hopper confounds the voyeur's crime: our stolen glimpse into other people's lives wasn't worth stealing. What we witness is too impersonal to be private, too inert to be engaging. At their most intimate, people are disappointingly themselves.

Hopper seems to be painting pictures in which nothing happens, but this isn't true: nothing doesn't look like this. Just as one projects the essence of emptiness not through silence but a series of echoes, so these scenes are crowded with objects that create a vacuum. In *Room in Brooklyn,* we're inside the apartment looking out, but the shift in perspective doesn't change the emotional climate. The horizontal and vertical lines formed by the three windows divide the available space into a vacant triptych. The central focus of the picture is a white vase of flowers that sits on a small table between two of the windows. The flowers are as vapid as the vase, yet both are made vivid by a shaft of glancing sunlight that provides a warm, sky-blue shadow. It is only after admiring the flowers that we notice the female occupant on the far right, her slumping head viewed from behind; she seems to be merging with the chair she sits in, just as the chair merges with a rust-colored tablecloth in the right foreground. The woman conforms to the room's overall pattern while the flowers defy it. Hopper's contrast makes his point discreetly: what sort of life can be upstaged by a handful of jonquils?

In *Hotel by a Railroad,* Hopper's bisecting game reaches an extreme; everything in the picture crowds everything else into insignificance. The older couple occupying the hotel room don't appear to be transient: staid to the point of inertia they could be part of the generic, nicked furniture that comes with the room, the dowdy woman in her soiled slip who reads without passion, the gaunt man who looks out the window without interest and smokes without pleasure. As if to confirm our impression, a mirror on the wall reflects only gray emptiness. The confined glimpse of train track visible from the window offers no escape; the man studies it over his spent cigarette with an expression devoid of all expectation; like the attendant in Hopper's *Gas,* he finds himself stuck beside a road that only others will travel.

Hopper's most celebrated use of visual segmenting is *Nighthawks:* his insomniacs occupy an illuminated wedge in a dark, sleeping world. The abandoned shops (*Early Sunday Morning* without the sunlight) that have surrendered to the night create a contrasting backdrop that makes this island of fluorescent light appear all the more detached. The four figures who occupy the restaurant replicate the isolation, defying sleep for no apparent reason: they aren't eating or working or talking. The crouching figure behind the counter is the only one who seems on the point of speaking, but then his paper hat and white frock compromise the gesture: if he speaks, questions are just part of his job. Sartre believed that hell was other people, but Hopper begs to differ by showing four who are completely alone together. If there's a concession stand in hell that sells coffee and pie, this is it.

Hopper once said, "It took me about ten years to get over Henri." Elsewhere, he said, "It took me ten years to get over Europe." These statements might lead one to assume there was a lot of unrequited love in the artist's temperament. I think instead it reveals a key aspect of Hopper's approach: his was a world less of omission than deletion. Like a great chess master, the man showed a willingness to make huge sacrifices a part of his strategy. In *Second Story Sunlight,* the two figures who comprise the focus of the scene occupy only the central third of the painting; the third on the right shows an anonymous forest, the third on the left, the shaded side of the building. A full third of *Seawatchers* is taken up by the dark side of a cottage, a space only relieved by a laundry line with three flapping beach towels. Beside Hopper, other painters appear unduly cluttered. This was no compositional quirk on the American's part; it allowed him to keep his figures at a dispassionate distance. The painter usually remains far enough away from his people for us to see their legs; the close-up wasn't a technique he favored.

Hopper's tendency to cede large tracts of his pictures gave him another expressive tool: he could interrupt a scene by superimposing something unrelated before it. The most famous example of this is *House by the Railroad,* where his staid Victorian mansion is abruptly cut off at the knees by a rusting horizontal line of train tracks. Hopper was unusually fond of this device and many of his pictures are bisected by the railroad. We never see the trains, but their implacable paths are enough to signal the authority of a new order.

Interrupting a picture in this way also allows the artist to get behind the façades he recorded so meticulously. In Hopper's wonderful watercolor *Skyline Near Washington Square,* we see a solitary brownstone rising above the functional detritus of a roof. The contrast between the official face of a building and the vents and chimney pots that make it work couldn't be starker. This unsightly foreground blocks our view of the lower floors of the brownstone; Hopper compromises our impression of the building even further by angling it so we see the abrupt blank of the side wall, a contrast that makes the ornate front appear all the more facile. Nothing undermines the illusion of a mask like the prominent ears and neck of the head hiding behind it.

Hopper's paintings can seem far simpler than they are because they communicate so directly, but the artist frequently adds elements that threaten to disrupt the impression he creates. One example of this is how colorfully he paints the drabbest scenes. The deep saturated hues Hopper favored resemble early Technicolor films: assertive reds, vibrant purples, glaring yellows, inky blacks.

A mundane restaurant is filled with the brown luster of mahogany trim; the lobby of a one-star hotel at least has a sumptuous green carpet; even at the Nighthawk Café, the two gleaming coffee urns show more vitality than all the human inhabitants combined.

Hopper can surprise a viewer in other ways. As confining as his apartment interiors look, he almost always provides a window with a glimpse of the vast world outside as an option. In *A Woman in the Sun,* the window he shows isn't the one that brightens the standing nude; rather it's another located beside her, one that reveals a knoll just brushed with an edge of that same sunrise. At other times, as in the highly peculiar *Excursion into Philosophy,* which shows a clothed, contrite man leaning away from an open book and his apparently just-sodomized female companion, the gentle field seen through the window on the extreme right goes largely unheeded.

For Hopper, society consisted entirely of windows: those on the inside look out, while we on the outside look in. For all their transparency, Hopper's windows both separate and liberate. A concrete wall creates a boundary that is imposed; the inhibitions of a sheet of glass, on the other hand, are more self-inflicted. We want to see the options we refuse to pursue; we like to know what lurks on the other side of the door we never open.

If all the inanimate specters who occupy Hopper's interiors appear incapable of opening that door, the problem might lie in the way they were painted. Hopper's humans are almost always stiff and unconvincing, the only generic element in a world of sharply observed specifics. His men seem to have tumbled out of a B movie, while his women look like something produced by Vargas with a hangover. It didn't help that he used his wife as the model for most of the female figures in his work; the same features keep cropping up like an outbreak of Down syndrome. The older he got, the more doll-like Hopper's people became (is that Ken and Barbie in *Sunlight in a Cafeteria?*). The lapse is odd, since his early sketches and watercolors show an artist with an innate feel for the dynamic possibilities of the human form. Just look at *L'Année Terrible: At the Barricades,* which shows a French fighter from behind just as he raises his rifle to shoot: it's an awkward pose gracefully rendered. The impressionistic style he dabbled with while studying in Europe enabled Hopper to catch moving figures with fleet precision; painting figures who never move could only neutralize this skill. The best one can say of the people in Hopper's paintings is that they confirm the banality of their settings.

Because Hopper's theme of dislocation is so exhaustively explored, a student of his work can easily assume that the theme never changed. It did change, dramatically, in the fifties and sixties. Hopper was always a painter who relished sunlight; in his later work, light takes on a more pronounced role. It goes beyond simply brightening objects and heightening colors; it becomes a force, a presence, a deity. It lures Hopper's lost souls into their doorways and onto their porches; they drop their newspapers, look up from their books, abandon their desks. While showing no pleasure in the experience, everyone looks strangely transfixed, like horned toads on a hot rock. In *People in the Sun,* or *High Noon,* or *Sunlight on Brownstones,* or a dozen other works, light is more than a phenomenon perceived by the eyes; Hopper's people seem to be listening to it. The pictures resemble the old Christian Annunciation scenes minus the articulating angel, or they could be a depiction of an Islamic call to prayer. Light fills the empty lives of Hopper's humanity, and, for once, his figures seem receptive to its gift.

While light possesses the power to penetrate the elaborate grids the artist has constructed around his people, there is nothing beatific in the process; the recipients are illuminated, but they remain unenlightened. A lesser artist would have invested all this with some higher meaning, but Hopper maintains his detachment. He shows the sun a pagan reverence. The source of all life warms the living for a moment, holding them briefly before they go back to wasting their lives. Just how impersonally Hopper viewed this element can be seen in one of his last paintings, *Sun in an Empty Room.* The people and furniture that populate Hopper's interiors have vanished. Only the sun remains to subdivide the space with brilliant geometric shapes. Without the human clutter, the scene is strangely optimistic, an apocalypse of light. No other image shows how utterly unsentimental this most popular artist really was. He once said, "I think I'm not very human," and the cumulative effect of his oeuvre seems to confirm the indictment. He recognized no allegiance; he respected no authority. His membership in the human race was entirely accidental and unsolicited. One feels that if he ever witnessed a meteorite crashing into a city, he would have made a mental note on how the flash of light bleached out the color of the buildings closest to the blast.

Hopper's very last painting was a double portrait of himself and his wife as two clowns taking a final bow. The curtain in the artist's theater has at last gone up, but the show is over. I've always found the picture uncharacteristically self-conscious and a little pat. Given the discomfort Hopper felt with the personal, it's not surprising that the formal self-portrait he painted forty years earlier isn't very successful either. He evinces a look of distracted study rather than introspection; this isn't the image of someone in the throes of discovery; rather this is how one studies the reflection of a pimple in a mirror. No, if I had to choose an image that summed up this artist, one of his least typical works would do, one of the lighthouses he painted throughout his career. They bear no relation to his established themes, but there is a definite affinity: a solitary presence standing at the furthest edge of land, scanning the dark void with a brilliant shaft of light. Was the light a warning, a search for survivors, or just a prurient glance? In a world in which we are all adrift, it could be all of the above.

ROBERT BOYERS

A Beauty

THE MOST BEAUTIFUL MAN I ever knew was Charles Newman,
the founding editor of the journal *TriQuarterly,* a gifted novelist
and man of letters. When I met him in the late 1970s he was almost forty, the possessor of a large, intelligent, perfectly ordered
face in which there was no discernible trace of turbulent emotion.
His hair lifted softly above an unruffled forehead, and though, as I
later learned, he had recently been through a period of stress and
agitation, his eyes were radiant with competence, unencumbered.
What might have been taken for indifference in another counte-
nance in his was clearly the conviction of a sumptuous sufficiency.
His beauty was carried lightly, as if he had never known the need
to tend or promote it. To win or shine was not his ambition. Somewhere, sometime, you felt, he had promised not to be vain. In his
own beauty he had discovered an endowment not to be overval-
ued or abused. What came to him as a result of his beauty would
be accepted gratefully, but with no accompanying sense that he
had done anything to deserve it.

I had known other men who seemed to me too beautiful, men
whose beauty overshadowed every other feature—of character or
wit or intelligence. Charlie's beauty did seem that way to some
of our friends. I'll not forget the words of a colleague who said,
half seriously, not a minute after she had set eyes on him for the
first time, that no man had a right to look that good. Who does
he think he is? she asked. Others, by far more numerous, were
impressed, struck dumb, or amused. Our friend Richard Howard

declared him impeccable. He looks, Richard said, the way a man ought to look.

Of course Charlie was not for him. Charlie was for women. At the Chinese restaurant on Fifty-Eighth Street before a dance performance at Lincoln Center, the striking twentysomething who showed us to our table carefully brushed his wrist when she handed around the menus. She likes you, I said, when she had moved a few steps away, but Charlie didn't answer. He took out his pipe and began to clean the bowl as if he hadn't noticed the young woman at all.

He was between marriages then, and his new girlfriend was away at a business conference in San Francisco. Renata was her name, and Charlie had brought her to us for a "quick impression" only a week or so after they met. She was a good deal younger than he was, late twenties, but you could see that there were some miles on her, and though she said that she'd never been married, or, for that matter, in love, I guessed that she wasn't in the market for anything permanent. Charlie was for her a trophy guy. With her long, bright red fingernails, and thick, reddish-brown hair tied back in an unfashionable ponytail, she laughed a lot, and batted her eyelashes at her benevolent, blue-eyed stallion.

I figured right away that the girl in the Chinese restaurant would know what to do with Charlie, whose beauty was a match for hers, and sure enough, she struck up a conversation with him about the duck she'd sliced before his quietly admiring eyes and asked whether the martini wasn't too dry. By the time we left the place an hour later, Charlie had jotted his unlisted phone number on the back of our bill and dropped it meaningfully in front of her. I'm not in the book, he said, but you can leave me a message anytime.

This was a scenario to which we'd grown accustomed. Charlie's beauty inspired intensities of admiration and interest. Though it might occasionally seem almost too good to be true, it was not intimidating. If his was an ideal beauty, a composite endowment of physical attributes that expressed poise, well-being, and lucidity, the beauty was at the same time, surely for most observers, entirely human, approachable. It conveyed little evidence, one way or another, of inveterate kindness or sensitivity, but it bespoke a measure of alertness and vulnerability that might in the long term prove an indispensable aspect of its charm. Women especially were drawn to this beauty as to a quality inordinately precious, as if being close to it might miraculously confer upon them a sense of comparable endowment not otherwise available to them, in spite of their own substantial attributes. In the great violet eyes of the Chinese beauty brooding gamely at our restaurant table we could see an avidity almost breathtaking in its hopefulness and candor.

Of course there are those for whom beauty resides only in the eye of the beholder. On this estimation, my friend was creditably beautiful only because he clearly moved others to declare him so and to cite as evidence their own sensations of pleasure and longing. I don't know how to contend against this view of beauty, which is in its way as unanswerable as the alternate view, which insists that beauty exists as an objective fact irrespective of any particular impressions or sensations it inspires. I am tempted to cite as authority on this matter Oscar Wilde, who famously quipped that "it is only shallow people who do not judge by appearances." But appearance is not quite as self-evident a quality as Wilde supposed. In his indispensable book on beauty, *Only a Promise of Happiness: The Place of Beauty in a World of Art,* Alexander Nehamas notes that "what counts as appearance doesn't remain constant," but proposes that appearance can be reliable as a gauge when accredited by "the members of a particular group with a similar background," who will agree "immediately when presented with the same phenomenon." This was, in my experience, the case with my friend Charlie, whose appearance was reliably compelling to all who knew him. With him it was as Arthur Danto observed when he wrote that beauty is "really as obvious as blue: one does not have to work at seeing it when it is there."

I knew Charles Newman for almost thirty years, and until he grew ill in his early sixties, I met no one who did not think him beautiful. Nothing remotely theoretical or problematic about it. In this sphere, the case for the more or less self-evident has long seemed compelling, if by no means flawless. Consider, as but one famous example, a passage from the *Phaedrus,* in which Plato describes the response of a man to beauty as follows: the man, he writes, "shudders in cold fear . . . But gradually his trembling gives way to a strange feverish sweat, stoked by the stream of beauty pouring into him through his eyes and feeding the growth of his soul's wings . . . He cares for nothing else . . . He gladly neglects everything else that concerns him." The inflamed language will no doubt seem to many of us excessive, and the superstructure Plato erects to exalt, or justify, the susceptibility to beauty—here reflected in the allusion to "his soul's wings"—may well seem irrelevant or spurious. But we ought not too readily to disdain the impression of a "stream of beauty pouring into him through his eyes." For Plato invites us to believe that there is in fact such a thing as beauty, and that beauty exists even where the theory to which we subscribe may tempt us to doubt it. Sophisticated people who pay little attention to beauty as an issue do nonetheless casually refer to the beauty of a familiar work of art—say the Lento movement of Dvorak's "American" Quartet or the *Primavera* of Botticelli, or the clean lines of a Marcel Breuer chair in a Bauhaus exhibition. When they do so, they do not think of the beauty to which they refer as in any way disputable. They believe in that which pours into them through their eyes or ears. Their ardor is real to them, and they know it to have been occasioned by something real for which they are grateful.

To be sure, there will always be persons who are indifferent to beauty, who regard it as superficial or refuse to be taken in by it. In an essay on Elias Canetti, Susan Sontag noted that "the great limit of Canetti's sensibility is the absence of the slightest trace of the aesthete. Canetti shows no love of art as such," she goes on, and "he does not love anything the mind fabricates for its own sake." Though Canetti was an "unregenerate . . . materialist," the merely material, fleshly beauty of Charles Newman would not have seemed to him at all irresistible. Would he have agreed, in the name of a hypothetically disinterested assessment, that my friend was endowed with the attributes conventionally associated with beauty? No doubt the very idea of such an assessment, mobilized simply to arrive at an empty verdict, would have seemed to Canetti irrelevant, adolescent. By contrast, Sontag herself was an insatiable beauty lover, and often she allowed herself to swoon—playfully, openly, generously, girlishly—at the mere sight of Charles Newman as he entered an auditorium or took a chair at the dining table in my own Saratoga Springs home. A 2002 e-mail from Sontag, responding to something I'd written her about Charlie's novel in progress, asks if he's "still beautiful."

Though I often disapproved of my friend, his beauty never seemed to me diminished by anything he said or did. Perhaps that marks a limitation in my own equipment, a flaw, or worse, in my own moral sensibility. The thing I liked least about Charlie was his way of carrying on with several women at a time and letting me in on what he was up to. In his fifties, when he was married to an obviously devoted and substantial woman, he was going around with a very attractive younger woman in St. Louis, where my wife and I often visited one of our children and his growing family. Though in New York Charlie lived with the wife—his fourth—in a high-rise near Lincoln Center, he spent the spring semester each year away from her, and had made the St. Louis companion something of a significant other there. The wife apparently had no idea what Charlie was up to, and though you might say that anyone married to Charlie who remained clueless about his predilections deserved whatever he handed out, it was hard for us to be cavalier about Charlie's cheating ways. We knew and liked Charlie's wife. We spent time with her and were pleased that she regarded us as friends to whom she could occasionally appeal for help or advice. She was an open and sometimes ebullient woman who might well, at the start of an intimate dinner party at their apartment, entertain her guests with fifteen or twenty minutes of a piano piece she had recently mastered. She obviously liked her husband and forgave him for what she took to be merely a habit of flirtation toward available women. Why shouldn't he flirt, the wife once asked us. He likes it, and the women all seem to like it, too. The wife knew herself to be both doting and beautiful, and Charlie had given her no reason to be insecure about their future together. He drank too much, but that, she felt, at least for the first years of the marriage, had little to do with his feelings toward her.

In truth, my wife and I often felt uncertain about what to do where Charlie and Edith were concerned. In spite of everything, Charlie continued to treat his wife with courtesy and affection. Often he spoke of her professional exploits at an architectural firm with unconcealed admiration. In their company it was remarkably easy to forget, at least for a while, that Charlie was also involved with the woman in St. Louis, and likely had other women he saw from time to time in New York as well. Even in decline, Charlie dressed elegantly and seemed in every way a refined, beautifully educated specimen, in bearing impeccably upright, correct, a pure example of the *danseur noble* type we would admire together at performances of the New York City Ballet.

But Charlie's beauty did not help us much when we were forced to confront his tall, willowy companion in St. Louis, or when he proposed that we all get together with our son and his family. Once we agreed to do this, and of course we all liked the girlfriend and thought Charlie remarkably comfortable with the situation. But later that night, on the phone, I told Charlie that none of this seemed to me a good idea, not where we were concerned. After all, we'd soon be seeing him with Edith in New York, or at our place in Saratoga Springs, and we'd have to pretend that we knew nothing about Jean.

You don't have to pretend anything, Charlie shot back, as he did again and again when we walked around in Central Park together later that spring. It's not as though Edith is going to ask you about my girlfriend and you'll be forced to lie. Jesus, he went on, you don't go around blurting everything to everyone you meet.

Bad faith, I said, reaching for a platinum-plated idea that Charlie and I had debated maybe twenty years earlier, when people still talked earnestly about such notions.

Bad faith my ass, Charlie said. Tell her anything you want. If you think Edith needs to hear from you about my love life, by all means, let her have it. It's not as if she hasn't harbored a suspicion or two. Might be good for her to think my best friends are looking out for her.

Sometimes you forgot that Charlie was, or could be, a gentle soul. But then you looked into those steady, steadying eyes of his and found something reassuring. Didn't know quite what to call it, but it did, you felt, have much to do with whatever in him continued to seem ineffably beautiful. He was not, to be sure, what typically passes for a beautiful character, not if that epithet is intended to identify an exalted moral stature. At times I felt that Charlie's beauty got in the way of any reasonable estimation I might make of him as a person, and I wondered—only a little—at my own ability to be moved, consoled, by a beauty that could seem, at such moments, mainly skin-deep.

It's not so easy to abandon the idea that beauty can never really be skin-deep, that genuine beauty is not only unproblematic but also somehow a sign of an essential goodness. "If the goodness of your heart was visible," Jenny Diski writes, "it would surely look like Audrey Hepburn or Johnny Depp." There was, I felt, in my friend, some indiscernible correspondence between his looks, his demeanor, and his true self, which had to be "good" in a way not always apparent even to those of us who loved him. I would not have known how to defend this impression had I been forced to do so, and it seemed to me the sort of lazy notion I typically despised.

Useful, perhaps, to recall something from Doris Lessing which may have some bearing on the question of beauty. Lessing noted what she called "a basic female ruthlessness" in herself, and went on to disdain the notion that gender is, in its essence, "socially constructed." How, she asked, did she acquire her husband? She stole him from another woman. And how did she feel about that? She felt, she said, that it was "my right": "When I've seen this creature emerge in myself, or in other women, I have felt awe." No need to pursue the question of what was, or was not, a "basic female ruthlessness" in Lessing. No need, in fact, to ask whether anything in Lessing's description has more to do with women than with men. Critical, however, to consider that the awe Lessing cites—a quality others might describe as pride, pride in being what one is—may well have much to do with the experience of oneself as a being sufficient, whole, indisputable, and yes, beautiful in one's felt disdain for standards not of one's own choosing, as for example moral standards that have something to say about a woman's setting out to steal another woman's husband. Lessing's awe rests upon an indifference to ways of feeling and judging that would interfere with the pure enjoyment or appreciation of a sublime self-approval aloof from the trivial misgivings of assorted scolds and moralists.

My friend Charlie was not—not in any way I could get terribly worked up about—a bad man. He took no special pleasure in causing pain. But betrayal was not for him—certainly in the domain of ordinary relations between men and women—an operant concept or lurking sentiment. Though he would not describe his own somewhat predatory attitude toward women as ruthless, he moved with the certain sense that he was somehow bound to behave as he did. I never heard him speak of the awe he felt at the display of his own seductive gifts, but he had about him an enviable freedom from the misgivings and reluctances that often inhibit the projects of less headstrong and confident lovers. If our sense of what is beautiful, truly beautiful, always derives from some idea or impression of what is natural, fully consistent with its own intrinsic laws, then it was legitimate for me to think of my friend as beautiful, even where his behavior seemed reprehensible.

Would I have continued to think him beautiful had he been openly or slyly flirtatious with my own very beautiful wife? No doubt my estimation of Charlie's beauty would then have been fatally compromised, for it would surely have seemed to me unnatural for this intimate friend of ours to ignore the obvious distress to which he would have blithely subjected both of us. The attentions in that case would then have seemed to me not an expression of supreme self-confidence but of a desire to wound, and it would have seemed to my wife not merely a testament to her own attractiveness but a symptom of Charlie's dark and complicated relation to me. In fact, the impression of our friend's beauty would then, I suppose, have given way to an impression of him as more than a little bit fucked-up, driven and unpredictable and reckless, rather than healthy in the steady pursuit of his own pleasures.

Natalie Angier, among many other science writers, has studied the correlation between health and the capacity to experience "unfettered joy." She notes that "sensations like optimism, curiosity and rapture . . . not only make life worth living, but also make life last longer." The surge of awe Lessing described in acknowledging her own right to proceed in accordance with her desires is, in this sense, rightly understood as entailing an optimism about her prospects. Lessing—so we may say—felt rapture at the absence of impediments associated with anxiety or reluctance. She seemed beautiful to herself precisely in her healthy, uncomplicated understanding of strength and appetite. Angier would appear to ratify this sense of the case when she writes that "real joy, far from being merely a lack of stress, has its own decidedly active state of possession, the ripe and gorgeous feeling that we are among the blessed celebrants of life. It is a delicious, as opposed to a vicious, spiral of emotions." If there does seem something primitive about the condition so described, health a state in which a whole range of civilized sentiments (guilt, regret, pity) are simply not in play, it aptly embodies what we witness when we are in the presence of certain kinds of beauty.

Think, for a moment, of Stendhal's extraordinary Sanseverina in *The Charterhouse of Parma,* a figure who seems to us worldly, witty, robust, and assertive, in every way a magnificent woman, indisputably beautiful while also scheming, corrupt, and openly disdainful of the standard moral sentiments. Her physical beauty we accept on the basis of the passions and transports she inspires, though, as a woman past thirty, she takes herself to be already "old" and to have passed beyond the stage at which mere looks in a woman will suffice. Stendhal is clearly in love with her, however much he pretends, playfully, to be appalled at her stratagems and duplicities. She seems to him, we feel, an epitome, the incarnation of everything that would make a woman desirable. Though she can be, at times, genuinely compassionate, she is by no means routinely so, and no one alert to the full range of her thoughts and propensities would think her conventionally nice or sweet. She is clever, to be sure, though Stendhal does not, clearly, regard her as an embodiment of spiritual beauty. Her attractiveness, all apart from the physical attributes duly noted by men and women of her acquaintance, has to do with her confident rejection of the fastidious conventions of feeling and manner associated with ordinary decent women. To be in her presence is to feel a certain uneasy gladness; our senses are preternaturally alerted to a beauty not uplifting but troubling. Though Gertrude Stein once said that to call a work of art beautiful is to say, in effect, that it is dead, there is nothing remotely dead about the Sanseverina, who is not, of course, a work of art, but who is in her way a perfected emblem of a beauty that is bracing, not at all superficial or ephemeral.

My friend Charlie was, in his way, a much more elementary embodiment of the beautiful, his physical endowments consoling, obvious. Admirers did not need, as readers of *Charterhouse* do, to overcome in themselves a reluctance to submit to this beauty. And I never felt that his beauty required of me an exercise of taste presumably lacking in others. Charlie's character simply did not play any part in our impression, perhaps because in most respects he was likable, not at all given to the plottings and subterfuges that so preoccupied Stendhal's Sanseverina. Charlie's was a more moderate temperament. His confidence required little in the way of testing or reinforcement. Though he was a learned and sophisticated man and knew that among educated persons the concept of the beautiful had become unpopular and retrograde, he could allow himself to take pleasure in beauty where he found it and did not regard the wish to ingratiate as a despicable sentiment. Had he been asked, he would not have agreed that the easy consolation derived by others from the contemplation of his own good looks was an unworthy satisfaction. No more would he have regarded the fact that judgments of beauty are often "subjective" as a reason to doubt their authenticity.

Charlie was, in the true and somewhat old-fashioned sense of the term, an art lover. A gifted, sometimes brilliant fiction writer and essayist, he worried over the fate of the arts in a culture he thought he had good reason to mistrust, and he devoted a controversial book-length study to what he called *The Post-Modern Aura*. There he displayed his own fondness for the difficult and his suspicion of the accessible pleasures afforded by straightforward realist fiction. He was a man in search of rarefied pleasures, and he appreciated that, in art especially, persons like himself were apt to regard as beautiful what others might regard as unduly complex or self-conscious.

At the same time, he was unapologetic about his own appetite for accredited masterpieces and insisted that beautiful was obviously preferable to ugly. Though he understood perfectly that works once thought to be awkward or ugly—from the poems of T. S. Eliot to the music of Igor Stravinsky—could in time come to seem "beautiful" by virtue of their familiarity or their status as revered modernist artifacts, he resisted the easy view that taste was merely a matter of convention and that efforts to differentiate between the beautiful and the ugly were hopelessly naive. Though he was an adept of interpretation, he was also drawn to Susan Sontag's famously provocative assertion that it was "the revenge of the intellect upon art," and he despised what she had designated the "overt contempt for appearances" that often figured so prominently in fashionably "advanced" readings of books and other artworks. In music he preferred the ravishing to the atonal and withholding, and he saw nothing limited or embarrassing in the canvases we examined together at an exhibition of Matisse's Moroccan paintings in New York. Theoretically he was inclined to agree with the critic Clement Greenberg that beauty, as commonly understood, is mostly irrelevant to the value of art. But he was, all the same, an inveterate beauty lover, and he was loath to accept that beauty has nothing to do with the success of particular artworks.

We were not at all surprised to learn, when Charlie died in

March of 2006, that he had left his money and possessions to the
Chamber Music Society of Lincoln Center, whose programs he
had enjoyed for many years. Did the beauty he found in the performances of chamber works by Schubert, Haydn, Ravel, and others inspire him to feel beautiful beyond what he felt upon casually
noting his own reflection in the mirror hung above his dressing
table? I would imagine so. Though Elaine Scarry may well be right
when she says "it does not appear to be the case that one who
pursues beauty becomes beautiful," Charlie was always inclined to
Plato's view in the *Symposium* that "life is worth living only in the
contemplation of beauty."

DUDLEY CLENDINEN

The Good Short Life

FROM *The New York Times Sunday Review*

I HAVE WONDERFUL FRIENDS. In this last year, one took me to Istanbul. One gave me a box of handcrafted chocolates. Fifteen of them held two rousing, pre-posthumous wakes for me. Several wrote large checks. Two sent me a boxed set of all the Bach sacred cantatas. And one, from Texas, put a hand on my thinning shoulder, and appeared to study the ground where we were standing. He had flown in to see me.

"We need to go buy you a pistol, don't we?" he asked quietly. He meant to shoot myself with.

"Yes, Sweet Thing," I said, with a smile. "We do."

I loved him for that.

I love them all. I am acutely lucky in my family and friends, and in my daughter, my work, and my life. But I have amyotrophic lateral sclerosis, or ALS, more kindly known as Lou Gehrig's disease, for the great Yankee hitter and first baseman who was told he had it in 1939, accepted the verdict with such famous grace, and died less than two years later. He was almost thirty-eight.

I sometimes call it Lou, in his honor, and because the familiar feels less threatening. But it is not a kind disease. The nerves and muscles pulse and twitch, and progressively, they die. From the outside, it looks like the ripple of piano keys in the muscles under my skin. From the inside, it feels like anxious butterflies, trying to get out. It starts in the hands and feet and works its way up and in, or it begins in the muscles of the mouth and throat and chest and abdomen, and works its way down and out. The second way is called bulbar, and that's the way it is with me. We don't live as long, because it affects our ability to breathe early on, and it just gets worse.

At the moment, for sixty-six, I look pretty good. I've lost twenty pounds. My face is thinner. I even get some "Hey, there, Big Boy," looks, which I like. I think of it as my cosmetic phase. But it's hard to smile, and chew. I'm short of breath. I choke a lot. I sound like a wheezy, lisping drunk. For a recovering alcoholic, it's really annoying.

There is no meaningful treatment. No cure. There is one medication, Rilutek, which might make a few months' difference. It retails for about $14,000 a year. That doesn't seem worthwhile to me. If I let this run the whole course, with all the human, medical, technological, and loving support I will start to need just months from now, it will leave me, in five or eight or twelve or more years, a conscious but motionless, mute, withered, incontinent mummy of my former self. Maintained by feeding and waste tubes, breathing and suctioning machines.

No, thank you. I hate being a drag. I don't think I'll stick around for the back half of Lou.

I think it's important to say that. We obsess in this country about how to eat and dress and drink, about finding a job and a mate. About having sex and children. About how to live. But we don't talk about how to die. We act as if facing death weren't one of life's greatest, most absorbing thrills and challenges. Believe me, it is. This is not dull. But we have to be able to see doctors and machines, medical and insurance systems, family and friends and religions as informative—not governing—in order to be free.

And that's the point. This is not about one particular disease or even about Death. It's about Life, when you know there's not much left. That is the weird blessing of Lou. There is no escape, and nothing much to do. It's liberating.

I began to slur and mumble in May 2010. When the neurologist gave me the diagnosis that November, he shook my hand with a cracked smile and released me to the chill, empty gray parking lot below.

It was twilight. He had confirmed what I had suspected through six months of tests by other specialists looking for other explanations. But suspicion and certainty are two different things. Standing there, it suddenly hit me that I was going to die. I'm not prepared for this, I thought. I don't know whether to stand here, get in the car, sit in it, or drive. To where? Why? The pall lasted about five minutes, and then I remembered that I did have a plan. I had a dinner scheduled in Washington that night with an old friend, a scholar and author who was feeling depressed. We'd been talking about him a lot. Fair enough. Tonight, I'd up the ante. We'd talk about Lou.

The next morning, I realized I did have a way of life. For twenty-two years, I have been going to therapists and twelve-step meetings. They helped me deal with being alcoholic and gay. They taught me how to be sober and sane. They taught me that I could be myself, but that life wasn't just about me. They taught me how to be a father. And perhaps most important, they taught me that I can do anything, one day at a time.

Including this.

I am, in fact, prepared. This is not as hard for me as it is for others. Not nearly as hard as it is for Whitney, my thirty-year-old daughter, and for my family and friends. I know. I have experience.

I was close to my old cousin, Florence, who was terminally ill. She wanted to die, not wait. I was legally responsible for two aunts, Bessie and Carolyn, and for Mother, all of whom would have died of natural causes years earlier if not for medical technology, well-meaning systems, and loving, caring hands.

I spent hundreds of days at Mother's side, holding her hand, trying to tell her funny stories. She was being bathed and diapered and dressed and fed, and for the last several years, she looked at me, her only son, as she might have at a passing cloud.

I don't want that experience for Whitney—nor for anyone who loves me. Lingering would be a colossal waste of love and money.

If I choose to have the tracheotomy that I will need in the next several months to avoid choking and perhaps dying of aspiration pneumonia, the respirator and the staff and support system necessary to maintain me will easily cost half a million dollars a year. Whose half a million, I don't know.

I'd rather die. I respect the wishes of people who want to live as long as they can. But I would like the same respect for those of us who decide—rationally—not to. I've done my homework. I have a plan. If I get pneumonia, I'll let it snuff me out. If not, there are those other ways. I just have to act while my hands still work: the gun, narcotics, sharp blades, a plastic bag, a fast car, over-the-counter drugs, oleander tea (the polite southern way), carbon monoxide, even helium. That would give me a *really* funny voice at the end.

I have found the way. Not a gun. A way that's quiet and calm.

Knowing that comforts me. I don't worry about fatty foods anymore. I don't worry about having enough money to grow old. I'm not going to grow old.

I'm having a wonderful time.

I have a bright, beautiful, talented daughter who lives close by, the gift of my life. I don't know if she approves. But she understands. Leaving her is the one thing I hate. But all I can do is to give her a daddy who was vital to the end, and knew when to leave. What else is there? I spend a lot of time writing letters and notes, and taping conversations about this time, which I think of as the Good Short Life (and Loving Exit), for WYPR-FM, the main NPR station in Baltimore. I want to take the sting out of it, to make it easier to talk about death. I am terribly behind in my notes, but people are incredibly patient and nice. And inviting. I have invitations galore.

Last month, an old friend brought me a recording of the greatest concert he'd ever heard, Leonard Cohen, live, in London, three years ago. It's powerful, haunting music, by a poet, composer, and singer whose life has been as tough and sinewy and loving as an old tree.

The song that transfixed me, words and music, was "Dance Me to the End of Love." That's the way I feel about this time. I'm dancing, spinning around, happy in the last rhythms of the life I love. When the music stops—when I can't tie my bow tie, tell a funny story, walk my dog, talk with Whitney, kiss someone special, or tap out lines like this—I'll know that Life is over.

It's time to be gone.

PAUL COLLINS

Vanishing Act

FROM *Lapham's Quarterly*

IN A NEW HAMPSHIRE APARTMENT during the winter of 1923, this typewritten notice was fastened squarely against a closed door:

> Nobody may come into this room if the door is shut tight (if it is shut not quite latched it is all right) without knocking. The person in this room if he agrees that one shall come in will say "come in," or something like that and if he does not agree to it he will say "not yet, please," or something like that. The door may be shut if nobody is in the room but if a person wants to come in, knocks and hears no answer that means there is no one in the room and he must not go in.
>   Reason. If the door is shut tight and a person is in the room the shut door means that the person in the room wishes to be left alone.

Through the door could be heard furious clacking and carriage returns: the sound, in fact, of an eight-year-old girl writing her first novel.

In 1923, typewriters were hardly a child's plaything, but to those following the family of critic and editor Wilson Follett, it was a grand educational experiment. He'd already written of his daughter Barbara in *Harper's*, describing a girl who by the age of three was consumed with letters and words. "She was always seeing A's in the gables of houses and H's in football goalposts," he recalled. One day she'd wandered into Wilson's office and discovered his typewriter.

"Tell me a story about it," she demanded.

This was Barbara's way of asking for any explanation, and after he demonstrated the wondrous machine, she took to it fiercely. A typewriter, her parents realized, could unleash a torrential flow of thoughts from a gifted child who still lacked the coordination to write in pencil.

"In a multitude of ways," Wilson Follett reported, "we become more and more convinced of the expediency of letting the typewriter be, so far as a machine can, the center and genesis of the first processes."

By five, Barbara was being homeschooled by her mother, and writing a tale titled *The Life of the Spinning Wheel, the Rocking-Horse, and the Rabbit.* Her fascination with flowers and butterflies bloomed from her typewriter into wild and exuberant poems and fairy tales. By 1922, at the age of seven, she was versifying upon music:

> When I go to orchestra rehearsals,
> there are often several passages for the
> Triangle and Tambourine
>   together.
> When they are together,
> they sound like a big piece of metal
> that has broken in thousandths
> and is falling to the ground.

The warning notice on her door the following year, though, marked a new project: young Barbara was attempting an entire novel. On some days the eight-year-old topped four thousand words. While her notes to her playmates and family overflowed with warmth, she was absolute in guarding her time to write. Neighboring children who didn't understand were brusquely dismissed.

"You don't understand why I have my work to do—because, at this particular time, you have none at all," she snapped in a letter to a complaining playmate.

As 1923 passed into another year and yet another, she wrote and rewrote her tale of a girl who ventures into the woods and vanishes into nature. Friends, when needed, could always be imagined. "I pretend," she once explained, "that Beethoven, the two Strausses, Wagner, and the rest of the composers are still living, and they go skating with me."

There's a peculiar comfort in imagining the companionship of great composers, for it is among them that a child prodigy is at home. Mozart rules the hopeful parent: homeschooled, composing harpsichord minuets at the age of five, playing the Viennese court at six, visiting Johann Christian Bach in London at age eight. He was one of the earliest celebrated child performers, and like Barbara, he was born to the profession—his father was a violin master. Then again, in some arts, there is almost an inevitability to the appearance of prodigies. Pablo Picasso's charming *Bullfight and Pigeons*—drawn in 1890, when he was nine years old—can still elicit admiration at exhibitions and wise nodding. *Ah, even then his talent shone through.*

And yet others pass by more quietly. We do not dwell upon Bobby Fischer, even though by the time he was eight his mother was having to write newspaper ads to find him worthy chess partners. And no parent today buys Zerah flash cards for their young genius, though math prodigy Zerah Colburn was once as famous as Mozart. The son of a Vermont carpenter, Zerah's talent was exhibited in 1810 at the age of five. Soon Zerah was gaining audiences with John Quincy Adams and letters of introduction from Washington Irving. By eight he mentally calculated in front of an audience that a Fermat number was not in fact prime, an almost unthinkable feat for even an adult mathematician. Yet the danger of Zerah's overbearing and hapless father was obvious enough that Bostonians raised a fund to educate the boy in New England. His father turned the money down: there was a bigger fortune waiting on the road.

Today, we hear of Mozart, but not of Colburn. Little Barbara might skate with one, but not the other.

By 1926—many drafts, one baby sister, and one manuscript-destroying house fire later—her book had the title *The House Without Windows*. It was, she explained, the tale of Eepersip, "a child who ran away from loneliness, to find companions in the woods—animal friends." The tale stretched to over forty thousand words.

"Daddy and I are correcting the manuscript," Barbara reported, "putting in and taking out, to copy it, and get it all ready to go to the printer."

It was to be a small vanity job, but her father had a suggestion. He'd been working for a while with Knopf in New York; what if he passed it along to them? When Knopf's response arrived addressed to Barbara—"a blue letter with the famous white BORZOI seal"—she wrote to a friend what happened next:

I simply threw myself on the floor and screamed, either with fear for what it might contain, with joy for getting it at last, or with terrific excitement of the whole thing. There is a feeling, after you have been waiting a long time for anything, there is a feeling that, when it really comes, it must be impossible—a dream—an optical illusion—a cross between those three things . . .

Now: "What doo zhoo fink???" It is Eepersip, *The House Without Windows,* my story, my story in New York, with the Knopfs, to be published!! . . . *published!!!!!!!!*

She had just turned twelve.

The House Without Windows appeared in February 1927 to overwhelming praise. "A Mirror of the Child Mind," announced a *New York Times* headline: "the most authentic and unalloyed document of a transient and hitherto unrecorded phase in plastic intelligence . . . [a] truly remarkable little book." They featured Barbara on the front page of that day's Photogravure Picture Section, showing her correcting a set of galley proofs.

The *Saturday Review of Literature* found the book "almost unbearably beautiful." It is not hard to see why. The opening lines evoke a fairy-tale isolation: "In a little brown shingled cottage on one of the foothills of Mt. Varcrobis, there lived with her father and mother, Mr. and Mrs. Eigleen, a little girl named Eepersip. She was rather lonely . . ." Eepersip emerges from the forest dressed in garlands to try to lure other children away, including her own younger sister:

"Look, I'd dress you like this, with ferns and flowers and butterflies . . . The bees gather honey from the flowers, which they would share with us."

"Bees sting," said Fleuriss, shrinking away; "they sting, and they hurt, Eepersip."

Unable to convince anyone to join her outdoors—in her "house without windows"—Eepersip eventually disappears altogether, transformed into a wood nymph. It is a haunting tale that merges archetypal myth with a childhood desire to run away.

Soon Barbara was being asked to review the latest A. A. Milne for the papers, and H. L. Mencken wrote to her parents that "you are bringing up the greatest critic we heard of in America." Follett's next plan—"to become a pirate" and take to the sea for her new book—was announced in the *Times*.

Barbara was famous.

CONGRATULATIONS MY DEAR EEPERSIP, one telegram arriving at the Follett house read. YOU HAVE DONE WHAT MANY AN ADULT HAS FAILED TO DO.

But one critic was unimpressed.

"I can conceive of no greater handicap for the writer between the ages of nineteen and thirty-nine," thundered Anne Carroll Moore in the *New York Herald Tribune*, "than to have published a successful book between the ages of nine and twelve."

The creator of the Children's Room at the New York Public Library and one of the most powerful critics of children's literature in America, Moore's qualms were not with Barbara's writing—"I have only words of praise for the story itself. *The House Without Windows* is exquisite"—but that it was published at all. "It is playing with fire," she warned. "What price will Barbara have to pay for her 'big days' at the typewriter?"

Barbara needed to be outside playing with children her own age, Moore declared—and to grow up unburdened by early fame. "There are no satisfactions comparable to a free and spacious childhood with a clear title to one's own good name at maturity."

Yet there was some precedent for Barbara's career. Seven years earlier, eleven-year-old Horace Wade published his thriller *In the Shadow of Great Peril*. More books followed, as well as encouraging letters from F. Scott Fitzgerald, and a job from William Randolph Hearst at the *Chicago American*. Wade's writing lacked Follett's aspirations—it was genre stuff, full of "chums" and dastardly outlaws—but it hinted that the child author could grow into success.

Others, though, were protected from their juvenilia. The most famous child author before Wade appeared just one year earlier, with Daisy Ashford and her ludicrous tale *The Young Visiters; or, Mr. Salteena's Plan*. Opening with the immortal line "Mr Salteena was an elderly man of 42 and was fond of asking peaple to stay with him," the book was a classic of unintentional hilarity. It was harmless to Ashford; she'd written the book as a nine-year-old in 1890, and published it from the safe distance of twenty-nine years later. She became a celebrity for having been a child, but was not a child celebrity.

But Barbara was having none of this, and none of Moore's criticism.

"It is surely very rash to slam down into the mud a childhood and a system of living that you know nothing about," she responded in a fiery letter. "I am very much amused at the favorable reviews which are being written—I do not take them at all seriously—but I do take seriously an article which distorts into a miserable caricature my living, my education, my whole personality."

To read her book "as if I were tyrannized over," Barbara wrote, insulted her and her parents. "The book," she insisted, "is an expression of joy—no more."

Even as reviews rolled in, Barbara planned an odyssey she'd long dreamed of: going to sea as a ship's crewman. That she was thirteen mattered little to her, and at length her parents found a lumber schooner to take her aboard as a passenger—one who insisted on doing chores.

Following her journey up to Nova Scotia, Follett's next book, *The Voyage of the Norman D,* was written at a white heat. The voyage took place in July, the final manuscript was in Knopf's hands by November, and the book was in stores by March. It is the work of an adult in the making: not just a charming prodigy, but an artist playing for keeps.

Follett sketches her first interview with the schooner's captain with droll eloquence:

> I spoke to the captain first of all, but very vaguely and dreamily, gazing about me—fascinated, enraptured, all the time. I looked at the long, huge booms, with the sails frapped closely round them; at the great, splendid masts; at the many ropes descending over blocks and made fast on belaying pins along the side of the boat; at the double and triple sheet blocks; and, above all, at the ratlines and shrouds, into which I longed to go up. The next minute I had jumped upon the spanker boom and crawled along to the very end, hanging slightly over the water, where I supported myself by one of the wire lifts.
>
> "Oh," said the captain, "I see you're a girl as likes to climb around."

The book's confidence stunned reviewers on both sides of the Atlantic. Follett was no longer a cute "child authoress": she was an author.

"Its ingeniousness is preserved, yet embellished, by a literary craftsmanship which would do credit to an experienced writer," the *Times Literary Supplement* marveled from London. The *Saturday Review* featured her book alongside Dorothy Parker's latest, and declared it "a fine, sustained, and vivid piece of writing." And yet, mused the *New York Times*, "Miss Barbara Newhall Follett celebrated her fourteenth birthday just twelve days before the publication."

But in that week before publication, Wilson Follett delivered devastating news. He'd recently turned forty, and—in a plot development he'd have struck down as painfully trite in any novel— he was leaving Barbara and her mother, Helen, for a younger woman.

"You say Helen needs me," Barbara pleaded to her father, "and right you are, but I need you, too." But at the moment of her greatest triumph, Barbara was abandoned by the man who had fostered her ambitions.

Wilson left them with little money. At first, Helen tried to spin necessity into adventure: they would take their typewriters to sea, sail to Tahiti, and write books! But by September 1929, Barbara found herself stranded and alone with family friends in Los Angeles. It was unbearable: she fled to San Francisco, hid in a hotel, and wrote poetry. But she'd been reported as a runaway, and when police burst into her room, they narrowly kept her from escaping through the window.

"I loathe Los Angeles," she explained to reporters.

The story made national news; a *Times* headline reminded readers, "Case of Barbara Follett Recalls Feats of Chopin, Mozart, and Others." Helen and Barbara were reunited in New York, but their finances were so dire that upon turning sixteen in March 1930, Barbara had to find work. Her timing was awful, coming months after the Wall Street crash. After a course in shorthand and business typing—a "decidedly more tawdry use of its magic," she mused—Barbara was getting up early every morning to ride the subway to a secretarial job.

"My dreams are going through their death flurries," she wrote that June. "I thought they were all safely buried, but sometimes they stir in their grave, making my heartstrings twinge. I mean no particular dream, you understand, but the whole radiant flock of them together—with their rainbow wings, iridescent, bright, soaring, glorious, sublime. They are dying before the steel javelins and arrows of a world of Time and Money."

Improbably, she kept writing: she took to waking up early before work to toil on a new book, *Lost Island*. Set around a New York couple who get shipwrecked on a deserted island, the book pivots on a dilemma: after they're discovered, the woman doesn't want to go back. *Lost Island*'s opening lines show a teenaged author turned older and abraded by Manhattan:

> Not even a cat was out. The rain surged down with a steady drone. It meant to harm New York and everyone there. The gutters could not contain it. Long ago they had despaired of the job and surrendered. But the rain paid no attention to them . . . New York people never lived in houses or even in burrows. They inhabited cells in stone cliffs. They timed the cooking of their eggs by the nearest traffic light. If the light went wrong, so did the eggs . . .
> "I don't like civilization," she said, to the rain.

By 1934, Follett had written her third and fourth books—*Lost Island,* and a brisk travelogue on the Appalachian Trail called *Travels Without a Donkey.* But worn down by six years without the encouragement of a father or an editor, the manuscripts finally stopped. Instead, she found a kindred soul in an outdoorsman named Nickerson Rogers, and they eloped.

America's next great novelist was now without a high-school degree, without work, and a teen bride. Yet she was not unhappy—at first. She backpacked through Europe, and between secretarial jobs in New York and Boston, she discovered dance classes. She took some summers off to travel west for dance classes at Mills College, which she loved: it was a taste of the college life that she'd been denied. But returning to her husband in Brookline, Massachusetts, in late 1939, she was shaken once again, worse even than by her father's abandonment.

"There *is* somebody else . . . ," she wrote to a friend. "I had it coming to me, I know." Her despair was so keen that she could only rest with the help of "sleeping stuff." Soon her correspondence darkened ominously: "On the surface things are terribly, terribly calm, and wrong . . . I still think there is a chance that the outcome will be a happy one, but I would have to think that anyway, in order to live; so you can draw any conclusions you like from that!"

The conclusion to be drawn was perhaps the worst one possible. On the evening of December 7, 1939, she and Nick quarreled, and by a friend's account she left later that evening.

She never returned.

Some prodigies flourish, some disappear. But Barbara Rogers did leave one last comment to the world about writing—a brief piece in a 1933 issue of the *Horn Book* that earnestly recommends that parents give their own children typewriters. "Perhaps there would simply be a terrific wholesale destruction of typewriters," she admits. "An effort would have to be made to impress upon children that a typewriter is magic." So is the child at it, but Follett doesn't hint that she had now been spending years battling poverty. The father who gave her that typewriter doesn't appear in the piece either. She'd been so angry at him in one letter that she snapped, "He isn't what you'd call a man."

But her tribulations were as appallingly timeless as the fairy tales that she so loved. Decades later, Bobby Fischer would be left by his mother at seventeen to essentially fend for himself, and while that may not have created his famed eccentricity, it hardly helped. Nor was the fact that she'd allowed him to drop out of school at the age of sixteen.

And what of the promising mathematical prodigy Zerah Colburn? After traveling to Europe to be exhibited by his father, the boy did not return for twelve years—his father now dead overseas, and Zerah himself nearly broke and his talents squandered. Financial straits might have led to his publication in 1833 of *A Memoir of Zerah Colburn, Written by Himself.* Unknown today, it is the first child-celebrity memoir. Colburn was so alienated from his existence that he wrote it in the third person—as if he, too, were gawking at this famed phenomenon called Zerah.

A washed-up performer at nineteen, he arrived back in Vermont and knocked on the door of his former home. "They inquired of an elderly woman who was at the door, if she knew where the widow Colburn lived? She replied that she was the woman . . . his own mother was as ignorant of the child she had nursed and provided for until he was six years old, as if she had never seen him before."

Zerah Colburn had also disappeared—so thoroughly that he couldn't reappear even when he wanted to.

Nick waited two weeks to go to the police, and another four months to request a missing persons bulletin: he claimed he was waiting for Barbara to return. Nobody in Boston's morgue matched her, and the bulletin, issued under her married name, went unnoticed by the press:

> Brookline. 139 4-22-40 3:38 PM Maccracken. Missing from Brookline since Dec. 7, 1939, Barbara Rogers, married, age 26, 5-7, 125, fair complexion, black eyebrows, brown eyes, dark auburn hair worn in a long bob, left shoulder slightly higher than right. Occasionally wears horn-rimmed glasses.

It wasn't until 1966, when Helen coauthored a slim academic study on her daughter, that the press realized Barbara Newhall Follett was missing at all.

In the intervening years, Wilson Follett wrote a peculiar anonymous essay for the *Atlantic* — "To a Daughter, One Year Lost," in May 1941 — which expressed muted guilt and amazement: "Could Helen Hayes be lost for ten days without a trace? Could Thomas Mann? Could Churchill? And now it is getting on toward forty times ten days . . ."

Helen, belatedly discovering how little Nickerson Rogers had looked for Barbara, spent 1952 urging police to seek someone now missing for thirteen years. "There is always foul play to be considered," she hinted to Brookline's police chief. To Nickerson, she was blunter: "All of this silence on your part looks as if you had something to hide concerning Barbara's disappearance . . . You cannot believe that I shall sit idle during my last few years and not make whatever effort I can to find out whether Bar is alive or dead, whether, perhaps, she is in some institution suffering from amnesia or nervous breakdown."

She never found her.

Extraordinary young talents are all the more dependent on the most ordinary sustenance. But instead of a home and a college education, what Barbara Follett got was author copies and yellowing newspaper clippings. This girl—who should have been America's next great literary woman—was abandoned by the two men she trusted, and her fame forgotten by a public that she never trusted in the first place. Her writings, out of print for many decades, only exist today in six archival boxes at Columbia University's library. Taken together, they are the saddest reading in all of American literature.

Then again, her work always was about escape. Her mysterious disappearance echoes with the final words of *The House Without Windows,* when the lonely Eepersip finally vanishes forever into the woods.

"She would be invisible forever to all mortals, save those few who have minds to believe, eyes to see," Follett wrote. "To these she is ever present, the spirit of Nature—a sprite of the meadow, a naiad of lakes, a nymph of the woods."

MARK DOTY

Insatiable

FROM *Granta*

I only hope we may sometime meet and I shall be able perhaps
to say what I cannot write.
  —Bram Stoker to Walt Whitman, February 1876

You did well to write to me so unconventionally, so fresh, so
manly, & so affectionately.
  —Walt Whitman to Bram Stoker, March 1876

ONLY A SENTENCE, casually placed as a footnote in the back
of Justin Kaplan's thick 2003 biography of Walt Whitman, but it
goes off like a little explosion: "Bram Stoker based the character
of Dracula on Walt Whitman."

Come again? The quintessential poet of affirmation, singer of
himself, celebrant of human vitality—what has he to do with the
parasitical phantom, the children of the night? The poet of "Song
of Myself" proclaims his solar confidence; he outgallops stallions,
is "plumb in the uprights" and "braced in the beams" and even the
smell of his own sweat famously delights him with "an aroma finer
than prayer."

He seems himself a kind of sun, radiant, generous, aglow with
an inner heat that seems composed of equal parts lust, good
health, and fellow feeling.

How could the embodiment of lunar pallor emerge from him?

What thrilled Whitman was vitality, and Bram Stoker—who'd
been championing the older man's poems since his days at Trin-
ity College, where he read them "with my door locked late at

night"—must have sensed this. He first found the expurgated edition that William Michael Rossetti had published in England, then
ordered an American edition of *Leaves of Grass,* and proceeded to
write Whitman a fan letter—really more of an outcry—about finding in the poems a kindred soul. "I thank you for all the love and
sympathy you have given me, in common with my kind," Stoker
wrote, and one can't help but read "my kind" in a number of ways,
which surely must have been what Stoker intended. The letter—a
longish late-adolescent gush, which seems practically to fall over
itself with hesitation, throat-clearing, and a tumult of feeling—was
charged enough for its author that he didn't manage to get it
into the post for four years, which must place it right up there
in the history of delayed correspondence. Whitman wrote an immediate reply; he was charmed by the letter and the note Stoker
sent with it. Who wouldn't be, by the description of himself Stoker
included, one such a "keen physiognomist" as Whitman might
desire?

> My friends call me Bram. I live at 43 Harcourt St., Dublin. I am
> a clerk in the service of the Crown on a small salary. I am twenty-
> four years old. Have been champion at our athletic sports (Trin-
> ity College, Dublin) and have won about a dozen cups. I have also
> been President of the College Philosophical Society and an art and
> theatrical critic of a daily paper. I am six feet two inches high and
> twelve stone weight naked and used to be forty-one or forty-two
> inches round the chest. I am ugly but strong and determined and
> have a large bump over my eyebrows. I have a heavy jaw and a big
> mouth and thick lips—sensitive nostrils—a snubnose and straight
> hair. I am equal in temper and cool in disposition and have a large
> amount of self control and am naturally secretive to the world. I take
> a delight in letting people I don't like—people of mean or cruel or
> sneaking or cowardly disposition—see the worst side of me. I have a
> large number of acquaintances and some five or six friends—all of
> which latter body care much for me. Now I have told you all I know
> about myself.

The novelist-to-be visited his hero the poet three times in the
1880s, when the theatrical company Stoker managed toured
America. And although their conversations were summarized
by Whitman's devoted amanuensis Horace Traubel, who would
collect his observations in the nine volumes of his *Walt Whit-*

man in Camden, I still find myself wondering what they talked about.

> Every atom belonging to me as good belongs to you.

I've always read Whitman's startling claim, at the beginning of his greatest poem, as a generous statement. But if Stoker indeed based his legend of appetite on the poet, then he turns this notion inside out: Every atom belonging to you is mine, your sweat, your tears, your lymphatic fluids, your semen if you're a man, your blood: I own you. That sentence in Kaplan's footnote shocks not because it's a stretch but because—despite the warmth we associate with Whitman and his legacy—it feels right somehow. I recognize him, the craving count, the barely bodied ancient thirst, inside the part of me that shares Whitman's love for the vital ember, the glowing health, the muscle and vigor of men. I wish I didn't. Every atom belonging to you: your semen, your blood. There he is in the mirror, shadow of the open-collared, slouch-hatted *camerado.*

Insatiable is unsustainable: I'm in the parking lot at the natural foods store when the bumper sticker on the Toyota beside me stops me in my tracks. In context it's about consumption and the environment, clearly—we can't go on using more and more resources, producing and shopping and throwing things away, not if there's going to be a lasting human presence on this planet.

I get that, but what shakes me is that I'm reading the slogan in another, not entirely unrelated way. Because I have been insatiable—have forgotten, actually, what it might feel like to be satiated, or perhaps (it hurts to admit this) even to be satisfied. "Satisfaction" is something I stopped seeking in sex, more or less, at least in a physical sense; what I wanted, in my long careening tour through the bodies of countless men, through bathhouse and sex club and online hookups and meth, was something difficult to grasp. The rhetoric of addiction would describe it as an urge to flee my own sense of lack, seeking and seeking to disguise or ignore or fill an emptiness within—something like the way Carl Jung is supposed to have said to Bill W., "You were reaching for spirit, you just reached for the wrong kind." And indeed that's one way to view a deep, compelling attraction to bodies, a longing to touch and touch and enter.

I was "partnered"—as postmodern parlance goes, or went, before same-sex marriage began to open different doors—to a man for sixteen years, and there was much pleasure and mutuality in our relation. And then there was, more clearly emergent over time, all that was left out, or wouldn't fit. I found this difficult to describe, this sense that not all of me could be expressed within our marriage. I began to use the metaphor of bandwidth, feeling even as I did so that it was partial, barely adequate.

If the self broadcasts on many channels, then Paul and I could clearly receive one another on, say, three of them, a nice midrange. Because we were both writers and thus shared a social and professional world of considerable fascination, a mandarin realm we could discuss at length with few others, and because we liked domestic tranquility and travel, and shared a deep pleasure in the work of description, trying to articulate what we saw—because of those things, we shared a mutual life. Outside of that: sex; adventure; the night; transgression; surprise; higher and lower pitches of experience. I need to be invited onto the back of a motorcycle and taken away now and then; I need a curtain pulled back, a hallway leading into some part of the world I've never seen. Paul feels that I have undervalued the midrange, the welcome and comfort of the intimacy that arose from our long association. My friend Carol says that's what marriage is, there's no way around it. Still, I can't help but be hungry for the broader range of experience, the higher frequencies and the depths; I need, for whatever reasons, to live on that broader spectrum, or wither. I am coming to accept this about myself.

The ex-con in construction boots and a towel, smoking a hash pipe, flicking tiny coals and bits of ash from the down of his belly outdoors by the pool, the water lights rippling over his torso.

The stoned, angelic young man, muscled and pale, opening his body to me and coaxing my fist inside him.

The oil worker who came in from days on the big oil rigs in the Gulf with his ears still ringing and his reddened skin hungry for touch.

The black man from the leather bar in Fresno who stood in front of me and came across my chest, then showed me a photo of his beautiful sixth-grade daughter and wept at how much he loved her.

The beautiful lean-muscled doctor—the first man I snorted crystal with—who whispered in my ear for hours about how he wanted me to infect him, covertly, without him knowing it, leaking virus into his bloodstream.

The landscaper who took me to his twenty-third-floor apartment, in a tower overlooking the park, and pissed on me on his terrace high above the lights of Houston while I lay on the concrete beneath him, entirely happy.

The bare-chested weightlifter in the gym, shorter than I was, thickly built, who stood behind me and guided my arms through a chest exercise as I pulled the cables taut in front of me and squeezed, and then pushed his chest into my back, and held me there, intently, without moving, so that I could feel his sweat and the pulse of his heart.

Men who wept about their fathers, their brothers, about bullies and gangs, about teachers and counselors and coaches, but fathers most of all, those fountainheads of male woundings, because they sensed I was someone in whose presence they could set down their guard, or just someone willing to listen without judgment. A beautiful, compact hairy young bear from New Jersey—forty-something but nonetheless very young anyway—who shook in my arms, wearing just a clean white jockstrap, because no one had ever genuinely loved him. I didn't judge; it was as if that were part of my purpose: I wanted to know the men who moved through my nights like passing comets, wanted them to feel the pleasure of being known.

But do I want to describe myself as a sex addict? Doesn't a label like that sit on one like a tight suit, an ill-fitting little cage of identity that must of necessity leave out so many of the regions of the self? That's how I felt, sitting in a twelve-step meeting, talking with groups of fellow users of methamphetamine about the drug we had decided not to use: that we were collectively defining our identities by what we would not do, and that such an act of definition was a strange, subtle kind of self-murder. I understand that such a radical act might be necessary, in the face of an intractable self-destructiveness, to save one's life—but nonetheless I can't bring myself not to describe it as a kind of murder, because in any such act of self-definition (I'm Mark and I'm an addict) the other selves, some of whom are not named because they don't belong in this context, and some of whom aren't named because they cannot be, but remain phantoms, potentialities, shadows, little streams into the larger liquidity—well, all those aspects of oneself are more or less banished from the conversation, and they retreat a little further away, and then a little further again.

Addiction is one way to think about it. But Lacan says that all desire is based in a sense of lack. Once we experienced ourselves as whole, separated neither from the world nor from ourselves by language, but once a self and other is perceived, or something is objectified by being named, then we fall from Eden, and forever after we'll have the sense of something missing, of the irretrievable object—wholeness, oneself and the motherworld that bore us all of a piece. Therefore the veil is the figure of desire; if we tear it away, desire tends to disappear, but as soon as the veil is restored, the well of longing fills again.

Behind every man I want to kiss lies that original desire, which it is my nature and my fate to displace. Though displacement seems hardly the right word, if there is nothing else one can do.

When you have a lot of sex, sex becomes increasingly less narrative. There's less of a story of connection and its development, and more a series of images, like the list I've just written, a photo album of sorts, in which still pictures stand for a succession of bodies in time, in their beautiful or awkward arcs or spasms. Like Cavafy's poems, these remembered snapshots contained rooms of eros: a man who lay back in a sling in his darkened third-floor apartment, his shining red motorcycle spotlit beside him. Two identical tattooed men, tattooed rugby players, on their backs, side by side in a bare room in Seattle.

A long green hallway, in an East Village apartment, down which one had to move laterally, since there wasn't room to walk straight ahead, and at the end of it, a room entirely lined with, of all things, midcentury American pottery, arrayed on walls the sun had never touched.

A list, is that what desire makes, finally? As in so many of Whitman's poems, where line after line spins out a careening catalogue of what the poet sees, or is, or wishes to be. Ask the collector, the curator, the accumulator of sexual experience, the person who touches and touches what he desires: he is making, on paper or in his head or in his dream life, a list.

To an American like Whitman (though there is no American like him, the progenitor of our hopes for ourselves too secret to quite name, the originator of the notion that democracy might be founded in the body, on the affection between bodies), elation in the face of the vital must have seemed an exhilarating rejection of the puritan heritage of division between body and soul. Was anyone ever so sanguine about sex? Blake, maybe, whose work Whitman read, though at what point in his career we don't quite know.

But to a European, perhaps this uprush of energy in the face of the body and its vital fluids had another cast altogether. For Stoker, it may have seemed that what was wan or dead in the self might be refreshed temporarily and, finally, horrifyingly, by the hot juices of those who were more immediately alive. Is vampirism a matter of the overly self-conscious being awakened to life by the vitality of those who are barely self-conscious at all? Is that why Whitman liked stevedores and streetcar conductors and Long Island baymen, the big guys at home in their bodies, who would never think to write a poem?

Or let's say Stoker, who married a woman Oscar Wilde had proposed to before Bram came along, found it necessary to suppress his own desires, to the degree that he would project them out onto a horrifying subhuman or posthuman creature, who has no firm foundation in biology, but must feed off the juices of others, without choice or sunlight. And in doing so, perhaps he reversed the gestures of his old idol. Where Whitman had written his beautiful poem of the sexual union between body and soul:

> I mind how once we lay, such a transparent summer morning,
> How you settled your head athwart my hips,
>   and gently turned over upon me,
> And parted the shirt from my bosom-bone,
>   and plunged your tongue to my bare-stript heart,
> And reached till you felt my beard, and reached till you held my feet.

Stoker has offered us a parallel physical situation with an entirely inverted tone:

> He pulled open his shirt, and with his long sharp nails opened a vein in his breast. When the blood began to spurt out, he took my hands in one of his, holding them tight, and with the other seized my neck and pressed my mouth to the wound, so that I must either suffocate or swallow.

Whitman fuses the erotic and the spiritual, as the kiss to the bare chest begins an epiphanic experience, a moment of peace and of understanding, whereas the mouth is brought to Dracula's chest in a kind of rape, a horrible force-feeding which can lead only to repulsion and contagion.

And so there it is: the intersection of the chosen and the compulsive, of consuming and being consumed, of the celebratory and of erasure.

Addiction is one way to think about it. But there's also what seems to have been Whitman's view—a mission, if you will, to seek out one's *cameradoes,* to join in the community of lovers, bound together by desire and affection, to find the common good in our common skin. This vision comes most clear in the Calamus poems, and in parts of "Song of Myself." It is primarily an imaginative union among men; Whitman's women, unfortunately, seem either afterthoughts or engines of procreation. He comes close to granting them freely moving sexual desires, and a position as democratic citizens, but he cannot really seem to desire them, and thus they are excluded from the essential bond—eros—that holds his *cameradoes* together in the new democratic union.

There are lists of men in Whitman's papers, with brief notations—an age, a bit of detail, a note about how they met. Not much. A collector's catalogue, a record of the body's travels? How else will I know the world, if not by touching as much of it as possible, finding in the bodies of my lovers and fellows my coordinates?

Or there's Teilhard de Chardin, brilliant radical Catholic, paleontologist, and physicist, who refashions the poet's claim on our shared atoms this way: "However narrowly the heart of an atom may be circumscribed," he writes, "its realm is co-extensive, at least potentially, with that of every other atom." We are all coextensive, and our work is to move toward union; evolution, de Chardin posits, is a collective motion toward greater consciousness. "No evolutionary future," he writes in *The Phenomenon of Man,* "awaits anyone except in association with everyone else." We must know our fellows in order for everything to move forward; it is our spiritual imperative to connect, or else the destiny of the world cannot be completed.

A theory of the popularity of vampire books and movies: we understand that in a consumer culture we are feasting on whatever brings us a feeling of life, that we hunger to be fed in this way, that our freedom to act upon our desires places us in the position of hungry consumers, seeking the next pleasure.

Buy anything and what you've brought into your life has made the world a little less vital someplace else.

And we consume our lovers, of course, as we know the world by mouth.

"By mouth" means to use our lips and tongues to touch, but also to speak, to name.

To consume as in tasting. Or as in absorbing, taking on their characteristics or vital energy.

Historians disagree about Whitman's sexual life; some suggest that he had actual congress with few, or none. I doubt that very much, though the evidence for my claim is based on feeling, on the rich and tender erotic force of the poetry, which seems to me composed out of the knowledge of skin. I would like to think he touched men, as he would say "long and long," and I would like to believe—of him and of myself—that this deep and attentive touching was a necessary sort of research, that his poems could not have come swimming into being from any other source but physical love, which he did not distinguish from the spiritual kind.

Great poets are, by definition, undead. The voice is preserved in the warm saline of ink and of memory. It cannot fade; time cannot take away a word of it. The personality, as it breathes through the preserved voice back into the world, is unmistakable: Walt Whitman sounds like no one else. And of all poets, he seems to have understood in the most uncanny of ways that his audience did not yet exist.

He was creating it, in his poems, summoning readers into being who could receive what he had to say. This is most clearly stated in "Crossing Brooklyn Ferry," a poem that has never failed to make me shiver, though I have read it countless times. Where is the speaker in the poem? On the ferry where in a few years the Brooklyn Bridge will stand, yes, in his own time, but also strangely present in our moment:

> It avails not, neither time or place—distance avails not,
> I am with you, you men and women of a generation, or ever so many
> generations hence,
> I project myself—also I return—I am with you, and know how it is.

Later in the poem, he returns to this sort of performative speech, willing himself outside of time—or is it further into it?—approaching his readers in their present moment, as if pushing upward through the skin of the page itself:

> Closer yet I approach you,
> What thought you have of me, I had as much of you—I laid in my
> stores in advance,
> I considered long and seriously of you before you were born.
>
> Who was to know what should come home to me?
> Who knows but I am enjoying this?
> Who knows but I am as good as looking at you now, for all you
> cannot see me?

There is perhaps one other poem like this in English, a fragment by John Keats that begins: "This living hand . . ." Who else would dare to speak this way, to write themselves into the condition of deathlessness?

Of the many poems that demonstrate Whitman's daring, "Trickle, Drops" is in its way the strangest. He placed it in the yearning, homoerotic Calamus sequence, for good reason, and I used to think it the creepiest page in *Leaves of Grass*. But in the light of Stoker, I begin to see it differently indeed, though I admit it still makes my skin crawl a little. Who's the vampire here?

O drops of me! trickle, slow drops,
Candid, from me falling—drip, bleeding drops,
From wounds made to free you whence you were prisoned,
From my face—from my forehead and lips,
From my breast—from within where I was concealed—
    Press forth, red drops—confession drops,
Stain every page—stain every song I sing, every word I say,
    bloody drops,
Let them know your scarlet heat—let them glisten,
Saturate them with yourself, all ashamed and wet,
Glow upon all I have written or shall write, bleeding drops,
Let it all be seen in your light, blushing drops.

With his characteristic, canny strangeness, Whitman has done what no one else would have thought to do. He's made the reader the vampire, feasting on the poems, which here expose, in their fierce confessional heat, the poet's naked life. And where "you," Whitman's ubiquitous second person, is nearly everywhere in his work, the reader he wishes to seduce and to claim, here he speaks, for once, to his own blood. He feeds it to us. I feel—as indeed he must have wanted his readers to feel—that he feeds it to me. How could I refuse him?

MARK EDMUNDSON

Who Are You and What Are You Doing Here?

FROM *The Oxford American*

WELCOME AND CONGRATULATIONS: getting to the first day of college is a major achievement. You're to be commended, and not just you, but the parents, grandparents, uncles, and aunts who helped get you here.

It's been said that raising a child effectively takes a village: well, as you may have noticed, our American village is not in very good shape. We've got guns, drugs, two wars, fanatical religions, a slime-based popular culture, and some politicians who—a little restraint here—aren't what they might be. To merely survive in this American village and to win a place in the entering class has taken a lot of grit on your part. So, yes, congratulations to all.

You now may think that you've about got it made. Amidst the impressive college buildings, in company with a high-powered faculty, surrounded by the best of your generation, all you need is to keep doing what you've done before: work hard, get good grades, listen to your teachers, get along with the people around you, and you'll emerge in four years as an educated young man or woman. Ready for life.

Do not believe it. It is not true. If you want to get a real education in America you're going to have to fight—and I don't mean just fight against the drugs and the violence and against the slime-based culture that is still going to surround you. I mean something a little more disturbing. To get an education, you're probably going to have to fight against the institution that you find yourself

in—no matter how prestigious it may be. (In fact, the more prestigious the school, the more you'll probably have to push.) You can
get a terrific education in America now—there are astonishing
opportunities at almost every college—but the education will not
be presented to you wrapped and bowed. To get it, you'll need to
struggle and strive, to be strong, and occasionally even to piss off
some admirable people.

I came to college with few resources, but one of them was an
understanding, however crude, of how I might use my opportunities there. This I began to develop because of my father, who
had never been to college—in fact, he'd barely gotten out of high
school. One night after dinner, he and I were sitting in our kitchen
at 58 Clewley Road in Medford, Massachusetts, hatching plans
about the rest of my life. I was about to go off to college, a feat
no one in my family had accomplished in living memory. "I think
I might want to be prelaw," I told my father. I had no idea what
being prelaw was. My father compressed his brow and blew twin
streams of smoke, dragonlike, from his magnificent nose. "Do you
want to be a lawyer?" he asked. My father had some experience
with lawyers, and with policemen, too; he was not well-disposed
toward either. "I'm not really sure," I told him, "but lawyers make
pretty good money, right?"

My father detonated. (That was not uncommon. My father detonated a lot.) He told me that I was going to go to college only
once, and that while I was there I had better study what I wanted.
He said that when rich kids went to school, they majored in the
subjects that interested them, and that my younger brother Philip
and I were as good as any rich kids. (We were rich kids minus the
money.) Wasn't I interested in literature? I confessed that I was.
Then I had better study literature, unless I had inside information
to the effect that reincarnation wasn't just hype, and I'd be able
to attend college thirty or forty times. If I had such info, prelaw
would be fine, and maybe even a tour through invertebrate biology could also be tossed in. But until I had the reincarnation stuff
from a solid source, I better get to work and pick out some English
classes from the course catalogue. "How about the science requirements?"

"Take 'em later," he said. "You never know."

My father, Wright Aukenhead Edmundson, Malden High
School class of 1948 (by a hair), knew the score. What he told me

that evening at the Clewley Road kitchen table was true in itself, and it also contains the germ of an idea about what a university education should be. But apparently almost everyone else—students, teachers, and trustees and parents—sees the matter much differently. They have it wrong.

Education has one salient enemy in present-day America, and that enemy is education—university education in particular. To almost everyone, university education is a means to an end. For students, that end is a good job. Students want the credentials that will help them get ahead. They want the certificate that will give them access to Wall Street, or entrance into law or medical or business school. And how can we blame them? America values power and money, big players with big bucks. When we raise our children, we tell them in multiple ways that what we want most for them is success—material success. To be poor in America is to be a failure—it's to be without decent health care, without basic necessities, often without dignity. Then there are those backbreaking student loans—people leave school as servants, indentured to pay massive bills, so that first job better be a good one. Students come to college with the goal of a diploma in mind—what happens in between, especially in classrooms, is often of no deep and determining interest to them.

In college, life is elsewhere. Life is at parties, at clubs, in music, with friends, in sports. Life is what celebrities have. The idea that the courses you take should be the primary objective of going to college is tacitly considered absurd. In terms of their work, students live in the future and not the present; they live with their prospects for success. If universities stopped issuing credentials, half of the clients would be gone by tomorrow morning, with the remainder following fast behind.

The faculty, too, is often absent: their real lives are also elsewhere. Like most of their students, they aim to get on. The work they are compelled to do to advance—get tenure, promotion, raises, outside offers—is, broadly speaking, scholarly work. No matter what anyone says, this work has precious little to do with the fundamentals of teaching. The proof is that virtually no undergraduate students can read and understand their professors' scholarly publications. The public senses this disparity and so thinks of the professors' work as being silly or beside the point. Some of it is. But the public also senses that because professors

don't pay full-bore attention to teaching they don't have to work
very hard—they've created a massive feather bed for themselves
and called it a university.

This is radically false. Ambitious professors, the ones who, like
their students, want to get ahead in America, work furiously. Scholarship, even if pretentious and almost unreadable, is nonetheless
labor-intensive. One can slave for a year or two on a single article
for publication in this or that refereed journal. These essays are
honest: their footnotes reflect real reading, real assimilation, and
real dedication. Shoddy work—in which the author cheats, cuts
corners, copies from others—is quickly detected. The people who
do this work have highly developed intellectual powers, and they
push themselves hard to reach a certain standard: that the results
have almost no practical relevance to the students, the public, or
even, frequently, to other scholars is a central element in the tragi-
comedy that is often academia.

The students and the professors have made a deal: neither of
them has to throw himself heart and soul into what happens in the
classroom. The students write their abstract, over-intellectualized
essays; the professors grade the students for their capacity to be abstract and over-intellectual—and often genuinely smart. For their
essays can be brilliant, in a chilly way; they can also be clipped
off the Internet, and often are. Whatever the case, no one wants
to invest too much in them—for life is elsewhere. The professor
saves his energies for the profession, while the student saves his
for friends, social life, volunteer work, making connections, and
getting in position to clasp hands on the true grail, the first job.

No one in this picture is evil; no one is criminally irresponsible.
It's just that smart people are prone to look into matters to see
how they might go about buttering their toast. Then they butter
their toast.

As for the administrators, their relation to the students often
seems based not on love but fear. Administrators fear bad pub-
licity, scandal, and dissatisfaction on the part of their customers.
More than anything else, though, they fear lawsuits. Throwing a
student out of college, for this or that piece of bad behavior, is
very difficult, almost impossible. The student will sue your eyes
out. One kid I knew (and rather liked) threatened on his blog to
mince his dear and esteemed professor (me) with a samurai sword
for the crime of having taught a boring class. (The class was *a little*

boring—I had a damned cold—but the punishment seemed a bit severe.) The dean of students laughed lightly when I suggested that this behavior might be grounds for sending the student on a brief vacation. I was, you might say, discomfited, and showed up to class for a while with my cell phone jiggered to dial 911 with one touch.

Still, this was small potatoes. Colleges are even leery of disciplining guys who have committed sexual assault, or assault plain and simple. Instead of being punished, these guys frequently stay around, strolling the quad and swilling the libations, an affront (and sometimes a terror) to their victims.

You'll find that cheating is common as well. As far as I can discern, the student ethos goes like this: if the professor is so lazy that he gives the same test every year, it's okay to go ahead and take advantage—you've both got better things to do. The Internet is amok with services selling term papers and those services exist, capitalism being what it is, because people purchase the papers—lots of them. Fraternity files bulge with old tests from a variety of courses.

Periodically the public gets exercised about this situation, and there are articles in the national news. But then interest dwindles and matters go back to normal.

One of the reasons professors sometimes look the other way when they sense cheating is that it sends them into a world of sorrow. A friend of mine had the temerity to detect cheating on the part of a kid who was the nephew of a well-placed official in an Arab government complexly aligned with the U.S. Black limousines pulled up in front of his office and disgorged decorously suited negotiators. Did my pal fold? Nope, he's not the type. But he did not enjoy the process.

What colleges generally want are well-rounded students, civic leaders, people who know what the system demands, how to keep matters light, not push too hard for an education or anything else; people who get their credentials and leave the professors alone to do their brilliant work, so they may rise and enhance the rankings of the university. Such students leave and become donors and so, in their own turn, contribute immeasurably to the university's standing. They've done a fine job skating on surfaces in high school—the best way to get an across-the-board outstanding record—and now they're on campus to cut a few more figure eights.

In a culture where the major and determining values are monetary, what else could you do? How else would you live if not by getting all you can, succeeding all you can, making all you can?

The idea that a university education really should have no substantial content, should not be about what John Keats was disposed to call Soul-making, is one that you might think professors and university presidents would be discreet about. Not so. This view informed an address that Richard Brodhead gave to the senior class at Yale before he departed to become president of Duke. Brodhead, an impressive, articulate man, seems to take as his educational touchstone the Duke of Wellington's precept that the Battle of Waterloo was won on the playing fields of Eton. Brodhead suggests that the content of the courses isn't really what matters. In five years (or five months, or minutes), the student is likely to have forgotten how to do the problem sets and will only hazily recollect what happens in the ninth book of *Paradise Lost*. The legacy of their college years will be a legacy of difficulties overcome. When they face equally arduous tasks later in life, students will tap their old resources of determination, and they'll win.

All right, there's nothing wrong with this as far as it goes—after all, the student who writes a brilliant forty-page thesis in a hard week has learned more than a little about her inner resources. Maybe it will give her needed confidence in the future. But doesn't the content of the courses matter at all?

On the evidence of this talk, no. Trying to figure out whether the stuff you're reading is true or false and being open to having your life changed is a fraught, controversial activity. Doing so requires energy from the professor—which is better spent on other matters. This kind of perspective-altering teaching and learning can cause the things which administrators fear above all else: trouble, arguments, bad press, etc. After the kid-samurai episode, the chair of my department not unsympathetically suggested that this was the sort of incident that could happen when you brought a certain intensity to teaching. At the time I found his remark a tad detached, but maybe he was right.

So, if you want an education, the odds aren't with you: the professors are off doing what they call their own work; the other students, who've doped out the way the place runs, are busy leaving the professors alone and getting themselves in position for bright and shining futures; the student-services people are trying to keep everyone content, offering plenty of entertainment and building another state-of-the-art workout facility every few months. The development office is already scanning you for future donations. The primary function of Yale University, it's recently been said, is to create prosperous alumni so as to enrich Yale University.

So why make trouble? Why not just go along? Let the profs roam free in the realms of pure thought, let yourselves party in the realms of impure pleasure, and let the student-services gang assert fewer prohibitions and newer delights for you. You'll get a good job, you'll have plenty of friends, you'll have a driveway of your own.

You'll also, if my father and I are right, be truly and righteously screwed. The reason for this is simple. The quest at the center of a liberal arts education is not a luxury quest; it's a necessity quest. If you do not undertake it, you risk leading a life of desperation—maybe quiet, maybe, in time, very loud—and I am not exaggerating. For you risk trying to be someone other than who you are, which, in the long run, is killing.

By the time you come to college, you will have been told who you are numberless times. Your parents and friends, your teachers, your counselors, your priests and rabbis and ministers and imams have all had their say. They've let you know how they size you up, and they've let you know what they think you should value. They've given you a sharp and protracted taste of what they feel is good and bad, right and wrong. Much is on their side. They have confronted you with scriptures—holy books that, whatever their actual provenance, have given people what they feel to be wisdom for thousands of years. They've given you family traditions—you've learned the ways of your tribe and your community. And, too, you've been tested, probed, looked at up and down and through. The coach knows what your athletic prospects are, the guidance office has a sheaf of test scores that relegate you to this or that ability quadrant, and your teachers have got you pegged. You are, as Foucault might say, the intersection of many evaluative and potentially determining discourses: you boy, you girl, have been made.

And—contra Foucault—that's not so bad. Embedded in all of the major religions are profound truths. Schopenhauer, who despised belief in transcendent things, nonetheless thought Christianity to be of inexpressible worth. He couldn't believe in the divinity of Jesus, or in the afterlife, but to Schopenhauer, a deep pessimist, a religion that had as its central emblem the figure of a man being tortured on a cross couldn't be entirely misleading. To the Christian, Schopenhauer said, pain was at the center of the understanding of life, and that was just as it should be.

One does not need to be as harsh as Schopenhauer to understand the use of religion, even if one does not believe in an otherworldly god. And all of those teachers and counselors and friends—and the prognosticating uncles, the dithering aunts, the fathers and mothers with their hopes for your fulfillment—or their fulfillment in you—should not necessarily be cast aside or ignored. Families have their wisdom. The question "Who do they think you are at home?" is never an idle one.

The major conservative thinkers have always been very serious about what goes by the name of common sense. Edmund Burke saw common sense as a loosely made, but often profound, collective work, in which humanity has deposited its hard-earned wisdom—the precipitate of joy and tears—over time. You have been raised in proximity to common sense, if you've been raised at all, and common sense is something to respect, though not quite—peace unto the formidable Burke—to revere.

You may be all that the good people who raised you say you are; you may want all they have shown you is worth wanting; you may be someone who is truly your father's son or your mother's daughter. But then again, you may not be.

For the power that is in you, as Emerson suggested, may be new in nature. You may not be the person that your parents take you to be. And—this thought is both more exciting and more dangerous—you may not be the person that you take yourself to be either. You may not have read yourself aright, and college is the place where you can find out whether you have or not. The reason to read Blake and Dickinson and Freud and Dickens is not to become more cultivated, or more articulate, or to be someone who, at a cocktail party, is never embarrassed (or who can embarrass others). The best reason to read them is to see if they may know you better than you know yourself. You may find your own suppressed and rejected thoughts flowing back to you with an "alienated majesty." Reading the great writers, you may have the experience that Longinus associated with the sublime: you feel that you have actually created the text yourself. For somehow your predecessors are more yourself than you are.

This was my own experience reading the two writers who have influenced me the most, Sigmund Freud and Ralph Waldo Emerson. They gave words to thoughts and feelings that I had never been able to render myself. They shone a light onto the world and what they saw, suddenly I saw, too. From Emerson I learned to trust my own thoughts, to trust them even when every voice seems to be on the other side. I need the wherewithal, as Emerson did, to say what's on my mind and to take the inevitable hits. Much more I learned from the sage—about character, about loss, about joy, about writing and its secret sources—but Emerson most centrally preaches the gospel of self-reliance and that is what I have tried most to take from him. I continue to hold in mind one of Emerson's most memorable passages: "Society is a joint-stock company, in which the members agree, for the better securing of his bread to each shareholder, to surrender the liberty and culture of the eater. The virtue in most request is conformity. Self-reliance is its aversion. It loves not realities and creators, but names and customs."

Emerson's greatness lies not only in showing you how powerful names and customs can be, but also in demonstrating how exhilarating it is to buck them. When he came to Harvard to talk about religion, he shocked the professors and students by challenging the divinity of Jesus and the truth of his miracles. He wasn't invited back for decades.

From Freud I found a great deal to ponder as well. I don't mean Freud the aspiring scientist, but the Freud who was a speculative essayist and interpreter of the human condition like Emerson. Freud challenges nearly every significant human ideal. He goes after religion. He says that it comes down to the longing for the father. He goes after love. He calls it "the overestimation of the erotic object." He attacks our desire for charismatic popular leaders. We're drawn to them because we hunger for absolute authority. He declares that dreams don't predict the future and that there's nothing benevolent about them. They're disguised fulfillments of repressed wishes.

Freud has something challenging and provoking to say about virtually every human aspiration. I learned that if I wanted to affirm any consequential ideal, I had to talk my way past Freud. He was—and is—a perpetual challenge and goad.

Never has there been a more shrewd and imaginative cartographer of the psyche. His separation of the self into three parts, and his sense of the fraught, anxious, but often negotiable relations among them (negotiable when you come to the game with a Freudian knowledge), does a great deal to help one navigate experience. (Though sometimes—and this I owe to Emerson—it seems right to let the psyche fall into civil war, accepting barrages of anxiety and grief for this or that good reason.)

The battle is to make such writers one's own, to winnow them out and to find their essential truths. We need to see where they fall short and where they exceed the mark, and then to develop them a little, as the ideas themselves, one comes to see, actually developed others. (Both Emerson and Freud live out of Shakespeare—but only a giant can be truly influenced by Shakespeare.) In reading, I continue to look for one thing—to be influenced, to learn something new, to be thrown off my course and onto another, better way.

My father knew that he was dissatisfied with life. He knew that none of the descriptions people had for him quite fit. He understood that he was always out of joint with life as it was. He had talent: my brother and I each got about half the raw ability he possessed and that's taken us through life well enough. But what to do with that talent—there was the rub for my father. He used to stroll through the house intoning his favorite line from Groucho Marx's ditty "Whatever it is, I'm against it." (I recently asked my son, now twenty-one, if he thought I was mistaken in teaching him this particular song when he was six years old. "No!" he said, filling the air with an invisible forest of exclamation points.) But what my father never managed to get was a sense of who he might become. He never had a world of possibilities spread before him, never made sustained contact with the best that had been thought and said. He didn't get to revise his understanding of himself, figure out what he'd do best that might give the world some profit.

My father was a gruff man, but also a generous one, so that night at the kitchen table at 58 Clewley Road he made an effort to let me have the chance that had been denied to him by both fate and character. He gave me the chance to see what I was all about, and if it proved to be different from him, proved even to be something he didn't like or entirely comprehend, then he'd deal with it.

Right now, if you're going to get a real education, you may have to be aggressive and assertive.

Your professors will give you some fine books to read, and they'll probably help you understand them. What they won't do, for reasons that perplex me, is to ask you if the books contain truths you could live your lives by. When you read Plato, you'll probably learn about his metaphysics and his politics and his way of conceiving the soul. But no one will ask you if his ideas are good enough to believe in. No one will ask you, in the words of Emerson's disciple William James, what their "cash value" might be. No one will suggest that you might use Plato as your bible for a week or a year or longer. No one, in short, will ask you to use Plato to help you change your life.

That will be up to you. You must put the question of Plato to yourself. You must ask whether reason should always rule the passions, philosophers should always rule the state, and poets should inevitably be banished from a just commonwealth. You have to ask yourself if wildly expressive music (rock and rap and the rest) deranges the soul in ways that are destructive to its health. You must inquire of yourself if balanced calm is the most desirable human state.

Occasionally—for you will need some help in fleshing out the answers—you may have to prod your professors to see if they take the text at hand—in this case the divine and disturbing Plato—to be true. And you will have to be tough if the professor mocks you for uttering a sincere question instead of keeping matters easy for all concerned by staying detached and analytical. (Detached analysis has a place—but, in the end, you've got to speak from the heart and pose the question of truth.) You'll be the one who pesters his teachers. You'll ask your history teacher about whether there is a design to our history, whether we're progressing or declining, or whether, in the words of a fine recent play, *The History Boys*, history's "just one fuckin' thing after another." You'll be the one who challenges your biology teacher about the intellectual conflict between evolution and creationist thinking. You'll not only question the statistics teacher about what *numbers* can explain but what they can't.

Because every subject you study is a language and since you may adopt one of these languages as your own, you'll want to know how to speak it expertly and also how it fails to deal with those concerns for which it has no adequate words. You'll be looking into the reach of every metaphor that every discipline offers, and you'll be trying to see around their corners.

The whole business is scary, of course. What if you arrive at college devoted to premed, sure that nothing will make you and your family happier than a life as a physician, only to discover that elementary school teaching is where your heart is?

You might learn that you're not meant to be a doctor at all. Of course, given your intellect and discipline, you can still probably be one. You can pound your round peg through the very square hole of medical school, then go off into the profession. And society will help you. Society has a cornucopia of resources to encourage you in doing what society needs done but that you don't much like doing and are not cut out to do. To ease your grief, society offers alcohol, television, drugs, divorce, and buying, buying, buying what you don't need. But all those, too, have their costs.

Education is about finding out what form of work for you is close to being play—work you do so easily that it restores you as you go. Randall Jarrell once said that if he were a rich man, he would pay money to teach poetry to students. (I would, too, for what it's worth.) In saying that, he (like my father) hinted in the direction of a profound and true theory of learning.

Having found what's best for you to do, you may be surprised how far you rise, how prosperous, even against your own projections, you become. The student who eschews medical school to follow his gift for teaching small children spends his twenties in low-paying but pleasurable and soul-rewarding toil. He's always behind on his student-loan payments; he still lives in a house with four other guys (not all of whom got proper instructions on how to clean a bathroom). He buys shirts from the Salvation Army, has intermittent Internet, and vacations where he can. But lo—he has a gift for teaching. He writes an essay about how to teach, then a book—which no one buys. But he writes another—in part out of a feeling of injured merit, maybe—and that one they do buy.

Money is still a problem, but in a new sense. The world wants him to write more, lecture, travel more, and will pay him for his efforts, and he likes this a good deal. But he also likes staying around and showing up at school and figuring out how to get this or that little runny-nosed specimen to begin learning how to read. These are the kinds of problems that are worth having and if you advance, as Thoreau said, in the general direction of your dreams, you may have them. If you advance in the direction of someone else's dreams—if you want to live someone else's life rather than yours—then get a TV for every room, buy yourself a lifetime supply of your favorite quaff, crank up the porn channel, and groove away. But when we expend our energies in rightful ways, Robert Frost observed, we stay whole and vigorous and we don't weary. "Strongly spent," the poet says, "is synonymous with kept."

JOSEPH EPSTEIN

Duh, Bor-ing

FROM *Commentary*

> Somewhere I have read that boredom is the torment of hell that
> Dante forgot.
> —Albert Speer, *Spandau: The Secret Diaries*

UNREQUITED LOVE, AS Lorenz Hart instructed us, is a bore, but
then so are a great many other things: old friends gone somewhat
dotty from whom it is too late to disengage, the important social-
science-based book of the month, 95 percent of the items on the
evening news, discussions about the Internet, arguments against
the existence of God, people who overestimate their charm, all
talk about wine, *New York Times* editorials, lengthy lists (like this
one), and, not least, oneself.

Some people claim never to have been bored. They lie. One
cannot be human without at some time or other having known
boredom. Even animals know boredom, we are told, though they
are deprived of the ability to complain directly about it. Some of us
are more afflicted with boredom than others. Psychologists make
the distinction between ordinary and pathological boredom; the
latter doesn't cause serious mental problems but is associated with
them. Another distinction is that between situational boredom
and existential boredom. Situational boredom is caused by the
temporary tedium everyone at one time or another encounters:
the dull sermon, the longueur-laden novel, the pompous gent extolling his prowess at the used-tire business. Existential boredom
is thought to be the result of existence itself, caused by modern
culture and therefore inescapable. Boredom even has some class
standing, and was once felt to be an aristocratic attribute. Ennui,
it has been said, is the reigning emotion of the dandy.

When bored, time slows drastically, the world seems logy and without promise, and reality itself can grow shadowy and vague. Truman Capote once described the novels of James Baldwin as "balls-achingly boring," which conveys something of the agony of boredom yet is inaccurate—not about Baldwin's novels, which are no stroll around the Louvre, but about the effect of boredom itself. Boredom is never so clearly localized. The vagueness of boredom, its vaporousness and its torpor, is part of its mild but genuine torment.

Boredom is often less pervasive in simpler cultures. One hears little of boredom among the Pygmies or the Trobriand Islanders, whose energies are taken up with the problems of mere existence. Ironically, it can be most pervasive where a great deal of stimulation is available. Boredom can also apparently be aided by overstimulation, or so we are all learning through the current generation of children, who, despite their vast arsenal of electronic toys, their many hours spent before screens of one kind or another, more often than any previous generation register cries of boredom. Rare is the contemporary parent or grandparent who has not heard these kids, when presented with a project for relief of their boredom—go outside, read a book—reply, with a heavy accent on each syllable, "Bor-ing."

My own experience of boredom has been intermittent, never chronic. As a boy of six or seven, I recall one day reporting to my mother that I was bored. A highly intelligent woman of even temperament, she calmly replied: "Really? May I suggest that you knock your head against the wall. It'll take your mind off your boredom." I never again told my mother that I was bored.

For true boredom, few things top life in a peacetime army. For the first eight weeks there, life consists of being screamed at while being put to tedious tasks: KP, guard duty, barracks cleanup, calisthenics, endless drilling. After those first two months, the screaming lets up but the tedium of the tasks continues. In my case, these included marching off in helmet liner and fatigues to learn to touch-type to the strains of the "Colonel Bogey March" from *The Bridge on the River Kwai;* later writing up cultural news (of which there wasn't any) at Fort Hood, Texas; in the evening, walking the streets of the nearby town of Killeen, where the entertainment on offer was a beer drunk, a hamburger, a tattoo, or an auto loan; and, later, typing up physical exams in an old bank building used as a recruiting station in downtown Little Rock, Arkansas. Was I bored? Yes, out of my gourd. But, then, so heavy is boredom in peacetime armies that, from the Roman Empire on, relief from it has often been a serious enticement on its own to war.

But, ah, the sweetness, the luxuriousness of boredom when the details of quotidian life threaten to plow one under through sheer aggravation, or real troubles (medical, familial, financial) are visited upon one, and supply, as Tacitus has it, "ample proof that the gods are indifferent to our tranquility but eager for our punishment." Except that most people cannot stand even gentle boredom for long.

"I have discovered that all evil comes from this," wrote Pascal, "man's being unable to sit still in a room." Failing precisely this test, that of the ability to sit quietly alone in a room, brought about *acedia*, a Greek word meaning "apathy," or "indifference," among hermit monks in North Africa in the fourth century C.E.

I come to this historical tidbit through reading *Boredom: A Lively History* (Yale University Press, 224 pages) by Peter Toohey, who teaches classics at Calgary University. His book and *A Philosophy of Boredom* (Reaktion Books, 124 pages) by Lars Svendsen are the two best contemporary works on the subject. Noteworthy that men living, respectively, in western Canada and Norway should be attracted to the subject of boredom; obviously their geography and occupations as academics qualify them eminently for the subject. A teacher, as I myself discovered after three chalk-filled decades, is someone who never says anything once—or, for that matter, never says anything a mere nine or ten times.

The radical difference between Toohey and Svendsen is that the former thinks boredom has its uses, while the latter is confident that boredom is *the* major spiritual problem of our day. "Is modern life," Svendsen asks, "first and foremost an attempt to escape boredom?" He believes it is, and also believes, I surmise, that this escape cannot be achieved. He holds that boredom is not merely an individual but a social, a cultural, finally a philosophical problem. He quotes Jean Baudrillard, the French philosopher, saying that the traditional philosophical problem used to be "why is there anything at all rather than nothing?" but that today the real question is "why is there just nothing, rather than something?" With Svendsen, we arrive at the exposition of existential boredom.

Svendsen remarks on the difficulty of portraying boredom in

literature. (In *The Pale King*, the unfinished novel that David Foster Wallace left at his desk after suicide at the age of forty-six, Wallace set out to explore all the facets of boredom, which, if reviewers are to be believed, he was, alas, unable to bring off.) Toohey would not quite agree and includes in the literature of boredom Ivan Goncharov's great novel *Oblomov*, whose first one hundred pages are about the inability of its title character to get out of bed and get dressed and do something, anything. But *Oblomov* is less about boredom than about sloth.

The difference is a reminder that boredom presents a semantic problem. One must discriminate and make distinctions when trying to define it. Ennui, apathy, depression, accidie, melancholia, *mal de vivre*—these are all aspects of boredom, but they do not quite define it. Perhaps the most serious distinction that needs to be made is that between boredom and depression. Toohey is correct when he argues that chronic boredom can bring about agitation, anger, and depression, but that boredom and depression are not the same. Boredom is chiefly an emotion of a secondary kind, like shame, guilt, envy, admiration, embarrassment, contempt, and others. Depression is a mental illness, and much more serious.

"Suicide," Toohey claims, "has no clear relationship with boredom," while it can have everything to do with depression. Perhaps. An exception is the actor George Sanders, who in 1972, at the age of sixty-five, checked into a hotel near Barcelona and was found dead two days later, having taken five bottles of Nembutal. He left behind a suicide note that read:

> Dear World, I am leaving because I am bored. I feel I have lived long enough. I am leaving you with your worries in this sweet cesspool. Good luck.

If boredom isn't easily defined—"a bestial and indefinable affliction," Dostoyevsky called it—it can be described. A "psychological Sahara," the Russian poet Joseph Brodsky called it. If one wants to experience it directly, I know no more efficient way than reading Martin Heidegger on the subject, specifically the sections on boredom in *The Fundamental Concepts of Metaphysics: World, Finitude, Solitude*. Boredom, for Heidegger, is valuable in that it rubs clear the slate of our mind and is, as Svendsen has it, "a privileged fundamental mood because it leads us directly into the very problem of time and being." Boredom, in this reading, readies the mind for profound vision. I could attempt to explain how, in Heidegger, this comes about, but your eyes, in reading it, would soon take on the glaze of a franchise doughnut. Besides, I don't believe it.

Neither does Toohey, who is excellent on drawing the line of the existentialist tradition of boredom that runs from the acedia of the early monks through Heidegger and Jean-Paul Sartre to the present day. Toohey holds that existentialist boredom is neither an emotion nor a feeling but a concept, one "constructed from a union of boredom, chronic boredom, depression, a sense of superfluity, frustration, surfeit, disgust, indifference, apathy, and feelings of entrapment." As such, existential boredom has become a philosophical sickness, not part of the human condition at all, but available exclusively to intellectuals given to moodiness and dark views.

The most notable novel in the existentialist boredom tradition is Sartre's *Nausea* (1938), whose main character, Antoine Roquentin, lives in a condition of overpowering indifference that Sartre calls "contingency," in which the universe is uncaring and one's existence is without necessity. After reading the philosophers taken up with the problems of being and existence, I cheer myself up by recalling the anecdote about the student in one of his philosophy courses at CCNY who asked Morris Raphael Cohen to prove that he, the student, existed. "Ah," replied Cohen in his Yiddish-accented English, "who's eskin'?"

In France, boredom is given a philosophical tincture; in England, an aristocratic one: Lord Byron, having seen and done it all, is the perfect type of the bored English aristocrat. George Santayana, traveling on a student fellowship from Harvard, made the discovery that the Germans had no conception of boredom whatsoever, which explains their tolerance for the *Ring* cycle and the novels of Hermann Broch, and for so many other lengthy productions in German high culture. In Italy, boredom can take on the coloration and tone of amusing decadence, an emotion perfectly embodied in several movies by Marcello Mastroianni.

Alberto Moravia's novel *Boredom* (1960) plays the subject for darkish laughs. A man in his thirties, a failed painter with a rich mother, hounded by boredom all his days, takes up with a young painter's model. He has regular and uncomplicated sex with her, but off the couch she bores him blue, until she begins cheating on him with another man, which arouses his interest in her. Preferring not to be interested, he concludes that his only solution is to marry her and give her a large number of children. Once she is his wife and he can ensure her fidelity, he can lapse back into comfortable boredom. "In this lack of all roots and responsibilities," he thinks, "in this utter void created by boredom, marriage, for me, was something dead and meaningless, and in this way it would at least serve some purpose." To "divorce, Italian style" Moravia adds "marriage, Italian style," though in the novel the painter does not finally marry the young woman.

Moravia's novel is also a reminder that perhaps as many marriages fail out of boredom as out of anything else. "Of all the primary relations," Robert Nisbet writes in *Prejudices: A Philosophical Dictionary,* "marriage is probably the most fertile in its yield of boredom, to a wife perhaps more than to a husband if only because prior to recent times, her opportunities to forestall or relieve boredom were fewer." In Nisbet's view, the changing nature of marriage, from an institution with an economic foundation designed primarily for procreation to one that has become an almost "purely personal relationship," has rendered it all the more susceptible to the incursions of boredom. Nisbet speculates that had God permitted Adam and Eve to remain in the Garden of Eden, their marriage, too, might have foundered on boredom.

Sameness and repetition are among the chief causes of boredom. If they haunt marriages, they are even more powerfully at work in the realm of vocation. Once work went beyond the artisanal state, where farmers and craftsmen had a personal hand in their productions, once the assembly line and its white-collar equivalent, the large bureaucratic office, came into being, work, owing to its repetitious nature, became one of the chief sources of boredom in the modern world.

Views on boredom and work alter with changing economic conditions. For my father's generation, arriving at maturity with the onset of the Depression, the notion of "interesting" in connection with work didn't come into play. Making a good living did. Unless the work was utterly degrading, my father could not understand leaving one job for another at a lesser salary. How different from today when a friend in California recently told me that he thought he might cease hiring young college graduates for jobs in his financial firm. "Their minds aren't in it," he said. "They all want to write screenplays."

One can also tell a great deal about a person by what bores him. Certainly this is so in my own case. After perhaps an hour of driving along the coast between Portland, Oregon, and Vancouver, British Columbia, encountering one dazzling landscape after another, I thought enough was enough; Mae West was wrong, you can get too much of a good thing; and I longed for the sight of a delicatessen stocked with febrile Jews.

Tolerance for boredom differs vastly from person to person. Some might argue that a strong intolerance for boredom suggests, with its need for constant action, impressive ambition. Others longing to be always in play have, as the old saying goes, ants in their pants, or, to use the good Yiddish word, *schplikes*.

No one longs to be bored, but if I am a useful example, as one grows older, one often finds oneself more patient with boredom. Pressureless, dull patches in life—bring them on. I recently read two very well-written but extremely boring novels by Barbara Pym—*A Glass of Blessings* and *A Few Green Leaves*. She is a writer I much admire, and I found myself quietly amused by how little happens in these novels. *A Few Green Leaves* contains the following sentence: "'It is an art all too seldom met with,' Adam declared, 'the correct slicing of cucumber.'"

Toohey suggests that boredom is good for us. We should, he feels, be less put off by it. For one thing, boredom can function as a warning sign, as angina warns of heart attack and gout of stroke, telling those who suffer unduly from it that they need to change their lives. For another, "boredom intensifies self-perception," by which I gather he means that it allows time for introspection of a kind not available to those who live in a state of continuous agitation and excitation. Boredom can also in itself function as a stimulant; boredom with old arguments and ideas can, in this view, presumably lead to freshened thought and creativity.

In the last chapter of *Boredom: A Lively History,* Toohey veers into a discussion of what brain science has to tell us about boredom. I almost wrote a "compulsory discussion," for with-it-ness now calls for checking in with what the neuroscientists have to say about your subject, whatever it might be. What they have to say is usually speculative, generally turns out to be based on studies of mice or chimps, and is never very persuasive. Boredom, neuroscientists believe, is thought to be experienced in the part of the brain called the "insula," where other secondary emotions are experienced, and which a neurologist named Arthur D. Craig calls the region of the brain that stands at "a crossroad of time and desire."

Having said this, one hasn't said much. Brain studies, critics of them argue, are still roughly at the stage that physiology was before William Harvey in the seventeenth century discovered the circulatory system. Boredom is after all part of consciousness, and about consciousness the neurologists still have much less to tell us than do the poets and the philosophers.

Boredom, like Parkinson's and Alzheimer's at a much higher level of seriousness, is a disease with no known cure, but Professor Toohey feels the need to supply possible ameliorations, or palliatives, for it. Among these are aerobic exercise (good, some say, for the restoration of brain cells), music (Mozart, it has been discovered, calms agitated elephants in captivity), and social activity (along with crossword puzzles, a recipe for aging well from Toohey's Aunt Madge). Even Toohey has to admit that these sound "corny," which they do. Worse, they sound boring. He does not dwell on those more expensive and dangerous palliatives for boredom: alcoholism, drug addiction, adultery, divorce, skydiving, bungee jumping, and psychotherapy.

Isaac Bashevis Singer once told an interviewer that the purpose of art was to eliminate boredom, at least temporarily, for he held that boredom was the natural condition of men and women. Not artists alone but vast industries have long been at work to eliminate boredom permanently. Think of twenty-four-hour-a-day cable television. Think of Steve Jobs, one of the current heroes of contemporary culture, who may be a genius, and just possibly an evil genius. With his ever more sophisticated iPhones and iPads, he is aiding people to distract themselves from boredom and allowing them to live nearly full-time in a world of games and information and communication with no time out for thought.

In 1989, Joseph Brodsky gave a commencement address at Dartmouth College on the subject of boredom that has a higher truth quotient than any such address I have ever heard (or, for that matter, have myself given). Brodsky told the eleven hundred Dartmouth graduates that although they may have had some splendid samples of boredom supplied by their teachers, these would be as nothing compared with what awaited them in the years ahead. Neither originality nor inventiveness on their part would suffice to defeat the endless repetition that life would serve up to them, as it has served up to us all. Evading boredom, he pointed out, is a full-time job, entailing endless change—of jobs, geography, wives and lovers, interests—and in the end a self-defeating one. Brodsky therefore advised: "When hit by boredom, go for it. Let yourself be crushed by it; submerge, hit bottom."

The lesson boredom teaches, according to Brodsky, is that of one's own insignificance, an insignificance brought about by one's own finitude. We are all here a short while, and then—*poof!*—gone and, sooner or later, usually sooner, forgotten. Boredom "puts your existence into perspective, the net result of which is precision and humility." Brodsky advised the students to try "to stay passionate," for passion, whatever its object, is the closest thing to a remedy for boredom. But about one's insignificance boredom does not deceive. Brodsky, who served eighteen months of hard labor in the Soviet Union and had to have known what true boredom is, closed by telling the students that "if you find this gloomy, you don't know what gloom is."

"Boredom," as Peter Toohey writes, "is a normal, useful, and incredibly common part of human experience." Boredom is also part of the human condition, always has been, and, if we are lucky, always will be.

Live with it.

JONATHAN FRANZEN

Farther Away

FROM *The New Yorker*

IN THE SOUTH PACIFIC OCEAN, five hundred miles off the coast of central Chile, is a forbiddingly vertical volcanic island, seven miles long and four miles wide, that is populated by millions of seabirds and thousands of fur seals but is devoid of people, except in the warmer months, when a handful of fishermen come out to catch lobsters. To reach the island, which is officially called Alejandro Selkirk, you fly from Santiago in an eight-seater that makes twice-weekly flights to an island a hundred miles to the east. Then you have to travel in a small open boat from the airstrip to the archipelago's only village, wait around for a ride on one of the launches that occasionally make the twelve-hour outward voyage, and then, often, wait further, sometimes for days, for weather conducive to landing on the rocky shore. In the 1960s, Chilean tourism officials renamed the island for Alexander Selkirk, the Scottish adventurer whose tale of solitary living in the archipelago was probably the basis for Daniel Defoe's novel *Robinson Crusoe,* but the locals still use its original name, Masafuera: Farther Away.

By the end of last fall, I was in some need of being farther away. I'd been promoting a novel nonstop for four months, advancing through my schedule without volition, feeling more and more like the graphical lozenge on a media player's progress bar. Substantial swaths of my personal history were going dead from within, from my talking about them too often. And every morning the same revving doses of nicotine and caffeine; every evening the same assault on my e-mail queue; every night the same drinking for the same brain-dulling pop of pleasure. At a certain point, hav-

ing read about Masafuera, I began to imagine running away and
being alone there, like Selkirk, in the interior of the island, where
nobody lives even seasonally.

I also thought it might be good, while I was there, to reread the
book generally considered to be the first English novel. *Robinson
Crusoe* was the great early document of radical individualism, the
story of an ordinary person's practical and psychic survival in profound isolation. The novelistic enterprise associated with individualism—the search for meaning in realistic narrative—went on to
become the culture's dominant literary mode for the next three
centuries. Crusoe's voice can be heard in the voice of Jane Eyre,
the Underground Man, the Invisible Man, and Sartre's Roquentin. All these stories had once excited me, and there persisted,
in the very word *novel,* with its promise of *novelty,* a memory of
more youthful experiences so engrossing that I could sit quietly
for hours and never think of boredom. Ian Watt, in his classic
The Rise of the Novel, correlated the eighteenth-century burgeoning of novelistic production with the growing demand for at-home
entertainment by women who'd been liberated from traditional
household tasks and had too much time on their hands. In a very
direct way, according to Watt, the English novel had risen from the
ashes of boredom. And boredom was what I was suffering from.
The more you pursue distractions, the less effective any particular
distraction is, and so I'd had to up various dosages, until, before
I knew it, I was checking my e-mail every ten minutes, and my
plugs of tobacco were getting ever larger, and my two drinks a
night had worsened to four, and I'd achieved such deep mastery
of computer solitaire that my goal was no longer to win a game
but to win two or more games in a row—a kind of meta-solitaire
whose fascination consisted not in playing the cards but in surfing
the streaks of wins and losses. My longest winning streak so far was
eight.

I made arrangements to hitch a ride to Masafuera on a small
boat chartered by some adventurous botanists. Then I indulged in
a little orgy of consumerism at REI, where the Crusovian romance
abides in the aisles of ultralightweight survival gear and, especially
perhaps, in certain emblems of civilization-in-wilderness, like the
stainless steel martini glass with an unscrewable stem. Besides a
new backpack, tent, and knife, I outfitted myself with certain late-
model specialty items, such as a plastic plate with a silicone rim

that flipped up to form a bowl, tablets to neutralize the taste of water sterilized with iodine, a microfiber towel that stowed in a marvelously small pouch, organic vegan freeze-dried chili, and an indestructible spork. I also assembled large stores of nuts, tuna, and protein bars, because I'd been told that if the weather turned bad I could be stranded on Masafuera indefinitely.

On the eve of my departure for Santiago, I visited my friend Karen, the widow of the writer David Foster Wallace. As I was getting ready to leave her house, she asked me, out of the blue, whether I might like to take along some of David's cremation ashes and scatter them on Masafuera. I said I would, and she found an antique wooden matchbox, a tiny book with a sliding drawer, and put some ashes in it, saying that she liked the thought of part of David coming to rest on a remote and uninhabited island. It was only later, after I'd driven away from her house, that I realized that she'd given me the ashes as much for my sake as for hers or David's. She knew, because I had told her, that my current state of flight from myself had begun soon after David's death, two years earlier. At the time, I'd made a decision not to deal with the hideous suicide of someone I'd loved so much but instead to take refuge in anger and work. Now that the work was done, though, it was harder to ignore the circumstance that, arguably, in one interpretation of his suicide, David had died of boredom and in despair about his future novels. The desperate edge to my own recent boredom: Might this be related to my having broken a promise to myself? The promise that, after I'd finished my book project, I would allow myself to feel more than fleeting grief and enduring anger at David's death?

And so, on the last morning of January, I arrived in heavy fog at a spot on Masafuera called La Cuchara (the Spoon), three thousand feet above sea level. I had a notebook, binoculars, a paperback copy of *Robinson Crusoe*, the little book containing David's remains, a backpack filled with camping gear, a grotesquely inadequate map of the island, and no alcohol, tobacco, or computer. Apart from the fact that, instead of hiking up on my own, I'd followed a young park ranger and a mule that was carrying my backpack, and that I'd also brought along, at various people's insistence, a two-way radio, a ten-year-old GPS unit, a satellite phone, and several spare batteries, I was entirely isolated and alone.

*

My first experience of *Robinson Crusoe* was having it read to me
by my father. Along with *Les Misérables*, it was the only novel that
meant anything to him. From the pleasure he took in reading it
to me, it's clear that he identified as deeply with Crusoe as he did
with Jean Valjean (which, in his self-taught way, he pronounced
"Gene Val Gene"). Like Crusoe, my father felt isolated from other
people, was resolutely moderate in his habits, believed in the superiority of Western civilization to the "savagery" of other cultures,
saw the natural world as something to be subdued and exploited,
and was an inveterate do-it-yourselfer. Self-disciplined survival on
a desert island surrounded by cannibals was the perfect romance
for him. He was born in a rough town built by his pioneer father
and uncles, and he'd grown up working in road-building camps in
the boreal swampland. In our basement in St. Louis, he kept an
orderly workshop in which he sharpened his tools, repaired his
clothes (he was a good seamster), and improvised, out of wood
and metal and leather, sturdy solutions to home maintenance
problems. He took my friends and me camping several times a
year, organizing our campsite by himself while I ran in the woods
with my friends, and making himself a bed out of rough old blankets beside our fiberfill sleeping bags. I think, to some extent, I
was an excuse for him to go camping.

My brother Tom, no less a do-it-yourselfer than my father, became a serious backpacker after he went away to college. Because
I was trying to emulate Tom in all things, I listened to his stories
of ten-day solo treks in Colorado and Wyoming and yearned to
be a backpacker myself. My first opportunity came in the summer I turned sixteen, when I persuaded my parents to let me take
a summer school course called Camping in the West. My friend
Weidman and I joined a busload of teenagers and counselors for
two weeks of "study" in the Rockies. I had Tom's obsolescent red
Gerry backpack and, for taking notes on my somewhat randomly
chosen area of study, lichens, a notebook identical to the one that
Tom carried.

On the second day of a trek into the Sawtooth Wilderness, in
Idaho, we were all invited to spend twenty-four hours by ourselves.
My counselor took me off to a sparse grove of ponderosa pine
and left me alone there, and very soon, although the day was
bright and unthreatening, I was cowering in my tent. Apparently,
all it took for me to become aware of the emptiness of life and

the horror of existence was to be deprived of human company for a few hours. I learned, the next day, that Weidman, though eight months older than me, had been so lonely that he hiked back to within sight of the base camp. What enabled me to stick it out—and to feel, moreover, that I could have stayed alone for longer than a day—was writing:

> Thursday July 3 This evening I begin a notebook. If anyone reads this, I trust they will forgive my overuse of "I." *I* can't stop it. *I*'m writing this.
>
> As I came back to my fire after dinner this afternoon there was a moment when I felt my aluminum cup a friend, sitting on a rock, considering me . . .
>
> I had a certain fly (at least I think it was the same one) buzz around my head for a goodly long while this afternoon. After a time I stopped thinking of it as an annoying, nasty insect & subconsciously came to think it an enemy that I was really quite fond of and that we were just playing with each other.
>
> Also this afternoon (this was my main activity) I sat out on a point of rock trying to set to words of a sonnet the different purposes of my life that I saw at different times (3—as in points of view). Of course I now see that I can't even do this in prose form so it was really futile. However, as I did this, I became convinced that life was a waste of time, or something like that. I was so sad and screwed up at the time that every thought was of despair. But then I looked at some lichens & wrote a bit about them & calmed down and figured out that my sorrow was due not to a loss of purpose but to the fact that I didn't know who I was or why I was and that I didn't show my love to my parents. I was coming close with my third point, but my next thought was a little off. I figured that the reason for the above was that ~~time~~ (life) is too short. This is, of course, true, but my sorrow wasn't caused by this. All of a sudden it hit me: I missed my family.

Once I'd diagnosed my homesickness, I was able to address it by writing letters. For the rest of the trip, I wrote in my journal every day and found myself moving away from Weidman and gravitating toward my female fellow campers; I'd never been so successful socially. What had been missing was some halfway secure sense of my own identity, a sense achieved in solitude by putting first-person words on a page.

I was keen for years afterward to do more backpacking, but

never quite keen enough to make it happen. The self I was discovering through writing turned out not to be identical to Tom's after all. I did hold on to his old Gerry backpack, although it was not a useful general-purpose piece of luggage, and I kept alive my dreams of wilderness by buying cheap nonessential camping gear, such as a jumbo bottle of Dr. Bronner's peppermint soap, which Tom periodically praised the virtues of. When I took a bus back to college for my senior year, I put the Dr. Bronner's in the backpack, and the bottle burst in transit, soaking my clothes and books. When I tried to rinse out the backpack in a dormitory shower, its fabric disintegrated in my hands.

Masafuera, as the boat approached it, was not inviting. My only map of the island was a letter-size printout of a Google Earth image, and I saw right away that I'd optimistically misinterpreted the contour lines on it. What had looked like steep hills were cliffs, and what had looked like gentle slopes were steep hills. A dozen or so lobsterman shacks were huddled at the bottom of a tremendous gorge, to either side of which the island's green shoulders rose thirty-five hundred feet into a cap of broodingly churning cloud. The ocean, which had seemed reasonably calm on the trip out, was beating in big swells against a gap in the rocks below the shacks. To get ashore, the botanists and I jumped down into a lobster boat, which motored to within a hundred yards of shore. There the boatmen hauled up the motor, and we took hold of a rope stretching out to a buoy and pulled ourselves farther in. As we neared the rocks, the boat lurched chaotically from side to side, water flooding into the stern, while the boatmen struggled to attach us to a cable that would drag us out. Onshore were breathtaking quantities of flies—the place's nickname is Fly Island. Competing boom boxes pumped North and South American music through the open doors of several shacks, pushing back against the oppressive immensity of the gorge and the coldly heaving sea. Adding to the stricken atmospherics was a grove of large, dead trees, aged to the color of bone, behind the shacks.

My companions for the trek to the interior were the young park ranger, Danilo, and a poker-faced mule. Considering the steepness of the island, I couldn't even pretend to be disappointed not to carry my own pack. Danilo had a rifle strapped across his back, in the hope of killing one of the nonnative goats that had survived a Dutch environmental foundation's recent effort to eradicate them. Under gray morning clouds that soon turned to fog, we hiked up interminable switchbacks and through a ravine lush with maquis, an introduced plant species that is used to repair lobster traps. There were discouraging quantities of old mule droppings on the trail, but the only moving things we saw were birds: a little gray-flanked cinclodes and several Juan Fernández hawks, two of Masafuera's five terrestrial bird species. The island is also the only known breeding site for two interesting petrels and one of the world's rarest songbirds, the Masafuera rayadito, which I was hoping to see. In fact, by the time I'd left for Chile, seeing new bird species was the only activity that I could absolutely count on not to bore me. The rayadito's population, most of which lives in a small, high-altitude area on the island called Los Inocentes, is now thought to number as few as five hundred. Very few people have ever seen one.

Sooner than I'd expected, Danilo and I arrived at La Cuchara and saw, in the fog, the outlines of a small *refugio,* or ranger's hut. We'd climbed three thousand feet in just over two hours. I'd heard that there was a *refugio* at La Cuchara, but I'd imagined a primitive shack and hadn't foreseen what a problem it would pose for me. Its roof was steep and tethered to the ground by cables, and inside it were a propane stove, two bunk beds with foam mattresses, an unappetizing but serviceable sleeping bag, and a cabinet stocked with dry pasta and canned foods; apparently, I could have brought along nothing but some iodine tablets and still survived here. The *refugio*'s existence made my already somewhat artificial project of solitary self-sufficiency seem even more artificial, and I resolved to pretend that it didn't exist.

Danilo took my pack off the mule and led me down a foggy path to a stream with enough water trickling in it to form a little pool. I asked him if it was possible to walk from here to Los Inocentes. He gestured uphill and said, "Yes, it's three hours, along the *cordones.*" I thought of asking if we could go there right now, so that I could camp nearer to the rayaditos, but Danilo seemed eager to get back to the coast. He departed with the mule and his gun, and I bent myself to my Crusovian tasks.

The first of these was to gather and purify some drinking water. Carrying a filtration pump and a canvas waterskin, I followed what I thought was the path to the pool, which I knew wasn't more than two hundred feet from the *refugio,* and I immediately got lost in the fog. When I finally located the pool, after trying several paths, the tube on my pump cracked. I'd bought the pump twenty years earlier, thinking it would come in handy if I was ever alone in the wilderness, and its plastic had since gone brittle. I filled up the skin with somewhat turbid water and, despite my resolution, entered the *refugio* and poured the water into a large cooking pot, along with some iodine tablets. This simple task had somehow taken me an hour.

Since I was in the *refugio* anyway, I changed out of my clothes, which had been soaked by the climb through dew and fog, and tried to dry the inside of my boots with the surfeit of toilet paper I'd brought. I discovered that the GPS unit, the one gadget that I didn't have spare batteries for, had been switched on and draining power all day, which triggered an anxiety that I assuaged by wiping all the mud and water off the *refugio's* floor with further wads of toilet paper. Finally, I ventured out onto a rocky promontory and scouted for a campsite beyond the *refugio's* penumbra of mule droppings. A hawk dived right over my head; a cinclodes called pertly from a boulder. After much walking and weighing of pros and cons, I settled on a hollow that afforded some protection from the wind and no view of the *refugio,* and there I picnicked on cheese and salami.

I'd been alone for four hours. I put up my tent, lashing the frame to boulders and weighing down the stakes with the heaviest rocks I could carry, and made some coffee on my little butane stove. Returning to the *refugio,* I worked on my footwear-drying project, pausing every few minutes to open windows and shoo out the flies that kept finding their way inside. I seemed to be no more able to wean myself from the *refugio's* conveniences than from the modern distractions that I was supposedly here to flee. I fetched another skin of water and used the big pot and the propane stove to heat some bathwater, and it was simply *much more pleasant,* after my bath, to go back inside and dry off with the microfiber towel and get dressed than to do this in the dirt and the fog. Since I was already so compromised, I went ahead and carried one of the foam mattresses down the promontory and put it in my tent "But that's it," I said to myself, aloud. "That's the end of it."

Except for the hum of flies and the occasional call of a cinclodes, the silence at my campsite was absolute. Sometimes the fog lifted a little, and I could see rocky hillsides and wet fern-filled valleys before the ceiling lowered again. I took out my notebook and jotted down what I'd done in the past seven hours: got water, had lunch, put up tent, took bath. But when I thought about writing confessionally, in an "I" voice, I found that I was too self-conscious. Apparently, in the past thirty-five years, I'd become so accustomed to narrativizing myself, to experiencing my life as a story, that I could now use journals only for problem solving and self-investigation. Even at fifteen, in Idaho, I hadn't written from within my despair but only after I was safely over it, and now, all the more so, the stories that mattered to me were the ones told—selected, clarified—in retrospect.

My plan for the next day was to try to see a rayadito. Simply knowing that the bird was on the island made the island interesting to me. When I go looking for new bird species, I'm searching for a mostly lost authenticity, for the remnants of a world now largely overrun by human beings but still beautifully indifferent to us; to glimpse a rare bird somehow persisting in its life of breeding and feeding is an enduringly transcendent delight. The next morning, I decided, I would get up at dawn and devote, if necessary, the entire day to finding my way to Los Inocentes and getting back. Cheered by the prospect of this not unchallenging quest, I made myself a bowl of chili, and then, although the daylight hadn't faded yet, I zipped myself inside my tent. On the very comfortable mattress, in a sleeping bag I'd owned since high school, and with a headlamp on my forehead, I settled down to read *Robinson Crusoe*. For the first time all day, I felt happy.

One of *Robinson Crusoe*'s biggest early fans was Jean-Jacques Rousseau, who, in *Émile,* proposed that it be the primary text for the education of children. Rousseau, in the fine tradition of French bowdlerization, didn't have in mind the entire text, just the long central section, in which Robinson relates his survival for a quarter century on a desert island. Few readers would dispute that this is the novel's most compelling section, next to which the adventures of Robinson before and after (being enslaved by a Turkish pirate, fending off the attacks of giant wolves) seem lusterless and rote. Part of the survival story's appeal is the specificity of Robinson's recounting of it: the "three . . . hats, one cap, and two shoes that were not fellows" that are all that remain of his drowned shipmates, the catalogue of useful gear that he salvages from the wrecked ship, the intricacies of stalking the feral goats that populate the island, the nuts and bolts of reinventing the homely arts of making furniture, boats, pottery, and bread. But what really animates these adventureless adventures, and makes them surprisingly suspenseful, is their accessibility to the imagination of the ordinary reader. I have no idea what I would do if I were enslaved by a Turk or menaced by wolves; I might very well be too scared to do what Robinson does. But to read about his practical solutions to the problems of hunger and exposure and illness and solitude is to be invited into the narrative, to imagine what I would do if I were similarly stranded, and to measure my own stamina and resourcefulness and industry against his. (I'm sure my father was doing this, too.) Until the larger world impinges on the island's isolation, in the form of marauding cannibals, there's just the two of us, Robinson and his reader, and it's very cozy. In a more action-packed narrative, the pages detailing Robinson's everyday tasks and emotions would be what the critic Franco Moretti wryly calls "filler." But, as Moretti notes, the dramatic expansion of this kind of "filler" was precisely Defoe's great innovation; such stories of the quotidian became a fixture of realist fiction, in Austen and Flaubert as in Updike and Carver.

Framing and to some extent interpenetrating Defoe's "filler" are elements of the other major forms of prose narrative that preceded it: ancient Hellenistic novels, which included tales of shipwrecks and enslavement; Catholic and Protestant spiritual autobiographies; medieval and Renaissance romances; and Spanish picaresques. Defoe's novel follows also in the tradition of narratives libelously based, or purporting to be based, on the lives of actual public personages; in Crusoe's case, the model was Alexander Selkirk. It has even been argued that Defoe intended the novel as a piece of utopianist propaganda, extolling the religious freedoms and economic opportunities of England's New World colonies. The heterogeny of *Robinson Crusoe* illuminates the difficulty, maybe even the absurdity, of talking about the "rise of the novel" and of identifying Defoe's work as the first individual of the species. *Don Quixote*, after all, was published more than a century earlier and is clearly a novel. And why not call the romances novels, too, since they were widely published and read in the seventeenth century and since, indeed, most European languages make no distinction between "romance" and "novel"? Early English novelists did often specifically stress that their own work was not "mere romance"; but, then, so had many of the romance writers themselves. And yet, by the early nineteenth century, when leading specimens of the form were first collected in authoritative sets by Walter Scott and others, the English not only had a very clear idea of what they meant by "novels" but were exporting large numbers of them, in translation, to other countries. A genre now definitely existed where none had before. So what exactly is a novel, and why did the genre appear when it did?

The most persuasive account remains the political-economic one that Ian Watt advanced fifty years ago. The birthplace of the novel, in its modern form, happens also to have been Europe's most economically dominant and sophisticated nation, and Watt's analysis of this coincidence is blunt but powerful, tying together the glorification of the enterprising individual, the expansion of a literate bourgeoisie eager to read about itself, the rise in social mobility (inviting writers to exploit its anxieties), the specialization of labor (creating a society of interesting *differences*), the disintegration of the old social order into a collection of individual isolates, and, of course, among the newly comfortable middle class, the dramatic increase in leisure for reading. At the same time, England was rapidly becoming more secular. Protestant theology had laid the foundations of the new economy by reimagining the social order as a collection of self-reliant individuals with a direct relationship with God, but by 1700, as the British economy thrived, it was becoming less clear that individuals needed God at all. It's true that, as any impatient child reader can tell you, many pages of *Robinson Crusoe* are devoted to its hero's spiritual journey. Robinson finds God on the island, and he turns to him repeatedly in moments of crisis, praying for deliverance and ecstatically thanking him for providing the means of it. And yet, as soon as each crisis has passed, he reverts to his practical self and forgets about God; by the end of the book, he seems to have been saved more by his own industry and ingenuity than by Providence. To read the story of Robinson's vacillations and forgetfulness is to see the genre of spiritual autobiography unraveling into realist fiction.

The most interesting aspect of the novel's origin may be the evolution of English culture's answers to the question of verisimilitude: should a strange story be accepted as true *because* it is strange, or should its strangeness be taken as proof that it is false? The anxieties of this question are still with us (witness the scandal of James Frey's "memoir"), and they were certainly in play in 1719, when Defoe published the first and best-known volume of *Robinson Crusoe*. The author's real name appeared nowhere in it. The book was identified, instead, as *The Life and Strange Surprizing Adventures of Robinson Crusoe . . . Written by Himself,* and many of its first readers took the story as nonfiction. Enough other readers doubted its authenticity, however, that Defoe felt obliged to defend its truthfulness when he published the third and last of the volumes, the following year. Contrasting his story with romances, in which "the story is feign'd," he insisted that his story, "though allegorical, is also historical," and he affirmed that "there is a man alive, and well known too, the actions of whose life are the just subject of these volumes." Given what we know of Defoe's real life—like Crusoe, he got into trouble by pursuing risky business schemes, such as raising civet cats for perfume, and he had intimate knowledge of isolation from the debtors' prison in which bankruptcy twice landed him—and given also his assertion, elsewhere in the volume, that "life in general is, or ought to be, but one universal act of solitude," it seems fair to conclude that the "well known" man is Defoe himself. (There is, strikingly, that "oe" at the end of both names.) We now understand a novel to be a mapping of a writer's experience onto a waking dream, and a crucial turn toward this understanding can be seen in Defoe's tentative assertion of a less than strictly historical kind of truth—the novelist's "truth."

The critic Catherine Gallagher, in her essay "The Rise of Fictionality," takes up a curious paradox related to this kind of truth: the eighteenth century was not only the moment when fiction writers, beginning (sort of) with Defoe, abandoned the pretense that their narratives weren't fictional; it was also the moment when they began taking pains to make their narratives seem *not* fictional—when verisimilitude became paramount. Gallagher's resolution of the paradox hinges on yet another aspect of modernity, the necessity of taking risks. When business came to depend on investment, you had to weigh various possible future outcomes; when marriages ceased to be arranged, you had to speculate on the merits of potential mates. And the novel, as it was developed in the eighteenth century, provided its readers with a field of play that was at once speculative and risk-free. While advertising its fictionality, it gave you protagonists who were typical enough to be experienced as possible versions of yourself and yet specific enough to remain, simultaneously, *not you*. The great literary invention of the eighteenth century was, thus, not simply a genre but an attitude *toward* that genre. Our state of mind when we pick up a novel today—our knowledge that it's a work of the imagination; our willing suspension of disbelief in it—is in fact one half of the novel's essence.

A number of recent scholarly studies have undermined the old notion that the epic is a central feature of all cultures, including oral cultures. Fiction, whether fairy tale or fable, seems mainly to have been a thing for children. In premodern cultures, stories were read for information or edification or titillation, and the more serious literary forms, poetry and drama, required a certain degree of technical mastery. The novel, however, was within reach of anyone with pen and paper, and the kind of pleasure it afforded was uniquely modern. Experiencing a made-up story purely for pleasure became an activity in which adults, too, could now indulge freely (if sometimes guiltily). This historical shift toward reading for pleasure was so profound that we can hardly even see it anymore. Indeed, as the novel has proliferated subgenerically into movies and TV shows and late-model video games—most of them advertising their fictionality, all of them offering characters at once typical and specific—it's hardly an exaggeration to say that what distinguishes our culture from all previous cultures is its saturation in entertainment. The novel, as a duality of thing and attitude-toward-thing, has so thoroughly transformed our attitude that the thing itself is at risk of no longer being needed.

On Masafuera's sister island—originally named Masatierra, or Closer to Land, and now called Robinson Crusoe—I had seen the damage wrought by a trio of mainland plant species, maquis and murtilla and blackberry, which have monotonously overrun entire hills and drainages. Particularly evil-looking was the blackberry, which can overwhelm even tall native trees and which spreads in part by shooting out thick runners that look like thorny fiber-optic cables. Two native plant species have already gone extinct, and unless a massive restoration project is undertaken many more will follow. Walking on Robinson, looking for delicate endemic ferns at the blackberry's margins, I began to see the novel as an organism that had mutated, on the island of England, into a virulent invasive that then spread from country to country until it conquered the planet.

Henry Fielding, in *Joseph Andrews*, referred to his characters as "species"—as something more than individual, less than universal. But, as the novel has transformed the cultural environment, species of humanity have given way to a universal crowd of individuals whose most salient characteristic is their being identically entertained. This was the monocultural specter that David had envisioned and set out to resist in his epic *Infinite Jest*. And the mode of his resistance in that novel—annotation, digression, nonlinearity, hyperlinkage—anticipated the even more virulent and even more radically individualistic invader that is now displacing the novel and its offspring. The blackberry on Robinson Crusoe Island was like the conquering novel, yes, but it seemed to me no less like the Internet, that BlackBerry-borne invasive, which, instead of mapping the self onto a narrative, maps the self onto the world. Instead of *the* news, *my* news. Instead of a single football game, the splintering of fifteen different games into personalized fantasy-league statistics. Instead of *The Godfather, My Cat's Funny Trick*. The individual run amok, everyman a Charlie Sheen. With *Robinson Crusoe*, the self had become an island; and now, it seemed, the island was becoming the world.

I was awakened in the night by the beating of the sides of my tent against my sleeping bag; a big wind had blown up. I deployed my earplugs, but I could still hear the beating and, later, a loud whapping. When day finally came, I found my tent partly disassembled, a pole segment dangling from its fly. The wind had dispersed the clouds below me, opening up a view of the ocean, startlingly close, with dawn breaking redly above its leaden water. Mustering the particular efficiency I can bring to the pursuit of a rare bird, I ate a quick breakfast, packed my knapsack with the radio and the satellite phone and enough food for two days, and, at the last minute, because the wind was so strong, collapsed my tent and weighted down its corners with large stones, so that it wouldn't blow away while I was gone. Time was short—mornings on Masafuera tend to be clearer than afternoons—but I made myself stop at the *refugio* and mark its coordinates on the GPS unit before hurrying on uphill.

The Masafuera rayadito is a larger, duller-plumaged cousin of the thorn-tailed rayadito, a striking little bird that I'd seen in several forests in mainland Chile before coming to the islands. How such a small species landed five hundred miles offshore in sufficient numbers to reproduce (and, subsequently, evolve) will never be known. The Masafueran species requires undisturbed native fern forest, and its population, never large, appears to be declining, perhaps because when it nests on the ground it is prone to predation by invasive rats and cats. (Ridding Masafuera of rodents would entail capturing and safeguarding the island's entire hawk population and then using helicopters to blanket its rugged terrain with poisoned bait, at a total cost of maybe five million dollars.) I'd been told that the rayadito isn't hard to see in proper habitat; the difficulty is in getting to the habitat.

The heights of the island were still in cloud, but I was hoping that the wind would soon clear it out. As well as I could tell from my map, I needed to ascend to about thirty-six hundred feet in order to skirt two deep canyons that blocked the way south to Los Inocentes. I was cheered by the fact that the hike's net altitude gain would be zero, but almost as soon as I'd left the *refugio* behind me, the clouds closed in again. Visibility dropped to a few hundred feet, and I began to stop every ten minutes to electronically mark my location, like Hansel leaving crumbs in the woods. For a while, I held to a trail marked with mule droppings, but the ground soon became too stony and scarred with goat tracks for me to be sure I was still on it.

At thirty-six hundred feet, I turned south and bushwhacked through dense, dripping ferns and found my way blocked by a drainage that ought to have been below me by now. I studied the map, but its Google Earth shadings hadn't become any less vague since the last time I'd studied it. I tried to work my way laterally around the sides of the canyon, but the fern cover concealed slippery rocks and deep holes, and the slope, as far as I could tell in the fog, seemed to be getting more vertical, and so I turned around and struggled back up to the ridge, orienting myself by GPS. An hour into my quest, I was thoroughly soaked and barely a thousand feet from where I'd started.

Checking the map, which was getting very wet, I recalled the unfamiliar word that Danilo had used. *Cordones:* it must mean ridges! I was supposed to follow the ridges! I charged uphill again, stopping only to scatter electronic bread crumbs, until I came to a solar-powered radio antenna, presumably a local summit. The wind, now stronger, was blowing cloud over the back side of the island, which I knew to consist of cliffs plunging three thousand feet down to the seal colony. I couldn't see them, but the mere thought of their proximity gave me vertigo; I'm very afraid of cliffs.

Fortunately, the *cordón* leading south from the antenna was fairly level and not too hard to pick my way along, even with high winds and near-zero visibility. I made good progress for half an hour, feeling elated to have deduced, from scant information, the right way to Los Inocentes. Eventually, however, the ridge began to branch, presenting me with choices between higher and lower routes. The map indicated pretty clearly that I should be at thirty-two hundred feet, not thirty-eight hundred. But when I followed the lower ridges, trying to reduce my elevation, I reached sickeningly precipitous dead ends. I returned to the high ridge, which had the added advantage of heading directly south toward Los Inocentes, and I felt gratified when it finally began to descend.

By now, the weather was really bad, the mist turning to rain and blowing horizontally, the wind gusting above forty miles an hour. As I picked my way down the ridge, it began to narrow alarmingly, until I found the way blocked by a small pinnacle. I could sort of make out that the ridge continued to descend on the far side of it, albeit very steeply. But how to get around it? If I scrambled around its leeward side, I risked being grabbed by a gust of wind and blown off. On the windward side, there was, for all I knew, a sheer three-thousand-foot drop; but at least, on this side, the wind would be pushing me against the rock, rather than pulling me off.

In my rain-filled boots, I edged out along the windward side, double-checking every foothold and handhold before relying on it. As I crept forward and was able to see a little farther, the ridge beyond the pinnacle began to look like another dead end, with nothing but dark space ahead and on either side of it. Although I was very determined to see the rayadito, there came a moment when I became afraid to take another step, and I was suddenly able to see myself: spread-eagled against a slippery rockface, in blinding rain and ferocious wind, with no assurance that I was going in the right direction. A sentence so clear that it seemed almost spoken popped into my head: *What you're doing is extremely dangerous.* And I thought of my dead friend.

David wrote about weather as well as anyone who ever put words on paper, and he loved his dogs more purely than he loved anything or anyone else, but nature itself didn't interest him, and he was utterly indifferent to birds. Once, when we were driving near Stinson Beach, in California, I'd stopped to give him a telescope view of a long-billed curlew, a species whose magnificence is to my mind self-evident and revelatory. He looked through the scope for two seconds before turning away with patent boredom. "Yeah," he said with his particular tone of hollow politeness, "it's pretty." In the summer before he died, sitting with him on his patio while he smoked cigarettes, I couldn't keep my eyes off the hummingbirds around his house and was saddened that he could, and while he was taking his heavily medicated afternoon naps, I was studying the birds of Ecuador for an upcoming trip, and I understood the difference between his unmanageable misery and my manageable discontents to be that I could escape myself in the joy of birds and he could not.

He was sick, yes, and in a sense the story of my friendship with him is simply that I loved a person who was mentally ill. The depressed person then killed himself, in a way calculated to inflict maximum pain on those he loved most, and we who loved him were left feeling angry and betrayed. Betrayed not merely by the failure of our investment of love but by the way in which his suicide took the person away from us and made him into a very public legend. People who had never read his fiction, or had never even heard of him, read his Kenyon College commencement address in the *Wall Street Journal* and mourned the loss of a great and gentle soul. A literary establishment that had never so much as short-listed one of his books for a national prize now united to declare him a lost national treasure. Of course, he *was* a national treasure, and, being a writer, he didn't "belong" to his readers any less than to me. But if you happened to know that his actual character was more complex and dubious than he was getting credit for, and if you also knew that he was more lovable—funnier, sillier, needier, more poignantly at war with his demons, more lost, more childishly transparent in his lies and inconsistencies—than the benignant and morally clairvoyant artist/saint that had been made of him, it was still hard not to feel wounded by the part of him that had chosen the adulation of strangers over the love of the people closest to him.

The people who knew David least well are most likely to speak of him in saintly terms. What makes this especially strange is the near-perfect absence, in his fiction, of ordinary love. Close loving relationships, which for most of us are a foundational source of meaning, have no standing in the Wallace fictional universe. What we get, instead, are characters keeping their heartless compulsions secret from those who love them; characters scheming to *appear* loving or to prove to themselves that what feels like love is really just disguised self-interest; or, at most, characters directing an abstract or spiritual love toward somebody profoundly repellent—the cranial-fluid-dripping wife in *Infinite Jest,* the psychopath in the last of the interviews with hideous men. David's fiction is populated with dissemblers and manipulators and emotional isolates, and yet the people who had only glancing or formal contact with him took his rather laborious hyperconsiderateness and moral wisdom at face value.

The curious thing about David's fiction, though, is how recognized and comforted, how *loved,* his most devoted readers feel when reading it. To the extent that each of us is stranded on his or her own existential island—and I think it's approximately correct to say that his most susceptible readers are ones familiar with the socially and spiritually isolating effects of addiction or compulsion or depression—we gratefully seized on each new dispatch from that farthest-away island which was David. At the level of content, he gave us the worst of himself: he laid out, with an intensity of self-scrutiny worthy of comparison to Kafka and Kierkegaard and Dostoyevsky, the extremes of his own narcissism, misogyny, compulsiveness, self-deception, dehumanizing moralism and theologizing, doubt in the possibility of love, and entrapment in footnotes-within-footnotes self-consciousness. At the level of form and intention, however, this very cataloguing of despair about his own authentic goodness is received by the reader as a gift of authentic goodness: we feel the love in the fact of his art, and we love him for it.

David and I had a friendship of compare and contrast and (in a brotherly way) compete. A few years before he died, he signed my hardcover copies of his two most recent books. On the title page of one of them, I found the traced outline of his hand; on the title page of the other was an outline of an erection so huge that it ran off the page, annotated with a little arrow and the remark "scale 100%." I once heard him enthusiastically describe, in the presence of a girl he was dating, someone else's girlfriend as his "paragon of womanhood." David's girl did a wonderfully slow double take and said, "*What?*" Whereupon David, whose vocabulary was as large as anybody's in the Western Hemisphere, took a deep breath and, letting it out, said, "I'm suddenly realizing that I've never actually known what the word 'paragon' means."

He was lovable the way a child is lovable, and he was capable of returning love with a childlike purity. If love is nevertheless excluded from his work, it's because he never quite felt that he deserved to receive it. He was a lifelong prisoner on the island of himself. What looked like gentle contours from a distance were in fact sheer cliffs. Sometimes only a little of him was crazy, sometimes nearly all of him, but, as an adult, he was never entirely not crazy. What he'd seen of his id while trying to escape his island prison by way of drugs and alcohol, only to find himself even more imprisoned by addiction, seems never to have ceased to be corrosive of his belief in his lovability. Even after he got clean, even decades after his late-adolescent suicide attempt, even after his slow and heroic construction of a life for himself, he felt undeserving. And this feeling was intertwined, ultimately to the point of indistinguishability, with the thought of suicide, which was the one sure way out of his imprisonment; surer than addiction, surer than fiction, and surer, finally, than love.

We who were not so pathologically far out on the spectrum of self-involvement, we dwellers of the visible spectrum who could imagine how it felt to go beyond violet but were not ourselves beyond it, could see that David was wrong not to believe in his lovability and could imagine the pain of not believing in it. How easy and natural love is if you are well! And how gruesomely difficult—what a philosophically daunting contraption of self-interest and self-delusion love appears to be—if you are not! And yet one of the lessons of David's work (and, for me, of being his friend) is that the difference between well and not well is in more respects a difference of degree than of kind. Even though David laughed at my much milder addictions and liked to tell me that I couldn't even conceive of how moderate I was, I can still extrapolate from these addictions, and from the secretiveness and solipsism and radical isolation and raw animal craving that accompany them, to the extremity of his. I can imagine the sick mental pathways by

which suicide comes to seem like the one consciousness-quench-
ing substance that nobody can take away from you. The need to
have something apart from other people, the need for a secret,
the need for some last-ditch narcissistic validation of the self's pri-
macy, and then the voluptuously self-hating anticipation of the last
grand score, and the final severing of contact with the world that
would deny you the enjoyment of your self-involved pleasure: I can
follow David there.

It is, admittedly, harder to connect with the infantile rage and
displaced homicidal impulses visible in certain particulars of his
death. But even here I can discern a fun-house-mirror Wallace
logic, a perverse sort of yearning for intellectual honesty and consistency. To deserve the death sentence he'd passed on himself,
the execution of the sentence had to be deeply injurious to someone. To prove once and for all that he truly didn't deserve to be
loved, it was necessary to betray as hideously as possible those who
loved him best, by killing himself at home and making them firsthand witnesses to his act. And the same was true of suicide as a
career move, which was the kind of adulation-craving calculation
that he loathed in himself and would deny (if he thought he could
get away with it) that he was conscious of making, and would then
(if you called him on it) laughingly or wincingly admit that, yeah,
okay, he was indeed capable of making. I imagine the side of David
that advocated going the Kurt Cobain route speaking in the seduc-
tively reasonable voice of the Devil in *The Screwtape Letters,* which
was one of David's favorite books, and pointing out that death by
his own hand would simultaneously satisfy his loathsome hunger
for career advantage and, because it would represent a capitula-
tion to the side of himself that his embattled better side perceived
as evil, further confirm the justice of his death sentence.

This is not to say that he spent his last months and weeks in
lively intellectual conversation with himself, à la Screwtape or the
Grand Inquisitor. He was so sick, toward the end, that every new
waking thought of his, on whatever subject, immediately cork-
screwed into the same conviction of his worthlessness, causing him
continual dread and pain. And yet one of his own favored tropes,
articulated especially clearly in his story "Good Old Neon" and in
his treatise on Georg Cantor, was the infinite divisibility of a single
instant in time. However continually he was suffering in his last
summer, there was still plenty of room, in the interstices between

his identically painful thoughts, to entertain the idea of suicide, to flash forward through its logic, and to set in motion the practical plans (of which he eventually made at least four) for effectuating it. When you decide to do something very bad, the intention and the reasoning for it spring into existence simultaneously and fully formed; any addict who's about to fall off the wagon can tell you this. Though suicide itself was painful to contemplate, it became—to echo the tide of another of David's stories—a sort of present to himself.

Adulatory public narratives of David, which take his suicide as proof that (as Don McLean sang of van Gogh) "this world was never meant for one as beautiful as you," require that there had been a unitary David, a beautiful and supremely gifted human being who, after quitting the antidepressant Nardil, which he'd been taking for twenty years, succumbed to major depression and was therefore *not himself* when he committed suicide. I will pass over the question of diagnosis (it's possible he was not simply depressive) and the question of how such a beautiful human being had come by such vividly intimate knowledge of the thoughts of hideous men. But bearing in mind his fondness for Screwtape and his demonstrable penchant for deceiving himself and others—a penchant that his years in recovery held in check but never eradicated—I can imagine a narrative of ambiguity and ambivalence truer to the spirit of his work. By his own account to me, he had never ceased to live in fear of returning to the psych ward where his early suicide attempt had landed him. The allure of suicide, the last big score, may go underground, but it never entirely disappears. Certainly, David had "good" reasons to go off Nardil—his fear that its long-term physical effects might shorten the good life he'd managed to make for himself; his suspicion that its psychological effects might be interfering with the best things in his life (his work and his relationships)—and he also had less "good" reasons of ego: a perfectionist wish to be less substance dependent, a narcissistic aversion to seeing himself as permanently mentally ill. What I find hard to believe is that he didn't have very bad reasons as well. Flickering beneath his beautiful moral intelligence and his lovable human weakness was the old addict's consciousness, the secret self, which, after decades of suppression by the Nardil, finally glimpsed its chance to break free and have its suicidal way.

This duality played out in the year that followed his quitting

Nardil. He made strange and seemingly self-defeating decisions about his care, engaged in a fair amount of bamboozlement of his shrinks (whom one can only pity for having drawn such a brilliantly complicated case), and in the end created an entire secret life devoted to suicide. Throughout that year, the David whom I knew well and loved immoderately was struggling bravely to build a more secure foundation for his work and his life, contending with heartbreaking levels of anxiety and pain, while the David whom I knew less well, but still well enough to have always disliked and distrusted, was methodically plotting his own destruction and his revenge on those who loved him.

That he was blocked with his work when he decided to quit Nardil—was bored with his old tricks and unable to muster enough excitement about his new novel to find a way forward with it—is not inconsequential. He'd loved writing fiction, *Infinite Jest* in particular, and he'd been very explicit, in our many discussions of the purpose of novels, about his belief that fiction is a solution, the *best* solution, to the problem of existential solitude. Fiction was his way off the island, and as long as it was working for him—as long as he'd been able to pour his love and passion into preparing his lonely dispatches, and as long as these dispatches were coming as urgent and fresh and honest news to the mainland—he'd achieved a measure of happiness and hope for himself. When his hope for fiction died, after years of struggle with the new novel, there was no other way out but death. If boredom is the soil in which the seeds of addiction sprout, and if the phenomenology and the teleology of suicidality are the same as those of addiction, it seems fair to say that David died of boredom. In his early story "Here and There," the brother of a perfection-seeking young man, Bruce, invites him to consider "how *boring* it would be to be perfect," and Bruce tells us:

> I defer to Leonard's extensive and hard-earned knowledge about being boring, but do point out that since being boring is an imperfection, it would by definition be impossible for a perfect person to be boring.

It's a good joke; and yet the logic is somehow strangulatory. It's the logic of "everything and more," to echo yet another of David's titles, and everything and more is what he wanted from and for his fiction. This had worked for him before, in *Infinite Jest*. But to try to add more to what is already everything is to risk having nothing: to become boring to yourself.

A funny thing about Robinson Crusoe is that he never, in twenty-eight years on his Island of Despair, becomes bored. He speaks, yes, of the drudgery of his early labors, he later admits to becoming "heartily tir'd" of searching the island for cannibals, he laments not having any pipes in which to smoke the tobacco he finds on the island, and he describes his first year of company with Friday as the "pleasantest year of all the life I led in this place." But the modern craving for *stimulation* is wholly absent. (The novel's most astonishing detail may be that Robinson makes "three large runlets of rum or spirits" last a quarter century; I would have drunk all three in a month, just to be done with them.) Although he never ceases to dream of escape, he soon comes to take "a secret kind of pleasure" in his absolute ownership of the island:

> I look'd now upon the world as a thing remote, which I had nothing to do with, no expectation from, and indeed no desires about: In a word, I had nothing indeed to do with it, nor was ever like to have; so I thought it look'd as we may perhaps look upon it hereafter.

Robinson is able to survive his solitude because he's lucky; he makes peace with his condition because he's ordinary and his island is concrete. David, who was extraordinary, and whose island was virtual, finally had nothing but his own interesting self to survive on, and the problem with making a virtual world of oneself is akin to the problem with projecting ourselves onto a cyberworld: there's no end of virtual spaces in which to seek stimulation, but their very endlessness, the perpetual stimulation without satisfaction, becomes imprisoning. To be everything and more is the Internet's ambition, too.

The vertiginous point where I turned back in the rain was less than a mile from La Cuchara, but the return hike took two hours. The rain was now not just horizontal but heavy, and I was having trouble staying upright in the wind. The GPS unit was giving me "Low Battery" messages, but I had to keep turning it on, because visibility was so poor that I couldn't maintain a straight line. Even when the unit showed that the *refugio* was a hundred and fifty feet away, I had to walk farther before I could make out its roofline.

I tossed my drenched knapsack into the *refugio,* ran down to my tent, and found it a basin of rainwater. I managed to wrestle out the foam mattress and get it back to the *refugio,* and then I went back and unstaked the tent and poured off the water and gathered the whole thing in my arms, trying to keep the things inside it half-way dry, and hustled it back uphill through the horizontal rain. The *refugio* was a disaster zone of soaked clothes and equipment. I spent two hours on various drying projects, followed by an hour of searching the promontory, to no avail, for a critical piece of tent hardware that I'd lost in my mad dash. And then, in a matter of minutes, the rain ended and the clouds blew off and I realized I'd been staying in the most dramatically beautiful spot I'd ever seen.

It was late afternoon, and the wind was blowing out over the in-sanely blue ocean, and it was time. La Cuchara seemed more sus-pended in the air than attached to the earth. There was a feeling of near infinity, the sun eliciting from the hillsides more shades of green and yellow than I'd suspected the visible spectrum of con-taining, a dazzling near infinity of colors, and the sky so immense that I wouldn't have been surprised to see the mainland on the eastern horizon. White shreds of remnant cloud came barreling down from the summit, whipped past me, and vanished. The wind was blowing out, and I began to cry, because I knew it was time and I hadn't prepared myself, had managed to forget. I went to the *refugio* and got the little box of David's ashes, the "booklet"—to use the term he'd amusingly applied to his not-short book about mathematical infinity—and walked back down the promontory with it, the wind at my back.

I was doing a lot of different things at every moment. Even as I was crying, I was also scanning the ground for the missing piece of my tent, and taking my camera out of my pocket and trying to capture the celestial beauty of the light and the landscape, and damning myself for doing this when I should have been purely mourning, and telling myself that it was *okay* that I'd failed in my attempt to see the rayadito in what would surely be my only visit to the island—that it was better this way, that it was time to accept finitude and incompleteness and leave certain birds forever un-seen, that the ability to accept this was the gift I'd been given and my beloved dead friend had not.

At the end of the promontory, I came to a pair of matching boulders that together formed a kind of altar. David had chosen to leave the people who loved him and give himself to the world of the novel and its readers, and I was ready to wish him well in it. I opened the box of ashes and threw them up into the wind. Some bits of gray bone came down on the slope below me, but the dust was caught in the wind and vanished into the blue vault of the sky, blowing out across the ocean. I turned and wandered back up the hill toward the *refugio,* where I would have to spend the night, because my tent was disabled. I felt done with anger, merely bereft, and done with islands, too.

Riding with me on the boat back to Robinson Crusoe were twelve hundred lobsters, a couple of skinned goats, and an old lobsterman who, after the anchor had been weighed, shouted to me that the sea was very rough. Yeah, I agreed, it was a little rough. *"No poco!"* he shouted seriously. *"Mucho!"* The boat's crew was tossing around the bloody goats, and I realized that instead of heading straight back toward Robinson we were angling forty-five degrees to the south, to keep from capsizing. I staggered down into a tiny, fetid bunkroom beneath the bow and heaved myself onto a bunk and there—after an hour or two of clutching the sides of the bunk to avoid becoming airborne, and trying to think about something, anything, that wasn't seasickness, and sweating off (as I later discovered) the antiseasickness patch I'd stuck behind my car, and listening to water slosh and hammer against the hull—I threw up into a Ziploc bag. Ten hours later, when I ventured back out on deck, I was expecting the harbor to be in sight, but the captain had done so much tacking that we were still five hours away. I couldn't face returning to the bunk, and I was still too sick to look at seabirds, and so I stood for five hours and did little but imagine changing my return flight, which I'd booked for the following week to allow for delays, and going home early.

I hadn't felt so homesick since, possibly, the last time I'd camped by myself. In three days, the California woman I live with would be going to watch the Super Bowl with friends of ours, and when I thought of sitting beside her on a sofa and drinking a martini and rooting for the Green Bay quarterback Aaron Rodgers, who'd been a star at California, I felt *desperate* to escape the islands. Before leaving for Masafuera, I'd already seen Robinson's two endemic land-bird species, and the prospect of another week there, with no chance of seeing something new, seemed suffocat-

ingly boring—an exercise in deprivation from the very busyness
that I'd been so intent on fleeing, a busyness whose pleasurability
I appreciated only now.

Back on Robinson, I enlisted my innkeeper, Ramón, to try to get
me on one of the following day's flights. Both flights turned out to
be full, but while I was eating lunch the local agent of one of the
air companies happened to walk into the inn, and Ramón pressed
her to let me fly on a third, cargo-only flight. The agent said no.
But what about the copilot seat? Ramón asked her. Couldn't he sit
in the copilot seat? No, the agent said, the copilot seat, too, would
be filled with cartons of lobster.

And so, although I no longer wanted it, or because I didn't
want it, I had the experience of being truly stranded on an island. I ate the same bad Chilean white bread at every meal, the
same nondescript fish served without sauce or seasoning at every
lunch and dinner. I lay in my room and finished *Robinson Crusoe*.
I wrote postcards in reply to the stack of mail I'd brought along.
I practiced mentally inserting into Chilean Spanish the *s*'s that its
speakers omitted. I got better views of the Juan Fernández fire-
crown, a splendid large, cinnamon-colored hummingbird severely
endangered by invasive plant and animal species. I hiked over the
mountains to a grassland where the island's annual cattle-branding
festival was being held, and I watched horseback riders drive the
village's herd into a corral. The setting was spectacular—sweeping
hills, volcanic peaks, whitecapped ocean—but the hills were de-
nuded and deeply gouged by erosion. Of the hundred-plus cattle,
at least ninety were malnourished, the majority of them so skeletal
it seemed remarkable that they could even stand up. The herd
had historically been a reserve source of protein, and the villagers
still enjoyed the ritual of roping and branding, but couldn't they
see what a sad travesty their ritual had become?

With three more days to fill and my knees worn out by downhill
hiking, I had no choice but to start reading Samuel Richardson's
first novel, *Pamela*, which I'd brought along mainly because it's
a lot shorter than *Clarissa*. All I'd known about *Pamela* was that
Henry Fielding had satirized it in *Shamela*, his own first venture
into novel writing. I hadn't known that *Shamela* was only one of
many works published in immediate response to *Pamela*, and that
Pamela, indeed, had been possibly the biggest news of any kind in
London in 1741. But as soon as I started reading it, I could see

why: the novel is compelling and electric with sex and class conflicts, and it details psychological extremes at a level of specificity
like nothing before it. Pamela Andrews isn't everything and more.
She's simply and uniquely Pamela, a beautiful servant girl whose
virtue is under sustained and ingenious assault by the son of her
late employer. Her story is told through her letters to her parents,
and when she finds out that these letters are being intercepted
and read by her would-be seducer, Mr. B., she continues to write
them *while knowing that Mr. B. will read them.* Pamela's piousness
and self-dramatizing hysterics were bound to infuriate a certain
kind of reader (one of the books published in response satirized
Richardson's subtitle, *Virtue Rewarded,* as *Feign'd Innocence Detected*),
but underneath her strident virtue and Mr. B.'s lascivious machinations is a fascinatingly rendered love story. The realistic power
of this story was what made the book such a groundbreaking sen-
sation. Defoe had staked out the territory of radical individualism, which has remained a fruitful subject for novelists as late as
Beckett and Wallace, but it was Richardson who first granted full
fictional access to the hearts and minds of individuals whose solitude has been overwhelmed by love for someone else.

Exactly halfway through *Robinson Crusoe,* when Robinson has
been alone for fifteen years, he discovers a single human footprint
on the beach and is literally made crazy by *"the fear of man."* After
concluding that the footprint is neither his own nor the Devil's
but, rather, some cannibal intruder's, he remakes his garden island into a fortress, and for several years he can think of little but
concealing himself and repelling imagined invaders. He marvels
at the irony that

> I whose only affliction was, that I seem'd banish'd from human so-
> ciety, that I was alone, circumscrib'd by the boundless ocean, cut off
> from mankind, and condemn'd to what I call'd silent life . . . that I
> should now tremble at the very apprehensions of seeing a man, and
> was ready to sink into the ground at but the shadow, or silent appear-
> ance of a man's having set his foot in the island.

Nowhere was Defoe's psychology more acute than in his imagination of Robinson's response to the rupture of his solitude. He gave
us the first realistic portrait of the radically isolated individual, and
then, as if impelled by novelistic truth, he showed us how sick and
crazy radical individualism really is. No matter how carefully we

defend ourselves, all it takes is one footprint of another real person to recall us to the endlessly interesting hazards of living relationships. Even Facebook, whose users collectively spend billions of hours renovating their self-regarding projections, contains an ontological exit door, the Relationship Status menu, among whose options is the phrase "It's complicated." This may be a euphemism for "on my way out," but it's also a description of all the other options. As long as we have such complications, how dare we be bored?

MALCOLM GLADWELL

Creation Myth

FROM *The New Yorker*

IN LATE 1979, a twenty-four-year-old entrepreneur paid a visit to a research center in Silicon Valley called Xerox PARC. He was the cofounder of a small computer startup down the road, in Cupertino. His name was Steve Jobs.

Xerox PARC was the innovation arm of the Xerox Corporation. It was, and remains, on Coyote Hill Road, in Palo Alto, nestled in the foothills on the edge of town, in a long, low concrete building, with enormous terraces looking out over the jewels of Silicon Valley. To the northwest was Stanford University's Hoover Tower. To the north was Hewlett-Packard's sprawling campus. All around were scores of other chip designers, software firms, venture capitalists, and hardware makers. A visitor to PARC, taking in that view, could easily imagine that it was the computer world's castle, lording over the valley below—and, at the time, this wasn't far from the truth. In 1970, Xerox had assembled the world's greatest computer engineers and programmers, and for the next ten years they had an unparalleled run of innovation and invention. If you were obsessed with the future in the seventies, you were obsessed with Xerox PARC—which was why the young Steve Jobs had driven to Coyote Hill Road.

Apple was already one of the hottest tech firms in the country. Everyone in the Valley wanted a piece of it. So Jobs proposed a deal: he would allow Xerox to buy a hundred thousand shares of his company for a million dollars—its highly anticipated IPO was just a year away—if PARC would "open its kimono." A lot of haggling ensued. Jobs was the fox, after all, and PARC was the henhouse. What would he be allowed to see? What wouldn't he be allowed to see? Some at PARC thought that the whole idea was lunacy, but, in the end, Xerox went ahead with it. One PARC scientist recalls Jobs as "rambunctious"—a fresh-cheeked, caffeinated version of today's austere digital emperor. He was given a couple of tours, and he ended up standing in front of a Xerox Alto, PARC's prized personal computer.

An engineer named Larry Tesler conducted the demonstration. He moved the cursor across the screen with the aid of a "mouse." Directing a conventional computer, in those days, meant typing in a command on the keyboard. Tesler just clicked on one of the icons on the screen. He opened and closed "windows," deftly moving from one task to another. He wrote on an elegant word-processing program, and exchanged e-mails with other people at PARC, on the world's first Ethernet network. Jobs had come with one of his software engineers, Bill Atkinson, and Atkinson moved in as close as he could, his nose almost touching the screen. "Jobs was pacing around the room, acting up the whole time," Tesler recalled. "He was very excited. Then, when he began seeing the things I could do onscreen, he watched for about a minute and started jumping around the room, shouting, 'Why aren't you doing anything with this? This is the greatest thing. This is revolutionary!'"

Xerox began selling a successor to the Alto in 1981. It was slow and underpowered—and Xerox ultimately withdrew from personal computers altogether. Jobs, meanwhile, raced back to Apple and demanded that the team working on the company's next generation of personal computers change course. He wanted menus on the screen. He wanted windows. He wanted a mouse. The result was the Macintosh, perhaps the most famous product in the history of Silicon Valley.

"If Xerox had known what it had and had taken advantage of its real opportunities," Jobs said, years later, "it could have been as big as IBM plus Microsoft plus Xerox combined—and the largest high-technology company in the world."

This is the legend of Xerox PARC. Jobs is the biblical Jacob and Xerox is Esau, squandering his birthright for a pittance. In the past thirty years, the legend has been vindicated by history. Xerox, once the darling of the American high-technology community, slipped from its former dominance. Apple is now ascendant, and the demonstration in that room in Palo Alto has come to symbolize the vision and ruthlessness that separate true innovators from also-rans. As with all legends, however, the truth is a bit more complicated.

After Jobs returned from PARC, he met with a man named Dean Hovey, who was one of the founders of the industrial-design firm that would become known as IDEO. "Jobs went to Xerox PARC on a Wednesday or a Thursday, and I saw him on the Friday afternoon," Hovey recalled. "I had a series of ideas that I wanted to bounce off him, and I barely got two words out of my mouth when he said, 'No, no, no, you've got to do a mouse.' I was, like, 'What's a mouse?' I didn't have a clue. So he explains it, and he says, 'You know, [the Xerox mouse] is a mouse that cost three hundred dollars to build and it breaks within two weeks. Here's your design spec: Our mouse needs to be manufacturable for less than fifteen bucks. It needs to not fail for a couple of years, and I want to be able to use it on Formica and my blue jeans.' From that meeting, I went to Walgreens, which is still there, at the corner of Grant and El Camino in Mountain View, and I wandered around and bought all the underarm deodorants that I could find, because they had that ball in them. I bought a butter dish. That was the beginnings of the mouse."

I spoke with Hovey in a ramshackle building in downtown Palo Alto, where his firm had started out. He had asked the current tenant if he could borrow his old office for the morning, just for the fun of telling the story of the Apple mouse in the place where it was invented. The room was the size of someone's bedroom. It looked as if it had last been painted in the Coolidge administration. Hovey, who is lean and healthy in a Northern California yoga-and-yogurt sort of way, sat uncomfortably at a rickety desk in a corner of the room. "Our first machine shop was literally out on the roof," he said, pointing out the window to a little narrow strip of rooftop covered in green outdoor carpeting. "We didn't tell the planning commission. We went and got that clear corrugated stuff and put it across the top for a roof. We got out through the window."

He had brought a big plastic bag full of the artifacts of that moment: diagrams scribbled on lined paper, dozens of different-size plastic mouse shells, a spool of guitar wire, a tiny set of wheels from a toy train set, and the metal lid from a jar of Ralph's preserves. He turned the lid over. It was filled with a waxlike substance, the middle of which had a round indentation in the shape of a small ball. "It's epoxy casting resin," he said. "You pour it, and then I put Vaseline on a smooth steel ball, and set it in the resin, and it hardens around it." He tucked the steel ball underneath the lid and rolled it around the tabletop. "It's a kind of mouse."

The hard part was that the roller ball needed to be connected to the housing of the mouse, so that it didn't fall out, and so that it could transmit information about its movements to the cursor on the screen. But if the friction created by those connections was greater than the friction between the tabletop and the roller ball, the mouse would skip. And the more the mouse was used, the more dust it would pick up off the tabletop, and the more it would skip. The Xerox PARC mouse was an elaborate affair, with an array of ball bearings supporting the roller ball. But there was too much friction on the top of the ball, and it couldn't deal with dust and grime.

At first, Hovey set to work with various arrangements of ball bearings, but nothing quite worked. "This was the 'aha' moment," Hovey said, placing his fingers loosely around the sides of the ball, so that they barely touched its surface. "So the ball's sitting here. And it rolls. I attribute that not to the table but to the oldness of the building. The floor's not level. So I started playing with it, and that's when I realized: I *want* it to roll. I don't want it to be supported by all kinds of ball bearings. I want to just barely touch it."

The trick was to connect the ball to the rest of the mouse at the two points where there was the least friction—right where his fingertips had been, dead center on either side of the ball. "If it's right at midpoint, there's no force causing it to rotate. So it rolls."

Hovey estimated their consulting fee at thirty-five dollars an hour; the whole project cost perhaps a hundred thousand dollars. "I originally pitched Apple on doing this mostly for royalties, as opposed to a consulting job," he recalled. "I said, 'I'm thinking fifty cents apiece,' because I was thinking that they'd sell fifty thousand, maybe a hundred thousand of them." He burst out laughing, because of how far off his estimates ended up being. "Steve's pretty savvy. He said no. Maybe if I'd asked for a nickel, I would have been fine."

Here is the first complicating fact about the Jobs visit. In the legend of Xerox PARC, Jobs stole the personal computer from Xerox. But the striking thing about Jobs's instructions to Hovey is that he *didn't want* to reproduce what he saw at PARC. "You know, there were disputes around the number of buttons—three buttons, two buttons, one-button mouse," Hovey went on. "The mouse at Xerox had three buttons. But we came around to the fact that learning to mouse is a feat in and of itself, and to make it as simple as possible, with just one button, was pretty important."

So was what Jobs took from Xerox the *idea* of the mouse? Not quite, because Xerox never owned the idea of the mouse. The PARC researchers got it from the computer scientist Douglas Engelbart, at Stanford Research Institute, fifteen minutes away on the other side of the university campus. Engelbart dreamed up the idea of moving the cursor around the screen with a stand-alone mechanical "animal" back in the mid-1960s. His mouse was a bulky, rectangular affair, with what looked like steel roller-skate wheels. If you lined up Engelbart's mouse, Xerox's mouse, and Apple's mouse, you would not see the serial reproduction of an object. You would see the evolution of a concept.

The same is true of the graphical user interface that so captured Jobs's imagination. Xerox PARC's innovation had been to replace the traditional computer command line with onscreen icons. But when you clicked on an icon, you got a pop-up menu: this was the intermediary between the user's intention and the computer's response. Jobs's software team took the graphical interface a giant step further. It emphasized "direct manipulation." If you wanted to make a window bigger, you just pulled on its corner and made it bigger; if you wanted to move a window across the screen, you just grabbed it and moved it. The Apple designers also invented the menu bar, the pulldown menu, and the trash can—all features that radically simplified the original Xerox PARC idea.

The difference between direct and indirect manipulation—between three buttons and one button, three hundred dollars and fifteen dollars, and a roller ball supported by ball bearings and a free-rolling ball—is not trivial. It is the difference between something intended for experts, which is what Xerox PARC had in mind, and something that's appropriate for a mass audience, which is what Apple had in mind. PARC was building a personal computer. Apple wanted to build a *popular* computer.

In a recent study, *The Culture of Military Innovation*, the military scholar Dima Adamsky makes a similar argument about the so-called revolution in military affairs. RMA refers to the way armies have transformed themselves with the tools of the digital age—such as precision-guided missiles, surveillance drones, and real-time command, control, and communications technologies—and Adamsky begins with the simple observation that it is impossible to determine who invented RMA. The first people to imagine how digital technology would transform warfare were a cadre of senior military intellectuals in the Soviet Union, during the 1970s. The first country to come up with these high-tech systems was the United States. And the first country to use them was Israel, in its 1982 clash with the Syrian air force in Lebanon's Bekaa Valley, a battle commonly referred to as "the Bekaa Valley turkey shoot." Israel coordinated all the major innovations of RMA in a manner so devastating that it destroyed nineteen surface-to-air batteries and eighty-seven Syrian aircraft while losing only a handful of its own planes.

That's three revolutions, not one, and Adamsky's point is that each of these strands is necessarily distinct, drawing on separate skills and circumstances. The Soviets had a strong, centralized military bureaucracy, with a long tradition of theoretical analysis. It made sense that they were the first to understand the military implications of new information systems. But they didn't do anything with it, because centralized military bureaucracies with strong intellectual traditions aren't very good at connecting word and deed.

The United States, by contrast, has a decentralized, bottom-up entrepreneurial culture, which has historically had a strong orientation toward technological solutions. The military's close ties to the country's high-tech community made it unsurprising that the U.S. would be the first to invent precision guidance and next-generation command-and-control communications. But those assets also meant that Soviet-style systemic analysis wasn't going to be a priority. As for the Israelis, their military culture grew out of a background of resource constraint and constant threat. In response, they became brilliantly improvisational and creative. But, as Adamsky points out, a military built around urgent, short-term "fire extinguishing" is not going to be distinguished by reflective theory. No one stole the revolution. Each party viewed the problem from a different perspective and carved off a different piece of the puzzle.

In the history of the mouse, Engelbart was the Soviet Union. He was the visionary, who saw the mouse before anyone else did. But visionaries are limited by their visions. "Engelbart's self-defined mission was not to produce a product, or even a prototype; it was an open-ended search for knowledge," Michael Hiltzik writes in *Dealers of Lightning* (1999), his wonderful history of Xerox PARC. "Consequently, no project in his lab ever seemed to come to an end." Xerox PARC was the United States: it was a place where things got made. "Xerox created this perfect environment," recalled Bob Metcalfe, who worked there through much of the 1970s, before leaving to found the networking company 3Com. "There wasn't any hierarchy. We built our own tools. When we needed to publish papers, we built a printer. When we needed to edit the papers, we built a computer. When we needed to connect computers, we figured out how to connect them. We had big budgets. Unlike many of our brethren, we didn't have to teach. We could just research. It was heaven."

But heaven is not a good place to commercialize a product. "We built a computer, and it was a beautiful thing," Metcalfe went on. "We developed our computer language, our own display, our own language. It was a gold-plated product. But it cost sixteen thousand dollars, and it needed to cost three thousand dollars." For an actual product, you need threat and constraint—and the improvisation and creativity necessary to turn a gold-plated three-hundred-dollar mouse into something that works on Formica and costs fifteen dollars. Apple was Israel.

Xerox *couldn't* have been IBM and Microsoft combined, in other words. "You can be one of the most successful makers of enterprise technology products the world has ever known, but that doesn't mean your instincts will carry over to the consumer market," the tech writer Harry McCracken recently wrote. "They're really different, and few companies have ever been successful in both." He was talking about the decision by the networking giant Cisco Systems, this spring, to shut down its Flip camera business, at a cost of many hundreds of millions of dollars. But he could just as easily have been talking about the Xerox of forty years ago, which was one of the most successful makers of enterprise technology the world has ever known. The fair question is whether Xerox, through its research arm in Palo Alto, found a better way to be Xerox—and the answer is that it did, although that story doesn't get told nearly as often.

One of the people at Xerox PARC when Steve Jobs visited was an optical engineer named Gary Starkweather. He is a solid and irrepressibly cheerful man, with large, practical hands and the engineer's gift of pretending that what is impossibly difficult is actually pretty easy, once you shave off a bit here, and remember some of your high school calculus, and realize that the thing that you thought should go in left to right should actually go in right to left. Once, before the palatial Coyote Hill Road building was constructed, a group that Starkweather had to be connected to was moved to another building, across the Foothill Expressway, half a mile away. There was no way to run a cable under the highway. So Starkweather fired a laser through the air between the two buildings, an improvised communications system that meant that, if you were driving down the Foothill Expressway on a foggy night and happened to look up, you might see a mysterious red beam streaking across the sky. When a motorist drove into the median ditch, "we had to turn it down," Starkweather recalled, with a mischievous smile.

   Lasers were Starkweather's specialty. He started at Xerox's East Coast research facility in Webster, New York, outside Rochester. Xerox built machines that scanned a printed page of type using a photographic lens and then printed a duplicate. Starkweather's idea was to skip the first step—to run a document from a computer directly into a photocopier, by means of a laser, and turn the Xerox machine into a printer. It was a radical idea. The printer, since Gutenberg, had been limited to the function of re-creation: if you wanted to print a specific image or letter, you had to have a physical character or mark corresponding to that image or letter. What Starkweather wanted to do was take the array of bits and bytes, ones and zeros that constitute digital images, and transfer them straight into the guts of a copier. That meant, at least in theory, that he could print anything.

"One morning, I woke up and I thought, Why don't we just print something out directly?" Starkweather said. "But when I flew that past my boss, he thought it was the most brain-dead idea he had ever heard. He basically told me to find something else to do. The feeling was that lasers were too expensive. They didn't work that well. Nobody wants to do this; computers aren't powerful enough. And I guess, in my naiveté, I kept thinking, He's just not right—there's something about this I really like. It got to be a frustrating situation. He and I came to loggerheads over the thing, about late 1969, early 1970. I was running my experiments in the backroom behind a black curtain. I played with them when I could. He threatened to lay off my people if I didn't stop. I was having to make a decision: do I abandon this, or do I try and go up the ladder with it?"

Then Starkweather heard that Xerox was opening a research center in Palo Alto, three thousand miles away from its New York headquarters. He went to a senior vice president of Xerox, threatening to leave for IBM if he didn't get a transfer. In January of 1971, his wish was granted, and within ten months, he had a prototype up and running.

Starkweather is retired now and lives in a gated community just north of Orlando, Florida. When we spoke, he was sitting at a picnic table inside a screened-in porch in his backyard. Behind him, golfers whirred by in carts. He was wearing white chinos and a shiny black short-sleeved shirt decorated with fluorescent images of vintage hot rods. He had brought out two large plastic bins filled with the artifacts of his research, and he spread the contents on the table: a metal octagonal disk, sketches on lab paper, a black plastic laser housing that served as the innards for one of his printers.

"There was still a tremendous amount of opposition from the Webster group, who saw no future in computer printing," he went on. "They said, 'IBM is doing that. Why do we need to do that?' and so forth. Also, there were two or three competing projects, which I guess I have the luxury of calling ridiculous. One group had fifty people and another had twenty. I had two." Starkweather picked up a picture of one of his in-house competitors, something called an "optical carriage printer." It was the size of one of those modular Italian kitchen units that you see advertised in fancy design magazines. "It was an unbelievable device," he said, with a rueful chuckle. "It had a ten-inch drum, which turned at five thousand rpm, like a super washing machine. It had characters printed on its surface. I think they only ever sold ten of them. The problem was that it was spinning so fast that the drum would blow out and the characters would fly off. And there was only this one lady in Troy, New York, who knew how to put the characters on so that they would stay.

"So we finally decided to have what I called a fly-off. There was a full page of text—where some of them were non-serif characters, Helvetica, stuff like that—and then a page of graph paper with grid lines, and pages with pictures and some other complex stuff, and everybody had to print all six pages. Well, once we decided on those six pages, I knew I'd won, because I knew there wasn't anything I couldn't print. Are you kidding? If you can translate it into bits, I can print it. Some of these other machines had to go through hoops just to print a curve. A week after the fly-off, they folded those other projects. I was the only game in town." The project turned into the Xerox 9700, the first high-speed, cut-paper laser printer in the world.

In one sense, the Starkweather story is of a piece with the Steve Jobs visit. It is an example of the imaginative poverty of Xerox management. Starkweather had to hide his laser behind a curtain. He had to fight for his transfer to PARC. He had to endure the indignity of the fly-off, and even then Xerox management remained skeptical. The founder of PARC, Jack Goldman, had to bring in a team from Rochester for a personal demonstration. After that, Starkweather and Goldman had an idea for getting the laser printer to market quickly: graft a laser onto a Xerox copier called the 7000. The 7000 was an older model, and Xerox had lots of 7000s sitting around that had just come off lease. Goldman even had a customer ready: the Lawrence Livermore laboratory was prepared to buy a whole slate of the machines. Xerox said no. Then Starkweather wanted to make what he called a photo-typesetter, which produced camera-ready copy right on your desk. Xerox said no. "I wanted to work on higher-performance scanners," Starkweather continued. "In other words, what if we print something other than documents? For example, I made a high-resolution scanner and you could print on glass plates." He rummaged in one of the boxes on the picnic table and came out with a sheet of glass, roughly six inches square, on which a photograph of a child's face appeared. The same idea, he said, could have been used to make "masks" for the semiconductor industry—the densely patterned screens used to etch the designs on computer chips. "No one would ever follow through, because Xerox said, 'Now you're in Intel's market; what are you doing that for?' They just could not seem to see that they were in the information business. This"—he lifted up the plate with the little girl's face on it—"is a copy. It's just not a copy of an office document." But he got nowhere. "Xerox had been infested by a bunch of spreadsheet experts who thought you could decide every product based on metrics. Unfortunately, creativity wasn't on a metric."

A few days after that afternoon in his backyard, however, Stark-weather e-mailed an addendum to his discussion of his experiences at PARC. "Despite all the hassles and risks that happened in getting the laser printer going, in retrospect the journey was that much more exciting," he wrote. "Often difficulties are just opportunities in disguise." Perhaps he felt that he had painted too negative a picture of his time at Xerox, or suffered a pang of guilt about what it must have been like to be one of those Xerox executives on the other side of the table. The truth is that Starkweather was a difficult employee. It went hand in hand with what made him such an extraordinary innovator. When his boss told him to quit working on lasers, he continued in secret. He was disruptive and stubborn and independent-minded—and he had a thousand ideas, and sorting out the good ideas from the bad wasn't always easy. Should Xerox have put out a special order of laser printers for Lawrence Livermore, based on the old 7000 copier? In *Fumbling the Future: How Xerox Invented, Then Ignored, the First Personal Computer* (1988)—a book dedicated to the idea that Xerox was run by the blind—Douglas Smith and Robert Alexander admit that the proposal was hopelessly impractical: "The scanty Livermore proposal could not justify the investment required to start a laser printing business . . . How and where would Xerox manufacture the laser printers? Who would sell and service them? Who would buy them and why?" Starkweather, and his compatriots at Xerox PARC, weren't the source of disciplined strategic insights. They were wild geysers of creative energy.

The psychologist Dean Simonton argues that this fecundity is often at the heart of what distinguishes the truly gifted. The difference between Bach and his forgotten peers isn't necessarily that he had a better ratio of hits to misses. The difference is that the mediocre might have a dozen ideas, while Bach, in his lifetime, created more than a thousand full-fledged musical compositions. A genius is a genius, Simonton maintains, because he can put together such a staggering number of insights, ideas, theories, random observations, and unexpected connections that he almost inevitably ends up with something great. "Quality," Simonton writes, is "a probabilistic function of quantity."

Simonton's point is that there is nothing neat and efficient about creativity. "The more successes there are," he says, "the more failures there are as well"—meaning that the person who had far more ideas than the rest of us will have far more bad ideas than the rest of us, too. This is why managing the creative process is so difficult. The making of the classic Rolling Stones album *Exile on Main St.* was an ordeal, Keith Richards writes in his new memoir, because the band had too many ideas. It had to fight from under an avalanche of mediocrity: "Head in the Toilet Blues," "Leather Jackets," "Windmill," "I Was Just a Country Boy," "Bent Green Needles," "Labour Pains," and "Pommes de Terre"—the last of which Richards explains with the apologetic, "Well, we were in France at the time."

At one point, Richards quotes a friend, Jim Dickinson, remembering the origins of the song "Brown Sugar":

> I watched Mick write the lyrics . . . He wrote it down as fast as he could move his hand. I'd never seen anything like it. He had one of those yellow legal pads, and he'd write a verse a page, just write a verse and then turn the page, and when he had three pages filled, they started to cut it. It was amazing.

Richards goes on to marvel, "It's unbelievable how prolific he was." Then he writes, "Sometimes you'd wonder how to turn the fucking tap off. The odd times he would come out with so many lyrics, you're crowding the airwaves, boy." Richards clearly saw himself as the creative steward of the Rolling Stones (only in a rock-and-roll band, by the way, can someone like Keith Richards perceive himself as the responsible one), and he came to understand that one of the hardest and most crucial parts of his job was to "turn the fucking tap off," to rein in Mick Jagger's incredible creative energy.

The more Starkweather talked, the more apparent it became that his entire career had been a version of this problem. Someone was always trying to turn his tap off. But someone *had* to turn his tap off: the interests of the innovator aren't perfectly aligned with the interests of the corporation. Starkweather saw ideas on their own merits. Xerox was a multinational corporation, with shareholders, a huge sales force, and a vast corporate customer base, and it needed to consider every new idea within the context of what it already had.

Xerox's managers didn't always make the right decisions when they said no to Starkweather. But he got to PARC, didn't he? And Xerox, to its great credit, *had* a PARC—a place where, a continent away from the top managers, an engineer could sit and dream, and get every purchase order approved, and fire a laser across the Foothill Expressway if he was so inclined. Yes, he had to pit his laser printer against lesser ideas in the contest. But he won the contest. And, the instant he did, Xerox canceled the competing projects and gave him the green light.

"I flew out there and gave a presentation to them on what I was looking at," Starkweather said of his first visit to PARC. "They really liked it, because at the time they were building a personal computer, and they were beside themselves figuring out how they were going to get whatever was on the screen onto a sheet of paper. And when I showed them how I was going to put prints on a sheet of paper, it was a marriage made in heaven." The reason Xerox invented the laser printer, in other words, is that it invented the personal computer. Without the big idea, it would never have seen the value of the small idea. If you consider innovation to be efficient and ideas precious, that is a tragedy: you give the crown jewels away to Steve Jobs, and all you're left with is a printer. But in the real, messy world of creativity, giving away the thing you don't really understand for the thing that you do is an inevitable tradeoff.

"When you have a bunch of smart people with a broad enough charter, you will always get something good out of it," Nathan Myhrvold, formerly a senior executive at Microsoft, argues. "It's one of the best investments you could possibly make—but only if you chose to value it in terms of successes. If you chose to evaluate it in terms of how many times you failed, or times you could have succeeded and didn't, then you are bound to be unhappy. Innovation is an unruly thing. There will be some ideas that don't get caught in your cup. But that's not what the game is about. The game is what you catch, not what you spill."

In the 1990s, Myhrvold created a research laboratory at Microsoft modeled in part on what Xerox had done in Palo Alto in the 1970s, because he considered PARC a triumph, not a failure. "Xerox did research outside their business model, and when you do that, you should not be surprised that you have a hard time dealing with it—any more than if some bright guy at Pfizer wrote a word processor. Good luck to Pfizer getting into the word-processing business. Meanwhile, the thing that they invented that was similar to their own business—a really big machine that spit paper out—they made a lot of money on it." And so they did. Gary Starkweather's laser printer made billions for Xerox. It paid for every other single project at Xerox PARC, many times over.

In 1988, Starkweather got a call from the head of one of Xerox's competitors, trying to lure him away. It was someone whom he had met years ago. "The decision was painful," he said. "I was a year from being a twenty-five-year veteran of the company. I mean, I'd done enough for Xerox that unless I burned the building down, they would never fire me. But that wasn't the issue. It's about having ideas that are constantly squashed. So I said, 'Enough of this,' and I left."

He had a good many years at his new company, he said. It was an extraordinarily creative place. He was part of decision making at the highest level. "Every employee from technician to manager was hot for the new, exciting stuff," he went on. "So, as far as buzz and daily environment, it was far and away the most fun I've ever had." But it wasn't perfect. "I remember I called in the head marketing guy and I said, 'I want you to give me all the information you can come up with on when people buy one of our products—what software do they buy, what business are they in—so I can see the model of how people are using the machines.' He looked at me and said, 'I have no idea about that.'" Where was the rigor? Then Starkweather had a scheme for hooking up a high-resolution display to one of his new company's computers. "I got it running and brought it into management and said, 'Why don't we show this at the tech expo in San Francisco? You'll be able to rule the world.' They said, 'I don't know. We don't have room for it.' It was that sort of thing. It was like me saying I've discovered a gold mine and you saying we can't afford a shovel."

He shrugged a little wearily. It was ever thus. The innovator says go. The company says stop—and maybe the only lesson of the legend of Xerox PARC is that what happened there happens, in one way or another, everywhere. By the way, the man who hired Gary Starkweather away to the company that couldn't afford a shovel? His name was Steve Jobs.

PETER HESSLER

Dr. Don

FROM *The New Yorker*

IN THE SOUTHWESTERN CORNER of Colorado, where the Uncompahgre Plateau descends through spruce forest and scrubland
toward the Utah border, there is a region of more than four thousand square miles which has no hospitals, no department stores,
and only one pharmacy. The pharmacist is Don Colcord, who lives
in the town of Nucla. More than a century ago, Nucla was founded
by idealists who hoped their community would become the "center of Socialistic government for the world." But these days it feels
like the edge of the earth. Highway 97 dead-ends at the top of
Main Street; the population is around seven hundred and falling. The nearest traffic light is an hour and a half away. When old
ranching couples drive their pickups into Nucla, the wives leave
the passenger's side empty and sit in the middle of the front seat,
close enough to touch their husbands. It's as if something about
the landscape—those endless hills, that vacant sky—makes a person appreciate the intimacy of a Ford F-150 cab.

Don Colcord has owned Nucla's Apothecary Shoppe for more
than thirty years. In the past, such stores played a key role in American rural health care, and this region had three more pharmacies, but all of them have closed. Some people drive eighty miles
just to visit the Apothecary Shoppe. It consists of a few rows of
grocery shelves, a gift-card rack, a Pepsi fountain, and a diabetes
section, which is decorated with the mounted heads of two mule
deer and an antelope. Next to the game heads is the pharmacist's
counter. Customers don't line up at a discreet distance, the way

city folk do; in Nucla they crowd the counter and talk loudly about health problems.

"What have you heard about sticking your head in a beehive?" This on a Tuesday afternoon, from a heavyset man suffering from arthritis and an acute desire to find low-cost treatment.

"It's been used, progressive bee-sting therapy," Don says. "When you get stung, your body produces cortisol. It reduces swelling, but it goes away. And you don't know when you're going to have that one reaction and go into anaphylactic shock and maybe drop dead. It's highly risky. You don't know where that bee has been. You don't know what proteins it's been getting."

"You're a helpful guy. Thank you."

"I would recommend hyaluronic acid. It's kind of expensive, about twenty-five dollars a month. But it works for some people. They make it out of rooster combs."

Somebody else asks about decongestants; a young woman inquires about the risk of birth defects while using a collagen stimulator. A preacher from the Abundant Life Church asks about drugs for a paralyzed vocal cord. ("When I do a sermon, it needs to last for thirty minutes.") Others stop by just to chat. Don, in addition to being the only pharmacist, is probably the most talkative and friendly person within four thousand square miles. The first time I visited his counter, he asked about my family, and I mentioned my newborn twin daughters. He filled a jar with thick brown ointment that he had recently compounded. "It's tincture of benzoin," he said. "Rodeo cowboys use it while riding a bull or a bronc. They put it on their hands; it makes the hands tacky. It's a respiratory stimulant, mostly used in wound care. You won't find anything better for diaper rash."

Don Colcord was born in Nucla, and he has spent all of his sixty years in Colorado, where community-minded individuals often develop some qualities that may seem contradictory. Don sells cigarettes at his pharmacy, because he believes that people have the right to do unhealthy things. He votes Democratic, a rarity in this region. He listens to Bocelli and drives a Lexus. At Easter, the Colcord family tradition is to dye eggs, line them up in a pasture, and fire away with a 25-06 Remington. A loyal NRA member, Don describes shooting as essentially peaceful. "Your arm moves

up and down every time you breathe, so you control your breath-
ing," he says. "It's very similar to meditation." He was once the star
marksman of the University of Colorado's rifle team, and for many
years he held a range record for standing shooting at the Air Force
Academy.

Calmness is one reason that he has such influence in the community. He's short and slight, with owlish glasses, and he seems
as comfortable talking to women as to men. "It's like Don looks
you in the eye and the rest of the world disappears," one local
tells me. Faith in Don's judgment is all but absolute. People sometimes telephone him at two o'clock in the morning, describe their
symptoms, and ask if they should call an ambulance for the two-
hour trip to the nearest hospital. Occasionally, they show up at his
house. A few years ago, a Mexican immigrant family had an eight-
year-old son who was sick; twice they visited a clinic in another
community, where they were told that the boy was dehydrated.
But the child didn't improve, and finally all eight family members
showed up one evening in Don's driveway. He did a quick evalua-
tion—the boy's belly was distended and felt hot to the touch. He
told the parents to take him to the emergency room. They went
to the nearest hospital, in Montrose, where the staff diagnosed severe brucellosis and immediately evacuated the boy on a plane to
Denver. He spent two weeks in the ICU before making a complete
recovery. One of the Denver doctors told Don that the boy would
have died if they had waited any longer to get him to a hospital.

At the Apothecary Shoppe, Don never wears a white coat. He
takes people's blood pressure, and he often gives injections; if it
has to be done in the backside, he escorts the customer into the
bathroom for privacy. Elderly folks refer to him as "Dr. Don," although he has no medical degree and discourages people from
using this title. He doesn't wear a name tag. "I wear old Levi's,"
he says. "People want to talk to somebody who looks like them,
talks like them, is part of the community. I know a lot of pharma-
cists wear a coat because it makes you look more professional. But
it's different here." He would rather be known as a druggist. "A
druggist is the guy who repairs your watch and your glasses," he
explains. "A pharmacist is the guy who works at Walmart."

He keeps watch-repair tools behind the counter, and he uses
them almost as frequently as he complains about Walmart, insurance companies, and Medicare Part D. Since 2006, the program

has provided prescription drug coverage for the elderly and disabled, ensuring that millions of people get their medication. But it's also had the unintended effect of driving rural pharmacies out of business. Instead of establishing a national formulary with standard drug prices, the way many countries do, the U.S. government allows private insurance plans to negotiate with drug providers. Big chains and mail-order pharmacies receive much better rates than independent stores, because of volume. Within the first two years of the program, more than five hundred rural pharmacies went out of business. Don gives the example of a local customer who needs Humira for rheumatoid arthritis. The insurance company reimburses $1,721.83 for a month's supply, but Don pays $1,765.23 for the drug. "I lose $43.40 every time I fill it, once a month," he says. Don's customer doesn't like using mail-order pharmacies; he worries about missing a delivery, and he wants to be able to ask a pharmacist questions face-to-face. "I like the guy," Don says. "So I keep doing it." Don's margins have grown so small that on three occasions he has had to put his savings into the Apothecary Shoppe in order to keep the doors open.

He is, by the strictest definition, a bad businessman. If a customer can't pay, Don often rings up the order anyway and tapes the receipt to the inside wall above his counter. "This one said he was covered by insurance, but it wasn't," he explains, pointing at a slip of paper on a wall full of them. "This one said he'll be in on Tuesday. This one is a patient who is going on an extended vacation." Most of his customers simply don't have the money. Each year, Don writes off between $10,000 and $20,000, and he estimates that he is owed around $300,000 in total. His annual salary is $65,000. Over the course of many days at the Apothecary Shoppe, I never saw a customer walk in whom Don doesn't know by name.

"It's just a cost of doing business in a small town," he says. "I don't know how you can look your neighbor in the eye and say, 'I know you're having a tough time, but I can't help you and your kid can't get well.'"

Settlers originally came to this remote place because they desired an alternative to capitalism. During the 1890s, a group called the Colorado Co-operative Colony hoped to build a utopian community in the region. Its Declaration of Principles explained that market-oriented competition makes it "almost impossible for an honest man or woman to make a comfortable living, and that a co-operative system, if properly carried out, will give the best opportunity to develop all that is good and noble in humanity." (The history of the colony and its values is described in a 2001 dissertation by Pamela J. Clark at the University of Wyoming.)

At the end of the nineteenth century, socialist communities weren't uncommon in the West. The arid landscape required extensive irrigation systems, and principles of shared labor made sense to people who were inspired by the theories of Karl Marx and Robert Owen. Anaheim, California, was settled through a cooperative water venture, as was nearby Riverside. Others failed but left idealistic names on the map: Equality, Freeland, Altruria. The Colorado Co-operative Colony published a newspaper called the *Altrurian,* which tracked the progress of the colony's founding project, an eighteen-mile irrigation ditch that was intended to carry water from the San Miguel River. Settlers also planned to do away with debt, interest, and rent. The *Altrurian* dreamed of a glorious fixture: "If a small colony of outlaws and refugees could build Rome and maintain the state for twelve hundred years, who could guess what a well organized colony of intelligent Americans may accomplish."

Within a year, they held their first purge. Ten members were expelled for being too communistic, and after that the newspaper often published aphorisms that clarified theories. ("Communism may be co-operation, but co-operation is not necessarily communism.") By the winter of 1898, settlers were running out of food. ("Competition is a product of Hell; Co-operation will make a paradise of earth.") In 1901, a member of the board revealed that the colony was bankrupt. A former president committed suicide. ("So long as you think of yourself alone, you cannot be a good cooperator.")

Eventually, the settlers abandoned the principle of shared labor and contracted out to private work crews. In 1904, water flowed through the completed ditch; six years later, they decided on the name Nucla, after *nucleus.* The socialist dreams were never realized, but the irrigation canal continues to function today. And there's still a Colorado Cooperative Company, which employs a full-time "ditch-rider" to monitor the system. His name is Dean

Naslund, and both his father and his grandfather worked on the ditch. Like most Nucla residents, Naslund doesn't talk about his ancestors in terms of sociopolitical theories. ("They called him Daddy Joe. He kinda cowboyed. He liked to hop around. Maybe play cards all week sometimes and then work a little.")

Nucla has a reputation as a tough town. It boomed in the 1950s and 1960s, when the region's uranium mining and processing thrived. But the nuclear industry collapsed after the Three Mile Island accident, in 1979, and the population continues to drop in Nucla and its sister town of Naturita, which is four miles away. In both these towns, the per capita income is less than $14,000 a year, a little higher than half the state figure, and only 8 percent of the adult population holds a college degree. This year, the school board decided to switch to a four-day school week because of lack of funds. There's only one restaurant in Nucla, one hamburger joint in Naturita, and one bar for both towns. It's called the 141 Saloon, named for the state highway that passes through Naturita. On a Thursday night I'm the only customer, and the bartender, a woman named Casey, tells me that she just bought a three-bedroom house in Nucla for $53,000. That's a mortgage of $250 a month.

"Only problem is the siding is asbestos," she says.

"Is that a big problem?"

"It's not a problem as long as you don't touch it. Asbestos lasts forever." She leans on the wooden bar. "What'll it be?"

"What do you have on tap?"

She smiles and says, "Only thing we got on tap is Jägermeister."

By the time Don Colcord was eight years old, he knew that he wanted to be a druggist. He grew up in Uravan, a mining town near Nucla, and his mother was a clerk in the pharmacy, where Don liked to hang around and watch the druggist. As a teenager, he began breaking into the place. Along with some friends, he stole beer, *Playboy,* and condoms. ("The condoms went to waste.") When the boys finally got caught, they were forced to pay for the goods by working at the store for twenty-five cents an hour, "Everybody knew why you were there," Don says. "It was probably the best thing that happened to me."

During his teenage years, Don shared a room with his brother,

Jim, and one day he found a magazine hidden under the bed. It featured photographs of naked men. When Jim came home, Don asked, "Is this yours?"

"Yes," said Jim, who didn't seem embarrassed. He took the magazine back, and neither of them mentioned it again.

Jim was three years older than Don. He was six feet three and well built, but he didn't enjoy sports or hunting, like most local kids. He spent a lot of time by himself, and in high school he became an excellent student. He was a source of disappointment to his father, who nagged at Jim to behave like a normal boy. In 1972, a couple of years after Jim left for college, he sent his family a letter explaining that he was gay and that he knew his father would never accept it. He asked them not to look for him; he was leaving Colorado for good. And for the next twelve years nobody heard from Jim.

At the age of eighteen, Don married his high school girlfriend, Kretha; eventually, they settled in Nucla and opened the Apothecary Shoppe. In 1983, Don's father died, and one of the first things his widow did was hire a private investigator. The detective found Jim in Chicago, where he was a clerk in the county court. He said he'd had a feeling that something had happened back home.

The following year, Jim made a four-day visit to Nucla. He went for long drives with his mother, who told him that she had always known he was gay and that she was sorry she hadn't been able to change his father's attitude. In the evenings, Jim and Don sat up late talking. One night, Jim told Don that he had been infected with HIV, and that his doctor said he was likely to develop full-blown AIDS. Jim told Don where he wanted his ashes scattered. And he asked him to visit Chicago, where Jim lived with his long-time boyfriend.

That year, they talked frequently on the phone. But whenever the topic of a Chicago visit came up, there was always a reason Don couldn't go: he was too busy at the store; his son and his daughter had school activities. Kretha tried to persuade him to make the trip, but he never did.

When Jim died, one of his colleagues telephoned with the news. She sent the ashes in a box, with a copy of Jim's will, some awards from work, and a few photographs. One of the pictures was taken at Wrigley Field, where Jim stands with his boyfriend in front of a GO CUBS sign. When Don looked at the photograph, he realized that he knew virtually nothing about his brother. He had seen Jim for all of four days in the past decade; he didn't even know his boyfriend's name. And he understood the real reason that he hadn't made a trip to Chicago. "I was angry with myself for not being comfortable in a house where two men were sleeping together," he says. "I didn't want to see two men kissing each other. It wouldn't bother me now, but it did then. I really regret it."

Along with his mother and his younger sister, Don scattered Jim's ashes at the juncture of the San Miguel and the Dolores Rivers. The Dolores flows from the south, where it crosses the great salt dome of Paradox Valley, and the water is saline and has no fish. If you swim there, you float as if you were in the ocean, a thousand miles away.

The last doctor in Naturita died fifteen years ago. There's a small health clinic, and recently it contracted with a doctor in another part of Colorado to visit two days a week. But the mainstay is Ken Jenks, a physician's assistant who is on call twenty-four hours a day. Jenks has lived in rural Colorado for a decade, and during that time he has learned that electrical tape is harder to remove from a wound than duct tape. Twice he has had patients suffer cervical fractures and drive themselves in to the clinic rather than wait for an ambulance. It's not unusual for somebody to sign out of the clinic AMA—against medical advice. A couple of times, Jenks has told heart attack victims that they needed to be evacuated by helicopter, only to have the patients decline because they believed they could get there cheaper. Jenks signed the forms, unhooked the IVs, and the patients got into their pickups to drive the two hours to a hospital. "And they made it," Jenks says. "So they were right!"

Jenks grew up in Salt Lake City, but he has spent most of his working life in small towns. "Maybe I can describe it this way," he says. "I like to play chess. I moved to a small town, and nobody played chess there, but one guy challenged me to checkers. I always thought it was kind of a simple game, but I accepted. And he beat me nine or ten games in a row. That's sort of like living in a small town. It's a simpler game, but it's played to a higher level." Jenks says that he is forced to have "a working relationship" with local methamphetamine users, treating their ailments in confidence. He explains that small towns might have a reputation for being closed-minded, but actually residents often learn to be non-judgmental, because contact is so intense. "Someday I might be on the side of the road, and the person who pulls me out is going to be a meth user," Jenks says. "The circle is much tighter." He believes there is less gossip than one would assume, simply because so much is already known.

One morning, a young woman arrives at the Apothecary Shoppe after spending the weekend in jail. She had an argument with her husband, who called the police; Colorado law requires officers to make an arrest whenever they respond to a domestic dispute. The law is intended to protect women from being coerced into dropping charges, but in this case the husband claimed that *he* had been attacked. In the drugstore, the woman is approached by half a dozen neighbors who have read about the arrest in the local newspaper.

"It's not what it sounds like," she tells one elderly woman. "He's lying about the whole thing, and he's going to get in trouble for that."

They stand at the pharmacy counter. "It's terrible when I have the criminal element in the store," Don jokes.

The young woman reads the police blotter in the newspaper. "He said I attacked him with a frying pan. He said I hit him in the arm. If I'd attacked him with a frying pan, I'd a hit him in the head."

"Let me tell you what you should do," the old woman says. She is in her seventies, with curly white hair and a sweet, grandmotherly smile. "Get you some wasp spray," she says. "It'll put their eyes out."

"I can't even have Mace, because it's a weapon."

With the wisdom of age, the elderly woman explains that wasp spray is not classified as a weapon and is thus available to people who are out on bail. "It's better than pepper spray," she says.

A while later, I see the young woman cutting out the arrest listing. "This way, if I'm ever stupid enough to think about taking him back, I'll look at this," she tells me. "I'll keep it in my scrapbook." (Eventually, all charges were dropped, and they divorced.)

At the store, Don never discusses anyone's situation with a third party, but he frequently mentions his own problems. Twenty years ago, Kretha was diagnosed with a rare degenerative form of spina bifida, and now she rarely leaves home. Their oldest son flies F-16s for the air force, but their daughter has struggled with alcoholism. After she had difficulties caring for her son, Gavin, Don and Kretha took custody of the boy. Don often mentions such issues to a customer. "If I'm dealing with somebody who has an alcoholic in the family, it helps for them to know about my daughter," he says. "You can't pretend that your family is perfect. My daughter is not perfect, but she's trying." He continues, "Almost all druggists in a small town will tell you the same thing. You are part and parcel of the community. Nobody's better, nobody's worse."

In Nucla, Wednesday is bowling-league night. The local alley shut down to the public long ago, because there are so few people left, but the facility opens twice a week for community leagues. The alley was built in 1962 and all its equipment is original, with an exuberant use of steel that you don't see anymore: long, shiny Brunswick ball racks, dining tables with heavy flared legs. Scorecards advertise businesses that have been dead for decades: Miracle Roofing and Insulation, Sir Speedy Instant Printing Center ("Instant Copies While You Wait!"). Don is the league's president, and he certifies the lanes every year. He took a course in Montrose in order to be licensed to use a bowling-lane micrometer.

Don's collection of certifications is impressively esoteric. He has taken CPR courses, and he's qualified to use an electric defibrillator. He has a pyrotechnics display license, so that Nucla can have fireworks on the Fourth of July. When he heard about a new type of hormone therapy, he flew to California to attend two days of classes, and now he compounds medicine for four transgendered patients who live in various parts of the West. Every three months, Don talks with them on the phone and prepares their drugs; he finds this interesting. On Friday nights, he announces Nucla High football games. They play eight-man ball, although if a bigger school comes to town, they switch numbers with every possession, so that each side can practice its plays. When Nucla is on offense, it's eight-on-eight, but it becomes eleven-on-eleven when the other team has the ball. Occasionally, somebody gets confused, and Don's voice rings out over the loudspeakers: "There's eleven white guys and eight blue guys, and that won't work." The football might not be first-rate, but the players' names are a novelist's dream. Nu-

cla has Seth Knob, Chad Stoner, and Seldon Riddle. Dove Creek
has a player named Tommy Fury. Blanding has Talon Jack and
Sterling Black, Tecohda Tom and Herschel Todachinnie. Shilo
Stanley, Terrance Tate, Dillon Daves: if alliteration ever needs an
offensive line, recruiting should begin around the Colorado-Utah
border.

When outsiders come to town—loners, drifters—they often
find their way to Don. A number of years ago, a man in his seventies named Tim Brick moved to Naturita and rented a mobile
home. He placed special orders at the Apothecary Shoppe: echi-
nacea, goldenseal, chamomile teas. He distrusted doctors and often had Don check his blood pressure. It was high, and eventually
Don persuaded him to get on regular medication. Soon, he was
visiting every four or five days, mostly to talk.

Don referred to him as Mr. Brick. He had no other local
friends, and he was cagey about his past, although certain details
emerged over time. His birth name had been Penrose Brick—he
was a descendant of the Penrose family, which came from Philadelphia and had made a fortune from mining claims around Cripple
Creek. But for some reason Mr. Brick had been estranged from all
his relatives for decades. He had changed his first name, and he
had spent most of his working life as an auto mechanic.

One day, his mobile home was broken into, and thieves made
off with some stock certificates. Mr. Brick had never used a bro-
ker—to him, they were just as untrustworthy as doctors—so he
went to the Apothecary Shoppe for help. Before long, Don was
making dozens of trips across Disappointment Valley, driving two
hours each way, in order to get documents certified at the bank in
Cortez, Colorado. Eventually, he sorted out Mr. Brick's finances,
but then the older man's health began to decline. Don managed
his care, helping him move out of various residences; on a couple of occasions, Mr. Brick lived at Don's house for an extended
stretch. At the age of ninety-one, Mr. Brick became seriously ill
and went to see a doctor in Montrose. The doctor said that pros-
tate cancer had spread to his stomach; with surgery, he might live
another six months. Mr. Brick said he had never had surgery and
he wasn't going to start now.

Don spent the next night at the old man's bedside. At one point
in the evening, Mr. Brick was lucid enough to have a conversation.
"I think you're dying," Don said.

"I'm not dying," Mr. Brick said. "I'm just going to pray now."

"Well, you better pray pretty hard," Don said. "But I think you're dying." He asked if Mr. Brick needed to see a lawyer. The old man declined; he said his affairs were in order.

Don found a hospice nurse, and within two days Mr. Brick died. Don arranged a funeral Mass, and then he went through boxes of Mr. Brick's effects. There was a collection of old highway maps, an antique cradle telephone, and a Catholic prayer stand. There were many photographs of naked men. Don found checkbooks under four different aliases. There were letters in Mr. Brick's handwriting asking friends if they could introduce him to other men who were "of the same type as me." But he must have lost courage, because those letters were never mailed. Don also found unopened letters that Mr. Brick's mother had sent more than half a century ago. One contained a ten-dollar bill and a message begging her son to make contact. The bill, from the 1940s, still looked brand-new, and seeing that crisp note made Don feel sad. Years ago, he had sensed that Mr. Brick was gay, and that this was the reason he was estranged from his family, but it wasn't a conversation they ever had.

In his will, Mr. Brick left more than half a million dollars in cash and stock to the local druggist. After taxes and other expenses, it came to more than $300,000, which was almost exactly what the community owed Don Colcord. But Don didn't seem to connect these events. He talked about all three subjects—neglecting his dying brother, offering credit to the townspeople, and helping Mr. Brick and receiving his gift—in different conversations that spanned more than a year. He probably never would have mentioned the money that was owed to him, but somebody in Nucla told me and I asked about it. From my perspective, it was tempting to apply a moral calculus, until everything added up to a neat story about redemption and reward in a former utopian community. But Don's experiences seemed to have taught him that there is something solitary and unknowable about every human life. He saw connections of a different sort: these people and incidents were more like the spokes of a wheel. They didn't touch directly, but each was linked to something bigger, and Don's role was to try to keep the whole thing moving the best he could.

*

Don Colcord's birthday is the Fourth of July. That's also when Nucla celebrates its annual Water Days, which commemorates the
completion of the town's irrigation system. Today, the theme is
"Where the Past Meets the Future," and Don announces the floats
for the parade down Main Street. After that, he helps out at the
barbecue in the park, and then he prepares to set off the town's
fireworks. All these events are sponsored by the Lions Club. When
Don joined the club, in 1978, he was the youngest member, and
he still is. Soon, the Lions Club will be disbanded because of lack
of members.

In the evening, we drive to the top of Nucla Hill. The view
is spectacular in all directions: westward, the slate-blue La Sal
Mountains, and the Uncompahgre Plateau to the east, where the
feathered tops of cottonwoods mark the long line of the irrigation ditch. Three remaining members of the Lions Club are here,
along with some volunteer firemen. Trucks and cars arrive from
town and park at the bottom of the hill to watch the show. When
darkness falls, the Lions prepare the fireworks in metal tubes, and
Don ignites them one by one. After it's over, we watch the pairs of
headlights glide in a neat line back up Main Street, dispersing as
drivers turn off toward home. Our attention drifts upward—now
that the fireworks and the headlights are gone, the stars seem brilliant, clustered together like the lights of some faraway city. Don
passes around a few bottles of beer. "I don't care if it is a small
town, we got good fireworks," he says. He sips his beer and gazes
up at the Milky Way. "When you see them from here, they look
so close together," he says. "It's hard to believe they're millions of
miles apart."

EWA HRYNIEWICZ-YARBROUGH

Objects of Affection

FROM *Ploughshares*

EACH SUMMER WHEN I'm in Kraków, I make weekly trips to a
flea market close to our apartment. This particular market also
sells antiques, but it doesn't aspire to a loftier name, because it also
peddles secondhand books, last year's issues of fashion magazines,
handmade jewelry, items that aren't old in the sense that antiques
are supposed to be. A valuable nineteenth-century chest of draw-
ers or a gilded mirror enjoys good neighborly relations with an
electric coffee grinder and rusty door handles. It would probably
be easier to attempt a list of things that aren't sold there than the
ones that are. If someone is looking for a rare item, his friends will
invariably suggest going to the flea market. When I was looking for
a desk, I first went there and bought a beautiful art nouveau table,
which recovered its former looks after being renovated. I love the
market because I love rummaging through old things and because
I usually will find something that I absolutely want to have. I love
running my fingers over the shapely back of a violin, tracing the
grooves in a century-old high-back chair, or gently tapping a por-
celain cup to hear it tinkle. I know that to some people viewing
old objects with something akin to reverence is a silly affectation.
But particularly there, in a country that wasn't spared violent en-
tanglements with History, an old photograph, a water pitcher, a
clock that stood on someone's mantelpiece and was miraculously
salvaged from a bombed-out building—those mute witnesses to
human life inspire awe and amazement at the mere fact of their
survival. They connect us to the past and its messy materiality by

making that past more concrete, more tangible. And in them we
see the reflected wisdom of our simple human order.

I was a child of the fifties, growing up in a communist country
beset by shortages of practically everything—food, clothes, furniture—and that circumstance may have been responsible for my
complicated attitude toward objects. We had few toys or books,
and we wore mostly hand-me-downs. A pair of mittens, a teddy
bear, and a chocolate bar for Christmas were enough. Once in a
while we also got skates, bikes, musical instruments. "Abundance"
had no place in our vocabulary and in our world, but we were
happy with what we had, in the way that only children can be.
We were unaware that our lives were in any way circumscribed,
although the reality we lived in trained us early on that there was
a huge gap between wanting something and getting it. After all,
even people with money had to hustle and resort to underhanded
maneuvers, including bribery, to buy things.

For many years I had only one doll, which my father somehow
managed to procure when I was four years old. Made in Germany,
Gabriela had two long braids. She was a beautiful doll, not like the
ones sold in toy stores, and although I had other dolls later, she remained special. When the mechanism responsible for her making
a crying sound broke, we took her to the doll clinic. At that time
nothing was thrown away if there was even a slight chance that it
could be repaired. I had Gabriela until I turned fourteen, when,
in a grown-up gesture, I bequeathed her to my young cousin.

By the time I graduated from high school, I was a person of
substance, or so I thought. The shortages never disappeared, but
it was easier to get things. I had a Chinese fountain pen and two
ballpoint pens, which I kept in my desk drawer and would only
use at home. I boasted several records that my sister and I listened
to on a gramophone she had been given as a name-day present a
few years before. Some of them were by the popular Polish rock
bands, and one was Beethoven's Fifth Symphony, the only classical
music record I had for a long time. I listened to it so often that
to this day I can hum the whole piece from beginning to end. I
also had a bookcase with a sliding glass front that was filled with
books. My parents' books were arrayed on three broad shelves in
the bottom part of a cupboard in what doubled as our living room
and their bedroom. Although both my parents were readers, they

rarely bought books, borrowing them instead from the public library. I was very possessive of the books I owned and only reluctantly loaned them to friends. When my younger sister took one out, I insisted she put it back in the exact same spot.

My possessiveness may have had a lot to do with how difficult books were to come by. They were published in small numbers, and there was such a huge demand for them among the intelligentsia that the good ones disappeared from stores very quickly. On my way back from school, I often made a detour and walked by the local bookstore to look in the window where new arrivals would be displayed. That was how I spotted a four-volume *War and Peace* that cost eighty zloty, not a negligible sum. I had only thirty. The clerk told me this was the only copy in the store. I knew the book would be sold soon, so I decided to go to my father's office and beg him for a loan, which he gave me at once. Clutching the money, I ran back to the bookstore, breathless and worried that the book would no longer be there. I realize that what I'm saying must seem pathetic to a person raised in the comforts of a free market economy, where it's enough to think of something to find it immediately in the store.

It might sound more poignant if I said that books and records helped me escape the surrounding grayness and drabness and that my hunting for them wasn't solely motivated by my newly developed acquisitiveness or a collector's instinct. But if I said that, I'd be practicing revisionist history. The truth is that we didn't see the grayness and drabness—not yet. This realization came much later. So if it was aesthetic escapism, it was the universal kind, not fueled by our peculiar political circumstances.

My youthful materialism thrived in a country where materialism—unless of the Marxist variety—was unanimously condemned as the ugly outgrowth of Western consumer societies. We knew this was just an ideological cover-up for the never-ending shortages. My brand of materialism didn't belong in a consumer society either, because it was a kind of disproportionate attachment to things that was caused by scarcity, something unheard-of in a market economy. I couldn't want more, new, or better. Such wanting was at best a futile and abstract exercise, so I learned to practice self-limitation. Paradoxically, however, I knew what I liked and wanted, and would have had no trouble making a choice had I been given the chance. When you're faced with overabundance, assaulted by

things and more things, it's often difficult to say what you like or
want, but that at least wasn't our problem. I don't mean to praise
privation or claim that we were somehow better or more virtu-
ous than people who inhabited a consumer heaven and whose
wishes could be automatically fulfilled. I'm only saying that my
relationship to things was developed under a different set of circumstances. I did care about possessions, no question about that. I
wanted to hang on to what I had and now and then replenish my
stock if I came across the right item. More often than not chance
ruled my acquisitions. I had to sift through what was available in
the hopes of finding something special among a slew of worthless
objects. That was also true of buying the so-called practical items. I
might have been walking by a shoe store when I spotted a delivery
truck. That sight would have been enough to make me stand in
line. If I was lucky, I might have ended up buying a pair of sneak-
ers. I might have also wasted my time because I liked none of the
shoes or couldn't get my size. People would often buy things they
didn't need or want, just in case. You could never tell when those
things might come in handy or be used to barter.

In the mid-eighties I came to America for an academic exchange
program. That wasn't my first visit to a Western country. In previous years, I'd spent some time in England and Germany and
a semester in Florida at the invitation of a Fulbright professor
who taught at my university. I saw stores overflowing with goods I
didn't know existed. But in 1984, three years after brutal martial
law that obliterated any hope for change, Poland experienced un-
precedented shortages, as if the communist government was doing everything in its power to punish the recalcitrant populace.
To buy meat we needed coupons, and the same was true of sugar.
Chocolate was rationed, too, but you had to have children to get
it. Grocery stores had shelves stacked only with vinegar and low-
quality tea, called Popularna—Popular, the irony of whose name
wasn't lost on us. Other necessities were so hard to get that serpen-
tine lines formed in front of the stores before daylight.
    A few days after I arrived in the United States, a friend took me
to a supermarket on Long Island where she lived. I knew what to
expect, but as I kept watching people piling item after item into
their shopping carts until they looked like elaborate pyramids, I
felt sick. Who needs so much food, I thought. This was almost

obscene. Soon my own shopping habits changed and began to resemble the American ones—if not in quantity, then in the way I
went about buying. But for many years I didn't quite shed my old
ways. For one thing, I attempted to have all broken items repaired.
I remember insisting that my husband take me to a repair shop
to have a strap reattached to a sandal that I'd bought a month
before. The sandals were cheap; I couldn't have paid more than
twenty dollars for them. To my dismay I discovered that fixing the
shoe would have cost me more than half that price. I gradually
learned the same was true of electronics and many other items of
daily use.

My reluctance to part with something that could possibly be
repaired, which, against my better judgment, I still exhibit, comes
from my grandmother. I can also attribute to her my preference
for well-made objects with a long life span ahead of them. I remember how she had often said that she couldn't afford poor
quality. By today's standards she had few clothes, and she wore her
coats, hats, and jackets for many long years. All her clothes were
made to last, carefully sewn of good-quality fabrics by a seamstress
or a tailor. The same can be said about her shoes. She had only
four pairs of them, a pair for each season, spring and fall counting
as one, and one pair of "going out" shoes that she'd wear to name-
day parties or family celebrations. She dutifully carried them to a
shoe repair shop if any of them needed new soles, straps, or buck-
les. Her apartment was furnished in what I came to call utilitarian
style: only the necessary items, simple, and functional, no bric-a-
brac, no trinkets of any kind. The only older object in her place
was an antique napkin holder, with a marble bottom and brass top,
whose origin I know nothing about. She must have developed this
unsentimental attitude after everything she owned perished in the
burning of her apartment building during the 1944 Warsaw Uprising.

After many days of hiding in the building's basement and the
subsequent defeat of the uprising, my grandmother was taken to
a camp in Pruszków with my aunt, who was barely a year old, and
my mother, eleven at the time. My grandfather had disappeared
at the beginning of the turmoil and found his wife and daughters
much later. Grandmother had a baby carriage, a suitcase with a
change of clothes, a handful of photos, and a silver sugar bowl that
at the last minute she snatched off the table. I never thought to

ask her about the sugar bowl, although I wondered why she took it. Besides the photos, that was the only item that had nothing to do with survival. I can see her hurriedly packing clothes, a mug, a spoon, maybe some Cream of Wheat for the baby. For a moment her eyes rest on the silver sugar bowl on the kitchen table, a wedding gift from her husband's aunt. She hesitates, then quickly wraps it in her daughter's blouse and puts it in the suitcase. Did she want to keep at least one thing from her apartment, as a reminder of the life she knew was about to end? Or did she just grab it thinking she might swap it for food or use it to bribe a German soldier?

Eventually, she ended up living for several months with a peasant family near Łowicz. They treated the survivors from Warsaw like their own kin, and Grandmother gave them the sugar bowl, the only thing she could give to repay their kindness. When Warsaw was freed by the Red Army, she went back, hoping that maybe her building was still there. She saw only its skeleton and her beloved city in ruins. Convinced that Warsaw would never be rebuilt, she decided then and there to move to the former East Prussia, now labeled the Recovered Territories. The family settled in a small town that was barely scathed by the war, with only a few ruins here and there. The majority of the apartment buildings and one-family houses were intact. Their former German owners fled in panic from the advancing Red Army. To save their lives they had to lose everything, abandon all the possessions they had accumulated over the years, just like Grandmother, who had to leave her apartment and all it contained. The difference, however, was that none of her possessions survived, while here the newly arrived, shipwrecked people moved into apartments that were furnished, had pots and pans, rugs, bedclothes, pictures, and all sorts of knickknacks.

I often wondered how my grandmother felt in a strange apartment where the smells of the previous owners still wafted in the air and the sheets were still warm from their bodies. Among strange furniture, saltshakers with the inscription *Salz*, faucets with Gothic script, she must have felt like an intruder. She missed her Warsaw apartment that she had patiently and lovingly decorated. Now she had nothing of her own, no objects imbued with memories, nothing to fill out the space and make it hers. She never felt comfortable surrounded by all these strange things, this post-German stuff as we came to call everything that had remained after the German exodus. She also sensed the wrongness of her situation, its moral illegality, even though it was done with official encouragement and approval. Contrary to the official propaganda, there was nothing she could recover in those "Recovered Territories."

When I was about ten, Grandmother, who, in the meantime, had divorced my grandfather, moved into her own small house on the outskirts of town. She took with her all the furniture that was in the apartment because that's what she had. She couldn't have just sold it and bought new items. To begin with, she didn't have the money, but even if she did, the rampant shortages of everything would have made buying new items difficult. She lived in that house for less than two years and hated the distance she had to walk to get to town. When she sold the house, this time she sold it with everything in it, and got a studio in a newly built apartment building that had the telltale look of communist-style residential architecture. She was relieved to get rid of all the post-German objects she'd never considered hers. Because her new place was tiny, she needed only a few items to furnish it. Those post-German items were more attractive and better made than what she had bought, but at last she had things that belonged to her. And once she furnished her place, she never replaced anything in it, and she lived to be ninety-three. Her furniture and all her other possessions were functional and practical, and that was all she cared about.

My grandmother passed away in the fall of 2001. My mother was no longer alive, so the task of dismantling Grandmother's apartment fell to my aunt. I told her I'd like to get something that belonged to my grandmother, a keepsake. My aunt was at a loss because Grandmother had none of the items that family members usually keep after a person's death. I ended up with a round glass paperweight and some photos. My aunt took the napkin holder and my sister a metal basket where Grandmother kept needles, receipts, and small change. Was the paperweight an object that was full of memories for me? Not really. I knew that it was hers and that it was in her apartment, but it wasn't like those things that overwhelm us with nostalgia when we hold them or look at them. I have a lot of memories attached to Grandmother's apartment, the many times I visited her, the meals she cooked for me in her cramped kitchen, and I know that these memories are more important than a trinket I could have inherited. But sometimes I do wish she had left behind some things she valued and loved, which I could keep now and later pass on to my daughters. My grandmother is still alive in my memories. My daughters' memories are limited, as we could visit her only in the summer. When I'm gone, she will die a second death. An object that belonged to her could then serve as a reminder of her life, a souvenir connecting the different generations.

When I came to America, I left behind everything I owned in Poland. I arrived with a large backpack and a suitcase the size of a carry-on, which contained my clothes and a few books. In this sense my situation was like my grandmother's, but there the resemblance ends. My circumstances weren't the result of a war or a historical upheaval. Yes, I did lose things I was attached to, but they didn't just disappear. They simply changed owners, and most of them remained in the family. And unlike my grandmother, I felt I needed things for my emotional well-being. My future husband had a lot of books and records, all of which I happily adopted as mine. Gradually, we filled our house with more books and records, more photos and photo albums, china, pictures, artwork, Christmas decorations. Some years later our daughters' dolls, teddy bears, drawings, seashells, rocks, homework, and school projects were added to the trove of important objects. I'm not a hoarder, but I'm sentimental about things.

My attachment to objects was put to a test the year of our cross-country move, from California to Massachusetts, where we live now. We knew we had to get rid of a lot of stuff. I decided to pack most of our belongings myself, separating the items of value from the ones relegated to the giveaway pile. The process was lengthy, and it exasperated my husband, who has a very down-to-earth, no-nonsense attitude toward possessions. He urged me to throw things away, since most of what I wanted to save I would never use or even look at. But with many objects I felt as if I had opened a sluice gate: I was flooded by memories. And once that happened, I knew I had to keep those items, no matter how trifling they would seem to someone else. I kept my daughters' newborn caps, their christening gowns, their first diaries with lockets, the cards they wrote to me on Mother's Day. I kept some folk art pictures, vases, plates, table runners I got from different relatives in Poland, even though I knew they would stay in the attic until the next inventory. And against my husband's advice to toss them, I even salvaged some items that he had as a child, like two model tractors he received at five from the Delta Implement Company in Indianola, Mississippi, and that now adorn the top of the bookshelf in his study. Will our daughters hang on to these things when the time comes to dismantle our house? I have no way of knowing. I do suspect, though, that they will want to keep our collection of books with its many first editions, the artwork, the photo albums, my mother's and my jewelry, a few antiques we have, and the Polish stoneware that I've been collecting for years. Maybe they will even keep some of the things that my husband wanted condemned to the junk pile. Maybe they'll be grateful to things for the delight they give us and the lessons they teach about the triumph and defeat of mortal matter.

Some years ago, in a world literature class, I was teaching Tadeusz Borowski's *This Way for the Gas, Ladies and Gentlemen.* One story in the collection, "The Man with the Package," a mere four pages long, provoked a very lively exchange. The story's main character is a Jew who has the position of a *Schreiber* in Birkenau's hospital—a position that for a long time offers him protection other prisoners don't have. Besides clerical work, his duties involve accompanying Jews selected for the gas chamber to the washroom, from which they are taken to the crematoria. One day the *Schreiber* himself comes down with the flu and is selected for the gas. On his way there he carries a cardboard box tied with a string; the box contains a pair of boots, a spoon, a knife, and a few other items. Seeing this, the story's narrator says: "He could show a little more good sense . . . He knows perfectly well . . . that within an hour or two he will go to the gas chamber, naked without his shirt, and without his package. What an extraordinary attachment to the last bit of property!" Just like the narrator, my students found the *Schreiber*'s behavior bizarre. They couldn't understand why, when faced with imminent death, he would hang on to what were to them worthless things. They hadn't yet learned that objects help us exorcise some of our fears, that they are stronger than we are, perfect and independent, that they give us a semblance of permanence and grant a stay against chaos, darkness, oblivion.

GARRET KEIZER

Getting Schooled

FROM *Harper's Magazine*

IN THE FALL OF 2010, after a fourteen-year hiatus from the classroom and at the unpropitious age of fifty-seven, I began a one-year job filling in for a teacher on leave from the same rural high school, in Orleans, Vermont, that I'd entered as a rookie thirty years before. I signed on mainly because my wife and I needed health insurance. The reason I had trained to be an English teacher in the first place was my parents' insistence that I graduate from college with a trade, "poet" falling short of the mark in their eyes. It's fair to say that I have never worked in a school with what might be called purity of heart, though much of what I know about purity of heart I learned there.

That I can say so without irony probably owes at least something to the fortunate working conditions of this past year. To describe those conditions in any detail will make many a teacher green with envy, if not downright incredulous. Most of the roughly four hundred students enrolled at the school were obliging and even friendly—I mean hold-open-the-door-and-ask-how-your-day's-going friendly. At no time did I feel threatened or in danger of violence. At no time did I feel inclined to regard any of my colleagues as lazy or inept—or feel they were insinuating similar judgments about me. My principal, recently and deservedly named Vermont's high school principal of the year, had been a student of mine at the same school. As he announced both to me at our first meeting and to the entire staff at its first meeting, he could not bring himself to address me by my first name. The vice principal, married to another of my former students, followed suit. My department head, though not a former student or at all disinclined to call me Garret, treated me like a peer and looked after me like a best friend. Of my five classes, none exceeded twenty students and three were sections of the same course, meaning they could usually be served with the same preparation. Not to rub it in, but I had all but one of these classes in the same room, both semesters, and a full forty minutes in which to eat my lunch. I could also eat my lunch alone in my classroom.

That said, I was nearly faint with hunger by the time lunch rolled around, for I ate my breakfast most days at 4:00 A.M. Not infrequently I would put in a twelve-hour day before heading home to work several additional hours after dinner, only to wake up the next morning feeling unprepared.

My immune system proved even rustier than my pedagogy. During the course of the school year I caught several colds plus one case each of flu, pneumonia, and conjunctivitis. After only two months on the job, I was compelled to put in a tedious session on a treadmill because of unspecified chest pains, though the technician assured me that my heart, however impure, belonged to a man twenty years my junior. This was a good thing to know given that I was frequently awakened by my heart pounding from a nightmare, invariably set in school. The bad dreams continue, but as I know from past experience, they will have subsided in ten years.

Except for a few precious hours on Friday nights, I had little of what is generally called a life. My wife and I seldom went out. My normally robust correspondence dwindled to nothing. I was unable to file our income taxes until July. Though I took pains not to appear so to my students, I was often despondent. One morning, when my wife remonstrated with me for picking up a drunk hitchhiker by myself on a lonely road late the night before—"What if he'd pulled a gun?"—I responded, half joking, that if I could just get myself shot, I might not have to correct any more papers.

My point here is that even under ideal circumstances, public school teaching is one of the hardest jobs a person can do. Most sensible people know that. Anyone who claims not to know that is either a scoundrel or a nincompoop; or, to put it another way, a typical expert on everything that's wrong with American public education and the often damaged children that it serves.

*

Like a war-wounded veteran unable to give his full trust to anyone who has never experienced the traumas of combat, I can find
it hard to respect the opinions of anyone who has never taught
school—not only in matters of education, which is reasonable
enough, but also in matters of philosophy and politics. John Adams, Samuel Johnson, and Henry David Thoreau, to name but
three who make the cut, tried their hand at "school mastering."
All three proved more or less dismal at it; all had greater things to
do in their lives than I, whose best accomplishments have arguably
taken place in a classroom. Still, I attribute the lack of illusion in
their thought, their disinclination to dogma on the one hand and
despair on the other, to the fact that they were tested as teachers.
They had encountered humanity in all its rawness and variety, and
with the dubious aim of "forming" it in some way. In the process,
they had beheld their own selves as naked as a human being can
get, and may in fact have achieved greatness partly out of fear of
being that naked again.

Ludwig Wittgenstein, of modern philosophers perhaps the
most sainted, served time as a schoolteacher. I am not surprised.
I am also not surprised that he resigned his position after hitting
an eleven-year-old boy in the head. I tried to remind myself of
that at least once a week throughout this past year, and not so I
could fancy myself superior to Wittgenstein. Rather, I wanted to
remember that what I had undertaken was by no means as safe or
as simple as redirecting the course of Western thought.

On the first day of school I begin my classes with John Coltrane's
"Welcome," at the closing bars of which a palpable attentiveness
comes over my chattering students, proof of what I've always believed about the source of Coltrane's genius and the wellspring
within even the dopiest-seeming kid. "This is nice music," one boy
remarks, and no one sneers. As I will do with the other musical
introductions I play throughout the year, all chosen to fit the interval between passing bells, I key in my selection on a purse-size
CD player, as quaint to the iPod generation as a Victrola is to me.
I write the name of each artist and piece on the blackboard, including the date of composition when I can find it, usually a year
predating that of my students' birth (circa 1995).

I wear a jacket and tie almost every day, one of the few adults at
school who do. To these I add a pair of well-oiled work boots, an

offhand expression of solidarity with the parents of our community but mostly a concession to my falling arches. For the first time in many years I have what can be called a "look"—like me and like the white-collar trade of teaching itself, a strange amalgam. A girl passing in the hall remarks that I always look "spiffy." I reply that I would have thought I looked old. "Hey, how old are you?" she counters. "Thirty?" I take this as a compliment and beam accordingly, though on reflection I wonder if she is simply trying to agree that I am old.

In this exchange and in countless other particulars, I find confirmation of the maxim that "kids are kids." I have been warned to expect big changes between now and the old days, but for the most part the students I meet are interchangeable with types I taught more than twenty years ago, even down to the baseball caps. I'm a bit surprised by the ubiquitous display of décolletage, the respectability of the word *sucks,* and the number of students who readily identify themselves as "attention deficit." If such a disorder exists, as I'm inclined to think it does, I'm glad there are medicines to treat it, although hearing someone say "I've got ADD" in a culture of such vast distractedness is a bit like having a fellow passenger on an ocean liner tell you that she feels afloat. Who doesn't?

As I expected, there have been a number of changes in the school itself. A sophisticated alarm system needs to be deactivated if you're the first person into the building and set again if you're the last to leave, and as I am reminded on one particularly flustered Saturday morning, it's linked to the Department of Homeland Security. In accordance with state standards, paragraphs are now called "constructed responses." A staff meeting to discuss students in academic jeopardy is called an EST (educational support team). A kid out of jeopardy is making AYP (adequate yearly progress). This profession-wide penchant for jargon in general and three-letter shorthand in particular, a pidgin derived from government commissions and gypsy consultants, makes the school seem forbiddingly foreign to me at first. My skepticism shrinks somewhat after attending my first morning EST and listening to my colleagues discuss how to make a more collaborative effort on behalf of the drowning students they share. Call it what you will, it can be a PIS (pretty impressive sight).

By far the most noticeable and happy improvement is the number of places to which students can turn for academic assistance.

What had previously been one highly stigmatized "special ed" room is now a bustling network of study areas, all staffed by unflappable, die-hard tutors, most of them proficient in several subjects. Some of these areas are devoted to students with identified special needs, but there's a laudable blurring of the boundaries, at least on the surface, that seems to make it easy for kids to feel comfortable in any given room. The word *retard* sadly persists in the hallways but is used mostly as an all-purpose, gender-neutral alternative to *peckerhead*.

Not surprisingly, many of the more salient changes are technological. The library looks like a NASA control center in which the controllers occasionally spend their break periods with a book. The proverbial dog who ate the homework is now a flash drive. Smoking in the boys' room is now texting in the boys' room, though to their lasting credit the addicts of yesteryear were usually able to survive at least an hour without a drag. I frequently hear the phrase "school of the twenty-first century" and understand it to mean the school with more wires. During one of the first staff-training days, the district superintendent tells us that 10 percent of all high school education will be computer based by 2014 and rise to 50 percent by 2019, the implication being how close to obsolescence our methods and we ourselves have become. No one ventures to ask what would seem to be the obvious question, which is what sort of high school education Bill Gates and Steve Jobs had and what they might have failed to accomplish without it.

Such caveats aside, I come to appreciate the advantages of a computerized grade book, though like other old-timers on the staff I keep an antique paper ledger "just in case." The end-of-marking-period all-nighter with a roped-in spouse doing backup duty on a calculator has mercifully gone the way of the mimeograph blues. Naturally, the resulting expectation is that the emancipated teacher will gather more assessments and record them in a more "timely" fashion.

In the increased emphasis on data and the imposed emphasis on standardized jargon and tests, including the standardized inanities that result (no student I meet seems to believe that the universe was formed in six days, but a disturbing number insist that an essay is always formed in five paragraphs), I sense the encroachment of the totalitarian "business model" that has destroyed family farming as a way of life, of the same itch for arcane nomenclature that has turned literary criticism into a pseudoscience. A veteran foreign-language teacher still going strong since my last stint at school says to me with a sigh, "I'm afraid the day of the teacher as artist is drawing to a close."

That seems to be the theme of the text we study together as a faculty. According to its authors, who shamelessly recount their exemplary and now franchised successes in a middle- to upper-middle-class high school, the day of the "lone wolf" teacher is done. We must shift from "an external focus on issues outside of the school" to a focus on what business consultant Jim Collins calls "the brutal facts" of our "organization." The notion that the very same teachers who made the greatest difference in my life need to be purged from the ranks is dispiriting enough, but the outrageous suggestion that the "brutal facts" of education have more to do with the schoolhouse than with the larger society in which my students live is enough to make me want to spit. Or teach.

What has definitely not changed since my first tenure at school is the degree of poverty and social dysfunction suffered by students in the region. Quite possibly it has gotten worse. I taught through the Reagan years and left during Clinton; I've come back during a catastrophic recession, the demon child of deregulation and its gory consort NAFTA.

The difference first comes home to me with the deceptively familiar FFA (Future Farmers of America). Back in the old days a kid who wore that gold-lettered dark blue corduroy jacket was as often as not a kid who came to school smelling like a barn, sometimes with manure in the tread of his boots. It takes me a while to realize that of the half dozen or so FFA members I have in my classes, only one lives on a farm; that is to say, the parents of the others have become lifetime members of the Past Farmers of America.

If you can imagine Silicon Valley running out of silicon, you have some inkling of what happens to an agricultural community when small-scale agriculture starts to die. In the early spring, when a young man's fancy turns to love, the front page of a single issue of the local newspaper headlines three stories: a twenty-eight-year-old man drowned after attempting to fly his snowmobile over the Connecticut River in a state of drunken delirium, a two-year-old boy accidentally shot to death by another child with a .22-caliber rifle, and a wretched holdout of a farmer charged with animal cruelty for housing his starving cows in a mire of their own accumulated excrement. How the farmer and his family were housed is not mentioned, but I doubt it will produce any arrests.

To teach with your eyes open in a region like this is ever to be on the verge of tears—though not always of pity or rage. By the metric of students qualifying for a reduced-price hot lunch, the high school where I teach ties for the third poorest in the state. Yet its standardized-test scores are among the very highest; the year before I came its scores in writing were *the* highest. What this means is that more than a few teachers and students are joined in a heroic effort. I see it all around me; I feel it every day. Back in the nineties I could arrive at 7:00 A.M. and be one of the first people in the building; this year I need to arrive half an hour before that merely to compete for the same distinction. And no one is cracking the whip; no merit-pay carrots are dangling in our faces. It takes one of my English-teaching colleagues two trips to get all his bulging crates and satchels of student papers to his car every day, three if his little girl has joined him after school. (And I never see that little girl without remembering what my daughter said when she was that age: "I wish I could make two daddies, a daddy to grade the kids' papers and a daddy to play pirates with me.") One fruit of these herculean labors is an understandable and, even to a jaded heart like mine, moving pride in the school. When the principal asks the student body "Who are we?" there is an unmistakable James Brown vibe as they say it LOUD: "Lake Region!"

I try not to think of the poisonous fruit growing on the same tree, especially as I am also laboring to make it grow (and shouting "Lake Region" with the best of them). If a kid from a poor school can do so well on a standardized test, then obviously it does not matter so much that she spent last winter living in an unheated trailer behind her grandmother's house or that he missed a week of school because of all the flea bites he picked up at his father's house. Hey, a baby sleeping in a stable might grow up to be the next Jesus Christ. Public education's commendable aim of creating "equal opportunity for all" is too easily subverted by the egregious aim of creating a clean conscience for the few. If everybody can "read at grade level," then we need not be overly concerned if some people get to read fabulous dividend statements and other people, who may be working twice as hard, get to read pink slips. All we need hope is that the latter sort never get to read Marx.

Along with poverty—I want to say arising from it, though I know the causal connection goes only so far—is widespread household turmoil. This was true in the past but feels nothing less than pandemic now. Day after day, "constructed response" after constructed response, I read unsolicited expressions of abandonment, bewilderment, and self-laceration. *If I wasn't so fat and was getting better grades maybe my dad wouldn't have left us.* A common complaint among students, I notice, is "all the drama." Ostensibly they are talking about school, the typical cliques and dustups of teenage life, but essentially they may be talking about home, where adolescence never dies.

Given my empirically based conviction that a stable home life is the single most reliable predictor of a student's success in school, I am surprised that the Republican Party, self-appointed champion of "family values," takes no pains to press the point. Of course, to do so would undermine its agenda of dismantling public education, hamstringing teachers' unions, denying same-sex couples the rights of marriage, preventing working mothers from achieving income parity, curtailing reproductive rights, outsourcing manufacturing jobs, and filling the coffers of the various charlatans who sell education in the form of standardized tests.

And of course the Republican Party is not the only faction holding a ten-foot pole against the question of what it means to be a responsible adult. That precious bourgeois squabble we referred to as the "culture wars"—all it means to me is two different ways of making war on children, two rival sects in the ancient religion of child-devouring Moloch: one that sacrificed and continues to sacrifice working-class children on the altar of American exceptionalism, and the other that sacrifices them to the frivolous exceptionalism of the "transgressive" lifestyle or the political escapism of the catchall canon. Shall we bomb the Taliban or put their writings on the syllabus? "It has been vivid to me for many years that what we call a race problem here is not a race problem at all," James Baldwin wrote many years ago. "The problem is rooted in the question of how one treats one's flesh and blood, especially one's children." The race problem, and just about every other problem that crosses a teacher's desk.

A child of our common flesh and blood bends over my desk examining one of the framed postcards I keep there to cheer me. "Wow, what is that place?" he asks. I tell him it is the great Reading Room of the New York Public Library, sent to me by a woman I used to teach. He's a bit of an operator, this one, the kind who can make you feel good even when you know you're being had, but I detect a heartfelt quality in the wistfulness with which he asks, "And you've been there?" I make a mental note to give him the picture at the end of the year. That never happens, though, because he is shunted to a new guardian and a new school before I can recall my intention. That's how it seems to go with many of the students I worry about most: they are whisked away, though few have enjoyed this kid's peculiar privilege of being referred to by a former foster parent—all in fun, I'm sure—as "my nigger slave."

I suppose I am willing to bet more money on this young man making it to the New York Public Library someday than I am on the likelihood of his taking a book off the shelves if he does. The same holds true for many of his classmates. I can't be sure if the resistance to reading that I encounter nearly every day marks a new development, because fourteen years is too long an interval for my memory to be trusted and because the sections I now teach are not the "honors" levels I taught in the past. Mine are "average" kids, but they are by no means stupid kids. Still, I do not remember feeling as frustrated then as I often feel now that so few of them want to read.

It's nothing new that some kids find reading a chore. What strikes me is the frequent lack of correlation between the ability to read and any inclination to do it. That, and the number of times I hear someone say, "I hate to read." A girl tells me so in private and sobs so preposterously that I worry I might laugh. After she calms down, I gently suggest that she read a passage aloud. Her fluency is impeccable; she could work for the BBC.

I realize that in some cases the reluctance to read has its basis in the lack of a suitable place to do it. I ask students to write a paragraph on "where I read," and get more than one account of how

hard it is to concentrate in a house "where people are always yell-
ing." Even at school, though, and even when the time and quiet
are provided, the book is not always read. I can't resist tipping
off two of my favorite rascals, who often visit with me before our
first-period class, that there might be a quiz on last night's reading assignment and that any young man less prepared than they
undoubtedly are would do well to use the next twenty minutes to
read it. The passage is short enough to finish in that time. Quicker
than I can wink, they pull out their books and turn to the assigned
pages, bending over them like monks in a scriptorium, doughnuts
in hand. In three minutes they put the books aside—enough of
that for one day—and go back to chatting. They flunk their quizzes.

Where the resistance to reading seems the strongest and proves
the most maddening is with major, long-term assignments, for
which I scrupulously supply written instructions, reading them
aloud and slowly to the entire class. I make extra handouts for
students who tend to lose things. But there is little else I can do
beyond repeating the mantra *What does the sheet say?* in response
to every bogus question, though often that takes the form of *Why
didn't you consult the sheet?* after the assignment has been handed
in.

I try to give the matter a political slant. When a rule is written
down, I tell the students, then the writer is bound by it no less
than the reader. That is why we have a Constitution. In an auto-
cratic state the king's whim is the law. Maybe one day he feels like
reading a six-hundred-word essay; the next day he feels like a six-
line poem. But in this case, I can't hold you accountable for any
requirement that isn't spelled out on the sheet. You can wave that
sheet in my face as evidence, and I can't win the argument simply by saying "I wrote the sheet." I have to win by pointing out to
your satisfaction what the words actually say. I seem to be getting
through—somebody's raising his hand.

"Do you want us to hand in our rough draft, too?"

A local pediatrician once told me, when I asked how he managed to keep his sanity in the face of so much needless grief, "I try
to remember that except for a very few psychopaths, most people
on most days are doing the best they can." I take that for my working motto, though I remain haunted by the thought that if "a kid

is just a kid," then a sixteen-year-old kid is a kid just two years away
from voting.

On the morning after Osama bin Laden is killed, I'm expecting
a barrage of comments, in anticipation of which I decide to let
Homer speak my piece. From top to bottom on my blackboard I
write a dozen lines from the *Odyssey*, what Odysseus says after he
has slain the suitors and his faithful servant Eurykleia is about to
rejoice. "No crowing aloud," he tells her, though he's willing to
add that the suitors got what they deserved. "To glory over slain
men is no piety." I leave the lines up for three days. No one asks
me what they mean or what they are doing on my blackboard. As
nearly as I can tell, no one reads them. For that matter, no one
mentions Osama bin Laden. At the close of the third day there is
nothing left for me to do but erase the lines and go for a haircut,
which in my case involves reducing a half inch of salt-and-pepper
thatch to a maintenance-free quarter and which I know will infal-
libly arouse keen interest and lively comment (all of it sweet) the
next day.

I never missed the school musical in my earlier years of teaching,
and I'm sure to be on hand for the one this year: a spirited vaude-
ville revue. Like all its precursors, it is performed in the town's old
auditorium, the school having no such place. There is that same
magic I remember from previous shows—and some of the same
teachers, still playing in the orchestra and doing makeup back-
stage, most of them gray-headed now—the magic of kids stepping
out of their daytime roles and into new ones, the latter sometimes
closer to their most authentic selves. Not always recognizable in
their costumes, still less so when they sing, they seem charmed and
immortal, happily lost in that thin place that is both school and
not-school because it exists outside the scheduled day. As the audience files out of the theater, mothers of actresses identifiable by
the bouquets in their hands, the vice principal calls me aside and
says that the principal wants to speak to all the faculty in the basement under the stage. When we gather, the principal announces
that a thirty-nine-year-old teacher on our staff, not at the play this
evening, has died suddenly from heart failure. Obviously shaken,
he wants us to be prepared. There is no mourning like mourning
in a school.

And there is nothing like a school to make one aware of mortality. You may be thinking of other professions where this is more the case, medicine or ministry for example, but I buried the dead and visited the dying for many years and do not recall ever leaving a hospital or a grave with a heightened awareness of my death; mostly what I felt was relief at being alive. But the relentless experience of finitude that is teaching, the angelus that rings—not three times a day, as in a monastery, but every forty-five minutes—remorselessly drives home one's sense of limited time on the earth, of diminishing chances to do the work and get it right. The kids are probably too young to feel it this way, and one hopes so, but they know what a deadline is, and they can hear the word *dead*.

If the bell schedule and the calendar are the body of a school, transcendence often comes as an out-of-body experience. When a classroom teacher can somehow manage to get kids "out of school," either physically or psychologically, then school can begin. Sometimes that happens simply by inviting students to stay after school, which can be difficult, though it helps if you have refreshments and a few students with nothing better to do at home. I have both. Sometimes it happens through a special project, the more hands-on the better—paradoxically, "out of body" often translates in practice to contact with the physical world, to running, drawing, making something *real*.

I hand out magic markers and invite students to deface enlarged photographs of my face, one blacked-out tooth or booger per part of speech accurately identified, and everybody wants to find a verb. I have them make a museum of projects based on the literature we have studied, and though I encourage the use of technology, their overwhelming preference is for projects made with tangible stuff, perhaps because more than one person can touch it at a time. Two boys team up and build a full-scale replica of the raft in *Huckleberry Finn*, using hand axes for authenticity, and cart it on a trailer to school. It seems the perfect symbol of our object: to get away from the prim Widow Douglas and float free for a while. Even so, we are no farther from the riverbank and its cruelties than Huck and Jim are, because not all the students have adults to help them with their projects or money to pay for materials; because one of the boys who builds the raft tells me he plans to join the marines after he graduates, and so mortality is still able to smirk at me over his tattooed shoulder.

Not surprisingly, the literature brings its own transcendence, especially when we get to drama and poetry, which I have injudiciously put off until the spring. I discover how much the students enjoy reading aloud; girls vie for the part of Emily in *Our Town;* the unlikeliest boys take a shot at Whitman's "Song of Myself." I come to suspect that it is not reading they hate so much as reading in isolation. The same radical privacy that I seek in books, my mind's way of eating its lunch alone, is what turns their stomachs. I learn of two girls in my class who got through *Ethan Frome* by reading aloud to each other over Skype, not unlike George Gibbs and Emily Webb chatting between their upstairs bedroom windows, just with different kinds of windows. They are acutely *social* creatures, these kids, and it is a slow learner indeed who fails to grasp that fact even as he prattles on about building a more social democracy.

Spring break marks the first school vacation when I have not been ill, and I celebrate with a free-for-all of physical work. I stack firewood. I burn brush. I prune trees, including the crabapple tree my expository-writing students gave to me in 1985 as a housewarming gift. It was about twenty inches high then and now stands a good twelve feet, with a span of branches almost as wide. It will be awash with white blossoms by the time of final exams. Plant trees when you're young, advised the Vermont poet James Hayford, so that when you're old, "you can walk in shade / That you and time together made." Several years ago I realized I had heard from no fewer than seven of my former students in a single month: a gay anarchist agitator, a hairdresser, a college professor, a guidance counselor, a dairy farmer, a Web designer, and a felon, three women and four men, all very different but all contributors to the shade that I and time together made. Sometimes I wonder how much richer my life might have been had I never left teaching. I wonder but I never ache with regret.

One of the more remarkable and, I think, telling things about the teaching trade is the number of people who need to believe that you love it. Ever since leaving the classroom in the mid-1990s and throughout the past year, I've found people asking if I missed teaching or had plans to take it up again. They didn't want to know; they wanted to hear me say yes. Some didn't bother to ask. "I know the pay is not the greatest, but you're doing what you love"—a sentiment that puts me in mind of the trope of the happy slave. In fact, our word *pedagogue* derives from a Greek word for a type of slave who led children to school. Jim is Huck Finn's teacher not only in spirit but in accordance with an ancient tradition. This is not to suggest that contemporary teachers are slaves or that I was ever treated like one, only that I am inclined to distrust people who expect me to work for love, or who need a sentimental mythology to gloss over the impossibilities of my job and the daily injustices it lays bare.

My principal, Mr. Messier, or Mr. Mess as the kids call him, never asks me if I love my job. He does say he hopes I am enjoying my year at Lake Region. He tells me that I was important to him when he was a high school student and that I am having a similar impact on students this year. He says that he thinks of me as the school's "artist in residence"; apparently he does not think the artisan teacher needs to die. He never hovers, yet I often feel him beside me, sometimes because he actually is, strolling nearby in the bustling halls until one of us notices the other and says hello, an effect that on certain days and in certain fragile states of mind can feel almost numinous. Well over six feet, with a halogen smile and the broadest shoulders I have ever seen on a human being, he is deferential, resolute, and charismatic to such a degree that he trumps my usual suspicions of charisma. At the close of every day, he walks the students to the buses, his figure unmistakable even with the hood of his Windbreaker up. He walks back into the building when the last bus is gone, and I feel that I know exactly what he is thinking, that he has seen his kids off for another day, only wishing he could see every one of them safely home, especially the ones who dread going.

Though my role in his formation is hypothetical at best—I first knew him as a fifteen-year-old farm boy and he would have made a fine principal then—I am unabashedly proud of him. I can't say with any conviction that I love teaching. But I do love him, and others I have taught who are very different from him. And I know I am not suited to be a teacher because even with that love and its incomparable satisfactions, I am counting off the days until I can go home for good.

Scores of days and hundreds of "teachable moments" remain before that can happen, however; every week something new. Babies in car seats begin to appear in the hallways, life-size baby dolls

as it turns out, a project for a class in parenting. I recall a similar assignment from my previous teaching stint, though then it
was done with a swaddled egg in a cigar box. The symbolism was
obvious, emphasizing the fragility of a newborn. In the updated,
higher-tech version, the students, all girls as far as I can tell, are
expected to attend to the artificial infant's simulated needs, responding promptly whenever it cries and keeping close watch over
it, though the dolls don't break as easily as the eggs did.

The parenting class is offered only to juniors and seniors, but
lo and behold a sophomore girl shows up in my last-period class
with baby and bucket in hand. It seems the "mother" has absented
herself from school for a day or two in order to handle her prodi-
gious prom arrangements and has left the baby with a round-the-
clock sitter, teasing out the simulation, to say nothing of the irony,
more than she probably knows. But I have to say, her choice of a
sitter is impeccable, a girl I'd surely have chosen were I needing
one for any child of mine. Meredith already has the experience
for one thing, routinely caring for her little niece, who lives with
her on the family farm. She also works part-time at McDonald's,
competes as an amateur wrestler (a pursuit I find hard to recon-
cile with her diminutive height and demure behavior, though I've
been told she can "beat the shit out of any boy in this school"),
reads her drowsy big brother's English assignments aloud to him
as he drives her to school in his truck (he's up at 2:00 A.M. doing
barn chores and occasionally nods off in my first-period class), and
can always be counted on to bring a pan of home-baked cookies
for afterschool study sessions (even when she herself can't stay)
and to deliver A+ speaking assignments, like the one on historical
infatuation entitled "How I Stalked JFK." A pearl of a girl, in other
words, so I'm glad she has charge of the "baby," not only because
she'll see it gets the right care but also because I hope she'll see,
if she hasn't already, that this is a burden she doesn't need for a
good long time.

Midway through the period the doll erupts in a fit of wailing.
My first thought is to ask who has their blasted cell phone on and
whatever possessed them to chose such a perverse ringtone. Then
I notice Meredith, clearly mortified by the outburst—this is a kid
who waits patiently by the electric pencil sharpener until everyone has finished speaking. Smiling, I offer to rock the doll for her

while I teach. "No," she says, "I'll take care of it," and hurries from the room.

Five minutes later I am still doing my teach-on-the-*Titanic* routine and the baby is still screaming out in the hall. Finally, one of the students says, "Mr. Keizer, I think maybe you better go out there."

When I do, I find Meredith frantically trying to turn a black plastic key into the control box at the back of the doll. She is visibly distressed. I feel a bit rattled myself at this point—the cry is "fake" but up close it arouses a very real and even primal response. I also try the key to no avail, noticing that there are written directions (and we know how much good they do) to turn the key clockwise. What I also discover is that the lady wrestler or some caretaker before her has succeeded in twisting the key into a worthless corkscrew of plastic. It turns only on itself. Can you get in touch with the student who gave this to you? I ask, raising my voice to be heard. She can't. She adds that if the crying is deactivated without turning the key it could compromise the other student's grade. I couldn't give a fig, I want to say, but instead ask if she knows the teacher in charge of the parenting class. No, she's somebody up at the career center ten miles to the north. The doll keeps wailing, louder it seems. I am indignant on behalf of Meredith and on my own behalf as well. We have been handed "a situation" for which we have not been prepared. Somewhat beyond what the assignment intends, we are feeling what every parent feels at one time or another: overwhelmed, clueless, and (needlessly) alone.

I tell Meredith what I think we should do and reluctantly she nods her head. I pop the voice box from the doll's plastic back. Like an image out of Poe, the box continues wailing in my hand as I stare at it dumbfounded. Wanting to stomp the thing under my boot, I pull the ribbon that expels the batteries and the noise finally stops.

But the simulation continues, at least for one deathly moment. In real life, in a predicament not too far removed from the experience of many of my students, I would not have been this girl's teacher. I would have been her boyfriend, perhaps the baby's father, perhaps not. I couldn't have pulled out the batteries, because there wouldn't have been any batteries to pull out. Instead, I would have taken up the infant in a fit of frustration and shaken it until it either died or became permanently eligible for special services. I, in turn, would have become eligible to have my deer-in-the-headlights mug shot appear in the police blotter of the local paper. Another stupid redneck bastard gets his. Or, if you prefer, another shaken, stunned, and stunted baby boy comes of age in the richest nation in the world.

I do not have to wonder if any of my students are thinking these same thoughts. I do not have to wonder because, when I step back into the classroom, I tell them exactly what I think.

Usually I was not so moralistic, believing as I still do that it was my duty to teach the curriculum and not to pontificate, to inspire debates, not to weigh in with verdicts. I did on one or two occasions tell my students they were living in a society that valued people of their age, region, and class primarily as cannon fodder, cheap labor, and gullible consumers, and that education could give them some of the weapons necessary to fight back. That I did say. I wish, though, that I had had a simple refrain, some terse slogan I could have repeated day after day, like the Roman senator Cato, who is supposed to have ended every speech by saying, "Carthage must be destroyed."

In fact, Cato's refrain would have done nicely. As it happens, the people of Carthage worshiped the same god their Phoenician ancestors had, a god they called Moloch. When the Romans eventually took Cato's advice, they found within the walls of the doomed city a multitude of clay urns containing the tiny charred bones of children. The Romans worshiped their own version of Moloch, needless to say, as do we if our poets are to be believed. "Moloch whose love is endless oil and stone! Moloch whose soul is electricity and banks!" A man named Allen Ginsberg wrote those lines decades before you were born, when your English teacher was a mere three years old. You see, my loves, I am still talking to you in my head, and though I rather hope you're reading something else these days, reading anything actually, here is what I wish I'd said before I said goodbye: *Carthage must be destroyed*—and you, for your part, must learn everything you can about Carthage.

DAVID J. LAWLESS

My Father/My Husband

FROM *Prism*

HE IS PREPARING the evening meal. Fried pork chops, rice, carrots from the garden, and a salad. A couple of rolls from the supermarket.

"Is my father coming for dinner?" she asks.

"No."

"Why not?"

"Because your father died forty-six years ago." He has given this answer several times a day for the past two or three years. He can't remember exactly how many times today, but he knows it is becoming more frequent.

"I know. I don't mean that father. I mean my other father."

"You, like anyone else, can have only one father. Your father died." He always answers her questions quietly.

"I mean my father-in-law."

"Your father-in-law is my father, and he died twenty-three years ago."

"Don't be stupid!" she says. "I mean the man who runs this house. That's my father! Where is he?"

"I run this house and I am not your father. I am your husband," he says calmly.

"My husband! You fool! I don't have a husband."

"I am your husband. You are my wife," he continues without looking up from the cooking. "We've been married for more than fifty years."

"Ha! You wish! I've never been married. And I certainly wouldn't marry an old man like you. Look at you. Gray hair. Big belly. Who would marry you?"

"Come and sit down and have something to eat," he says.

"I'm not going to eat with you. You pig!"

"Then I'll bring it over to you and you can eat while you watch TV."

"I'm not going to eat this garbage!"

"Then at least take your pills. I'll bring a glass of water. You can eat later or I'll save the supper till morning."

"I've already had my pills. You're trying to poison me. Do you know how many pills I've taken today?"

"Yes. And you have to take these and a couple more before you go to bed."

She requires medication on a regular daily schedule for a number of disabilities.

She accepts them, under protest.

"Come up to bed," she calls from the top of the stairs.

"No. It's too early for me," he calls back. "It's only ten after eight. You go to bed. I'll catch up with you later." He continues to read news and articles on the Internet.

A few minutes later she comes out again. "I can't sleep by myself. I need you with me. I can't sleep alone. Come up."

"No. Not yet. Try to go to sleep. I'll come up in a while."

"I can't sleep."

"Then just rest."

Ten minutes pass.

Zzzzz. The sound of the chair lift coming downstairs.

She comes into his den. "Come up to bed."

"Not yet. It's too early."

She sits next to him, holding his arm with both hands and leaning on his shoulder. "What are you watching on the TV?"

"This is not TV. I'm reading things. Here, I'll get you ABC España."

He clicks on ABC and a headline comes up about Zapatero. He scrolls down to an article about Princess Letizia, which she reads. Then to some photos about the Duquesa de Alba, whom she despises.

"Let's go up to bed," she says. "I'm very tired."

"Not yet. It's early. I want to watch the news. Here. It's time to take the nitro patch off your shoulder."

"I already took it off."

"When?"

"Before supper."

"It's not supposed to come off till eight o'clock. It's supposed to be on for twelve hours. From eight in the morning till eight at night. It controls your irregular heartbeat."

"It was itchy," she says.

She clings to him throughout the night. Her fingers and feet are always cold. It is the effect of metoprolol, a medication she takes for heart failure that draws the blood from her extremities. He is always warm, sometimes sweaty. They have to arrange the bed-clothes to suit each of them, and he has to leave his feet sticking out because of the heavy blankets and duvet.

She wakes him at four thirty in the morning.

"Are we in Spain?"

"No. Canada," he says.

"Is this Madrid?"

"No, Calgary. Go to sleep."

"Why are we in Calgary?"

"Because we live here."

"Why?"

"Because I came here for a job."

"Are we going to stay here?"

"Yes. Go to sleep."

"Why don't we live in Spain?"

"We have pensions here. We have medical insurance here. Because taxes are lower here. Because our children live here. Because we have a house here. Now go to sleep."

"Is this our house?"

"Yes. We own it. We had it built for us thirteen years ago."

"I don't remember. Are we married?"

"Yes. We married over fifty years ago. Now go to sleep."

"I don't remember. Where did we marry?"

"In Victoria."

"Why in Victoria? Why not in Madrid?"

"Because in those days we couldn't afford to travel to Madrid from Vancouver to marry in your parish church, so we went to Victoria to marry in my parish church. Do you remember?"

"Sort of."

Pause.

"Do we have children?"

"Yes. Six children."

"Six! That's a lot. What are their names?"

He lists their names and the cities in which they live, their wives and husbands and children. It is almost a nightly ritual, a middle-of-the-night ritual. "Now go to sleep."

She pulls close to him in the bed and holds him tight.

He makes her a cup of coffee in the morning, passes her the morning newspaper, gives her an iron pill, and puts the nitro patch onto her shoulder.

"Can you give me the telephone number of my father? I can't find my telephone book."

He has hidden all telephone directories and phone lists because she has phoned so many people, numbers, and directories all over the world in the past year or so, asking for the telephone number of her father. It became too expensive and her sisters in Spain grew exasperated at receiving phone calls in the middle of the night.

"No. I can't. Your father died forty-five years ago."

"Then give me the number of the store. I'll phone the store."

"There is no store. Your father sold the store before he died."

"He died?"

"Yes. In 1964. Do you remember? You went to visit him in Madrid a few months before he died. He had this growth on his neck, remember?" He draws a line down the side of his neck. "It was cancer. He died a few months later."

"Yes, I remember. My poor father! Who looks after the store?"

"Your father sold the store before he died."

"Who has the store now?"

"I don't know."

"I have to go there. I have to open the store."

"No. There is no store. We live in Canada. There is no store in Madrid."

*

She goes to the front door, opens it and looks out, then comes to the kitchen, where he is preparing the evening meal. This is another ritual. She goes to open the front door several times a day to check whether her father or husband is coming.

"Is my father coming for dinner?"

"No."

"Why not?"

"Because your father died in 1964."

"I know that. I meant my father-in-law."

"Your father-in-law was my father. He died in 1985."

"No. No. I meant my other father."

"A person can have only one father. Your father was Emilio. My father was John. They both died a long time ago." He has made this statement so many times over the past few years that the entire dialogue has become automatic and predictable.

"I know that. I mean the man who looks after this house."

"I am the man who looks after this house. I am your husband."

"My husband? You wish! I never married you!"

"Yes you did. We married more than fifty years ago."

"I never married anyone."

He goes to the mantel and takes down a silver-framed photo from their wedding. "Here. This is a photo of our wedding. Here we are. Just married. Do you remember?"

"That's not you. That's my husband. Give it to me! Don't touch it!" She snatches it from him.

He points to the photo. "That's you . . . with me . . . in the church . . . in 1958."

"That's not you, fool! That's my husband."

"Well, I must admit that I've changed over the past fifty years. But that's me."

"That's my husband. Wait till he comes home. He'll throw you out."

He is making her a cup of Nescafé as she settles into the sofa early in the morning to watch TV.

"Where is your husband?" she asks.

"I don't have a husband," he says. This is fairly routine in the morning. "Men don't have husbands. Men have wives. You are my wife."

"Don't be stupid! Where is your husband? Did he go to open the store?"

"There is no store."

"Don't be stupid, I said. Did my father go to open the store?"

"There is no store. Your father sold the store before he died. Many years ago."

"My father died?"

"More than forty-five years ago."

"He died?" she says. "Why didn't anyone tell me?" She begins to weep.

"*You* told *me*. It was a long time ago."

"I don't remember."

He hugs her. "I'm sorry. It was a long time ago."

"I don't remember. I don't know what's wrong. I don't remember things." A tear runs down her cheek. She clings to him.

"I know. Don't worry."

"I'm losing my memory."

"Don't worry." He gives her a kiss.

He wakes in the middle of the night. A few years ago he put in a night-light so that she could get up to go to the toilet without having to stumble or run into things. The bed moves and he can feel her sitting up. He can see the shadows cast on the wall by the night-light. She comes around to his side of the bed. She runs her hand gently around his head and face.

"Who are you?" she asks.

"Your husband."

"You're not my husband. Are you my father?"

"No. Your husband."

"You're not my husband. I don't have a husband. What are you doing in my bed?"

"This is my bed. Our bed," he says. "Come back to bed. Come back to sleep."

She turns on the main lights, picks up her walking cane, and starts to beat him.

"Get out! Get out of here!"

"Stop that! Stop it!" He wrenches the cane from her hands. "Now just settle down and come back to bed."

She leaves the room.

Zzzzz. He hears the chair lift going downstairs.

She'll settle down in a while and come back to bed in an hour or so, he thinks. She usually does. He drifts off to a fitful sleep.

"Excuse me, sir."

He wakes up. There is a police officer standing over his bed. Then he sits up, startled.

"What is it? What happened?"

"We had a call about an intruder."

"What?" He rubs his eyes. "An intruder? My wife called?"

"Yes, sir. She says you are an intruder."

"Aaaagh!" He gets out of bed and puts on his slippers. "I'm sorry. My wife is sick. She has Alzheimer's and dementia. She gets over it in a few hours. I have medication for her but it is impossible to give it to her when she is like this. Maybe I can get you to give it to her. She won't take it from me when she's in this state."

"Sorry, sir, we can't do that. I'm going to have to ask you for identification."

"Okay, okay, okay. Let's go downstairs. It's in my office."

They pass the living room where his wife is sitting and talking with the second police officer.

"Are you all right?" he asks her as they look up.

"Yes," she says. "I phoned them to come." She had phoned the operator, who had put her through to 911.

"Come with me," he says to the first officer, leading him to his den. "Please come inside. I want to close the door."

The officer hesitates.

"I have to close the door. I can't let her see where I conceal the papers."

Reluctantly, the officer enters and allows the door to be closed.

"Now, what papers would you like to see? I have to keep them under lock and key or she will take them, hide them, destroy them. I keep everything locked up. My wallet, my money, my glasses, my watch, my driver's license, passports, marriage certificate, birth certificates, the whole works. What would you like to see?"

"Passports would be fine."

He takes the key from its secret place, opens the filing cabinet, and produces the passports.

The officer takes the passports to the living room.

"Is this you?" he asks.

She looks closely. "Yes."

"Is this your husband?"

She looks closely again, hesitates, and eventually answers, "Yes."

"Good," her husband says. "Now can we finally get to bed and let these people go back to their work?"

"I'm sorry," she says, tears forming in her eyes.

He leans over to kiss her and she clings to him.

He returns from his daily five-kilometer walk, sweating slightly, and takes off his shoes.

She comes into the hallway. "Did she leave?"

"Did who leave?" he asks.

"That woman. That fat, ugly woman."

"There was no one in the house today other than you and I."

"There was a woman. She was here this morning."

"No woman. No one. No one has been here. Just you and I."

"She came in while you were out for your walk. She said she was the cleaning woman. She said you hired her. You asked her to come. She had the key."

"No. No cleaning woman. No one was in the house."

"I told her to leave. She went upstairs. My pearls are missing. I can't find them anywhere. She went into the kitchen and made a sandwich and a cup of tea. I told her to get out. I told her I would call the police."

"I think it was a dream."

"No. She was here. She was impertinent. Where are my pearls? I think she took one of my handbags."

"I'll look for your pearls and your handbag," he says. He has been through this little scenario before in a number of variations.

"She took them! That bitch!"

"Don't worry. I'll find them. I'll get them back."

"You can't go out like that and leave me alone."

"I was gone less than an hour and you were lying down when I went out."

"You can't leave me alone."

A search turns up the missing handbag. The pearls are inside, wrapped in Kleenex.

*

"Are we in Madrid?"

It is four thirteen in the morning, according to his bedside clock.

"No. This is Calgary. In Canada."

"Why are my paintings on the wall? This is Madrid. I bought these paintings in Madrid."

"This is Calgary. Those are prints you and I bought at the Prado. We had them framed and brought them to Canada."

"I bought this furniture in Madrid."

"No. We bought it at Thomasville when we came to Calgary in 1996."

"I bought this chandelier on the Gran Via. It was a good price."

In fact, he had bought it at an antique auction in Winnipeg in 1968.

"Okay. Go to sleep now."

"This is my mirror. These are my paintings. This is my chandelier. This is my chair. This is my lamp. I bought them in Madrid."

"Okay. Let's go to sleep." It is all nonsense, of course. She often inventories the furniture, the china, the silver, and other household items, claiming that they are hers and stating that she bought them in Madrid. Most of it they bought in Canada, but he wants to go to sleep.

"I need to go to my sister's house in the morning. You can drive me, can't you?"

"No. I can't. Sorry. Tere lives in Madrid. We live in Calgary."

"I'll take a taxi. You have to give me the money. I don't have any money."

"You can't take a taxi to Madrid. It's thousands of miles away and across the ocean."

"Where are we now?"

"In Calgary. In Canada."

"Why are we here?"

"We live here."

"Why?"

"Because I came here for a job."

"Are we going to stay here?"

"Yes."

"For how long?"

"For the rest."

"Why don't we go to Madrid?"

"We have a house here. We don't have a house in Madrid. We would have to sell our house here and all our furniture and buy a house and furniture in Madrid. It would cost us a fortune."

"We could live with my parents. They have a big house on Claudio Coello in the Barrio de Salamanca."

"Your parents died many years ago. They left the house on Claudio Coello in 1959, soon after we were married. Go back to sleep."

She remains sitting up for a long time staring into the shadows at the wall hangings and the chandelier.

It is five o'clock in the evening. She is watching TV in the family room.

"Here are your pills for your heart and your blood. And here is a glass of water."

"I've already taken them," she says.

"No. Not these ones. You have to take them at five o'clock."

"Who says so? You are not my doctor."

"All your doctors say that you have to take them."

"I've taken enough pills today. I'm not going to take any more."

"Sorry. You have to."

She takes them reluctantly.

Later she goes to open the front door and looks out for a few minutes, leaning on her cane, then comes to the kitchen, where he is preparing the evening meal.

"Is my father coming for dinner?"

"No."

"Why not?"

"Because your father died many years ago."

"What? My father was here this morning. What are you talking about? You fool!"

"Sorry. Your father died."

"He died? My father died?" She breaks into tears. "Why didn't anyone tell me? I loved him. He was such a wonderful man. So clever. So educated. He had a doctorate. He taught at the university."

He feels humbled and honored. He knows she is talking of him. Her father had never gone to university. He holds her gently.

"Where is my mother?"

"Your mother died a long time ago."

"You mean both my parents are dead?"

"Yes. I'm sorry."

"Then who are you?"

"I'm your husband."

"My husband? I never had a husband! I was never married. Who are you? What are you doing in my house?"

"Like it or not, I've been your husband and you've been my wife for more than fifty years."

"You fool! I've never been married. Never."

"Come to bed," she calls from upstairs.

"No. It's too early for me. It's only twenty past seven. Go to sleep. I'll catch up with you later."

Zzzzz. She comes down on the chair lift.

"Come up to bed. I don't like to be alone."

"It's too early. Then you'll wake me up at four thirty in the morning and ask all kinds of questions."

"Come up. I've made the bed. You can sleep with me in the big bed."

"I sleep with you in that bed every night. We've slept together in the same bed for more than fifty years."

"Really? In the same bed? That's not possible."

"Yes it is. We've been married for more than fifty years, and other than a few business trips and visits to your family, we've slept together every night."

"Are you my husband?" She sits beside him.

"I certainly am. Are you my wife?" He asks playfully.

"I don't know. Are we married?" She folds her hands around his arm and smiles.

"Yes, we are. For a long time."

"Do we have children?"

"Yes. Six."

"I don't remember. Tell me." She puts her head on his shoulder and closes her eyes.

He rhymes off the names, cities of residence, spouses, and grandchildren's names.

"Yes. Now I remember."

They go up to bed. He gives her her nighttime pills.

At 3:30 A.M. he hears her get up to go to the toilet. She comes back in the semidarkness and runs her hand across his face.

"Are you my father?" she asks.

"No. Your husband."

"Are you sure?"

"Quite sure. Come back to bed."

"I thought you were my father."

"You don't sleep with your father. You sleep with your husband. Come back to bed."

She crawls into the bed and clings to him. "I'm losing my memory."

"I know. That's all right."

"Don't leave me. Don't ever leave me."

"I won't."

"Promise?"

"Promise. Now go to sleep."

She pulls as close as she can and kisses him.

He is in the home office, his den, when she comes in from the family room.

"What are you doing here?" she asks.

"Checking a few things on the Net."

"This is my father's office. You have no right to be here."

"This is my office."

"You liar! This is my father's TV."

"This is not a TV. This is a computer screen."

"My father bought this."

"Computers like this didn't exist when your father died."

"I bought this table for my father." She is talking loudly and aggressively.

"You and I bought this table in Madrid fifteen years after your father died, and we brought it to Canada," he says.

"I bought this chair for my father."

"You bought this chair for me, for Christmas, two years ago."

"These are my paintings. I bought them in Madrid," she insists.

"Your sister bought them for us as a gift when we were in Madrid in 1971."

"This is my bookcase. I bought it for my father."

"We bought it at an auction in Winnipeg, long after your father died."

"You liar! This is my cabinet."

"This was our daughter's cabinet. She left it with us when she moved to Ontario."

"You lie! You lie! Why are you wearing my father's slippers? That is my father's shirt! I bought it for him. You have no right to wear it. What do you think you are doing here? Get out of my house!"

She storms out of the room and returns quickly holding a framed photo of him sitting beside Mother Teresa. "This is my father!" she proclaims triumphantly.

"That's a photo of me. Your father was never in Calcutta. He never met Mother Teresa."

"You're a liar!"

He remains silent as she continues the outburst. Eventually she goes to the family room to pick up the phone. She forgets what she was going to do or say, puts down the phone, and turns on the TV.

They lay in bed for an afternoon nap.

"My hands are very cold," she says.

"It's the medication. Bring them here. Put them under my shirt. Under my arms."

He unbuttons his shirt and brings her hands in. Her fingers are yellow and her hands are like ice. It takes a few minutes before they come back to normal.

She has congestive heart failure and takes a large number of medications to control it.

"Don't ever leave me," she says.

"I won't."

"Did we ever marry?"

"More than fifty years ago."

"I don't remember. Do we have children?"

"Yes. Six."

"Tell me their names."

He rhymes off their names, their spouses, their cities of residence, the names of the grandchildren.

*

He prepares a coffee for her in the morning and sets out her medication.

"Where is my father? Did he go to open the store?"

"Your father died forty-five years ago. He sold the store before he died. There is no store."

"He died?"

"Yes. You remember the growth he had on his neck? It was cancerous."

"My poor father! I loved him. He was a beautiful man. Very educated. He was the president of a university. He was very intelligent."

He feels humbled.

"Is my mother coming?"

"No. Your mother died in 1986. In La Granja. Heart."

"Oh, yes. I remember. She had a bad heart. Then I am an orphan."

"Yes. Sorry about that. So am I."

"Your father and mother died?"

"Yes."

"Were they very old?"

"Ninety-four and ninety-three."

"Where is my husband?"

"I am your husband. Here, give me a kiss."

"You are not my husband. I never had a husband."

"Yes, I am." He taps his cheek and leans toward her.

She kisses his cheek and they both smile.

ALAN LIGHTMAN

The Accidental Universe

FROM *Harper's Magazine*

IN THE FIFTH CENTURY B.C.E., the philosopher Democritus proposed that all matter was made of tiny and indivisible atoms, which came in various sizes and textures—some hard and some soft, some smooth and some thorny. The atoms themselves were taken as givens. In the nineteenth century, scientists discovered that the chemical properties of atoms repeat periodically (and created the periodic table to reflect this fact), but the origins of such patterns remained mysterious. It wasn't until the twentieth century that scientists learned that the properties of an atom are determined by the number and placement of its electrons, the subatomic particles that orbit its nucleus. And we now know that all atoms heavier than helium were created in the nuclear furnaces of stars.

The history of science can be viewed as the recasting of phenomena that were once thought to be accidents as phenomena that can be understood in terms of fundamental causes and principles. One can add to the list of the fully explained: the hue of the sky, the orbits of planets, the angle of the wake of a boat moving through a lake, the six-sided patterns of snowflakes, the weight of a flying bustard, the temperature of boiling water, the size of raindrops, the circular shape of the sun. All these phenomena and many more, once thought to have been fixed at the beginning of time or to be the result of random events thereafter, have been explained as *necessary* consequences of the fundamental laws of nature—laws discovered by human beings.

This long and appealing trend may be coming to an end. Dramatic developments in cosmological findings and thought have led some of the world's premier physicists to propose that our universe is only one of an enormous number of universes with wildly varying properties, and that some of the most basic features of our particular universe are indeed mere *accidents*—a random throw of the cosmic dice. In which case, there is no hope of ever explaining our universe's features in terms of fundamental causes and principles.

It is perhaps impossible to say how far apart the different universes may be, or whether they exist simultaneously in time. Some may have stars and galaxies like ours. Some may not. Some may be finite in size. Some may be infinite. Physicists call the totality of universes the "multiverse." Alan Guth, a pioneer in cosmological thought, says that "the multiple-universe idea severely limits our hopes to understand the world from fundamental principles." And the philosophical ethos of science is torn from its roots. As put to me recently by Nobel Prize–winning physicist Steven Weinberg, a man as careful in his words as in his mathematical calculations, "We now find ourselves at a historic fork in the road we travel to understand the laws of nature. If the multiverse idea is correct, the style of fundamental physics will be radically changed."

The scientists most distressed by Weinberg's "fork in the road" are theoretical physicists. Theoretical physics is the deepest and purest branch of science. It is the outpost of science closest to philosophy, and religion. Experimental scientists occupy themselves with observing and measuring the cosmos, finding out what stuff exists, no matter how strange that stuff may be. Theoretical physicists, on the other hand, are not satisfied with observing the universe. They want to know *why*. They want to explain all the properties of the universe in terms of a few fundamental principles and parameters. These fundamental principles, in turn, lead to the "laws of nature," which govern the behavior of all matter and energy. An example of a fundamental principle in physics, first proposed by Galileo in 1632 and extended by Einstein in 1905, is the following: all observers traveling at constant velocity relative to one another should witness identical laws of nature. From this principle, Einstein derived his theory of special relativity. An example of a fundamental parameter is the mass of an electron, considered one of the two dozen or so "elementary" particles of nature. As far as physicists are concerned, the fewer the fundamental principles and parameters, the better. The underlying hope and belief of this enterprise has always been that these basic principles are so restrictive that only one, self-consistent universe is possible, like a crossword puzzle with only one solution. That one universe would be, of course, the universe we live in. Theoretical physicists are Platonists. Until the past few years, they agreed that the entire universe, the one universe, is generated from a few mathematical truths and principles of symmetry, perhaps throwing in a handful of parameters like the mass of the electron. It seemed that we were closing in on a vision of our universe in which everything could be calculated, predicted, and understood.

However, two theories in physics, eternal inflation and string theory, now suggest that the *same* fundamental principles from which the laws of nature derive may lead to many *different* self-consistent universes, with many different properties. It is as if you walked into a shoe store, had your feet measured, and found that a size 5 would fit you, a size 8 would also fit, and a size 12 would fit equally well. Such wishy-washy results make theoretical physicists extremely unhappy. Evidently, the fundamental laws of nature do not pin down a single and unique universe. According to the current thinking of many physicists, we are living in one of a vast number of universes. We are living in an accidental universe. We are living in a universe incalculable by science.

"Back in the 1970s and 1980s," says Alan Guth, "the feeling was that we were so smart, we almost had everything figured out." What physicists had figured out were very accurate theories of three of the four fundamental forces of nature: the strong nuclear force that binds atomic nuclei together, the weak force that is responsible for some forms of radioactive decay, and the electromagnetic force between electrically charged particles. And there were prospects for merging the theory known as quantum physics with Einstein's theory of the fourth force, gravity, and thus pulling all of them into the fold of what physicists called the theory of everything, or the final theory. These theories of the 1970s and 1980s required the specification of a couple dozen parameters corresponding to the masses of the elementary particles, and another half dozen or so parameters corresponding to the strengths of the fundamental forces. The next step would then have been to derive most of the elementary particle masses in terms of one or two fundamental masses and define the strengths of all the fundamental forces in terms of a single fundamental force.

There were good reasons to think that physicists were poised to take this next step. Indeed, since the time of Galileo, physics has been extremely successful in discovering principles and laws that have fewer and fewer free parameters and that are also in close agreement with the observed facts of the world. For example, the observed rotation of the ellipse of the orbit of Mercury, 0.012 degrees per century, was successfully calculated using the theory of general relativity, and the observed magnetic strength of an electron, 2.002319 magnetons, was derived using the theory of quantum electrodynamics. More than any other science, physics brims with highly accurate agreements between theory and experiment.

Guth started his physics career in this sunny scientific world. Now sixty-four years old and a professor at MIT, he was in his early thirties when he proposed a major revision to the Big Bang theory, something called inflation. We now have a great deal of evidence suggesting that our universe began as a nugget of extremely high density and temperature about fourteen billion years ago and has been expanding, thinning out, and cooling ever since. The theory of inflation proposes that when our universe was only about a trillionth of a trillionth of a trillionth of a second old, a peculiar type of energy caused the cosmos to expand very rapidly. A tiny fraction of a second later, the universe returned to the more leisurely rate of expansion of the standard Big Bang model. Inflation solved a number of outstanding problems in cosmology, such as why the universe appears so homogeneous on large scales.

When I visited Guth in his third-floor office at MIT one cool day in May, I could barely see him above the stacks of paper and empty Diet Coke bottles on his desk. More piles of paper and dozens of magazines littered the floor. In fact, a few years ago Guth won a contest sponsored by the *Boston Globe* for the messiest office in the city. The prize was the services of a professional organizer for one day. "She was actually more a nuisance than a help. She took piles of envelopes from the floor and began sorting them according to size." He wears aviator-style eyeglasses, keeps his hair long, and chain-drinks Diet Cokes. "The reason I went into theoretical physics," Guth tells me, "is that I liked the idea that we could understand everything—i.e., the universe—in terms of mathematics and logic." He gives a bitter laugh. We have been talking about the multiverse.

While challenging the Platonic dream of theoretical physicists, the multiverse idea does explain one aspect of our universe that has unsettled some scientists for years: according to various calculations, if the values of some of the fundamental parameters of our universe were a little larger or a little smaller, life could not have arisen. For example, if the nuclear force were a few percentage points stronger than it actually is, then all the hydrogen atoms in the infant universe would have fused with other hydrogen atoms to make helium, and there would be no hydrogen left. No hydrogen means no water. Although we are far from certain about what conditions are necessary for life, most biologists believe that water is necessary. On the other hand, if the nuclear force were substantially weaker than what it actually is, then the complex atoms needed for biology could not hold together. As another example, if the relationship between the strengths of the gravitational force and the electromagnetic force were not close to what it is, then the cosmos would not harbor any stars that explode and spew out life-supporting chemical elements into space or any other stars that form planets. Both kinds of stars are required for the emergence of life. The strengths of the basic forces and certain other fundamental parameters in our universe appear to be "fine-tuned" to allow the existence of life. The recognition of this fine-tuning led the British physicist Brandon Carter to articulate what he called the anthropic principle, which states that the universe must have the parameters it does because we are here to observe it. Actually, the word *anthropic,* from the Greek for "man," is a misnomer: if these fundamental parameters were much different from what they are, it is not only human beings who would not exist. No life of any kind would exist.

If such conclusions are correct, the great question, of course, is *why* these fundamental parameters happen to lie within the range needed for life. Does the universe care about life? Intelligent design is one answer. Indeed, a fair number of theologians, philosophers, and even some scientists have used fine-tuning and the anthropic principle as evidence of the existence of God. For example, at the 2011 Christian Scholars' Conference at Pepperdine University, Francis Collins, a leading geneticist and director of the National Institutes of Health, said, "To get our universe, with all of its potential for complexities or any kind of potential for any kind of life-form, everything has to be precisely defined on this knife edge of improbability . . . You have to see the hands of a creator who set the parameters to be just so because the creator was interested in something a little more complicated than random particles."

Intelligent design, however, is an answer to fine-tuning that does not appeal to most scientists. The multiverse offers another explanation. If there are countless different universes with different properties—for example, some with nuclear forces much stronger than in our universe and some with nuclear forces much weaker—then some of those universes will allow the emergence of life and some will not. Some of those universes will be dead, lifeless hulks of matter and energy, and others will permit the emergence of cells, plants and animals, minds. From the huge range of possible universes predicted by the theories, the fraction of universes with life is undoubtedly small. But that doesn't matter. We live in one of the universes that permits life because otherwise we wouldn't be here to ask the question.

The explanation is similar to the explanation of why we happen to live on a planet that has so many nice things for our comfortable existence: oxygen, water, a temperature between the freezing and boiling points of water, and so on. Is this happy coincidence just good luck, or an act of Providence, or what? No, it is simply that we could not live on planets without such properties. Many other planets exist that are not so hospitable to life, such as Uranus, where the temperature is −371 degrees Fahrenheit, and Venus, where it rains sulfuric acid.

The multiverse offers an explanation to the fine-tuning conundrum that does not require the presence of a Designer. As Steven Weinberg says: "Over many centuries science has weakened the hold of religion, not by disproving the existence of God but by invalidating arguments for God based on what we observe in the natural world. The multiverse idea offers an explanation of why we find ourselves in a universe favorable to life that does not rely on the benevolence of a creator, and so if correct will leave still less support for religion."

Some physicists remain skeptical of the anthropic principle

and the reliance on multiple universes to explain the values of the fundamental parameters of physics. Others, such as Weinberg and Guth, have reluctantly accepted the anthropic principle and the multiverse idea as together providing the best possible explanation for the observed facts.

If the multiverse idea is correct, then the historic mission of physics to explain all the properties of our universe in terms of fundamental principles — to explain why the properties of our universe must *necessarily* be what they are — is futile, a beautiful philosophical dream that simply isn't true. Our universe is what it is because we are here. The situation could be likened to a school of intelligent fish who one day began wondering why their world is completely filled with water. Many of the fish, the theorists, hope to prove that the entire cosmos necessarily has to be filled with water. For years, they put their minds to the task but can never quite seem to prove their assertion. Then, a wizened group of fish postulate that maybe they are fooling themselves. Maybe there are, they suggest, many other worlds, some of them completely dry, and everything in between.

The most striking example of fine-tuning, and one that practically demands the multiverse to explain it, is the unexpected detection of what scientists call dark energy. Little more than a decade ago, using robotic telescopes in Arizona, Chile, Hawaii, and outer space that can comb through nearly a million galaxies a night, astronomers discovered that the expansion of the universe is accelerating. As mentioned previously, it has been known since the late 1920s that the universe is expanding; it's a central feature of the Big Bang model. Orthodox cosmological thought held that the expansion is slowing down. After all, gravity is an attractive force; it pulls masses closer together. So it was quite a surprise in 1998 when two teams of astronomers announced that some unknown force appears to be jamming its foot down on the cosmic accelerator. The expansion is speeding up. Galaxies are flying away from each other as if repelled by antigravity. Says Robert Kirshner, one of the team members who made the discovery: "This is not your father's universe." (In October, members of both teams were awarded the Nobel Prize in Physics.)

Physicists have named the energy associated with this cosmological force dark energy. No one knows what it is. Not only invisible, dark energy apparently hides out in empty space. Yet, based on our observations of the accelerating rate of expansion, dark energy constitutes a whopping three-quarters of the total energy of the universe. It is the invisible elephant in the room of science.

The amount of dark energy, or more precisely the amount of dark energy in every cubic centimeter of space, has been calculated to be about one hundred-millionth (10^{-8}) of an erg per cubic centimeter. (For comparison, a penny dropped from waist high hits the floor with an energy of about three hundred thousand—that is, 3×10^5—ergs.) This may not seem like much, but it adds up in the vast volumes of outer space. Astronomers were able to determine this number by measuring the rate of expansion of the universe at different epochs—if the universe is accelerating, then its rate of expansion was slower in the past. From the amount of acceleration, astronomers can calculate the amount of dark energy in the universe.

Theoretical physicists have several hypotheses about the identity of dark energy. It may be the energy of ghostly subatomic particles that can briefly appear out of nothing before self-annihilating and slipping back into the vacuum. According to quantum physics, empty space is a pandemonium of subatomic particles rushing about and then vanishing before they can be seen. Dark energy may also be associated with an as-yet-unobserved force field called the Higgs field, which is sometimes invoked to explain why certain kinds of matter have mass. (Theoretical physicists ponder things that other people do not.) And in the models proposed by string theory, dark energy may be associated with the way in which extra dimensions of space—beyond the usual length, width, and breadth—get compressed down to sizes much smaller than atoms, so that we do not notice them.

These various hypotheses give a fantastically large range for the *theoretically possible* amounts of dark energy in a universe, from something like 10^{115} ergs per cubic centimeter to -10^{115} ergs per cubic centimeter. (A negative value for dark energy would mean that it acts to *decelerate* the universe, in contrast to what is observed.) Thus, in absolute magnitude, the amount of dark energy actually present in our universe is either very, very small or very, very large compared with what it could be. This fact alone is surprising. If the theoretically possible positive values for dark energy were marked out on a ruler stretching from here to the sun, with zero at one end of the ruler and 10^{115} ergs per cubic centimeter at the other end, the value of dark energy actually found in our universe (10^{-8} ergs per cubic centimeter) would be closer to the zero end than the width of an atom.

On one thing most physicists agree: if the amount of dark energy in our universe were only a little bit different than what it actually is, then life could never have emerged. A little more and the universe would accelerate so rapidly that the matter in the young cosmos could never pull itself together to form stars and thence form the complex atoms made in stars. And, going into negative values of dark energy, a little less and the universe would decelerate so rapidly that it would recollapse before there was time to form even the simplest atoms.

Here we have a clear example of fine-tuning: out of all the possible amounts of dark energy that our universe might have, the actual amount lies in the tiny sliver of the range that allows life. There is little argument on this point. It does not depend on assumptions about whether we need liquid water for life or oxygen or particular biochemistries. As before, one is compelled to ask the question: why does such fine-tuning occur? And the answer many physicists now believe: the multiverse. A vast number of universes may exist, with many different values of the amount of dark energy. Our particular universe is one of the universes with a small value, permitting the emergence of life. We are here, so our universe must be such a universe. We are an accident. From the cosmic lottery hat containing zillions of universes, we happened to draw a universe that allowed life. But then again, if we had not drawn such a ticket, we would not be here to ponder the odds.

The concept of the multiverse is compelling not only because it explains the problem of fine-tuning. As I mentioned earlier, the possibility of the multiverse is actually predicted by modern theories of physics. One such theory, called eternal inflation, is a revision of Guth's inflation theory developed by Andrei Linde, Paul Steinhardt, and Alex Vilenkin in the early and mid-1980s. In regular inflation theory, the very rapid expansion of the infant universe is caused by an energy field, like dark energy, that is temporarily trapped in a condition that does not represent the lowest possible energy for the universe as a whole—like a marble sitting in a small dent on a table. The marble can stay there, but if it is jostled it will roll out of the dent, roll across the table, and then fall to the floor (which represents the lowest possible energy level). In the theory of eternal inflation, the dark energy field has many different values at different points of space, analogous to lots of marbles sitting in lots of dents on the cosmic table. Moreover, as space expands rapidly, the number of marbles increases. Each of these marbles is jostled by the random processes inherent in quantum mechanics, and some of the marbles will begin rolling across the table and onto the floor. Each marble starts a new Big Bang, essentially a new universe. Thus, the original, rapidly expanding universe spawns a multitude of new universes, in a never-ending process.

String theory, too, predicts the possibility of the multiverse. Originally conceived in the late 1960s as a theory of the strong nuclear force but soon enlarged far beyond that ambition, string theory postulates that the smallest constituents of matter are not subatomic particles like the electron but extremely tiny one-dimensional "strings" of energy. These elemental strings can vibrate at different frequencies, like the strings of a violin, and the different modes of vibration correspond to different fundamental particles and forces. String theories typically require seven dimensions of space in addition to the usual three, which are compacted down to such small sizes that we never experience them, like a three-dimensional garden hose that appears as a one-dimensional line when seen from a great distance. There are, in fact, a vast number of ways that the extra dimensions in string theory can be folded up, and each of the different ways corresponds to a different universe with different physical properties.

It was originally hoped that from a theory of these strings, with very few additional parameters, physicists would be able to explain all the forces and particles of nature—all of reality would be a manifestation of the vibrations of elemental strings. String theory would then be the ultimate realization of the Platonic ideal of a fully explicable cosmos. In the past few years, however, physicists have discovered that string theory predicts not a unique universe but a huge number of possible universes with different properties. It has been estimated that the "string landscape" contains 10^{500} different possible universes. For all practical purposes, that number is infinite.

It is important to point out that neither eternal inflation nor string theory has anywhere near the experimental support of many previous theories in physics, such as special relativity or quantum electrodynamics, mentioned earlier. Eternal inflation or string theory, or both, could turn out to be wrong. However, some of the world's leading physicists have devoted their careers to the study of these two theories.

Back to the intelligent fish. The wizened old fish conjecture that there are many other worlds, some with dry land and some with water. Some of the fish grudgingly accept this explanation. Some feel relieved. Some feel like their lifelong ruminations have been pointless. And some remain deeply concerned. Because there is no way they can prove this conjecture. That same uncertainty disturbs many physicists who are adjusting to the idea of the multiverse. Not only must we accept that basic properties of our universe are accidental and incalculable. In addition, we must believe in the existence of many other universes. But we have no conceivable way of observing these other universes and cannot prove their existence. Thus, to explain what we see in the world and in our mental deductions, we must believe in what we cannot prove.

Sound familiar? Theologians are accustomed to taking some beliefs on faith. Scientists are not. All we can do is hope that the same theories that predict the multiverse also produce many other predictions that we can test here in our own universe. But the other universes themselves will almost certainly remain a conjecture.

"We had a lot more confidence in our intuition before the discovery of dark energy and the multiverse idea," says Guth. "There will still be a lot for us to understand, but we will miss out on the fun of figuring everything out from first principles."

One wonders whether a young Alan Guth, considering a career in science today, would choose theoretical physics.

SANDRA TSING LOH

The Bitch Is Back

FROM *The Atlantic*

DURING MENOPAUSE, A woman can feel like the only way she can continue to exist for ten more seconds inside her crawling, burning skin is to walk screaming into the sea—grandly, epically, and terrifyingly, like a fifteen-foot-tall Greek tragic figure wearing a giant, pop-eyed wooden mask. Or she may remain in the kitchen and begin hurling objects at her family: telephones, coffee cups, plates. Or, as my mother did in the 1970s, she may just eerily disappear into her bedroom, like a tide washing out—curtains drawn, door locked, dead to the world, for days, weeks, months (some moms went silent for years). Oh, for a tribal cauldron to dive into, a harvest moon to howl at, or even an online service that provides—here's an idea!—demon gypsy lovers.

But no, this is twenty-first-century America, so there is no ancient womyn's magic for us but rather, as usual for female passages, a stack of medically themed self-help books. (I ask you: Where are the vampire novels for perimenopausal women? Werewolf tales? Pirate movies?) That's right—to fully get our crone on, we're supposed to *read*, even though it may feel, what with the giant Greek chthonic headpiece, that one can barely see out the eyeholes. (Who can focus on words on a page? Who can even remember where she left her giant octagonal Medea-size reading glasses?) Rest assured, though: I'm here to help. Gentle reader, if you are a female of transitional age, which can apparently be anywhere from thirty-five to sixty-five these days, let me be your Virgil to the literature of menopause. Long have I wandered through the dry riverbeds, long have I suffered; now I've come back to share my wisdom.

To set the stage, here is a selection of titles from my local bookstore's women's section: *Could It Be . . . Perimenopause?; Before Your Time: The Early Menopause Survival Guide; The Natural Menopause Plan; Second Spring; Menopause Reset!: Reverse Weight Gain, Speed Fat Loss, and Get Your Body Back in 3 Simple Steps;* and the slightly ominously titled *What Nurses Know . . . Menopause* (two words: *atrophic vaginitis*). On the cover of a typical menopause book, instead of the perhaps more-to-the-point fanged woman with the Medusa do, one is far more likely to see a lone flower—a poppy, perhaps a daisy. Curious choice? Well, no, because as one begins to read the war stories of the MD, PhD, and RN (atrophic vaginitis!) authors who dominate this genre, one sees narratives that are indeed Stuart Smalley–esque. Here's a pastiche:

> Mary Anne, age forty-eight, came into my office feeling overweight and bloated. She hadn't been sleeping, work was stressful, her husband had just gone on disability, and he required daily care. Mary Anne complained to me of lower-back problems and gastritis, and also cramping during sex, which had become more and more infrequent. She was extremely depressed about moving her eighty-four-year-old mother to a nursing home, and upon examination I noticed vaginal inflammation.

As unappetizing as that just was to read, be glad you saw only one such passage—I must have read a hundred. Because clearly, from the medical-professional point of view, menopause, or really the run-up to it called perimenopause, is a parade of baleful, bloated middle-aged women ("Lisa, fifty-two," "Carolyn, forty-seven," "Suzanne, sixty-one") trudging into their doctors' offices complaining of lower-back pain and family caregiving issues and diminished libidos and personal dryness and corns. As they sit wanly on the tables in their paper gowns, they arduously count out their irregular periods—from thirty-five days to forty-four days to fifty-seven, going heavy to light, light to heavy, sometimes with spotting, sometimes with flooding, sometimes flood-spotting, sometimes spot-flooding. Why this variation? So easy to understand, really. The simple science: ovarian production of the estrogens and progesterone becomes erratic during perimenopause, with unpredictable fluctuations in levels, which in turn can result in many different symptoms, including major mood swings. But sometimes not. You may never feel any of this! Because here's the key: *all women are different.*

And yet, even though we all are different, the list of prescriptions for us seems to be very much the same, and none of it's fun. If one *must* tinker with hormone replacement therapy, one may—briefly, in moderation. But from this point on, the Change is about a healthy lifestyle. We're all to get more exercise, drink more water, do yoga stretches before bed, cut out alcohol and caffeine, and yet (and how does this follow?) reduce stress. Even the flirty exhortations to have more sex feel like yet another job on life's chore wheel (given that it's supposed to be with your mate of twenty years rather than with Johnny Depp). And don't forget all the deep sensory pleasures of a reduced-calorie diet. *Menopause Reset!* at least initially seemed to promise a nutritional miracle cure for that mysterious spare beach floaty that arrives after forty. I for one was excited to see that, instead of *Black Swan*-ing it until dinner, as apparently so many of us women do (in order to heap our measly fifteen hundred calories together into one meal a person might actually want to eat), you're supposed to eat many tiny meals constantly. Hurray! But alas, after reading much dietary advice for menopausal women, I concluded that, in the horrible new metrics of midlife, each of the following constitutes a *meal:*

Meal No. 1 (8:00 A.M.)
2 tsp. nonfat yogurt

Meal No. 2 (10:00 A.M.)
3 almonds (unsalted)

Meal No. 3 (12:00 P.M.)
2 oz. low-fat barley soufflé (see Appendix D)

Meal No. 4 (2:00 P.M.)
small bell pepper
1 tsp. flaxseed

Just staying *awake* all day to *eat* the food—while of course getting in those fifteen reps an hour of sex with your fiftysomething husband—seems a challenge. No wine, though: best to pair vaginal dryness with buckwheat tempeh. Oh! Oh! Oh! Where is the plate-glass window to hurl the phone through? Why is life worth living? Ouch, my corns!

So that's the basic physiological landscape of menopause. Dry as the riverbeds can seem, though, one menopause book does rise like Mount Etna above the rest. Now celebrating its tenth anniversary, it is the bible of middle-aged womanhood: *The Wisdom of Menopause,* by Christiane Northrup, MD. Having recently spent (twenty? fifty? eighty?) hours with it, I've come to believe that *The Wisdom of Menopause* is a masterwork. Weighing in at two pounds and 656 pages, it is an astonishingly complete, mind-bogglingly detailed orrery of the achingly complex, wheels-and-dials-filled Ptolemaic universe that is Womanhood. Featuring, arch-conventionally, its smiling doctor/author on a soothing pastel cover, the book is very much of the genre, and yet explodes it. Northrup presents both a celebration of Western medical practice and a revolt against it. Three times as big as the others, *Wisdom* is no less than the Jupiter in the menopause-book solar system, our *Gravity's Rainbow.*

Let me now gloriously unbutton my too-tight mom jeans, wave my Hadassah arms (even more hideous term heard recently—*bat wings*), and wax on. Are you grasping, yet, the scope of this thing? *Wisdom* is a Homeric poem of modern femalehood. No stone from Western or Eastern (or Southern or Northern) medicine is left unturned, from folic acid to breast exams to personal dancing to selenium to feng shui to cosmetic surgery (Northrup allows it, while counseling discretion as a protection against judgmental friends). Woo-woo passages on Motherpeace Tarot cards and the chakra work of the astrologer Barbara Hand Clow alternate with biological analyses of an almost kidney-squeezing complexity. Which is not to say there isn't tons of news you can use:

> I highly recommend a snack at around four in the afternoon, right during the time when blood sugar, mood, and serotonin tend to plummet.

This totally hit home. Although the Hour of the Wolf is typically considered four o'clock in the morning, for many mothers of school-age children, how many of our inner wolves appear at afternoon carpool time?

Even Suze Orman makes a guest appearance, in a TV green-room (the place where all modern witches gather):

> She told me that you can see people's ill health in their money and cash flow first because money has nowhere to hide an energy imbalance. You either have positive cash flow or you have debt. Simple. Sooner or later, if the behavior patterns and beliefs that create money problems are not addressed, they will manifest as health problems in the body.

I couldn't help gasping in recognition again and penciling in the margin, like Woody Allen's "Whore of Mensa," "Yes, very true." You see? *Wisdom* is of such a multitasking, infinitely varied scope that I think few men could tolerate it, or even maintain consciousness through it. But they remain ignorant at their peril!

All of that said, even under my inspiring leadership, it is unlikely the targeted demographic of women will ever engage in Bloomsday-like readings of *Wisdom,* as is done with Joyce's *Ulysses.* (Groused a girlfriend to whom I was manically recommending it: "Why should I bother? Every day of menopause *already* feels like you're reading a six-hundred-page book.") So, for the bloated and tired, let me give you the CliffsNotes.

Today women between the ages of forty-four and sixty-five are the largest demographic group. So it's no surprise that Northrup considers menopause a major cultural event. Without going into the sometimes arduous detail other feminist texts do (the rising or falling number of women in government, the social architecture of food-sharing collectives), Northrup suggests this gigantic demographic transition will change society—somehow—for the better. All well and good, no arguments there, but now here comes the juicy core of *Wisdom:*

> A woman once told me that when her mother was approaching the age of menopause, her father sat the whole family down and said, "Kids, your mother may be going through some changes now, and I want you to be prepared. Your Uncle Ralph told me that when your Aunt Carol went through the change, she threw a leg of lamb right out the window!" Although this story fits beautifully into the stereotype of the "crazy" menopausal woman, it should not be overlooked that throwing the leg of lamb out the window may have been Aunt Carol's outward expression of the process going on within her soul: the reclaiming of self. Perhaps it was her way of saying how tired she

was of waiting on her family, of signaling to them that she was past the cook/chauffeur/dishwasher stage of life. For many women, if not most, part of this reclamation process includes getting in touch with anger and, perhaps, blowing up at loved ones for the first time.

Woo-woo! Duck, Uncle Ralph! Go, Aunt Carol!

In short, never mind the wavy-graph technicalities of all those estrogen/progesterone/FSH fluctuations. Opines the doctor:

> I think it's useful to get your hormone levels tested. But it's far more useful to tune in to how you're feeling than to focus on a lab test, which gives, after all, just a single snapshot of an ever-changing process.

What the phrase *wisdom of menopause* stands for, in the end, is that, as the female body's egg-producing abilities and levels of estrogen and other reproductive hormones begin to wane, so does the hormonal cloud of our nurturing instincts. During this huge biological shift, our brain, temperament, and behaviors will begin to change—as then must, alarmingly, our relationships. As one Northrup chapter title tells it, "Menopause Puts Your Life Under a Microscope," and the message, painful as it is, is: "Grow . . . or die."

It's intriguing to ponder this suggested reversal of what has traditionally been thought to be the woman's hormonal cloud. A sudden influx of hormones is not what causes fifty-year-old Aunt Carol to throw the leg of lamb out the window. Improperly balanced hormones were probably the culprit. Fertility's amped-up reproductive hormones helped Aunt Carol thirty years ago to begin her mysterious automatic weekly ritual of roasting lamb just so and laying out twelve settings of silverware with an OCD-like attention to detail while cheerfully washing and folding and ironing the family laundry. No normal person would do that—look at the rest of the family: they are reading the paper and lazing about like rational, sensible people. And now that Aunt Carol's hormonal cloud is finally wearing off, it's not a tragedy, or an abnormality, or her going crazy—it just means she can rejoin the rest of the human race: she can be the same selfish, nonnurturing, nonbonding type of person everyone else is. (And so what if get-well casseroles won't get baked, PTAs will collapse, and in-laws will go for decades without being sent a single greeting card? Paging Aunt Carol! The *old* Aunt Carol!)

One could further argue that all of these menopausal women, in fact, represent a major evolutionary shift. Owing to women's greatly lengthened life span (from about forty in 1900 to eighty in 2000 in the U.S.), even the notion of what a woman's so-called normal state is can be questioned: Northrup notes that before this time in history, most women never reached menopause — they died before it could arrive. If, in an eighty-year life span, a female is fertile for about twenty-five years (let's call it ages fifteen to forty), it is not menopause that triggers the mind-altering and hormone-altering variation; the hormonal "disturbance" is actually *fertility*. Fertility is the Change. It is during fertility that a female loses herself and enters that cloud overly rich in estrogen. And of course, simply chronologically speaking, over the whole span of her life, the self-abnegation that fertility induces is not the norm — the more standard state of selfishness is.

Which is to say, if it comes at the right time, menopause *is* wisdom. For Northrup — whose own passage through menopause included a traumatic divorce, a narrative she relates with regret, but little apology — this seemed to be so. Menopause's liberating narrative dovetails elegantly with a typical baby boomer female's biological and chronological clock. When a woman gets married in her twenties, has children in her late twenties or early thirties, and begins to detach in her forties, look where her nuclear family is by the time she reaches her menopausal wanderlust-filled fifties: her grown-up (say eighteen-year-old) children are leaving the nest; her perhaps slightly older (say sixtyish) husband is transitioning into gardening and fishing; her aged parents have conveniently died (let's say back — and wouldn't it be lovely? — when they slipped and injured a hip at, oh, seventy-eight).

Compare that timeline, however, with the clock of my own generation of late-boomer/Gen X women. Putting our careers and our Selves first, we adventured and traveled in our twenties, settled down and got married in our thirties, got pregnant (or tried to — fertility problems being the first surprising biological wall we hit) in our late thirties or even early forties . . . and now what scenario will we face when we hit menopause?

In my case, when it arrived at forty-nine, perimenopause was terrifying, and like nothing I had ever before physically experienced. It was not just the hot flashes; it was the mood swings, although the phrase *mood swings* sounds far too cartoonlike and teen-girlish. I would describe it as the sudden onset of a crippling, unreasoning gloom. It is like resting one's hand on the familiar wall of one's day—helping kids with homework, some grocery shopping, hurtling along on a favorite freeway, listening to Miles Davis—and then feeling the hand suddenly push through the wall, through foam spongy as the flesh of a drowned corpse, into . . . nothingness.

You experience anxiety at the notion of being face-to-face with your loved ones, because they will immediately read from your dull eyes that which you can no longer hide—that you don't love them, never will again. (And note that I had already divorced my husband of several decades and had run off with my demon gypsy lover . . . Now I felt repulsion upon hearing the squeaky wheels of the recycling bin he was dutifully rolling out to the curb.) At one time, the sweet smell of your baby's head was your whole world; now you can feel the clanging chime of her ten-year-old voice, note by note, draining your will to live. Where once you coordinated seventy volunteers and thousands of dollars of fundraising with four- and fivefold Excel spreadsheets at your kids' school, now the mere thought of trying to figure out how to pay the United Visa bill online makes you so depressed, you can't get out of bed. Your chemistry has changed—*and that is no small thing.*

Even more unsettling is how, at night, the depression and anxiety are so much stranger and more intense than the minor quotidian irritants that seem to be tipping you off into hopelessness (the overflowing laundry basket, the $530 car repair bill, the fact that the scale says you're up—what is it?—eight pounds). The other night, I was awake at 3:24 A.M. as usual (melatonin, Tylenol PM, Ambien, forget it—I could take them all at once, paired with a bottle of wine, and still drive an eighteen-wheeler). As I lay in the darkness, all at once, the name *Brian Hong* surfaced in my consciousness, and I experienced not a passing wave of despair, but despair simply moving in as a cold, straight tide.

I have no idea who Brian Hong is—I was filled with gloom simply because of the name. Perhaps there is, in fact, a lone forgotten yellow Post-it, somewhere on my rolltop desk with its gas bills and Discover-card solicitations and Blue Cross health insurance forms, that reads BRIAN HONG. Perhaps Brian Hong is the head of a small Asian nonprofit who several months ago earnestly if a bit keeningly e-mailed me, citing as a referral the name of a mutual friend, to ask if I would drive an hour down to San Pedro to give a free speech at a fundraising benefit for a flailing youth center for depressed gay minority teens at 10:00 A.M. three months from now on a cloudy Wednesday.

On the one hand, as a longtime veteran of the nonprofit world, I can no longer afford to humor the endless requests to do everything for free, particularly because no one treats you worse than the penniless. On the other hand, though, for me to categorically say no seems like a kick in the teeth to all the kids in the world who are already down; the result of this discomfiting indecision being that I NEVER REPLIED TO BRIAN HONG AT ALL, and so now, like that forgotten spongy corpse, he has come after me in the middle of the night to gently (because that is Brian Hong's passive-aggressive way) but persistently (because that is also Brian Hong's passive-aggressive way) haunt me. Brian Hong! Brian Hong! Brian Hong!

And of course, you can only expect it to get worse. I am a member of the "sandwich" generation, that group that must simultaneously care for elderly parents and support children. Never mind that I have lost the dreamlike fortyish haze I was in during nursing and babyhood and toddlerhood, when the peach fuzz of my daughters' cheeks made for a heady narcotic, when my heart thrilled at all their colorful pieces of kinderart, when I honestly enjoyed—oh the novelty, for someone who had pursued abstract subjects in college and graduate school for ten years!—baking birthday cakes. Fiftyish now, when I squat over to pick up their little socks and snip quesadillas into little bowls and yank fine hair out of their brushes, as I have now for the thousandth time, I feel like I'm in a dream, but a very bad, very sour-scented dream. I am fast losing patience with the day job of motherhood. Worse yet, I'll be in the full fires of menopause just when my girls are in the full fires of adolescence! (As my good friend, the family therapist Wendy Mogel, observes, in her calm Zen/Torah–like way, "What wonderful insight you'll have into their mood swings.")

Meanwhile, my Shanghai-born father is ninety years old, has Parkinson's, and is in a wheelchair . . . But that doesn't mean, with his eerily Jack LaLanne–like resting pulse of thirty-eight, he isn't frighteningly willful and able. Every day, my dad wheels himself down to the bus, shouting at his Malibu neighbors and at passing Mexican day laborers to help him; three hours later (via a trip that involves several bus transfers and all the shouting for help that comes with), he arrives at the UCLA campus, where he crashes chemistry and neurobiology lectures, wheeling himself to the front row, asking loud questions, disrupting the class, then going to the bathroom, getting stuck in the stall, and ordering PhD students to help him. The bewildered science departments have been calling us, as well as the UCLA campus police, asking us to remove him or at least assign him a caregiver. We have to reply that we *do* have a full-time caregiver, but my father is impatient to get out in the mornings, won't wait, and indeed, just as often, enjoys the sport of evading capture. I myself have chauffeured my father around, but eventually found myself unwilling, when the men's room was five feet away, to continue to (manually) help him urinate on the street.

In light of my father's situation, I have to question some of the clear-seeming lines Northrup draws. As she puts it:

> Learn the difference between care and overcare. True care of others, from a place of unconditional love, enhances our health . . . That's one reason why volunteering and community service feel good and are associated with improved health. Overcare and burnout result from not including ourselves on the list of people who require care . . . The way to tell the difference between the two is to be aware of how caring for another makes you feel. You must also be 100 percent honest about what you're getting out of excessive care giving.

Pretty easy for you to say! The problem is, "overcare" is the only thing that ensures functioning lives for the many people who depend on the average woman. Sure, I *could* give it up—but the police and neighbors call every single day of the week, *every single day.* Who's going to do the caring if I don't overcare?

How often do I feel, midlife, as though I am in a strange *Island of Doctor Moreau*–like science experiment? My preteen daughters are flashing more and more midriff as they cavort to the (PG or R? If I could only make out the LYRICS!) gangsta rap of Radio Disney. My ridiculously old father is a giant baby who wheels his own crib into traffic, pees into a Starbucks cup, and still wields, intact, his own power of attorney. As I grow ever more sullen about it all, I feel I should be living alone in a perimenopausal cave.

So, who will supply all the caregiving when a whole sandwich generation of fiftyish women checks out? Maybe it will be men: related and hired men. I think of a phalanx of us standing recently in my father's dining room in Malibu, trying to figure out a schedule for his care—or at the very least, for his capture. (From their homes in Northern California, my brother and sister provide all the financial and emotional support to all the caregivers, which is considerable.) In the room at that moment were my Chinese stepmother (seventy-four), myself (forty-nine), Filipino Nurse No. 1 (female, sixty), Filipino Nurse No. 2 (female, fifty-nine), and Filipino Nurse No. 3 (male, forty-one). Which of us were going to take care of my dad? Since all of the women in the room knew all too well the difference between care and overcare, essentially everyone has now quit except for the forty-one-year-old male, who alone has the strength to heft my dad's wheelchair in traffic, needs the money to support his own family of six, and is paid accordingly (which is to say well, far better than many young college graduates I know). I think also, thank heaven, of my girls' fifty-something father, he who holds up the other end of the fifty-fifty custody balance beam. He is unfailingly calm and patient, buys them fashionable new jeans and tennies, braids their hair, punches new holes in their pink belts, takes them camping, cooks them baked beans, and butters their corn on the cob. By a natural chronology that doesn't imprison *him* in this *Island of Doctor Moreau*–like timeline—given that he would not have dreamed of wanting to do all this as a touring musician of twenty-five—my ex, I think, became a father at just the right stage, which is to say older. At his age, my girls have such a wonderfully nurturing father, he might as well be a mother.

I finally went for some estrogen replacement to the woman who would turn out to be my fabulous new gynecologist, Valerie—who is *not* in my Anthem Blue Cross PPO plan, but whom my demon lover insisted I go to anyway because that was our lesbian neighbors' recommendation.

With kind blue eyes and a comfortingly patterned knit cardigan, exuding an air that you might expect from a Scandinavian maiden aunt, Valerie gently interviewed me—while continually handing me tissues—as I sat on the archetypal metal table in my own paper gown, weeping for what seemed like an hour. And I must tell you—as a middle-aged woman who labors mightily every day to wear the mask of being sane, admitting to experiencing only the narrowest spectrum of emotions, from good-humored cheer to only the lightest irritation, a mood soothed easily with a good chuckle thanks to NPR—that it is beyond delicious to ramble aloud about the infinite varieties, colors, and shades of one's depressions and to discuss, ad nauseam, a month's worth of various panic attacks (going heavy to light, light to heavy). Valerie, listening quietly, wrote down the dates of my periods on a tablet, lending my ravings a reassuring scientific structure, then she gave me one of the most deeply comforting speeches I have ever heard (who from central casting would you get to do it? Streep? Mirren? Lansbury?).

"Sandra," she said, "I have this theory. Let me see if I can describe it for you. I think some girls are paper-plate girls, and some are Chinets. Paper plates collapse even if they have nothing on them; Chinets can take a lot heaped on them and never break. Yes, right now things feel very unstable, and you're having an emotional response to what is a purely physiological phenomenon. But I think, at heart"—and here she leaned forward—"you're a Chinet girl. What we'd like to do now is take some of the stressors off your plate, while at the same time temporarily strengthening its foundation." And with that, she gently smeared the tiniest dot of clear estrogen gel on the inside of my wrist, and even though she said it would take a few weeks to take effect, I *instantly* felt high!

In conclusion, gentle reader, here are some handy tips, from women who have survived the Change. (These come after the project of draining your parents' savings so Medicare can pay Filipino male orderlies to do everything.)

The first is a fantastically freeing gambit called "Now That I'm Fifty." As my friend Denise puts it, "Now that I'm fifty, I don't visit my fighting in-laws in Cleveland anymore. My husband can go off and see them if he wants to, but I've been doing it for twenty years, and you know what? Never again." (Beat.) "I'm fifty!"

Another is one of my own invention that I call "Stuff It, Barbara

Ehrenreich." For years, I was afraid to hire domestic help, because Barbara Ehrenreich wrote in *Nickel and Dimed* that to have a Third World woman scrub your toilets is to oppress a fellow sister. But now that I can afford it, and I've come out of denial over the fact that to have a house cleaned professionally is unbelievably fantastic, once every three weeks, I bring in Marta—whom I refer to sometimes as Marta, and sometimes, baldly, as "the maid"—and when I do so, I silently flip Barbara Ehrenreich the finger. I'm (just about) fifty!

A third, related, survival tip is to have no shame. The middle-aged women I know, clawing their way one day at a time through this passage, have no rules—they glue themselves together with absolutely anything they can get their hands on. They do estrogen cream, progesterone biocompounds, vaginal salves, coffee in the morning, big sandwiches at lunch. They drink water all day; they work out twice a week, hard, with personal trainers. They take Xanax to get over the dread of seeing their personal trainers; they take Valium to settle themselves before the first Chardonnay of happy hour. They may do with just a half a line of coke before a very small martini, while knitting and doing some crosswords. If there are cigarettes and skin dryness, there are also collagen and Botox, and the exhilaration of flaming an ex on Facebook. And finally, as another woman friend of mine counseled with perfect sincerity and cheer: "Just gain the twenty-five pounds. I really think I would not have survived menopause—AND the death of my mother—without having gained these twenty-five pounds."

Sure, we're supposed to take calcium pills to avoid brittle bones and hip injuries at ninety, but who worries about living long when we're just trying to get through the day? In the end, the *real* wisdom of menopause may be in questioning how fun or even sane this chore wheel called modern life actually is. And if what works is black cohosh tea with a vodka chaser, and an overturned Greek chthonic head as a chocolate-fondue fountain, then bottoms up! Avast, ye vampires and werewolves and pirates! *Arrrr!*

KEN MURRAY

How Doctors Die

FROM *Zocalo Public Square*

YEARS AGO, CHARLIE, a highly respected orthopedist and a mentor of mine, found a lump in his stomach. He had a surgeon explore the area, and the diagnosis was pancreatic cancer. This surgeon was one of the best in the country. He had even invented a new procedure for this exact cancer that could triple a patient's five-year-survival odds—from 5 percent to 15 percent—albeit with a poor quality of life. Charlie was uninterested. He went home the next day, closed his practice, and never set foot in a hospital again. He focused on spending time with family and feeling as good as possible. Several months later, he died at home. He got no chemotherapy, radiation, or surgical treatment. Medicare didn't spend much on him.

It's not a frequent topic of discussion, but doctors die, too. And they don't die like the rest of us. What's unusual about them is not how much treatment they get compared to most Americans, but how little. For all the time they spend fending off the deaths of others, they tend to be fairly serene when faced with death themselves. They know exactly what is going to happen, they know the choices, and they generally have access to any sort of medical care they could want. But they go gently.

Of course, doctors don't want to die; they want to live. But they know enough about modern medicine to know its limits. And they know enough about death to know what all people fear most: dying in pain, and dying alone. They've talked about this with their families. They want to be sure, when the time comes, that no heroic measures will happen—that they will never experience, during their last moments on earth, someone breaking their ribs in an attempt to resuscitate them with CPR (that's what happens if CPR is done right).

Almost all medical professionals have seen what we call "futile care" being performed on people. That's when doctors bring the cutting edge of technology to bear on a grievously ill person near the end of life. The patient will get cut open, perforated with tubes, hooked up to machines, and assaulted with drugs. All of this occurs in the intensive care unit at a cost of tens of thousands of dollars a day. What it buys is misery we would not inflict on a terrorist. I cannot count the number of times fellow physicians have told me, in words that vary only slightly, "Promise me if you find me like this that you'll kill me." They mean it. Some medical personnel wear medallions stamped "NO CODE" to tell physicians not to perform CPR on them. I have even seen it as a tattoo.

To administer medical care that makes people suffer is anguishing. Physicians are trained to gather information without revealing any of their own feelings, but in private, among fellow doctors, they'll vent. "How can anyone do that to their family members?" they'll ask. I suspect it's one reason physicians have higher rates of alcohol abuse and depression than professionals in most other fields. I know it's one reason I stopped participating in hospital care for the last ten years of my practice.

How has it come to this—that doctors administer so much care that they wouldn't want for themselves? The simple, or not-so-simple, answer is this: patients, doctors, and the system.

To see how patients play a role, imagine a scenario in which someone has lost consciousness and been admitted to an emergency room. As is so often the case, no one has made a plan for this situation, and shocked and scared family members find themselves caught up in a maze of choices. They're overwhelmed. When doctors ask if they want "everything" done, they answer yes. Then the nightmare begins. Sometimes, a family really means "do everything," but often they just mean "do everything that's reasonable." The problem is that they may not know what's reasonable, nor, in their confusion and sorrow, will they ask about it or hear what a physician may be telling them. For their part, doctors told to do "everything" will do it, whether it is reasonable or not.

The above scenario is a common one. Feeding into the problem are unrealistic expectations of what doctors can accomplish.

Many people think of CPR as a reliable lifesaver when, in fact, the results are usually poor. I've had hundreds of people brought to me in the emergency room after getting CPR. Exactly one, a healthy man who'd had no heart troubles (for those who want specifics, he had a "tension pneumothorax"), walked out of the hospital. If a patient suffers from severe illness, old age, or a terminal disease, the odds of a good outcome from CPR are infinitesimal, while the odds of suffering are overwhelming. Poor knowledge and misguided expectations lead to a lot of bad decisions.

But of course it's not just patients making these things happen. Doctors play an enabling role, too. The trouble is that even doctors who hate to administer futile care must find a way to address the wishes of patients and families. Imagine, once again, the emergency room with those grieving, possibly hysterical, family members. They do not know the doctor. Establishing trust and confidence under such circumstances is a very delicate thing. People are prepared to think the doctor is acting out of base motives, trying to save time, or money, or effort, especially if the doctor is advising against further treatment.

Some doctors are stronger communicators than others, and some doctors are more adamant, but the pressures they all face are similar. When I faced circumstances involving end-of-life choices, I adopted the approach of laying out only the options that I thought were reasonable (as I would in any situation) as early in the process as possible. When patients or families brought up unreasonable choices, I would discuss the issue in layman's terms that portrayed the downsides clearly. If patients or families still insisted on treatments I considered pointless or harmful, I would offer to transfer their care to another doctor or hospital.

Should I have been more forceful at times? I know that some of those transfers still haunt me. One of the patients of whom I was most fond was an attorney from a famous political family. She had severe diabetes and terrible circulation, and, at one point, she developed a painful sore on her foot. Knowing the hazards of hospitals, I did everything I could to keep her from resorting to surgery. Still, she sought out outside experts with whom I had no relationship. Not knowing as much about her as I did, they decided to perform bypass surgery on her chronically clogged blood vessels in both legs. This didn't restore her circulation, and the surgical wounds wouldn't heal. Her feet became gangrenous, and she endured bilateral leg amputations. Two weeks later, in the famous medical center in which all this had occurred, she died.

It's easy to find fault with both doctors and patients in such stories, but in many ways all the parties are simply victims of a larger system that encourages excessive treatment. In some unfortunate cases, doctors use the fee-for-service model to do everything they can, no matter how pointless, to make money. More commonly, though, doctors are fearful of litigation and do whatever they're asked, with little feedback, to avoid getting in trouble.

Even when the right preparations have been made, the system can still swallow people up. One of my patients was a man named Jack, a seventy-eight-year-old who had been ill for years and undergone about fifteen major surgical procedures. He explained to me that he never, under any circumstances, wanted to be placed on life-support machines again. One Saturday, however, Jack suffered a massive stroke and got admitted to the emergency room unconscious, without his wife. The doctors did everything possible to resuscitate him and put him on life support in the ICU. This was Jack's worst nightmare. When I arrived at the hospital and took over Jack's care, I spoke to his wife and to hospital staff, bringing in my office notes with his care preferences. Then I turned off the life-support machines and sat with him. He died two hours later.

Even with all his wishes documented, Jack hadn't died as he'd hoped. The system had intervened. One of the nurses, I later found out, even reported my unplugging of Jack to the authorities as a possible homicide. Nothing came of it, of course; Jack's wishes had been spelled out explicitly, and he'd left the paperwork to prove it. But the prospect of a police investigation is terrifying for any physician. I could far more easily have left Jack on life support against his stated wishes, prolonging his life, and his suffering, a few more weeks. I would even have made a little more money, and Medicare would have ended up with an additional $500,000 bill. It's no wonder many doctors err on the side of overtreatment.

But doctors still don't overtreat themselves. They see the consequences of this constantly. Almost anyone can find a way to die in peace at home, and pain can be managed better than ever. Hospice care, which focuses on providing terminally ill patients with comfort and dignity rather than on futile cures, provides most people with much better final days. Amazingly, studies have found that people placed in hospice care often live longer than people with the same disease who are seeking active cures. I was struck to hear on the radio recently that the famous reporter Tom Wicker had "died peacefully at home, surrounded by his family." Such stories are, thankfully, increasingly common.

Several years ago, my older cousin Torch (born at home by the light of a flashlight—or torch) had a seizure that turned out to be the result of lung cancer that had gone to his brain. I arranged for him to see various specialists, and we learned that with aggressive treatment of his condition, including three to five hospital visits a week for chemotherapy, he would live perhaps four months. Ultimately, Torch decided against any treatment and simply took pills for brain swelling. He moved in with me.

We spent the next eight months doing a bunch of things that he enjoyed, having fun together like we hadn't had in decades. We went to Disneyland, his first time. We hung out at home. Torch was a sports nut, and he was very happy to watch sports and eat my cooking. He even gained a bit of weight, eating his favorite foods rather than hospital food. He had no serious pain, and he remained high-spirited. One day, he didn't wake up. He spent the next three days in a comalike sleep and then died. The cost of his medical care for those eight months, for the one drug he was taking, was about twenty dollars.

Torch was no doctor, but he knew he wanted a life of quality, not just quantity. Don't most of us? If there is a state of the art of end-of-life care, it is this: death with dignity. As for me, my physician has my choices. They were easy to make, as they are for most physicians. There will be no heroics, and I will go gentle into that good night. Like my mentor Charlie. Like my cousin Torch. Like my fellow doctors.

FRANCINE PROSE

Other Women

FROM *Granta*

THIS IS THE STORY I tell: In the spring of 1972, I was twenty-five years old, unhappily married, and living in Cambridge, Massachusetts. Like many women I knew then, I joined a feminist consciousness-raising group, to which I belonged for six months until I left my husband and moved across the country. A year later, when I briefly returned to pick up some possessions, I learned that, after my departure, my husband had serially and systematically slept with all the women in my group.

He'd been my college boyfriend and was a graduate student in mathematics. We'd gotten married during my senior year. The day before the wedding, my mother said, "You can still call it off." Though I would have liked to, it seemed like too much trouble. I knew the marriage was a mistake. The hot buzz of romance had worn off, and there we were, stuck with each other at a historical moment when—or so we heard—the so-called sexual revolution was boiling all around us.

Another mistake: after college, I went to graduate school, where I spiraled into a long, persistent, low-grade nervous breakdown. Officially, I was a PhD candidate in medieval English literature. Unofficially, I was a semi-agoraphobic stoner who stayed in bed for days watching TV and tried never to leave the house except to attend an intermediate Latin class I needed to fulfill a language requirement. The class was on Ovid's *Metamorphoses,* which I truly loved, but I failed all the quizzes and eventually stopped going.

Among my terrors was the fear of a certain street near my apartment. For some reason the block had become an impromptu gathering spot for flashers, who sat in cars and exposed themselves to young women passing by. What scared me was not the sight of their pink, innocent-looking genitals but the looks on their faces, the paradoxical mix of shame and goofy ecstatic triumph.

Feminism was big news then; a groundswell political movement. Gloria Steinem was a star. Literary celebrities—Kate Millett, Germaine Greer—were created overnight; lost classics were resurrected. There were public and private conversations about the truly egregious ways in which women were underpaid, underrated, excluded from certain professions, and restricted to others. Such things were debated on talk shows!

One thing people said was: the personal is political. It was an attractive idea because it suggested that the most quotidian events were reflective and emblematic of the dramas enacted in the wider world. Of course, this is true, and it isn't. Having a stranger assume you are stupid simply because you have a vagina is related to the problem but is *not the same problem* as being subjected to an involuntary clitoridectomy. Sometimes it wasn't clear to me how well this difference was understood, but the general feeling was that if you looked at (and got together and talked about) how women were treated as second-class citizens in the home and office and classroom, your perspective would broaden to include societies in which women were bought, sold, altered, bred, and worked like barnyard animals.

Everywhere, women were staging protests, issuing manifestos, publishing newsletters that represented a broad spectrum from separatist radical lesbians to moderates who wanted respect, equal pay, and a seat at the table. Like any social change, this one whipped up a mini-tornado of opposition: Norman Mailer had no problem writing that books by women (including Virginia Woolf) were humorless, sentimental, narrow-minded, and unreadable. The more judicious worried about the damage to the American family if moms put their kids in day care and went out and got jobs. To be fair, there were excesses on both sides: women used words like *foremother* and *phallocratic* with straight faces and had debates about makeup.

I, too, began to question certain things I'd taken for granted. I noted, for example, the passive hostility of the distinguished professor who asked me, with disinterested curiosity, why women students were always in the dead middle of the class and never at the top or the bottom. Why couldn't I remember once seeing my father clear the table, even though he and my mother both worked long hours as doctors? Was my slide into marriage, graduate school, and madness the result of an early indoctrination by *Cinderella* and *Jane Eyre*? Were the flashers on Kirkland Street only the psycho-expression of the outer reaches of men's true feelings about women?

And so it happened that I joined a consciousness-raising group. A possible explanation for my psychic decline had suggested itself: the too-early marriage, the too-easy path, the phobias, and the weed. Had I wound up in this sorry state *because I was a woman?* This was the sort of question a women's group was supposed to address as we compared our experiences with those of our newfound sisters.

I don't know what I expected. A new way of being, I guess. Once we identified and divested ourselves of the bogus values imposed on us by the patriarchy, everyone would be equal and helpful and *nice to each other.* Our consciousnesses would be raised!

Half a dozen women, all in their twenties or early thirties, met in each other's homes (I always tried to persuade them to meet in my apartment) to talk about feminism in general and our lives in particular, to discuss the books and essays that had become iconic, and to report on our successes or failures in teaching our boyfriends or husbands how to use a vacuum cleaner.

Though I have hazy memories of some women in the group, I'm fairly sure that most were connected to the university or living with someone who was. Some were working or looking for the sort of young-people jobs (arts administrator, lab assistant) that suggest that adulthood will have some relation to one's college major. As I recall, only one of us had a child: a sweet woman with a nice husband; they both seemed overwhelmed. I remember two slightly older married women with stable lives and nicer apartments and a maternal but slightly judgmental air that made the rest of us want to please them. Then there was the pretty one, who'd brought me into the group.

The first disappointment was the rapidity with which we fell into roles that replicated junior high. As much as we critiqued the ways in which male culture had taught us to objectify our bodies, the same hierarchies applied: the plump deferred to the thin, the short to the tall, the homely to the handsome. The older women exerted a subtle maternal leadership, though the actual mother, the overburdened one, was considered slightly pitiful for having gotten herself into that situation. I also assumed a familiar role, a fallback position from grade school. Self-protective, watchful, stiff with social discomfort, at once too proud, too removed, and too lazy to mention the phobias, the cannabis, the TV, the forlorn marriage, the secret novel forever "in progress."

None of that rose to the surface as I joined my sisters in complaining about the patriarchal creepiness of the men I knew. I described how my husband used to torment me by staring theatrically and somewhat apishly at every beautiful woman we passed until he was sure I noticed, and then he would give me a horrible smile, like the rictus grin of the Kirkland Street flashers. I wondered why the other women so often rose to his defense and asked why I was being so hard on a guy who was tall, reasonably nice, intelligent, and so forth.

If I'd imagined that the group would collectively generate a higher *consciousness* about ourselves in relation to other women and men, I soon realized we'd re-created in microcosm the Darwinian power relationships of the boardroom, the cabinet meeting, the office, the nursery school.

We, too, had our outcast: the future social worker's wife. Objectively, she was as smart and attractive as anyone else. But her mistake was being too honest and unguarded about her motivation for joining the group.

She made the mistake of saying what no one else would admit. She was sick of her marriage. Her perfectly pleasant husband had been her first lover. And to quote John Berryman, she was heavy bored. My guess is that all of us were bored and erotically restless; my sense is that the madly-in-love didn't rush to join women's groups. But the obsessiveness and nakedness of this woman's discontent allowed the rest of us to pity her, to condescend and patronize her for focusing on something trivial and self-indulgent. When conversation lagged, the meetings devolved into scenarios in which she bemoaned her romantic ennui while the rest of us rolled our eyes and smirked. Watching her, I was reminded of the schoolyard lesson about the risks of volunteering too much information. But secrecy has its drawbacks, too—it can make you feel cornered.

Backed into a corner, I began to joke around—some of my jokes were funny, some not, some appropriate, some not. Some were probably hostile. No one else thought they were funny. I remember suggesting we read Valerie Solanas's *SCUM Manifesto,* a book I still think is hilariously weird. I especially loved Solanas's fantastic suggestion (I might be getting this slightly wrong) that the only way for men to rehabilitate themselves was to gather in groups and ritually chant in unison, "I am a lowly abject turd!"

I remember telling this to the group. I recall no one laughing. A current joke was: How many feminists does it take to change a light bulb? Answer: That's not funny. But it wasn't the women's fault. None of them were stupid. Some had a sense of humor. They could tell that I wasn't trying to amuse but to provoke.

All this time, though sick with loathing and doubt, I was working on my novel. I wrote a first draft and put it away and rewrote it from scratch. Eventually, I got brave enough to show it to a former college professor.

Then, an unexpected event occurred. An editor called from New York. My former professor had sent him my novel, and he wanted to publish it.

A single phone call affected my brain like a jolt of ECT without the mouth guard, the electrodes, or the memory loss. It was a miracle cure. I moved to San Francisco.

And so I returned a year later to collect my things. And that was when I found out that my husband had, so to speak, worked his way through the group. One of the women told me and excused herself; she wasn't the only one! No wonder he'd always seemed so pleased when the group met at our house. No wonder they'd always taken his side.

In fact, this was not how it happened. In fact, I'm pretty sure that my husband only slept with two of the women in the group.

I don't know why I tell this story, or tell it the way I do. Obviously, saying *all the women in the group* makes a better story than saying *two of the women in the group.* But under the circumstances, two seems like more than two; two seems like more than twice as much as one. It seems like a *statement,* which it was. I know he slept with the pretty one and (I think) one of the maternal know-it-alls and for good measure both of the girls who lived in the apartment upstairs in our weathered Cambridge three-decker.

If our true desires and disappointments are buried deep in our dreams, they're closer to the surface in the stories we tell and re-tell, in the mythologies we ourselves have come to believe. Does saying *all the women* express how betrayed I felt by my husband and my feminist sisters?

Actually, I was surprised by how little it upset me. Though I hadn't had the encyclopedic sexual experience that people of my generation are supposed to have had, I'd had enough to know: sex trumps politics, common sense, and better judgment. And my husband's bad behavior wasn't entirely unexpected. One gift of a faltering marriage is a heightened sensitivity to the frequencies of flirtation. And however misused, the word *liberation* was very much in the air, often to mean having sex with someone because it was more trouble to say no.

The truth is that when I think of that time, I feel neither out-rage nor betrayal but gratitude: my consciousness was raised. Do I think that women are better than men and that the world would be a better place if women ran it? I can thank my Cambridge wom-en's group (along with Margaret Thatcher and Indira Gandhi) for having cured me of the notion that women are no more or less likely than men to treat people well or badly. Perhaps the problem lies with institutions rather than people, and a group, no matter how small, is an institution.

Yet somehow, in the process, I became a feminist. Almost forty years later, feminism is as basic to my sense of self as the fact that I have brown eyes, as integral to my sense of the world as the fact that gravity keeps us from flying off the planet.

Do I think that women deserve equal pay for equal work? Do I think women are as smart and capable as men? Do I think that women are still being discriminated against in obvious and subtle ways? Does it disturb me to meet young women who imagine that the playing field is level and that feminism is irrelevant to their domestic lives and careers? Do I think women need to help one another? Have I noticed that there are men who inevitably and consciously or unconsciously treat women like idiots, babies, or witches? Of course, the answer to these questions is an emphatic yes.

*

No matter how much or how little happened in those conscious-ness-raising groups, they were part of a formative era that opened the eyes and changed the minds of women like myself. Living through that time persuaded me not to think that gender dis-crimination is the unavoidable product of boys being boys. Along with consciousness came the faint consolation of knowing that certain slights and omissions, certain unenlightened attitudes and intended or unintended insults are neither purely personal nor in our imaginations.

I feel fortunate to have spent my adult life in the company of a (second) husband and two sons who actually like women—or, any-way, some women. But frequently when I venture beyond my do-mestic bubble, I'm reminded of the degree to which the weather is still chilly out there for the ladies.

Recently, I participated in a reading tribute to an important (dead white male) American writer. A friend sent me a link to an online literary site in which the presumably young male blog-ger noted (inaccurately, but whatever) that I was *taller* than any of my fellow readers, all male. Even as I was persuading myself that a similar comment might have been made about a five-foot nine-inch man (Gee, Philip Roth is tall!), I read further, to find myself described as acting like a "socialite." A *socialite? Me?* Don't socialites organize charity balls and nibble low-cal salad lunches and make cameo appearances on *Real Housewives of New York City?* Did he mean *sophisticate? Aristocrat?* Was he trying to be nice and got the wrong word? No matter how I parsed it, I couldn't imagine a male writer of my age with a similar publication record being described as a tall socialite. Or was it that the sight of a tall, rea-sonably competent woman inspired the blogger to think of Tom Wolfe's social x-rays and lemon tarts—women asking the waiter to bring the dressing on the side?

If I still belonged to my women's group, I could tell them that story and perhaps be heartened by stories of similar things that happened to them. Who knows where they are now? If their prob-lems were solved or not, if they found jobs or not, had kids or not, left their boring boyfriends or not? All are older, some may be grandmothers and some may be long dead.

It makes for a better story to say that they all slept with my hus-band. But whatever symbolic or metaphoric truth the fictive ver-sion exhumes, I don't much care if it happened that way or not. I learned more than I would have if my feminist sisters had loyally resisted my former husband's advances. Gender doesn't confer moral superiority, nor the opposite, needless to say.

In retrospect, my women's group provided a political education, though not exactly the one that the women's movement intended. I learned not to follow a party line; I learned not to take things for granted or at face value; I learned to assume that situations may not be what they appear—all useful lessons for a novelist and a human being.

I don't know how much the group helped confirm my inconvenient determination to keep talking about the unpleasant or abysmal ways in which girls and women are treated. That inequalities and horrors continue to plague women is a fact, not my opinion. Though it is also true that many women's lives are vast improvements over what they would have been in 1972.

I remember asking my husband why he slept with all those women, and I remember him saying that he'd wanted to, all along. He gave me that wicked little smile, like the men in the cars.

By *all those women,* we meant *two women.* For me to claim that he slept with them all is not only untrue but also unfair. But it's the sort of embellishment that shines light on some deeper truth, in this case the peculiar truth of a long-ago skirmish in the ongoing, counterproductive war of men against women.

RICHARD SENNETT

Humanism[1]

FROM *The Hedgehog Review*

IN THIS ESSAY, I want to explore some dimensions of what the term *humanism* means—what it meant in the past and what it means today. In particular, I would like to consider the relation of displacement and humanism—a cultural ideal on the one hand, a social fact on the other. The two seem to have nothing in common. Yet I want to argue that they do; at the dawn of the modern era, a person's capacity to manage and master displacement formed part of the humanist project, and, I argue, it continues to do so today, but on very different terms. In a world filled with mobile people—economic immigrants and political exiles in particular—an old humanist ideal might help them to give shape to their lives.

Baruch Spinoza was the humanist philosopher whom we immediately think of as experiencing this connection firsthand. He was exiled from Amsterdam because he was accused of heresy, of violating Judaism. From the thirteenth century on, many Christians also began to be persecuted for the same supposed crime, that is, heresy. One of the greatest of Spinoza's Christian brothers was the humanist philosopher Pico della Mirandola, who lived from 1463 to 1494, the younger son of a minor aristocratic family driven first from Italy to France for heresy, then imprisoned in France for that crime, who then returned to Florence to die, thanks to the protection of Lorenzo de' Medici.

It was Pico who first made explicit the connection between displacement and the humanist project. His touchstone was the phrase, "Man is his own Maker," which appeared in his brief essay "Oration on the Dignity of Man," written, it is now thought, while Pico was in prison. Pico imagines God as "the master-builder [who] by the laws of his secret wisdom fabricated this house, this world which we see."[2] But God, whom Pico calls the "Master Artisan," then created mankind as a "work of indeterminate form." Pico imagines God the Master Artisan speaking to Adam, his unfinished creation, as follows: "In conformity with thy free judgement, in whose hands I have placed thee, thou art confined by no bounds; and thou wilt fix limits of nature for thyself."[3] These words had the personal meaning to Pico that, as a displaced person, he would have to make up a life for himself.

Freedom, then, to do anything and to become anyone? Informality and spontaneity as the ends of life? Pico emphatically rejected this. Born indeterminate, he says, human beings have to find unity in their lives; a person must make him- or herself coherent. In Renaissance humanism, this quest meant uniting conflicting ancient ideals by bridging the Hellenic and the Christian mindset; in Pico's own philosophy, it meant making the one and the many cohere, or as philosophers would put it today, discovering unity in the midst of difference. Spinoza, two centuries later, was grounded in just this humanist project.

What does the humanist quest for unity in the midst of difference mean for us today? Here a contrast between Pico and Spinoza is all-important. Spinoza emphasized unities transcending time—timeless unities in mental space—whereas Pico dwelt on the fact of shifting time, and shifting time in everyday experience. Pico dwelt, we would now say, on the phenomenon of life narrative: can the events and accidents of life add up to a coherent story? That is every migrant's question. And since these events and accidents are beyond an uprooted person's control, the unity of a life story has to reside in the person telling it; unity, we would say, lies in the quality of the narrator's voice. The narrator, following Pico's precept, must learn how to tell about disorder and displacement in his or her own life in such a way that he or she does not become confused or deranged by the telling.

Voice

Pico's humanism has mattered to me greatly in the work I do as a sociologist. When I began studying labor in the early 1970s, the life histories of the people I interviewed resembled well-made plots, determinate and constricted rather than experimental. The American manual laborers on whom I and Jonathan Cobb reported in *The Hidden Injuries of Class* (1972), for instance, served only a few employers during the course of their lives and hoped to better themselves by small, incremental gains in salary and status. White-collar employees higher up the job scale even more orchestrated their lives in order to climb up a fixed corporate ladder. These real-life narratives were shaped by big, well-defined institutions: corporations with elaborate bureaucracies, powerful unions, an intrusive welfare state.

In the last quarter century, modern capitalism has changed so that this determinate life narrative is weakening. Profound forces deregulate people's experience of time: new technologies, global markets, new forms of bureaucratic organization. They orient economic activity to the short term rather than the long term; they challenge continuity and duration as institutional goals. One instance may suffice: in 1960 the "profit horizon" investors used for evaluating corporations was three years; in 1999 it was typically three months.

How this changing frame of time affects work can be illuminated by two early usages in the English language. In Chaucer's day, a "career" meant a well-laid, well-mapped roadway on which to travel; a "job" meant a lump of something, coal or wood, that could be moved around indiscriminately from place to place. Today, in the labor market, Chaucerian jobs rather than careers define work. The young, middle-level university graduate can expect to change employers at least twelve times in the course of a working life, and to change his or her "skills base" at least three times; the skills he or she must draw on at forty are not the skills learned in school. Job change no longer flows within the Chaucerian trajectory of a career; without a fixed corporate structure, job change follows a more erratic path.

My studies of workers—both manual and white-collar—have led me to the conclusion that they are profoundly unhappy simply to narrate these erratic shifts as their own life stories. The flux of time is weakening their powers as narrators; they can see their working lives only in bits and pieces. Without a clear sense of how to structure work in time, people become confused, if not depressed, about what they should do. The flexible workplace itself seems illegible; the chameleon character of organizations, for instance, makes it hard for people to calculate what will happen if they change jobs.

There is a social dimension as well to chaotic, deregulated time. Short-term organizations tend to reduce commitment: how could you be loyal to a fickle corporation? I have found that middle-aged workers who have developed loyalties to particular companies feel betrayed that these commitments now count for so little. Nor does work experience, or sheer seniority, mean what it once did, given employers' preference for younger, cheaper, and more pliable workers. One way to summarize the conflict between short-term, deregulated time and the human life course is that, as work experience accumulates, it diminishes in economic value. Another summary is that modern capitalism is turning everyone into a work migrant, and many into work exiles.

If you are a writer or reader of a certain temperament, you celebrate the "postmodern condition," in which the flux and flow of events dethrone the narrator's assured voice. If you are a scholar exploring "posthumanism," you might believe that the human subject can no longer speak as the master of circumstances. Yet if you are an ordinary worker, you need to find your voice. You need, like our Renaissance forebears, to find principles of continuity and unity in how you account for your material experience.

"Voice" is both a personal and a social issue. To hold fragmentary experiences together in time requires the capacity to step back from the power of each event to hurt or to disorient. To find one's voice requires establishing some distance from the immediate, from the noumenal; sheer surrender to the moment weakens one's voice. Of course in the midst of the most traumatic events, like a civil war, stepping back can occur only after the event is over. But in the sort of traumas to which I have devoted my studies, as in the moments when people are tested at work—told, for instance, they are losing a job—the capacity to stand in and out of a situation at the same time is a practical strategy for survival—with long-term consequences. Workers who can manage this duality are better able to fashion a sustaining long-term narrative for their lives.

The social anthropologist can detect this containing narrative in many ways: People able to step back are able to put in long-term context a particular trauma like being passed over for promotion; the scale of the trauma shrinks. They become better at strategic thinking, since, by stepping back, they are able to reason why a failure occurred. On the positive side, and more ethically, they are able to frame modestly any particular achievement; it becomes one event among many diverse ones. If I had to name one quality of this sustaining, difference-registering voice—at least the prime quality of voice I have detected in conducting interviews over the last forty years—it lies in renouncing the search for a denouement in one's life history. Continuity is established, relating different events by scale and context, but the person whose voice is empowered does not expect a catharsis to come or a sudden, blinding revelation of wholeness.

Humanism, it is sometimes said, put Man at the center of experience, men and women as masters, rather than God. But of course no one, ever, is master in his or her own house. The historical Renaissance knew this full well, which is why humanists of that time emphasized *Fortuna,* the goddess of chance. Today, similarly, a humane outlook requires the embrace of chance and rupture; humanism refers in part to the self's determination to make continuities of these ill-fitting pieces of experience, through standing both within and outside them. The social challenge people face in doing so comes from those workplaces, political regimes, religions, and ethnic cultures that demand absolute immersion and total engagement. As I shall later show, these demands are becoming ever stronger in modern society; surrender of self to circumstance is a cultural fact as well as an economic fact. To resist surrendering, we need an idea of ourselves as both engaged and detached at any one moment.

These precepts reflect, if they do not precisely mirror, Pico's understanding of Man as his own Maker. What his humanism says to us is that the human subject should stand apart from his or her circumstances emotionally and intellectually, even as he or she experiences the flux of Fortuna—the Chaucerian "job" writ large in a life—and the mesmerizing power of the moment. Only in this can we find our voice.

Difference

The historian Jacob Burckhardt lived most of his life in nineteenth-century Basel. If he is read today at all, it is for his *Civiliza-*

tion of the Renaissance in Italy, which still makes compelling reading. Burckhardt made his historical figures seem living presences. He worked the same verbal magic on ancient Rome. And though he seldom left his study, he was keenly in the living presence of those close to home; he was the friend and sometimes protector of Friedrich Nietzsche in Basel.

The human presences of the Renaissance, whom he summoned so vividly on the page, were complex individuals, their experience cut loose from fixed traditions, people who were experimenting with their lives. No doubt he idealized. Burckhardt celebrated Renaissance men and women who moved between different milieux, who experienced different cultures; they deepened themselves in the process. As we might put it today, he celebrated the impact of difference upon the self. In the same spirit, he applied Pico's idea of Man as his own Maker to statecraft; he described the Renaissance state as "a work of art," meaning that politics can be shaped, fashioned, and created rather than just follow inherited forms.

There was a practical side to these humanist values focused on difference; it appeared in the Renaissance workshop. The medieval guild workshop morphed, during the fifteenth and sixteenth centuries, into a broader institution: it became a laboratory, open to experimentation with materials, tools, and new uses of technology. By Spinoza's time, for instance, the craft of lens grinding had become an experimental activity in which there was constant experimentation with the glass substance, shape, and polishing of lens. Since Burckhardt's time, more exacting historians of science have confirmed that the technological urge to experiment was inextricably bound up with cultural beliefs that revolved around the human being as a work in progress; Steven Shapin speaks of Renaissance humanism as a "self-embrace of the yet to be known."

Today, most politically correct people celebrate the fact of racial, ethnic, or religious differences, but we do not believe in them as our humanist ancestors did. We focus on toleration, particularly on the rights of people who differ from us, but toleration can be itself a form of mutual indifference, leaving one another alone, each in his or her own sphere, as a version of getting along together. Our humanist forebears, particularly those of a practical bent, thought of difference, as it were, making more of a difference. True, the differences they had in mind were different views of material things and what could be done with them. True, also, the early modern era imposed its own Christian culture on the peoples outside Europe it subjugated or enslaved. But the technological and scientific mentality of humanism formulated a simple precept about the experience of difference that, I think, remains powerful in thinking about alternatives to the mere toleration of cultural differences today.

The precept ruling the early modern workshop was that informal, open-ended cooperation is how best to experience difference. Each of the terms in this precept matters. "Informal" means that contacts between people of differing skills or interests are rich when messy, weak when they become regulated, like boring meetings run strictly on formal rules of order. "Open-ended" means you want to find out what another person is about without knowing where it will lead; put another way, you want to avoid the iron rule of utility that establishes a fixed goal—a product, a policy objective—in advance. "Cooperation" is the simplest and most important term. You suppose that different parties all gain by exchanging, rather than one part gaining at the expense of others.

In high-tech laboratories today, the elements of this precept produce innovation, just as they did in the late Renaissance workshops of the past. But the precept seems entirely alien to social life and the complex differences modern society contains. Imagine a modern exile in Spinoza's condition: Would we allow him to live undocumented, informally among us? Would our experience of him focus on open-ended exchanges? Would our impulse be to cooperate with him? None of these, I think. We would treat an exile differently than we treat a scientific experiment; at best, we would tolerate his presence, without much interaction. For these reasons, the humanist's laboratory/workshop provides one standard for the word *inhumane*.

In the research I have done both on workplaces and on urban life, I have taken this standard to heart. Offices and streets become inhumane when rigidity, utility, and competition rule; they become humane when they promote informal, open-ended, and cooperative interactions. Our physical environment suggests why attacks on the humanist tradition want to have it both ways. These attacks want to dethrone the power of the human subject, Man as the measure, etc., yet when environments are produced that lack human scale, when buildings or places are created that lack warmth, the projects are criticized as "inhumane."

Again, it is under the aegis of the duality inhumane/humane that we make sociological sense of the powers of the voice. Accounts of one's life governed by rigidity, utility, and competition are arid, thin, and weak; moreover, if they tell what happened to a person, they give little sense of what the happenings meant to him or her. Their model is the abstract personnel file, an inhumane narrative. This inhumanity, I want to stress, is not the narrator's fault; rather, an inhumane social reality has been mirrored, all too accurately, in the way the self understands itself. Where life narratives in which difference has been experienced on informal, open-ended, and cooperative terms become what the anthropologist Clifford Geertz once called "thick descriptions," the narrator is conveying a more complex, and engaging, social reality.

Burckhardt's Paradox

I have made heavy intellectual weather about humanist values of personal time and social space, for an ultimate reason. Today it is widely believed that advanced technologies and machines are dethroning humanist values. The robot with a life of its own, the computer whose brain is better than ours—this scenario seems to mark a gulf between ourselves and our forebears who worked by hand, who relied on their biological powers. It is a story in which material advance seems to eclipse the human.

This self-dethroning story about technology and society was questioned by Jacob Burckhardt in an unusual way. The historian was certainly pessimistic about modern times; he described the modern era as an "age of brutal simplifiers." But in his view, the epithet "an age of brutal simplifiers" propounds a paradox: as society's material conditions become ever more complex, its social relationships become ever more crude.

In Burckhardt's own time, the nationalism nascent in the nineteenth century seemed to the historian to usher in the "age of brutal simplifiers," nationalism denying the mixture of peoples and the multiple identities of individuals in each nation. The paradox appears because the nineteenth century was also the great age of industrial development, of productive technology. His paradox connected these two developments, technology and nationalism,

with industrial technology tending to the complex and nationalism tending to the brutally simple.

If radios had existed in Burckhardt's time, the stark us-against-
them language on right-wing American talk shows would have
served him to define "crude"; if Burckhardt could have websurfed,
he would have found similar evidence in blogs of all political per-
suasions all over the world. We could use another value-soaked
word to understand what Burckhardt was getting at: society becomes more primitive, the more people see themselves categorically, in terms of fixed identities.

Whether social relations were once more complex is a question
we should set aside; it is an exercise in nostalgia. We should refo-
cus this paradox just as a proposition in itself; refocused, it suggests most simply that technical innovations run ahead of people's
ability to use the innovations well. This simple version has been
true through the history of technology: human beings have invented new tools before they knew what to do with them. There is,
though, a sharper version of the paradox: the first impulse in using a new tool is to simplify the social relations that existed before.

We are in just that condition, I believe, at the present moment.
Our generation is living through a revolution in communications technology, but this revolution so far has reduced the quality of communications in the same measure it has increased their
quantity. Those enslaved to e-mail will know exactly what I mean.
Composing one hundred carefully considered letters a day would
take up the whole of the day; a single, well-thought-out letter can
require hours in itself. For this reason, as the technologist Jaron
Lanier observes, speed is replacing depth in communications. I
would add that the communication occurring in e-mails tends to
the denotative rather than the connotative; it focuses on sheer information. A professional writer will spend hours on situating a
piece of information, finding just the right words to convey irony
or conviction; so, too, in face-to-face conversations, silences and
pauses, nonverbal glances and bodily gestures transform the information contained in raw words. The brutalist fault, I want to emphasize, lies not in the technology itself, but in the uses to which it
has been put.

I experienced Burckhardt's paradox close-up, in which the issue of narrative appeared in a computerized form. I belonged to
a group beta-testing Google Wave, a software program encourag-

ing serious cooperation online. Real-time voices and images were organized onscreen in clear ways; Google Wave archived the flow of contributions, so that nothing was lost in time, as things are frequently forgotten in the flux of face-to-face conversation. Yet the programmers had imagined cooperation in a project simply as an interactive narrative that should move ineluctably toward a practical denouement; stray, suggestive thoughts and the kind of surprising discoveries we call "thinking outside the box" were banished to the archives. People who made these stray comments or thought outside the box gradually ceased to participate, as our project—analyzing immigration to London—moved inexorably toward its policy goals onscreen. We became frustrated collaborators, as online cooperation was giving us less and less innovation; we resorted in the end to airplanes—the most sadistic of all modern machines—to meet and work productively together. Google Wave proved equally inhibiting to other beta-testing groups, and this sleek, technologically sophisticated program was abandoned after only a year on the market.

The fault here lay in the programming engineers' imagination of what cooperation is about. They had streamlined—that is, simplified—the process. They had made communication easier, more user-friendly. But in working together, we were after complexity, not friendliness. Burckhardt's paradox is a way of naming just this gap.

You can understand the issue again purely mechanically, in terms of the difference between replicants and robots. A replicant is a machine that mimics the human body, for instance, a pacemaker for the heart, or the perfect artificial humans in the film *The Stepford Wives*. A robot proper does not mimic the human body; as in the robots used in auto construction, the machines follow a physical and computational logic of their own.

When we worry about machines replacing human beings, we are focused more on these alien robots than on mimetic replicants. Yet the programming of robots can, as the engineer Cecil Balmond observes, make their proper use obscure and dysfunctional, just because we have no guiding measure of what they should do for us. Neither Lanier nor Balmond are back-to-nature romantics; they are raising questions of purpose and value in the design of machines, questions they think can only be answered by returning to the human subject. It is exactly the same question technicians in Spinoza's generation posed about the value of the double concave lens he was a master in fabricating.

I have wanted, in sum, to explain in this essay why the label "humanist" is a badge of honor, rather than the name for an exhausted worldview. Humanism's emphasis on life narratives, on the enriching experience of difference, and on evaluating tools in terms of human rather than mechanical complexity are all living values—and more, I would say, these are critical measures for judging the state of modern society. Looking back to the origins of these values is not an exercise in nostalgia; it is rather to remind us that we are engaged in a project, still in process, a humanism yet to be realized, of making social experience more open, engaging, and layered.

Notes

1. This essay is based on a paper presented at the "After Humanism" conference, sponsored by the Oakley Center for the Humanities and Social Sciences, Williams College, September 23–24, 2010.
2. Giovanni Pico della Mirandola, *On the Dignity of Man,* trans. Charles Glenn Wallis, Paul J. W. Miller, and Douglas Carmichael (Cambridge, MA: Hackett, 1965), 4.
3. Pico della Mirandola, 5.

LAUREN SLATER

Killing My Body to Save My Mind

FROM *Elle*

MY BLOOD IS IN A BLENDER. It's just about the only bit of brightness in this drab office of a life insurance company that, before betting on my body, wants to sample its various fluids. First, it was urine in a tiny pleated cup, and now in some sort of centrifuge, my blood. It begins circling slowly, before picking up speed and whipping around until, at last, the lipids separate from the fresh red liquid and rise to the top. That's cholesterol I'm seeing, a custardy yellow substance that reminds me of the pudding my mother used to make. Damn my mother! It's her cakes and tarts and tortes that have put me in this position, which is precisely . . . what? I'm a forty-plus fatso with a penchant for Belgian waffles. In truth, though, it's neither my mother nor the waffles that are responsible for my body's breakdown. Isn't the term odd? *Breakdown.* My body is having a breakdown, for sure, yet instead of atomizing into pieces and parts, I'm doing just the opposite. I'm acquiring a perverse sort of solidity that belies the real crux of the matter. Certainly no breeze will blow me over, but that doesn't mean I'm robust. My breakdown is a kind of hyperplastic excess that renders me easily winded—and possibly worse—and has exiled me to the plus-size section of clothing stores. Once I was five feet (I'm still five feet) and weighed a pert one hundred pounds. What has happened here?

"Do you think they'll insure me?" I ask the phlebotomist as we both peer at my spinning blood and the lipids lining its surface.

"I see this with lots of folks," the kind man says to me. But I'm not reassured. I am now a member—along with "lots of folks"—of the American obesity club, a club I'd do almost anything to leave, the badge stuck to my bulk with an adhesive that is out-of-this-world strong.

This is not a story about how hard it is to get life insurance when your cholesterol, like mine, registers at 405—healthy is anything below 200—and your triglycerides are over 800, or 650 mg/dL higher than they should be. In fact, I got the life insurance, but that didn't change my predicament. Every night I take a handful of pills, all of them psychotropics. Way back when, in my lean, clean twenties, I needed only one pill to keep my mind aloft, but the brain is a sneaky, needy organ, and even though the psychiatric profession likes to deny it, it's an organ that becomes tolerant to the chemicals you ingest—often necessitating what is called "polypharmacy," or, more colloquially, "the cocktail." My cocktail at this point consists of 300 mg of Effexor XR, 300 mg of Wellbutrin XL, 90 mg of Vyvanse, 2 mg of Suboxone, 1 mg of Klonopin, and, last but not least, 7.5 mg of the fattening drug called Zyprexa.

Nearly all psychotropics cause some weight gain, but Zyprexa is in a class by itself. It was prescribed to me last year during a horrific depression. I saw black hats roll across roads and heard the crying of a child I could never find. At night, the darkness was intense, all-consuming, like liquid coal I tried to move through.

I'd always known, at least for as long as I've had my psychology degree, that severe depression can have psychotic features. But knowing is one thing, experience so entirely something else, that I was humbled, thinking I'd ever understood. In the summer, the psychosis worsened, in part because I could not stand the contrast between my blackness and all the beauty everywhere around me and utterly inaccessible. From the window of the kitchen I could see my garden, full of bee balm and mint, loosestrife and arctic daisies—big wheels of white with florid amber navels packed with pollen. My garden bloomed profusely all that summer, calling to it butterflies and bees and birds with yellow vests. And yet this beauty seemed somehow menacing to me. The flowers—some had the heads of serpents, others flamed in the high heat, causing the air to warble, as though the whole world were wavering. If I stared at my garden long enough, it would dissolve into thousands of Pissarro points that then lost their shapes and dripped downward.

That was when my psychopharmacologist, alarmed at my state, decided to add another drug to my mix. First he put me on Abilify, which is used in some cases to boost the efficacy of Effexor XR and Prozac. It didn't do the trick. Next he prescribed Geodon, also used to punch up Prozac and its close companions, the SSRIs. Geodon also failed. The third SSRI amplifier was Zyprexa, a name that made me think of an instrument, or a scooter.

Of all the so-called atypical antipsychotics, which are often prescribed as adjuncts when your plain old antidepressant fizzles out, Zyprexa is most associated with weight gain, and the weight gain, in turn, is linked to a host of dangerous conditions—diabetes, for one.

At the time I was given Zyprexa, I was so desperate I couldn't have cared less about diabetes, and my doctor's warning that I might plump up as a side effect of the drug fell on fairly deaf ears. What did it matter to me that in every study I saw comparing "weight-gain liabilities" among the atypical antipsychotics, Zyprexa always fared worst, with some patients gaining more than one hundred pounds. I knew how bad a rap Zyprexa had; I'd seen a friend pop those pills and go practically elephantine. But from my point of view just then, I would've rather been a happy elephant than a miserable hominid. Thus, I filled my script ASAP. I took my first white pill the same night. Three pills and three days later, my depression lifted, just lifted like a wet velvet curtain, heavy and dripping and hauled up high above me, so I could see the air and my garden and my entire life as it once was—no, even better. Zyprexa seemed to add a little zip, a little zing, so the edges of everything had a merry sparkle, and I could laugh. I did laugh, finding my children's antics delightful, loving the way my dogs danced for their food.

Food. *Food.* For the first time in months I had my appetite back, and everything looked good; it looked downright delicious, in fact, the lasagna steaming in its pan, the hot melted cheese crisped at the outer edges and bubbling on top. I couldn't get enough; I had the hunger of a wolf after winter, when he's gone a whole season with no prey. I was insatiable, every bite packed with complex flavors: a simple pistachio nut both fruity and salty, with the wet tang of earth in the background. I rose each morning full of enthusiasm, my desire for food spilling over onto other things, each day filled with appetizing possibilities, as if I were choosing from a delectable buffet. I packed my children's lunches in the morning and licked the Fluffernutter off the knife's blade, the taste of sweetness and sunlight. Once the kids were headed off to camp, I began my own breakfast, practically panting with excitement. Some mornings I might make oatmeal, seasoning it with cinnamon and nutmeg and several dark drops of vanilla, which gave it such a fine scent I had to have seconds, even thirds. At this point I wasn't giving much thought to my increase in appetite or weight, focused almost solely on how happy I was to have my life back, though I did register it as odd that my stomach could hold so much food.

I kept going.

There were baked apple crisps with brown-sugar topping; ice creams filled with chunks of fresh peach; french fries, the outside browned, the inside soft and white—I ate it all. And then more. As with many drugs I've taken, Zyprexa's side effects were more intense in the beginning; I gained about fifty pounds before coming up for air. What happened is, I saw myself. I was walking down the street toward a glass door reflecting my image back to me, and it took me several seconds to recognize myself, to realize that the woman I was seeing was me. I'd grown so stout, my cheekbones were buried in slabs of fat. I thought, Oh my God. I went to the gym and StairMastered in a frenzy, but the exercise didn't seem to help. By this time I'd been on Zyprexa for many months, and its appetite-heightening effects had diminished, yet I was still gaining weight. "I swear to God I'm eating less than twelve hundred calories a day," I told my psychopharmacologist. He plainly didn't believe me. "We always eat more than we think we do," he responded. I responded by keeping a food diary to prove him wrong, and I did prove him wrong, although I think he doubted the integrity of my reportage.

Some researchers say that, indeed, Zyprexa makes you fat because it radically alters how the body metabolizes calories, not just because it stimulates appetite. Others—most, in fact—aren't convinced. "Although Zyprexa may alter metabolism to some degree," says Alexander Vuckovic, MD, a psychiatrist at McLean Hospital in Belmont, Massachusetts, "the main problem is the relentless hunger it causes. You can't stop eating." My experience, of course, contradicts this. After seeing my enormity in the reflection, I went back to eating bunny food—sliced carrots and salted celery and diet drinks for dinner—and still the scale went up, the digital red numbers burning in their black display, even my feet widening so my shoe size went from 7 to 7½. My fingers, according to my eleven-year-old girl, look like "sausages." I find I am shy around my husband, and not in a flirtatious, come-hither way. "Could you have sex with a fat woman?" I asked him the other day. To his incredible credit, he smiled softly and said, "I'm sure willing to give it a try." I'm not. Damn that drug! Why does it have to work this way?

It doesn't really matter why Zyprexa makes you fat. The bottom line is that it does, and with the excess of adipose tissue comes a raft of health issues. At 180 pounds, I have a body mass index of 35.1, which means that I'm more likely than a person with a normal BMI to develop diabetes and something called metabolic syndrome, which is essentially a collection of risk factors for heart disease and stroke ranging from hypertension and elevated triglyceride levels to a waistline of 35 inches or more (for women). I also have a higher risk of contracting most cancers, according to the American Cancer Society—cancers of the colon and gastrointestinal system among them. So many patients have become diabetic or suffered from cardiovascular problems on Zyprexa that its maker, Eli Lilly, agreed in January 2007 to pay up to $500 million to settle lawsuits from plaintiffs who claimed they became ill after taking the drug. Many more suits are still pending.

I'm certainly not going to sue Eli Lilly for making a drug that saved my life, even as it may be leaching it away. I went into this with my eyes wide open. I do not feel fooled or tricked. Still, I'm not at all happy about the news I received after my most recent doctor visit, that my blood sugar is high enough to render me prediabetic. What does this mean? At some point, the nurse practitioner told me, I'll likely be officially diabetic. The standard advice for prediabetics is to exercise and lose weight, but while the nurse recommended I take those steps, there is no guarantee I'll be able to reverse the impact of my Zyprexa.

Zyprexa raises some interesting, if painful, philosophical issues along with its fleshy miseries. Well before Zyprexa or any psychotropic hit the scene, Descartes, in 1641, famously came to conceive of the body as one thing and the soul, or mind, as another. According to his reasoning, one could be sure he had a mind because he could think; not so the body, because a person could dream it up, or be under the influence of a delusion created by an evil spirit. And thus, the French philosopher concluded, the mind and body were so different as to practically exist in separate realms. Dualism was born, or, specifically, Cartesian dualism, and it ruled the intellectual roost until, in the twentieth century, we all grew hip to the notion that mind and brain could not be separated; that mind, like body, was matter.

Zyprexa, or the experience of taking Zyprexa, moves one out of the twenty-first century and back to the age of reason. It makes clear to the patient taking it that she must choose between her mind and her flesh. The result of my choice is that I often feel as if I live hunched up in my head, which has to drag this offending, unfamiliar carcass all around town. "Go! Go now!" my mind orders the lipidinous tyrant, the carcass I've had to disown, but she only laughs long and hard.

So while Zyprexa has helped at least some of its twenty million users worldwide to banish depression and even psychosis, at the same time it's ushered in a whole new/old way of living: divided. I could go on for quite a while about this (the history of dualism, its appearance in the book of Genesis, in Plato's writings, the role of the pineal gland in Descartes's mind-body split), but it would just be a form of evasion. What matters in the here and now is not some philosophical construct unwittingly resurrected by big pharma but rather what it feels like living with the consequences of that construct. I'm killing my body to save my mind—and it's downright scary. I can practically feel the sugar in my blood, practically hear the crystals clanking. I can feel myself living at the cusp of some physical mishap, perhaps even disaster. I can't see what I might do about this, about any of these facts, other than accept them as the manifestation of my decision to do dualism, to side with my mind while sending my flesh down the river.

Because of Zyprexa, I no longer see my life too far into the future. When I was trim and healthy, I silently assumed, due to the ever-increasing advances in medical care and my level of fitness, that I'd live well into my nineties. I had for inspiration my maternal grandparents, who entered their tenth decade swimming laps and playing cards on their screened-in porch. Thus being thirty, forty, forty-five—it all still seemed young, the road ahead unfurling, its endpoint still impossible to see. I even toyed with the idea that I might be a centenarian, what with thinkers like Ray Kurzweil and Aubrey de Grey suggesting that, with a few tweaks to our telomeres, we could reverse the aging process radically. On the February 21, 2011, cover of *Time* was the picture of a cyborg under the headline: "2045: The Year Man Becomes Immortal." Once, I would have read the accompanying article with gusto, but now I read it as a curious and wistful onlooker, as a woman who does not see herself surviving past her seventies if she's—if *I'm*—lucky.

My potentially foreshortened time on the planet isn't all bad, however. I take my days more seriously. I touch my children whenever I can. In a so far unsuccessful effort to reverse the effects of Zyprexa, I exercise hard almost every day, with the result that now my weight has stabilized, albeit at a very high number. Every day I step on that scale and every day it stays the same, no matter how many buckets I sweat. But that's just one sort of scale. In reality, my life is full of scales, what one might call the measure of our days, and on that scale I think I'm winning. I am tremendously grateful to be free of the mind-distorting depression. I take my raft of medicines at night. I always take the Zyprexa last. It's just a plain white pill—who would've guessed it could resurrect Descartes in addition to treating mental illness? The other drugs I slug down fast, sometimes two or three at a time, but when it comes to the Zyprexa, I put the one pill in the center of my palm. I put it right on my lifelines, smack in their center—a reminder, a reassertion that this is the choice I've made—and then I send it down the chute, while high up in my head I look all around. My bedroom is white, my curtains so sheer they seem to be made of mist. My child comes in and wants to sleep as a sandwich tonight—can he? He asks to be between me and his father, for no particular reason, and I tell him yes. Of course. When we turn out the light, I hear my husband on the far side snoring, and my little boy talking in his sleep of sailboats and sand. With all this hubbub, I'll probably be up all night. It's all right. The crickets call. A car booms as it backfires. Somewhere the ocean surges. I lie very still, surrounded. I listen, hard, to life.

JOSE ANTONIO VARGAS

Outlaw

FROM *The New York Times Magazine*

ONE AUGUST MORNING nearly two decades ago, my mother woke me and put me in a cab. She handed me a jacket. *"Baka malamig doon"* were among the few words she said. ("It might be cold there.") When I arrived at the Philippines' Ninoy Aquino International Airport with her, my aunt, and a family friend, I was introduced to a man I'd never seen. They told me he was my uncle. He held my hand as I boarded an airplane for the first time. It was 1993, and I was twelve.

My mother wanted to give me a better life, so she sent me thousands of miles away to live with her parents in America—my grandfather (*Lolo* in Tagalog) and grandmother *(Lola).* After I arrived in Mountain View, California, in the San Francisco Bay Area, I entered sixth grade and quickly grew to love my new home, family, and culture. I discovered a passion for language, though it was hard to learn the difference between formal English and American slang. One of my early memories is of a freckled kid in middle school asking me, "What's up?" I replied, "The sky," and he and a couple of other kids laughed. I won the eighth-grade spelling bee by memorizing words I couldn't properly pronounce. (The winning word was *indefatigable.*)

One day when I was sixteen, I rode my bike to the nearby DMV office to get my driver's permit. Some of my friends already had their licenses, so I figured it was time. But when I handed the clerk my green card as proof of U.S. residency, she flipped it around, examining it. "This is fake," she whispered. "Don't come back here again."

Confused and scared, I pedaled home and confronted Lolo. I remember him sitting in the garage, cutting coupons. I dropped my bike and ran over to him, showing him the green card. *"Peke ba ito?"* I asked in Tagalog. ("Is this fake?") My grandparents were naturalized American citizens—he worked as a security guard, she as a food server—and they had begun supporting my mother and me financially when I was three, after my father's wandering eye and inability to properly provide for us led to my parents' separation. Lolo was a proud man, and I saw the shame on his face as he told me he purchased the card, along with other fake documents, for me. "Don't show it to other people," he warned.

I decided then that I could never give anyone reason to doubt I was an American. I convinced myself that if I worked enough, if I achieved enough, I would be rewarded with citizenship. I felt I could earn it.

I've tried. Over the past fourteen years, I've graduated from high school and college and built a career as a journalist, interviewing some of the most famous people in the country. On the surface, I've created a good life. I've lived the American dream.

But I am still an undocumented immigrant. And that means living a different kind of reality. It means going about my day in fear of being found out. It means rarely trusting people, even those closest to me, with who I really am. It means keeping my family photos in a shoebox rather than displaying them on shelves in my home, so friends don't ask about them. It means reluctantly, even painfully, doing things I know are wrong and unlawful. And it has meant relying on a sort of twenty-first-century underground railroad of supporters, people who took an interest in my future and took risks for me.

Last year I read about four students who walked from Miami to Washington to lobby for the DREAM Act, a nearly decade-old immigration bill that would provide a path to legal permanent residency for young people who have been educated in this country. At the risk of deportation—the Obama administration has deported almost 800,000 people in the last two years—they are speaking out. Their courage has inspired me.

There are believed to be eleven million undocumented immigrants in the United States. We're not always who you think we are. Some pick your strawberries or care for your children. Some are in high school or college. And some, it turns out, write news articles you might read. I grew up here. This is my home. Yet even though I think of myself as an American and consider America my country, my country doesn't think of me as one of its own.

My first challenge was the language. Though I learned English in the Philippines, I wanted to lose my accent. During high school, I spent hours at a time watching television (especially *Frasier, Home Improvement,* and reruns of *The Golden Girls*) and movies (from *Goodfellas* to *Anne of Green Gables*), pausing the VHS to try to copy how various characters enunciated their words. At the local library, I read magazines, books, and newspapers—anything to learn how to write better. Kathy Dewar, my high school English teacher, introduced me to journalism. From the moment I wrote my first article for the student paper, I convinced myself that having my name in print—writing in English, interviewing Americans—validated my presence here.

The debates over "illegal aliens" intensified my anxieties. In 1994, only a year after my flight from the Philippines, Governor Pete Wilson was reelected in part because of his support for Proposition 187, which prohibited undocumented immigrants from attending public school and accessing other services. (A federal court later found the law unconstitutional.) After my encounter at the DMV in 1997, I grew more aware of anti-immigrant sentiments and stereotypes: *they don't want to assimilate; they are a drain on society.* They're not talking about me, I would tell myself. I have something to contribute.

To do that, I had to work—and for that, I needed a Social Security number. Fortunately, my grandfather had already managed to get one for me. Lolo had always taken care of everyone in the family. He and my grandmother emigrated legally in 1984 from Zambales, a province in the Philippines of rice fields and bamboo houses, following Lolo's sister, who married a Filipino American serving in the American military. She petitioned for her brother and his wife to join her. When they got here, Lolo petitioned for his two children—my mother and her younger brother—to follow them. But instead of mentioning that my mother was a married woman, he listed her as single. Legal residents can't petition for their married children. Besides, Lolo didn't care for my father. He didn't want him coming here, too.

But soon Lolo grew nervous that the immigration authorities

reviewing the petition would discover my mother was married, thus derailing not only her chances of coming here but those of my uncle as well. So he withdrew her petition. After my uncle came to America legally in 1991, Lolo tried to get my mother here through a tourist visa, but she wasn't able to obtain one. That's when she decided to send me. My mother told me later that she figured she would follow me soon. She never did.

The "uncle" who brought me here turned out to be a coyote, not a relative, my grandfather later explained. Lolo scraped together enough money—I eventually learned it was $4,500, a huge sum for him—to pay him to smuggle me here under a fake name and fake passport. (I never saw the passport again after the flight and have always assumed that the coyote kept it.) After I arrived in America, Lolo obtained a new fake Filipino passport, in my real name this time, adorned with a fake student visa, in addition to the fraudulent green card.

Using the fake passport, we went to the local Social Security Administration office and applied for a Social Security number and card. It was, I remember, a quick visit. When the card came in the mail, it had my full, real name, but it also clearly stated: "Valid for work only with INS authorization."

When I began looking for work, a short time after the DMV incident, my grandfather and I took the Social Security card to Kinko's, where he covered the "INS authorization" text with a sliver of white tape. We then made photocopies of the card. At a glance, at least, the copies would look like copies of a regular, unrestricted Social Security card.

Lolo always imagined I would work the kind of low-paying jobs that undocumented people often take. (Once I married an American, he said, I would get my real papers, and everything would be fine.) But even menial jobs require documents, so he and I hoped the doctored card would work for now. The more documents I had, he said, the better.

While in high school, I worked part-time at Subway, then at the front desk of the local YMCA, then at a tennis club, until I landed an unpaid internship at the *Mountain View Voice*, my hometown newspaper. First I brought coffee and helped around the office; eventually I began covering city hall meetings and other assignments for pay.

For more than a decade of getting part-time and full-time jobs, employers have rarely asked to check my original Social Security card. When they did, I showed the photocopied version, which they accepted. Over time, I also began checking the citizenship box on my federal I-9 employment eligibility forms. (Claiming full citizenship was actually easier than declaring permanent resident "green card" status, which would have required me to provide an alien registration number.)

This deceit never got easier. The more I did it, the more I felt like an impostor, the more guilt I carried—and the more I worried that I would get caught. But I kept doing it. I needed to live and survive on my own, and I decided this was the way.

Mountain View High School became my second home. I was elected to represent my school at school board meetings, which gave me the chance to meet and befriend Rich Fischer, the superintendent for our school district. I joined the speech and debate team, acted in school plays, and eventually became coeditor of the *Oracle,* the student newspaper. That drew the attention of my principal, Pat Hyland. "You're at school just as much as I am," she told me. Pat and Rich would soon become mentors, and over time, almost surrogate parents for me.

After a choir rehearsal during my junior year, Jill Denny, the choir director, told me she was considering a Japan trip for our singing group. I told her I couldn't afford it, but she said we'd figure out a way. I hesitated, and then decided to tell her the truth. "It's not really the money," I remember saying. "I don't have the right passport." When she assured me we'd get the proper documents, I finally told her. "I can't get the right passport," I said. "I'm not supposed to be here."

She understood. So the choir toured Hawaii instead, with me in tow. (Mrs. Denny and I spoke a couple of months ago, and she told me she hadn't wanted to leave any student behind.)

Later that school year, my history class watched a documentary on Harvey Milk, the openly gay San Francisco city official who was assassinated. This was 1999, just six months after Matthew Shepard's body was found tied to a fence in Wyoming. During the discussion, I raised my hand and said something like: "I'm sorry Harvey Milk got killed for being gay . . . I've been meaning to say this . . . I'm gay."

I hadn't planned on coming out that morning, though I had

known that I was gay for several years. With that announcement, I became the only openly gay student at school, and it caused turmoil with my grandparents. Lolo kicked me out of the house for a few weeks. Though we eventually reconciled, I had disappointed him on two fronts. First, as a Catholic, he considered homosexuality a sin and was embarrassed about having "*ang apo na bakla*" ("a grandson who is gay"). Even worse, I was making matters more difficult for myself, he said. I needed to marry an American woman in order to gain a green card.

Tough as it was, coming out about being gay seemed less daunting than coming out about my legal status. I kept my other secret mostly hidden.

While my classmates awaited their college acceptance letters, I hoped to get a full-time job at the *Mountain View Voice* after graduation. It's not that I didn't want to go to college, but I couldn't apply for state and federal financial aid. Without that, my family couldn't afford to send me.

But when I finally told Pat and Rich about my immigration "problem"—as we called it from then on—they helped me look for a solution. At first, they even wondered if one of them could adopt me and fix the situation that way, but a lawyer Rich consulted told him it wouldn't change my legal status because I was too old. Eventually they connected me to a new scholarship fund for high-potential students who were usually the first in their families to attend college. Most important, the fund was not concerned with immigration status. I was among the first recipients, with the scholarship covering tuition, lodging, books, and other expenses for my studies at San Francisco State University.

As a college freshman, I found a job working part-time at the *San Francisco Chronicle*, where I sorted mail and wrote some freelance articles. My ambition was to get a reporting job, so I embarked on a series of internships. First I landed at the *Philadelphia Daily News*, in the summer of 2001, where I covered a drive-by shooting and the wedding of the 76ers star Allen Iverson. Using those articles, I applied to the *Seattle Times* and got an internship for the following summer.

But then my lack of proper documents became a problem again. The *Times* recruiter, Pat Foote, asked all incoming interns to bring certain paperwork on their first day: a birth certificate, or a passport, or a driver's license plus an original Social Security card. I panicked, thinking my documents wouldn't pass muster. So before starting the job, I called Pat and told her about my legal status. After consulting with management, she called me back with the answer I feared: I couldn't do the internship.

This was devastating. What good was college if I couldn't then pursue the career I wanted? I decided then that if I was to succeed in a profession that is all about truth telling, I couldn't tell the truth about myself.

After this episode, Jim Strand, the venture capitalist who sponsored my scholarship, offered to pay for an immigration lawyer. Rich and I went to meet her in San Francisco's financial district.

I was hopeful. This was in early 2002, shortly after Senators Orrin Hatch, the Utah Republican, and Dick Durbin, the Illinois Democrat, introduced the DREAM Act—Development, Relief, and Education for Alien Minors. It seemed like the legislative version of what I'd told myself: if I work hard and contribute, things will work out.

But the meeting left me crushed. My only solution, the lawyer said, was to go back to the Philippines and accept a ten-year ban before I could apply to return legally.

If Rich was discouraged, he hid it well. "Put this problem on a shelf," he told me. "Compartmentalize it. Keep going."

And I did. For the summer of 2003, I applied for internships across the country. Several newspapers, including the *Wall Street Journal*, the *Boston Globe,* and the *Chicago Tribune,* expressed interest. But when the *Washington Post* offered me a spot, I knew where I would go. And this time, I had no intention of acknowledging my "problem."

The *Post* internship posed a tricky obstacle: it required a driver's license. (After my close call at the California DMV, I'd never gotten one.) So I spent an afternoon at the Mountain View Public Library, studying various states' requirements. Oregon was among the most welcoming—and it was just a few hours' drive north.

Again, my support network came through. A friend's father lived in Portland, and he allowed me to use his address as proof of residency. Pat, Rich, and Rich's longtime assistant, Mary Moore, sent letters to me at that address. Rich taught me how to do three-point turns in a parking lot, and a friend accompanied me to Portland.

The license meant everything to me—it would let me drive, fly, and work. But my grandparents worried about the Portland trip and the Washington internship. While Lola offered daily prayers so that I would not get caught, Lolo told me that I was dreaming too big, risking too much.

I was determined to pursue my ambitions. I was twenty-two, I told them, responsible for my own actions. But this was different from Lolo's driving a confused teenager to Kinko's. I knew what I was doing now, and I knew it wasn't right. But what was I supposed to do?

I was paying state and federal taxes, but I was using an invalid Social Security card and writing false information on my employment forms. But that seemed better than depending on my grandparents or on Pat, Rich, and Jim—or returning to a country I barely remembered. I convinced myself all would be okay if I lived up to the qualities of a "citizen": hard work, self-reliance, love of my country.

At the DMV in Portland, I arrived with my photocopied Social Security card, my college ID, a pay stub from the *San Francisco Chronicle,* and my proof of state residence—the letters to the Portland address that my support network had sent. It worked. My license, issued in 2003, was set to expire eight years later, on my thirtieth birthday, on February 3, 2011. I had eight years to succeed professionally, and to hope that some sort of immigration reform would pass in the meantime and allow me to stay.

It seemed like all the time in the world.

My summer in Washington was exhilarating. I was intimidated to be in a major newsroom but was assigned a mentor—Peter Perl, a veteran magazine writer—to help me navigate it. A few weeks into the internship, he printed out one of my articles, about a guy who recovered a long-lost wallet, circled the first two paragraphs, and left it on my desk. "Great eye for details—awesome!" he wrote. Though I didn't know it then, Peter would become one more member of my network.

At the end of the summer, I returned to the *San Francisco Chronicle.* My plan was to finish school—I was now a senior—while I worked for the *Chronicle* as a reporter for the city desk. But when the *Post* beckoned again, offering me a full-time, two-year paid internship that I could start when I graduated in June 2004, it was too tempting to pass up. I moved back to Washington.

About four months into my job as a reporter for the *Post*, I began feeling increasingly paranoid, as if I had "illegal immigrant" tattooed on my forehead—and in Washington, of all places, where the debates over immigration seemed never-ending. I was so eager to prove myself that I feared I was annoying some colleagues and editors—and worried that any one of these professional journalists could discover my secret. The anxiety was nearly paralyzing. I decided I had to tell one of the higher-ups about my situation. I turned to Peter.

By this time, Peter, who still works at the *Post*, had become part of management as the paper's director of newsroom training and professional development. One afternoon in late October, we walked a couple of blocks to Lafayette Square, across from the White House. Over some twenty minutes, sitting on a bench, I told him everything: the Social Security card, the driver's license, Pat and Rich, my family.

Peter was shocked. "I understand you one hundred times better now," he said. He told me that I had done the right thing by telling him, and that it was now our shared problem. He said he didn't want to do anything about it just yet. I had just been hired, he said, and I needed to prove myself. "When you've done enough," he said, "we'll tell Don and Len together." (Don Graham is the chairman of the Washington Post Company; Leonard Downie Jr. was then the paper's executive editor.) A month later, I spent my first Thanksgiving in Washington with Peter and his family.

In the five years that followed, I did my best to "do enough." I was promoted to staff writer, reported on video game culture, wrote a series on Washington's HIV/AIDS epidemic, and covered the role of technology and social media in the 2008 presidential race. I visited the White House, where I interviewed senior aides and covered a state dinner—and gave the Secret Service the Social Security number I obtained with false documents.

I did my best to steer clear of reporting on immigration policy but couldn't always avoid it. On two occasions, I wrote about Hillary Clinton's position on driver's licenses for undocumented immigrants. I also wrote an article about Senator Mel Martinez of Florida, then the chairman of the Republican National Committee, who was defending his party's stance toward Latinos after only one Republican presidential candidate—John McCain, the coauthor of a failed immigration bill—agreed to participate in a debate sponsored by Univision, the Spanish-language network.

It was an odd sort of dance: I was trying to stand out in a highly competitive newsroom, yet I was terrified that if I stood out too much, I'd invite unwanted scrutiny. I tried to compartmentalize my fears, distract myself by reporting on the lives of other people, but there was no escaping the central conflict in my life. Maintaining a deception for so long distorts your sense of self. You start wondering who you've become, and why.

In April 2008, I was part of a *Post* team that won a Pulitzer Prize for the paper's coverage of the Virginia Tech shootings a year earlier. Lolo died a year earlier, so it was Lola who called me the day of the announcement. The first thing she said was, "*Anong mangyari kung malaman nang tao?*"

What will happen if people find out?

I couldn't say anything. After we got off the phone, I rushed to the bathroom on the fourth floor of the newsroom, sat down on the toilet, and cried.

In the summer of 2009, without ever having had that follow-up talk with top *Post* management, I left the paper and moved to New York to join the *Huffington Post*. I met Arianna Huffington at a Washington Press Club Foundation dinner I was covering for the *Washington Post* two years earlier, and she later recruited me to join her news site. I wanted to learn more about web publishing, and I thought the new job would provide a useful education.

Still, I was apprehensive about the move: many companies were already using E-Verify, a program set up by the Department of Homeland Security that checks if prospective employees are eligible to work, and I didn't know if my new employer was among them. But I'd been able to get jobs in other newsrooms, I figured, so I filled out the paperwork as usual and succeeded in landing on the payroll.

While I worked at the *Huffington Post*, other opportunities emerged. My HIV/AIDS series became a documentary film called *The Other City*, which opened at the Tribeca Film Festival last year and was broadcast on Showtime. I began writing for magazines and landed a dream assignment: profiling Facebook's Mark Zuckerberg for *The New Yorker*.

The more I achieved, the more scared and depressed I became. I was proud of my work, but there was always a cloud hanging over it, over me. My old eight-year deadline—the expiration of my Oregon driver's license—was approaching.

After slightly less than a year, I decided to leave the *Huffington Post*. In part, this was because I wanted to promote the documentary and write a book about online culture—or so I told my friends. But the real reason was, after so many years of trying to be a part of the system, of focusing all my energy on my professional life, I learned that no amount of professional success would solve my problem or ease the sense of loss and displacement I felt. I lied to a friend about why I couldn't take a weekend trip to Mexico. Another time I concocted an excuse for why I couldn't go on an all-expenses-paid trip to Switzerland. I have been unwilling, for years, to be in a long-term relationship because I never wanted anyone to get too close and ask too many questions. All the while, Lola's question was stuck in my head: what will happen if people find out?

Early this year, just two weeks before my thirtieth birthday, I won a small reprieve: I obtained a driver's license in the state of Washington. The license is valid until 2016. This offered me five more years of acceptable identification—but also five more years of fear, of lying to people I respect and institutions that trusted me, of running away from who I am.

I'm done running. I'm exhausted. I don't want that life anymore.

So I've decided to come forward, own up to what I've done, and tell my story to the best of my recollection. I've reached out to former bosses and employers and apologized for misleading them—a mix of humiliation and liberation coming with each disclosure. All the people mentioned in this article gave me permission to use their names. I've also talked to family and friends about my situation and am working with legal counsel to review my options. I don't know what the consequences will be of telling my story.

I do know that I am grateful to my grandparents, my Lolo and Lola, for giving me the chance for a better life. I'm also grateful to my other family—the support network I found here in America—for encouraging me to pursue my dreams.

It's been almost eighteen years since I've seen my mother. Early on, I was mad at her for putting me in this position, and then mad at myself for being angry and ungrateful. By the time I got to college, we rarely spoke by phone. It became too painful; after a while it was easier to just send money to help support her and my two half siblings. My sister, almost two years old when I left, is almost twenty now. I've never met my fourteen-year-old brother. I would love to see them.

Not long ago, I called my mother. I wanted to fill the gaps in my memory about that August morning so many years ago. We had never discussed it. Part of me wanted to shove the memory aside, but to write this article and face the facts of my life, I needed more details. Did I cry? Did she? Did we kiss goodbye?

My mother told me I was excited about meeting a stewardess, about getting on a plane. She also reminded me of the one piece of advice she gave me for blending in: if anyone asked why I was coming to America, I should say I was going to Disneyland.

WESLEY YANG

Paper Tigers

FROM *New York Magazine*

SOMETIMES I'LL GLIMPSE my reflection in a window and feel astonished by what I see. Jet-black hair. Slanted eyes. A pancake-flat surface of yellow-and-green-toned skin. An expression that is nearly reptilian in its impassivity. I've contrived to think of this face as the equal in beauty to any other. But what I feel in these moments is its strangeness to me. It's my face. I can't disclaim it. But what does it have to do with me?

Millions of Americans must feel estranged from their own faces. But every self-estranged individual is estranged in his own way. I, for instance, am the child of Korean immigrants, but I do not speak my parents' native tongue. I have never called my elders by the proper honorific, "big brother" or "big sister." I have never dated a Korean woman. I don't have a Korean friend. Though I am an immigrant, I have never wanted to strive like one.

You could say that I am, in the gently derisive parlance of Asian Americans, a banana or a Twinkie (yellow on the outside, white on the inside). But while I don't believe our roots necessarily define us, I do believe there are racially inflected assumptions wired into our neural circuitry that we use to sort through the sea of faces we confront. And although I am in most respects devoid of Asian characteristics, I do have an Asian face.

Here is what I sometimes suspect my face signifies to other Americans: An invisible person, barely distinguishable from a mass of faces that resemble it. A conspicuous person standing apart from the crowd and yet devoid of any individuality. An icon of so much that the culture pretends to honor but that it in fact patronizes and exploits. Not just people "who are good at math" and play the violin, but a mass of stifled, repressed, abused, conformist quasi-robots who simply do not matter, socially or culturally.

I've always been of two minds about this sequence of stereotypes. On the one hand, it offends me greatly that anyone would think to apply them to me, or to anyone else, simply on the basis of facial characteristics. On the other hand, it also seems to me that there are a lot of Asian people to whom they apply.

Let me summarize my feelings toward Asian values: Fuck filial piety. Fuck grade grubbing. Fuck Ivy League mania. Fuck deference to authority. Fuck humility and hard work. Fuck harmonious relations. Fuck sacrificing for the future. Fuck earnest, striving middle-class servility.

I understand the reasons Asian parents have raised a generation of children this way. Doctor, lawyer, accountant, engineer: these are good jobs open to whoever works hard enough. What could be wrong with that pursuit? Asians graduate from college at a rate higher than any other ethnic group in America, including whites. They earn a higher median family income than any other ethnic group in America, including whites. This is a stage in a triumphal narrative, and it is a narrative that is much shorter than many remember. Two-thirds of the roughly 14 million Asian Americans are foreign-born. There were less than 39,000 people of Korean descent living in America in 1970, when my elder brother was born. There are around 1 million today.

Asian American success is typically taken to ratify the American dream and to prove that minorities can make it in this country without handouts. Still, an undercurrent of racial panic always accompanies the consideration of Asians, and all the more so as China becomes the destination for our industrial base and the banker controlling our burgeoning debt. But if the armies of Chinese factory workers who make our fast fashion and iPads terrify us, and if the collective mass of high-achieving Asian American students arouse an anxiety about the laxity of American parenting, what of the Asian American who obeyed everything his parents told him? Does this person really scare anyone?

Earlier this year, the publication of Amy Chua's *Battle Hymn of the Tiger Mother* incited a collective airing out of many varieties of race-based hysteria. But absent from the millions of words written in response to the book was any serious consideration of whether

Asian Americans were in fact taking over this country. If it is true that they are collectively dominating in elite high schools and universities, is it also true that Asian Americans are dominating in the real world? My strong suspicion was that this was not so, and that the reasons would not be hard to find. If we are a collective juggernaut that inspires such awe and fear, why does it seem that so many Asians are so readily perceived to be, as I myself have felt most of my life, the products of a timid culture, easily pushed around by more assertive people, and thus basically invisible?

A few months ago, I received an e-mail from a young man named Jefferson Mao, who after attending Stuyvesant High School had recently graduated from the University of Chicago. He wanted my advice about "being an Asian writer." This is how he described himself: "I got good grades and I love literature and I want to be a writer and an intellectual; at the same time, I'm the first person in my family to go to college, my parents don't speak English very well, and we don't own the apartment in Flushing that we live in. I mean, I'm proud of my parents and my neighborhood and what I perceive to be my artistic potential or whatever, but sometimes I feel like I'm jumping the gun a generation or two too early."

One bright, cold Sunday afternoon, I ride the 7 train to its last stop in Flushing, where the storefront signs are all written in Chinese and the sidewalks are a slow-moving river of impassive faces. Mao is waiting for me at the entrance of the Main Street subway station, and together we walk to a nearby Vietnamese restaurant.

Mao has a round face, with eyes behind rectangular wire-frame glasses. Since graduating, he has been living with his parents, who emigrated from China when Mao was eight years old. His mother is a manicurist; his father is a physical therapist's aide. Lately, Mao has been making the familiar hour-and-a-half ride from Flushing to downtown Manhattan to tutor a white Stuyvesant freshman who lives in Tribeca. And what he feels, sometimes, in the presence of that amiable young man is a pang of regret. Now he understands better what he ought to have done back when he was a Stuyvesant freshman: "Worked half as hard and been twenty times more successful."

Entrance to Stuyvesant, one of the most competitive public high schools in the country, is determined solely by performance on a test: the top 3.7 percent of all New York City students who take the

Specialized High Schools Admissions Test hoping to go to Stuyvesant are accepted. There are no set-asides for the underprivileged
or, conversely, for alumni or other privileged groups. There is no
formula to encourage "diversity" or any nebulous concept of "well-
roundedness" or "character." Here we have something like pure
meritocracy. This is what it looks like: Asian Americans, who make
up 12.6 percent of New York City, make up 72 percent of the high
school.

This year, 569 Asian Americans scored high enough to earn
a slot at Stuyvesant, along with 179 whites, 13 Hispanics, and 12
blacks. Such dramatic overrepresentation, and what it may be
read to imply about the intelligence of different groups of New
Yorkers, has a way of making people uneasy. But intrinsic intelligence, of course, is precisely what Asians don't believe in. They believe—and have proved—that the constant practice of test taking
will improve the scores of whoever commits to it. All throughout
Flushing, as well as in Bayside, one can find "cram schools," or
storefront academies, that drill students in test preparation after
school, on weekends, and during summer break. "Learning math
is not about learning math," an instructor at one called Ivy Prep
was quoted in the *New York Times* as saying. "It's about weightlift-
ing. You are pumping the iron of math." Mao puts it more specifically: "You learn quite simply to nail any standardized test you
take."

And so there is an additional concern accompanying the rise
of the Tiger Children, one focused more on the narrowness of
the educational experience a non-Asian child might receive in the
company of fanatically preprofessional Asian students. Jenny Tsai,
a student who was elected president of her class at the equally
competitive New York public school Hunter College High School,
remembers frequently hearing that "the school was becoming too
Asian, that they would be the downfall of our school." A couple
of years ago, she revisited this issue in her senior thesis at Harvard, where she interviewed graduates of elite public schools and
found that the white students regarded the Asian students with
wariness. (She quotes a music teacher at Stuyvesant describing the
dominance of Asians: "They were mediocre kids, but they got in
because they were coached.") In 2005, the *Wall Street Journal* reported on "white flight" from a high school in Cupertino, California, that began soon after the children of Asian software engineers

had made the place so brutally competitive that a B average could place you in the bottom third of the class.

Colleges have a way of correcting for this imbalance: the Princeton sociologist Thomas Espenshade has calculated that an Asian applicant must, in practice, score 140 points higher on the SAT than a comparable white applicant to have the same chance of admission. This is obviously unfair to the many qualified Asian individuals who are punished for the success of others with similar faces. Upper-middle-class white kids, after all, have their own elite private schools, and their own private tutors, far more expensive than the cram schools, to help them game the education system.

You could frame it, as some aggrieved Asian Americans do, as a simple issue of equality and press for race-blind quantitative admissions standards. In 2006, a decade after California passed a voter initiative outlawing any racial engineering at the public universities, Asians composed 46 percent of UC Berkeley's entering class; one could imagine a similar demographic reshuffling in the Ivy League, where Asian Americans currently make up about 17 percent of undergraduates. But the Ivies, as we all know, have their own private institutional interests at stake in their admissions choices, including some that are arguably defensible. Who can seriously claim that a Harvard University that was 72 percent Asian would deliver the same grooming for elite status its students had gone there to receive?

Somewhere near the middle of his time at Stuyvesant, a vague sense of discontent started to emerge within Mao. He had always felt himself a part of a mob of "nameless, faceless Asian kids," who were "like a part of the décor of the place." He had been content to keep his head down and work toward the goal shared by everyone at Stuyvesant: Harvard. But around the beginning of his senior year, he began to wonder whether this march toward academic success was the only, or best, path.

"You can't help but feel like there must be another way," he explains over a bowl of pho. "It's like, we're being pitted against each other while there are kids out there in the Midwest who can do way less work and be in a garage band or something—and if they're decently intelligent and work decently hard in school . . ."

Mao began to study the racially inflected social hierarchies at Stuyvesant, where, in a survey undertaken by the student newspaper this year, slightly more than half of the respondents reported that their friends came from within their own ethnic group. His attention focused on the mostly white (and Manhattan-dwelling) group whose members seemed able to manage the crushing workload while still remaining socially active. "The general gist of most high school movies is that the pretty cheerleader gets with the big dumb jock, and the nerd is left to bide his time in loneliness. But at some point in the future," he says, "the nerd is going to rule the world, and the dumb jock is going to work in a carwash.

"At Stuy, it's completely different: if you looked at the pinnacle, the girls and the guys are not only good-looking and socially affable, they also get the best grades and star in the school plays and win election to student government. It all converges at the top. It's like training for high society. It was jarring for us Chinese kids. You got the sense that you had to study hard, but it wasn't enough."

Mao was becoming clued in to the fact that there was another hierarchy behind the official one that explained why others were getting what he never had—"a high-school sweetheart" figured prominently on this list—and that this mysterious hierarchy was going to determine what happened to him in life. "You realize there are things you really don't understand about courtship or just acting in a certain way. Things that somehow come naturally to people who go to school in the suburbs and have parents who are culturally assimilated." I pressed him for specifics, and he mentioned that he had visited his white girlfriend's parents' house the past Christmas, where the family had "sat around cooking together and playing Scrabble." This ordinary vision of suburban American domesticity lingered with Mao: here, at last, was the setting in which all that implicit knowledge "about social norms and propriety" had been transmitted. There was no cram school that taught these lessons.

Before having heard from Mao, I had considered myself at worst lightly singed by the last embers of Asian alienation. Indeed, given all the incredibly hip Asian artists and fashion designers and so forth you can find in New York, it seemed that this feeling was destined to die out altogether. And yet here it was in a New Yorker more than a dozen years my junior. While it may be true that sections of the Asian American world are devoid of alienation, there are large swaths where it is as alive as it has ever been.

A few weeks after we meet, Mao puts me in touch with Daniel Chu, his close friend from Stuyvesant. Chu graduated from Wil-

liams College last year, having won a creative writing award for
his poetry. He had spent a portion of the $18,000 prize on a trip
to China, but now he is back living with his parents in Brooklyn
Chinatown.

Chu remembers that during his first semester at Williams, his
junior adviser would periodically take him aside. Was he feeling all
right? Was something the matter? "I was acclimating myself to the
place," he says. "I wasn't totally happy, but I wasn't depressed." But
then his new white friends made similar remarks. "They would say,
'Dan, it's kind of hard, sometimes, to tell what you're thinking.'"

Chu has a pleasant face, but it would not be wrong to character-
ize his demeanor as reserved. He speaks in a quiet, unemphatic
voice. He doesn't move his features much. He attributes these
traits to the atmosphere in his household. "When you grow up in
a Chinese home," he says, "you don't talk. You shut up and listen
to what your parents tell you to do."

At Stuyvesant, he had hung out in an exclusively Asian world
in which friends were determined by which subway lines you traveled. But when he arrived at Williams, Chu slowly became aware of
something strange: the white people in the New England wilderness walked around smiling at each other. "When you're in a place
like that, everyone is friendly."

He made a point to start smiling more. "It was something that
I had to actively practice," he says. "Like, when you have a trans-
action at a business, you hand over the money—and then you
smile." He says that he's made some progress but that there's still
plenty of work that remains. "I'm trying to undo eighteen years of
a Chinese upbringing. Four years at Williams helps, but only so
much." He is conscious of how his father, an IT manager, is treated
at work. "He's the best programmer at his office," he says, "but
because he doesn't speak English well, he is always passed over."

Though Chu is not merely fluent in English but is officially the
most distinguished poet of his class at Williams, he still worries
that other aspects of his demeanor might attract the same kind
of treatment his father received. "I'm really glad we're having this
conversation," he says at one point—it is helpful to be remembering these lessons in self-presentation just as he prepares for job
interviews.

"I guess what I would like is to become so good at something
that my social deficiencies no longer matter," he tells me. Chu is a

bright, diligent, impeccably credentialed young man born in the United States. He is optimistic about his ability to earn respect in the world. But he doubts he will ever feel the same comfort in his skin that he glimpsed in the people he met at Williams. That kind of comfort, he says—"I think it's generations away."

While he was still an electrical engineering student at Berkeley in the nineties, James Hong visited the IBM campus for a series of interviews. An older Asian researcher looked over Hong's résumé and asked him some standard questions. Then he got up without saying a word and closed the door to his office.

"Listen," he told Hong, "I'm going to be honest with you. My generation came to this country because we wanted better for you kids. We did the best we could, leaving our homes and going to graduate school not speaking much English. If you take this job, you are just going to hit the same ceiling we did. They just see me as an Asian PhD, never management potential. You are going to get a job offer, but don't take it. Your generation has to go farther than we did, otherwise we did everything for nothing."

The researcher was talking about what some refer to as the "bamboo ceiling"—an invisible barrier that maintains a pyramidal racial structure throughout corporate America, with lots of Asians at junior levels, quite a few in middle management, and virtually none in the higher reaches of leadership.

The failure of Asian Americans to become leaders in the white-collar workplace does not qualify as one of the burning social issues of our time. But it is a part of the bitter undercurrent of Asian American life that so many Asian graduates of elite universities find that meritocracy as they have understood it comes to an abrupt end after graduation. If between 15 and 20 percent of every Ivy League class is Asian, and if the Ivy Leagues are incubators for the country's leaders, it would stand to reason that Asians would make up some corresponding portion of the leadership class.

And yet the numbers tell a different story. According to a recent study, Asian Americans represent roughly 5 percent of the population but only 0.3 percent of corporate officers, less than 1 percent of corporate board members, and around 2 percent of college presidents. There are nine Asian American CEOs in the Fortune 500. In specific fields where Asian Americans are heavily represented, there is a similar asymmetry. A third of all software engineers in Silicon Valley are Asian, and yet they make up only 6 percent of board members and about 10 percent of corporate officers of the Bay Area's twenty-five largest companies. At the National Institutes of Health, where 21.5 percent of tenure-track scientists are Asians, only 4.7 percent of the lab or branch directors are, according to a study conducted in 2005. One succinct evocation of the situation appeared in the comments section of a website called Yellowworld: "If you're East Asian, you need to attend a top-tier university to land a good high-paying gig. Even if you land that good high-paying gig, the white guy with the pedigree from a mediocre state university will somehow move ahead of you in the ranks simply because he's white."

Jennifer W. Allyn, a managing director for diversity at PricewaterhouseCoopers, works to ensure that "all of the groups feel welcomed and supported and able to thrive and to go as far as their talents will take them." I posed to her the following definition of parity in the corporate workforce: if the current crop of associates is 17 percent Asian, then in fourteen years, when they have all been up for partner review, 17 percent of those who are offered partner will be Asian. Allyn conceded that PricewaterhouseCoopers was not close to reaching that benchmark anytime soon—and that "nobody else is either."

Part of the insidious nature of the bamboo ceiling is that it does not seem to be caused by overt racism. A survey of Asian Pacific American employees of Fortune 500 companies found that 80 percent reported they were judged not as Asians but as individuals. But only 51 percent reported the existence of Asians in key positions, and only 55 percent agreed that their firms were fully capitalizing on the talents and perspectives of Asians.

More likely, the discrepancy in these numbers is a matter of unconscious bias. Nobody would affirm the proposition that tall men are intrinsically better leaders, for instance. And yet while only 15 percent of the male population is at least six feet tall, 58 percent of all corporate CEOs are. Similarly, nobody would say that Asian people are unfit to be leaders. But subjects in a recently published psychological experiment consistently rated hypothetical employees with Caucasian-sounding names higher in leadership potential than identical ones with Asian names.

Maybe it is simply the case that a traditionally Asian upbringing is the problem. As Allyn points out, in order to be a leader, you must have followers. Associates at PricewaterhouseCoopers are initially judged on how well they do the work they are assigned. "You have to be a doer," as she puts it. They are expected to distinguish themselves with their diligence, at which point they become "super-doers." But being a leader requires different skill sets. "The traits that got you to where you are won't necessarily take you to the next level," says the diversity consultant Jane Hyun, who wrote a book called *Breaking the Bamboo Ceiling*. To become a leader requires taking personal initiative and thinking about how an organization can work differently. It also requires networking, self-promotion, and self-assertion. It's racist to think that any given Asian individual is unlikely to be creative or risk-taking. It's simple cultural observation to say that a group whose education has historically focused on rote memorization and "pumping the iron of math" is, on aggregate, unlikely to yield many people inclined to challenge authority or break with inherited ways of doing things.

Sach Takayasu had been one of the fastest-rising members of her cohort in the marketing department at IBM in New York. But about seven years ago, she felt her progress begin to slow. "I had gotten to the point where I was overdelivering, working really long hours, and where doing more of the same wasn't getting me anywhere," she says. It was around this time that she attended a seminar being offered by an organization called Leadership Education for Asian Pacifics.

LEAP has parsed the complicated social dynamics responsible for the dearth of Asian American leaders and has designed training programs that flatter Asian people even as it teaches them to change their behavior to suit white American expectations. Asians who enter a LEAP program are constantly assured that they will be able to "keep your values, while acquiring new skills," along the way to becoming "culturally competent leaders."

In a presentation to fifteen hundred Asian American employees of Microsoft, LEAP president and CEO J. D. Hokoyama laid out his grand synthesis of the Asian predicament in the workplace. "Sometimes people have perceptions about us and our communities which may or may not be true," Hokoyama told the audience. "But they put those perceptions onto us, and then they do something that can be very devastating: they make decisions about us not based on the truth but based on those perceptions." Hokoyama argued that it was not sufficient to rail at these unjust perceptions. In the end, Asian people themselves would have to assume responsibility for unmaking them. This was both a practical matter, he argued, and, in its own way, fair.

Aspiring Asian leaders had to become aware of "the relationship between values, behaviors, and perceptions." He offered the example of Asians who don't speak up at meetings. "So let's say I go to meetings with you and I notice you never say anything. And I ask myself, Hmm, I wonder why you're not saying anything. Maybe it's because you don't know what we're talking about. That would be a good reason for not saying anything. Or maybe it's because you're not even interested in the subject matter. Or maybe you think the conversation is beneath you. So here I'm thinking, because you never say anything at meetings, that you're either dumb, you don't care, or you're arrogant. When maybe it's because you were taught when you were growing up that when the boss is talking, what are you supposed to be doing? Listening."

Takayasu took the weeklong course in 2006. One of the first exercises she encountered involved the group instructor asking for a list of some qualities that they identify with Asians. The students responded: upholding family honor, filial piety, self-restraint. Then the instructor solicited a list of the qualities the members identify with leadership, and invited the students to notice how little overlap there is between the two lists.

At first, Takayasu didn't relate to the others in attendance, who were listing typical Asian values their parents had taught them. "They were all saying things like 'Study hard,' 'Become a doctor or lawyer,' blah, blah, blah. That's not how my parents were. They would worry if they saw me working too hard." Takayasu had spent her childhood shuttling between New York and Tokyo. Her father was an executive at Mitsubishi; her mother was a concert pianist. She was highly assimilated into American culture, fluent in English, poised and confident. "But the more we got into it, as we moved away from the obvious things to the deeper, more fundamental values, I began to see that my upbringing had been very Asian after all. My parents would say, 'Don't create problems. Don't trouble other people.' How Asian is that? It helped to explain why I don't reach out to other people for help." It occurred to Takayasu that she was a little bit "heads down" after all. She was willing to take on difficult assignments without seeking credit for herself. She was reluctant to "toot her own horn."

Takayasu has put her new self-awareness to work at IBM, and she now exhibits a newfound ability for horn tooting. "The things I could write on my résumé as my team's accomplishments, they're really impressive," she says.

The law professor and writer Tim Wu grew up in Canada with a white mother and a Taiwanese father, which allows him an interesting perspective on how whites and Asians perceive each other. After graduating from law school, he took a series of clerkships, and he remembers the subtle ways in which hierarchies were developed among the other young lawyers. "There is this automatic assumption in any legal environment that Asians will have a particular talent for bitter labor," he says, and then goes on to define the word *coolie*, a Chinese term for "bitter labor." "There was this weird self-selection where the Asians would migrate toward the most brutal part of the labor."

By contrast, the white lawyers he encountered had a knack for portraying themselves as above all that. "White people have this instinct that is really important: to give off the impression that they're only going to do the really important work. You're a quarterback. It's a kind of arrogance that Asians are trained not to have. Someone told me not long after I moved to New York that in order to succeed, you have to understand which rules you're supposed to break. If you break the wrong rules, you're finished. And so the easiest thing to do is follow all the rules. But then you consign yourself to a lower status. The real trick is understanding what rules are not meant for you."

This idea of a kind of rule-governed rule breaking—where the rule book was unwritten but passed along in an innate cultural sense—is perhaps the best explanation I have heard of how the bamboo ceiling functions in practice. LEAP appears to be very good at helping Asian workers who are already culturally competent become more self-aware of how their culture and appearance impose barriers to advancement. But I am not sure that a LEAP course is going to be enough to get Jefferson Mao or Daniel Chu the respect and success they crave. The issue is more fundamental, the social dynamics at work more deeply embedded, and the remedial work required may be at a more basic level of comportment.

What if you missed out on the lessons in masculinity taught in the gyms and locker rooms of America's high schools? What if life has failed to make you a socially dominant alpha male who runs the American boardroom and prevails in the American bedroom? What if no one ever taught you how to greet white people and make them comfortable? What if, despite these deficiencies, you no longer possess an immigrant's dutiful forbearance for a secondary position in the American narrative and want to be a player in the scrimmage of American appetite right now, in the present?

How do you undo eighteen years of a Chinese upbringing?

This is the implicit question that J. T. Tran has posed to a roomful of Yale undergraduates at a Master's Tea at Silliman College. His answer is typically Asian: practice. Tran is a pickup artist who goes by the handle Asian Playboy. He travels the globe running "boot camps," mostly for Asian male students, in the art of attraction. Today, he has been invited to Yale by the Asian American Students Alliance.

"Creepy can be fixed," Tran explains to the standing-room-only crowd. "Many guys just don't realize how to project themselves." These are the people whom Tran spends his days with, a new batch in a new city every week: nice guys, intelligent guys, motivated guys, who never figured out how to be successful with women. Their mothers had kept them at home to study rather than let them date or socialize. Now Tran's company, ABCs of Attraction, offers a remedial education that consists of three 4-hour seminars, followed by a supervised night out "in the field," in which J.T., his assistant Gareth Jones, and a tall blond wing-girl named Sarah force them to approach women. Tuition costs $1,450.

"One of the big things I see with Asian students is what I call the Asian poker face—the lack of range when it comes to facial expressions," Tran says. "How many times has this happened to you?" he asks the crowd. "You'll be out at a party with your white friends, and they will be like—'Dude, are you angry?'" Laughter fills the room. Part of it is psychological, he explains. He recalls one Korean American student he was teaching. The student was a very dedicated schoolteacher who cared a lot about his students. But none of this was visible. "Sarah was trying to help him, and she was like, 'C'mon, smile, smile,' and he was like . . ." And here Tran mimes the unbearable tension of a face trying to contort itself into a simulacrum of mirth. "He was so completely unpracticed at smiling that he literally could not do it." Eventually, though, the student fought through it, "and when he finally got to smiling he was, like, really cool."

Tran continues to lay out a story of Asian American male distress that must be relevant to the lives of at least some of those who have packed Master Krauss's living room. The story he tells is one of Asian American disadvantage in the sexual marketplace, a disadvantage that he has devoted his life to overturning. Yes, it is about picking up women. Yes, it is about picking up white women. Yes, it is about attracting those women whose hair is the color of the midday sun and eyes are the color of the ocean, and it is about having sex with them. He is not going to apologize for the images of blond women plastered all over his website. This is what he prefers, what he stands for, and what he is selling: the courage to pursue anyone you want, and the skills to make the person you desire desire you back. White guys do what they want; he is going to do the same.

But it is about much more than this, too. It is about altering the perceptions of Asian men—perceptions that are rooted in the ways they behave, which are in turn rooted in the way they were raised—through a course of behavior modification intended to teach them how to be the socially dominant figures that they are not perceived to be. It is a program of, as he puts it to me later, "social change through pickup."

Tran offers his own story as an exemplary Asian underdog. Short, not good-looking, socially inept, sexually null. "If I got a B, I would be whipped," he remembers of his childhood. After college, he worked as an aerospace engineer at Boeing and Raytheon, but internal politics disfavored him. Five years into his career, his entire white cohort had been promoted above him. "I knew I needed to learn about social dynamics, because just working hard wasn't cutting it."

His efforts at dating were likewise "a miserable failure." It was then that he turned to "the seduction community," a group of men on Internet message boards like alt.seduction.fast. It began as a "support group for losers" and later turned into a program of self-improvement. Was charisma something you could teach? Could confidence be reduced to a formula? Was it merely something that you either possessed or did not possess, as a function of the experiences you had been through in life, or did it emerge from specific forms of behavior? The members of the group turned their computer science and engineering brains to the question. They wrote long accounts of their dates and subjected them to collective scrutiny. They searched for patterns in the raw material and filtered these experiences through social-psychological research. They eventually built a model.

This past Valentine's Day, during a weekend boot camp in New York City sponsored by ABCs of Attraction, the model is being played out. Tran and Jones are teaching their students how an alpha male stands (shoulders thrown back, neck fully extended, legs planted slightly wider than the shoulders). "This is going to feel very strange to you if you're used to slouching, but this is actually right," Jones says. They explain how an alpha male walks (no shuffling; pick your feet up entirely off the ground; a slight sway in the shoulders). They identify the proper distance to stand from "targets" (a slightly bent arm's length). They explain the importance of "kino escalation." (You must touch her. You must not be afraid to do this.) They are teaching the importance of subcommunication: what you convey about yourself before a single word has been spoken. They explain the importance of intonation. They explain what intonation is. "Your voice moves up and down in pitch to convey a variety of different emotions."

All of this is taught through a series of exercises. "This is going to feel completely artificial," says Jones on the first day of training. "But I need you to do the biggest shit-eating grin you've ever made in your life." Sarah is standing in the corner with her back to the students—three Indian guys, including one in a turban, three Chinese guys, and one Cambodian. The students have to cross the room, walking as an alpha male walks, and then place their hands on her shoulder—firmly but gently—and turn her around. Big smile. Bigger than you've ever smiled before. Raise your glass in a toast. Make eye contact and hold it. Speak loudly and clearly. Take up space without apology. This is what an alpha male does.

Before each student crosses the floor of that bare white cubicle in midtown, Tran asks him a question. "What is good in life?" Tran shouts.

The student then replies, in the loudest, most emphatic voice he can muster: "To crush my enemies, see them driven before me, and to hear the lamentation of their women—in my bed!"

For the intonation exercise, students repeat the phrase "I do what I want" with a variety of different moods.

"Say it like you're happy!" Jones shouts. ("I do what I want.") Say it like you're sad! ("I do what I want." The intonation utterly unchanged.) Like you're sad! ("I . . . do what I want.") Say it like you've just won five million dollars! ("I do what I want.")

Raj, a twenty-six-year-old Indian virgin, can barely get his voice to alter during the intonation exercise. But on Sunday night, on the last evening of the boot camp, I watch him cold-approach a set of women at the Hotel Gansevoort and engage them in conversation for a half-hour. He does not manage to "number close" or "kiss close." But he had done something that not very many people can do.

Of the dozens of Asian Americans I spoke with for this story, many were successful artists and scientists; or good-looking and socially integrated leaders; or tough, brassy, risk-taking, street-smart entrepreneurs. Of course, there are lots of such people around—do I even have to point that out? They are no more morally worthy than any other kind of Asian person. But they have figured out some useful things.

The lesson about the bamboo ceiling that James Hong learned from his interviewer at IBM stuck, and after working for a few years at Hewlett-Packard, he decided to strike out on his own. His first attempts at entrepreneurialism failed, but he finally struck pay dirt with a simple, not terribly refined idea that had a strong primal appeal: hotornot.com. Hong and his cofounder eventually sold the site for roughly $20 million.

Hong ran hotornot.com partly as a kind of incubator to seed in his employees the habits that had served him well. "We used to hire engineers from Berkeley—almost all Asian—who were on the cusp of being entrepreneurial but were instead headed toward jobs at big companies," he says. "We would train them in how to take risk, how to run things themselves. I remember encouraging one employee to read *The Game*"—the infamous pickup-artist textbook—"because I figured growing the *cojones* to take risk was applicable to being an entrepreneur."

If the bamboo ceiling is ever going to break, it's probably going to have less to do with any form of behavior assimilation than with the emergence of risk takers whose success obviates the need for Asians to meet someone else's behavioral standard. People like Steve Chen, who was one of the creators of YouTube, or Kai and Charles Huang, who created Guitar Hero. Or Tony Hsieh, the founder of Zappos.com, the online shoe retailer that he sold to Amazon for about a billion dollars in 2009. Hsieh is a short Asian man who speaks tersely and is devoid of obvious charisma. One cannot imagine him being promoted in an American corporation. And yet he has proved that an awkward Asian guy can be a formidable CEO and the unlikeliest of management gurus.

Hsieh didn't have to conform to Western standards of comportment because he adopted early on the Western value of risk taking. Growing up, he would play recordings of himself in the morning practicing the violin, in lieu of actually practicing. He credits the experience he had running a pizza business at Harvard as more important than anything he learned in class. He had an instinctive sense of what the real world would require of him, and he knew that nothing his parents were teaching him would get him there.

You don't, by the way, have to be a Silicon Valley hotshot to break through the bamboo ceiling. You can also be a chef like Eddie Huang, whose little restaurant on the Lower East Side, Bao-Haus, sells delicious pork buns. Huang grew up in Orlando with a hard-core Tiger Mom and a disciplinarian father. "As a kid, psychologically, my day was all about not getting my ass kicked," he says. He gravitated toward the black kids at school, who also knew something about corporal punishment. He was the smallest member of his football team, but his coach named him MVP in the seventh grade. "I was defensive tackle and right guard because I was just mean. I was nasty. I had this mentality where I was like, 'You're going to accept me or I'm going to fuck you up.'"

Huang had a rough twenties, bumping repeatedly against the bamboo ceiling. In college, editors at the *Orlando Sentinel* invited him to write about sports for the paper. But when he visited the offices, "the editor came in and goes, 'Oh, no.' And his exact words:

'You can't write with that face.'" Later, in film class at Columbia, he wrote a script about an Asian American hot dog vendor obsessed with his small penis. "The screenwriting teacher was like, 'I love this. You have a lot of Woody Allen in you. But do you think you could change it to Jewish characters?'" Still later, after graduating from Cardozo School of Law, he took a corporate job, where other associates would frequently say, "You have a lot of opinions for an Asian guy."

Finally, Huang decided to open a restaurant. Selling food was precisely the fate his parents wanted their son to avoid, and they didn't talk to him for months after he quit lawyering. But Huang understood instinctively that he couldn't make it work in the professional world his parents wanted him to join. "I've realized that food is one of the only places in America where we are the top dogs," he says. "Guys like David Chang or me—we can hang. There's a younger generation that grew up eating Chinese fast food. They respect our food. They may not respect anything else, but they respect our food."

Rather than strive to make himself acceptable to the world, Huang has chosen to buy his way back in, on his own terms. "What I've learned is that America is about money, and if you can make your culture commodifiable, then you're relevant," he says. "I don't believe anybody agrees with what I say or supports what I do because they truly want to love Asian people. They like my fucking pork buns, and I don't get it twisted."

Sometime during the hundreds of hours he spent among the mostly untouched English-language novels at the Flushing branch of the public library, Jefferson Mao discovered literature's special power of transcendence, a freedom of imagination that can send you beyond the world's hierarchies. He had written to me seeking permission to swerve off the traditional path of professional striving—to devote himself to becoming an artist—but he was unsure of what risks he was willing to take. My answer was highly ambivalent. I recognized in him something of my own youthful ambition. And I knew where that had taken me.

Unlike Mao, I was not a poor, first-generation immigrant. I finished school alienated both from Asian culture (which, in my hometown, was barely visible) and the manners and mores of my white peers. But like Mao, I wanted to be an individual. I had refused both cultures as an act of self-assertion. An education spent dutifully acquiring credentials through relentless drilling seemed to me an obscenity. So did adopting the manipulative cheeriness that seemed to secure the popularity of white Americans.

Instead, I set about contriving to live beyond both poles. I wanted what James Baldwin sought as a writer—"a power which outlasts kingdoms." Anything short of that seemed a humiliating compromise. I would become an aristocrat of the spirit, who prides himself on his incompetence in the middling tasks that are the world's business. Who does not seek after material gain. Who is his own law.

This, of course, was madness. A child of Asian immigrants born into the suburbs of New Jersey and educated at Rutgers cannot be a law unto himself. The only way to approximate this is to refuse employment, because you will not be bossed around by people beneath you, and shave your expenses to the bone, because you cannot afford more, and move into a decaying Victorian mansion in Jersey City, so that your sense of eccentric distinction can be preserved in the midst of poverty, and cut yourself free of every form of bourgeois discipline, because these are precisely the habits that will keep you chained to the mediocre fate you consider worse than death.

Throughout my twenties, I proudly turned away from one institution of American life after another (for instance, a steady job), though they had already long since turned away from me. Academe seemed another kind of death—but then again, I had a transcript marred by as many F's as A's. I had come from a culture that was the middle path incarnate. And yet for some people, there can be no middle path, only transcendence or descent into the abyss.

I was descending into the abyss.

All this was well deserved. No one had any reason to think I was anything or anyone. And yet I felt entitled to demand this recognition. I knew this was wrong and impermissible; therefore I had to double down on it. The world brings low such people. It brought me low. I haven't had health insurance in ten years. I didn't earn more than $12,000 for eight consecutive years. I went three years in the prime of my adulthood without touching a woman. I did not produce a masterpiece.

I recall one of the strangest conversations I had in the city. A woman came up to me at a party and said she had been moved by a piece of writing I had published. She confessed that prior to reading it, she had never wanted to talk to me, and had always been sure, on the basis of what she could see from across the room, that I was nobody worth talking to, that I was in fact someone to avoid.

But she had been wrong about this, she told me: it was now plain to her that I was a person with great reserves of feeling and insight. She did not ask my forgiveness for this brutal misjudgment. Instead, what she wanted to know was—why had I kept that person she had glimpsed in my essay so well hidden? She confessed something of her own hidden sorrow: she had never been beautiful and had decided, early on, that it therefore fell to her to "love the world twice as hard." Why hadn't I done that?

Here was a drunk white lady speaking what so many others over the years must have been insufficiently drunk to tell me. It was the key to many things that had, and had not, happened. I understood this encounter better after learning about LEAP, and visiting Asian Playboy's boot camp. If you are a woman who isn't beautiful, it is a social reality that you will have to work twice as hard to hold anyone's attention. You can either linger on the unfairness of this or you can get with the program. If you are an Asian person who holds himself proudly aloof, nobody will respect that, or find it intriguing, or wonder if that challenging façade hides someone worth getting to know. They will simply write you off as someone not worth the trouble of talking to.

Having glimpsed just how unacceptable the world judges my demeanor, could I, too, strive to make up for my shortcomings? Practice a shit-eating grin until it becomes natural? Love the world twice as hard?

I see the appeal of getting with the program. But this is not my choice. Striving to meet others' expectations may be a necessary cost of assimilation, but I am not going to do it.

Often I think my defiance is just delusional, self-glorifying bullshit that artists have always told themselves to compensate for their poverty and powerlessness. But sometimes I think it's the only thing that has preserved me intact, and that what has been preserved is not just haughty caprice but in fact the meaning of my life. So this is what I told Mao: In lieu of loving the world twice as hard, I care, in the end, about expressing my obdurate singularity at any cost. I love this hard and unyielding part of myself more than any other reward the world has to offer a newly brightened and ingratiating demeanor, and I will bear any costs associated with it.

The first step toward self-reform is to admit your deficiencies. Though my early adulthood has been a protracted education in them, I do not admit mine. I'm fine. It's the rest of you who have a problem. Fuck all y'all.

Amy Chua returned to Yale from a long, exhausting book tour in which one television interviewer had led off by noting that Internet commenters were calling her a monster. By that point, she had become practiced at the special kind of self-presentation required of a person under public siege. "I do not think that Chinese parents are superior," she declared at the annual gathering of the Asian American Students Alliance. "I think there are many ways to be a good parent."

Much of her talk to the students, and indeed much of the conversation surrounding the book, was focused on her own parenting decisions. But just as interesting is how her parents parented her. Chua was plainly the product of a brute-force Chinese education. *Battle Hymn of the Tiger Mother* includes many lessons she was taught by her parents—lessons any LEAP student would recognize. "Be modest, be humble, be simple," her mother told her. "Never complain or make excuses," her father instructed. "If something seems unfair at school, just prove yourself by working twice as hard and being twice as good."

In the book, Chua portrays her distaste for corporate law, which she practiced before going into academe. "My entire three years at the firm, I always felt like I was play-acting, ridiculous in my suit," she writes. This malaise extended even earlier, to her time as a student. "I didn't care about the rights of criminals the way others did, and I froze whenever a professor called on me. I also wasn't naturally skeptical and questioning; I just wanted to write down everything the professor said and memorize it."

At the AASA gathering at Yale, Chua made the connection between her upbringing and her adult dissatisfaction. "My parents didn't sit around talking about politics and philosophy at the dinner table," she told the students. Even after she had escaped from corporate law and made it onto a law faculty, "I was kind of lost. I just didn't feel the passion." Eventually, she made a name for herself as the author of popular books about foreign policy and became an award-winning teacher. But it's plain that she was no better prepared for legal scholarship than she had been for corporate law. "It took me a long, long time," she said. "And I went through lots and lots of rejection." She recalled her extended search for an academic post, in which she was "just not able to do a good interview, just not able to present myself well."

In other words, *Battle Hymn* provides all the material needed to refute the very cultural polemic for which it was made to stand. Chua's Chinese education had gotten her through an elite schooling, but it left her unprepared for the real world. She does not hide any of this. She had set out, she explained, to write a memoir that was "defiantly self-incriminating"—and the result was a messy jumble of conflicting impulses, part provocation, part self-critique. Western readers rode roughshod over this paradox and made of Chua a kind of Asian minstrel figure. But more than anything else, *Battle Hymn* is a very American project—one no traditional Chinese person would think to undertake. "Even if you hate the book," Chua pointed out, "the one thing it is not is meek."

"The loudest duck gets shot" is a Chinese proverb. "The nail that sticks out gets hammered down" is a Japanese one. Its Western correlative: "The squeaky wheel gets the grease." Chua had told her story and been hammered down. Yet here she was, fresh from her hammering, completely unbowed.

There is something salutary in that proud defiance. And though the debate she sparked about Asian American life has been of questionable value, we will need more people with the same kind of defiance, willing to push themselves into the spotlight and to make some noise, to beat people up, to seduce women, to make mistakes, to become entrepreneurs, to stop doggedly pursuing official paper emblems attesting to their worthiness, to stop thinking those scraps of paper will secure anyone's happiness, and to dare to be interesting.

Contributors' Notes

BENJAMIN ANASTAS is the author of two novels, *An Underachiever's Diary* and *The Faithful Narrative of a Pastor's Disappearance*, and his memoir, *Too Good to Be True*, will be published in October 2012. His short fiction, journalism, essays, and reviews have appeared in the *Paris Review*, the *New York Times Magazine*, *Harper's Magazine*, and *Bookforum*. He teaches in the undergraduate writing program at Columbia University and is a member of the core faculty at the Bennington Writing Seminars.

MARCIA ANGELL, MD, is senior lecturer in social medicine at Harvard Medical School and former editor in chief of the *New England Journal of Medicine*. She is the author of two books for the public, *The Truth About the Drug Companies: How They Deceive Us and What to Do About It* and *Science on Trial: The Clash of Medical Evidence and the Law in the Breast Implant Case*, as well as many articles on medical issues. Along with Arnold S. Relman, she received the George Polk Award for Magazine Reporting for their 2002 article in the New Republic, "The Insatiable Greed of the Pharmaceutical Industry." In 1997, *Time* magazine named her one of the twenty-five most influential Americans.

MIAH (MARY) ARNOLD is a native of Myton, Utah. Her first novel, *Sweet Land of Bigamy*, was released in July 2012. Her stories and essays have been published in the *Michigan Quarterly Review*, *Cite*, *NANO Fiction*, *Confrontation*, *Painted Bride Quarterly*, and the *South Dakota Review*. She has received a Barthelme Prize, an Inprint/Diana P. Hobby Award, and a Houston Arts Alliance Established Artist Grant for her work. She is a graduate of Carleton College and received a PhD in literature and creative writing from the University of Houston. She lives in Houston with her husband, Raj Mankad, and her children, Lila and Vishwa.

GEOFFREY BENT has published several pieces of Shakespearean criticism with Oxford University Press and the *Antioch Review,* one of which was reprinted in the international anthology *Shakespearean Criticism.* He has also published essays on art and book reviews in *Boulevard, North American Review, Pleiades,* and *Southern Review.* His novel *Silent Partners* appeared in 2003. He has written sixteen books and painted five hundred oils, and his paintings have been exhibited in museums and galleries in nineteen states. He lives in Glen Ellyn, Illinois, with his wife, Jeanette, and their daughter, Emily, and is currently working on a collection of his essays on art and artists.

ROBERT BOYERS is the editor of *Salmagundi,* director of the New York State Summer Writers Institute, and professor of English at Skidmore College. He is the author of nine books, including *Excitable Women, Damaged Men* (a collection of short stories) and *The Dictator's Dictation: Essays on the Politics of Novels and Novelists.* "A Beauty" will be included as a chapter in a just-completed memoir titled *Anecdotage and Polemic: Memoir of a Life in Ideas.*

DUDLEY CLENDINEN, a journalist and author who particularly relished his years as a columnist for the *St. Petersburg Times,* and a national correspondent and later editorial writer for the *New York Times,* had a daughter, friends, a house, and an independent life in Baltimore that he loved, but not nearly enough money or income, in 2010, when he turned sixty-six. He needed a compelling new book subject. Those problems were solved when he was diagnosed that November with amyotrophic lateral sclerosis, or Lou Gehrig's disease, which has no treatment or cure, and wrote this essay about knowing how to live and when to die the following summer for the *New York Times Sunday Review.* In response to his essay, he received almost a thousand letters and calls and messages, from all over the world, and a book contract with Algonquin Press. He does not expect to be alive when this anthology is published. He just hopes he is able to finish the book. *Dudley Clendinen died on May 30, 2012, at the age of sixty-seven.—Ed*

PAUL COLLINS is a writer specializing in history, memoir, and antiquarian literature. His seven books have been translated into eleven languages; his most recent is *The Murder of the Century* (2011). In addition to appearing on NPR's *Weekend Edition* as its "literary detective" on odd and forgotten old books, he edits the Collins Library imprint of McSweeney's Books. Collins lives in Oregon, where he teaches nonfiction in the MFA program at Portland State University.

MARK DOTY'S essay "Insatiable" will appear in *What Is the Grass,* a forthcoming book-length meditation on Walt Whitman, desire, and the ecstatic.

A winner of the National Book Award for Poetry, Doty teaches at Rutgers University and lives in New York City.

MARK EDMUNDSON is the author of seven books, including *Why Read?*, *The Fine Wisdom and Perfect Teachings of the Kings of Rock and Roll*, and *Teacher*. His newest book, *Fellow Teachers, Fellow Students,* is forthcoming and will contain "Who Are You and What Are You Doing Here?" He teaches at the University of Virginia.

A new collection of JOSEPH EPSTEIN's, called *Essays in Biography,* will be published this autumn. He has begun work on a book on charm.

JONATHAN FRANZEN was educated in the Missouri public schools and at Swarthmore College. He is the author of the novels *The Twenty-Seventh City, Strong Motion, The Corrections,* and *Freedom,* along with a collection of essays, *How to Be Alone,* and *The Discomfort Zone: A Personal History.* He lives in New York City.

MALCOLM GLADWELL is a staff writer for *The New Yorker.* He is also the author of four books, *The Tipping Point: How Little Things Can Make a Big Difference* (2000); *Blink: The Power of Thinking Without Thinking* (2005); *Outliers: The Story of Success* (2008); and *What the Dog Saw: And Other Adventures* (2009).

PETER HESSLER is a staff writer at *The New Yorker* and has written three books about China. He lived in southwestern Colorado for a number of years but is now a resident of Cairo, Egypt.

EWA HRYNIEWICZ-YARBROUGH is a literary translator and essayist. Her essays have appeared in the *Normal School, Ploughshares,* the *American Scholar, TriQuarterly,* the *Threepenny Review,* and the *San Francisco Chronicle.* Her most recent book of translations is *They Carry a Promise,* a collection of poems by Janusz Szuber published in 2009. A native of Poland, she divides her time between Boston and Kraków.

GARRET KEIZER is the author of *Privacy* (2012), *The Unwanted Sound of Everything We Want: A Book About Noise, Help, The Enigma of Anger, God of Beer, A Dresser of Sycamore Trees,* and *No Place but Here.* His work has appeared in *The Best American Science and Nature Writing 2002, The Best American Poetry 2005,* and *The Best American Essays 2007* and *2009.* A contributing editor at *Harper's Magazine* and a recent Guggenheim Fellow, he is currently at work on a book based on the essay that appears in this volume. He and his wife live in northeastern Vermont.

DAVID J. LAWLESS is president emeritus of St. Mary's University College in Calgary, Alberta. He was its founding president after retiring as president of St. Francis Xavier University in Nova Scotia. He also served as vice president (academic) of the University of Manitoba. He met his wife, Maria-Pilar Ruiz, who was from Madrid, Spain, while he was a graduate student at the University of British Columbia in Vancouver. They were married for more than fifty years and had six children. Maria-Pilar died suddenly in 2010 after a lengthy illness. Dr. Lawless is the author of textbooks and research papers in psychology. This is his first published work outside his professional field. He was born in Victoria, British Columbia, a long time ago. He now lives in Calgary and is an avid vegetable gardener.

ALAN LIGHTMAN is a novelist, essayist, and physicist, with a PhD in theoretical physics. He has served on the faculties of Harvard University and MIT and was the first person to receive dual faculty appointments at MIT in science and in the humanities. His essays and articles have appeared in *Harper's Magazine,* the *Atlantic, The New Yorker, Granta,* and other publications. Lightman's *Einstein's Dreams* was an international bestseller and has been translated into thirty languages. His novel *The Diagnosis* was a finalist for the National Book Award for Fiction. His latest book is *Mr g,* a novel about the Creation as told by God.

SANDRA TSING LOH is a contributing editor at the *Atlantic,* a frequent commentator on public radio, and a monologist who has performed several solo shows off-Broadway. Her books include *Depth Takes a Holiday, A Year in Van Nuys, Aliens in America,* and *Mother on Fire.* Her next book, tentatively titled *The Bitch Is Back (or Menopalooza),* inspired by this essay, is scheduled to be published next year.

KEN MURRAY was a family doctor and clinical assistant professor of family medicine in Los Angeles until his retirement in 2006. He is a regular contributor to *Zocalo Public Square* and was adviser to "Weekly Briefings from the *New England Journal of Medicine.*" He was a contributor to the seminal book *How to Report Statistics in Medicine* by Thomas Lang and Michelle Secic. His volunteer activities in water quality led to his sharing in the 2011 U.S. Water Prize.

FRANCINE PROSE is the author of more than twenty books. Her most recent is a novel, *My New American Life.* She is a distinguished visiting writer at Bard College, a contributing editor at *Harper's Magazine,* and a member of the American Academy of Arts and Sciences and the American Academy of Arts and Letters.

RICHARD SENNETT teaches at New York University and at the London School of Economics. His most recent book is *Together: The Rituals, Pleasures and Politics of Co-operation* (2012).

LAUREN SLATER is the author of *Opening Skinner's Box: Great Psychological Experiments of the Twentieth Century, Prozac Diary, Lying: A Metaphorical Memoir,* and several other books of fiction and nonfiction. She publishes regularly in *Elle, More,* the *New York Times Magazine,* and *O Magazine.* Her most current book is *The $60,000 Dog: My Life with Animals,* to be published in November 2012. This is Slater's fourth appearance in *The Best American Essays,* and she served as its guest editor in 2006. Slater lives with her family on Sitting Rock Farm in Harvard, Massachusetts.

JOSE ANTONIO VARGAS, a multimedia storyteller, is the founder of Define American, a media campaign that seeks to elevate the immigration conversation. He has written for *The New Yorker, Rolling Stone,* and the *Atlantic* and covered technology, culture, HIV/AIDS, and the 2008 presidential campaign for the *Washington Post,* where he shared a Pulitzer Prize for coverage of the Virginia Tech massacre. He's working on a memoir inspired by his essay "Outlaw."

WESLEY YANG is a contributing editor at *New York.* His writing has also been published in the *New York Times, n+1, Bookforum,* and *Tablet Magazine,* among others, and he has won a National Magazine Award. He lives in New York and is working on his first book.

Notable Essays of 2011

SELECTED BY ROBERT ATWAN

MARCIA ALDRICH
    Of Pumps and Death, *Normal School*, Spring.
SUE ALLISON
    Made to Measure, *Antioch Review*, Winter.
JACOB M. APPEL
    An Absence of Jello, *Southwest Review*, vol. 96, no. 2.
CHRIS ARTHUR
    Reading Life, *Southwest Review*, vol. 96, no. 4.

MATTHEW JAMES BABCOCK
    The Handicap Bug, *Fiddleback*, vol. 1, no. 6.
CHRIS BACHELDER
    The Dead Chipmunk, *Believer*, February.
NICHOLSON BAKER
    Why I'm a Pacifist, *Harper's Magazine*, May.
POE BALLANTINE
    Hope, *Ecotone*, Spring.
ELIZABETH BANICKI
    Wrong Side of the Track, *Slake*, no. 2.
HELEN BAROLINI
    My Bernini Box, *Southwest Review*, vol. 96, no. 3.

CHARLES BAXTER
    Hatching Monsters, *Lapham's Quarterly*, Winter.
JOHN BERGER
    One Message Leading to Another, *Massachusetts Review*, vol. 52, no. 3–4.
EMILY BERNARD
    The Refuge of the Classroom, *Oxford American*, no. 74.
SVEN BIRKETS
    The Mother of Possibility, *Lapham's Quarterly*, Spring.
TOM BISSELL
    The Last Lion, *Oustide*, October.
CHARLES BOWDEN
    The Lives of the Saints, *Aperture*, Winter.
ANDREW BOYD
    First Empty Your Cup, *Sun*, December.
MICHAEL P. BRANCH
    Freebirds, *Orion*, November/December.

BILL CAPOSSERE
    Fog, *Alaska Quarterly Review*, Spring/Summer.
RON CAPPS
    Yellow, *JMWW*, Fall.

JOHN HALES
Helpline, *Missouri Review,*
Spring.
JEFFREY HAMMOND
Thirteen Ways of Looking at a
Blackboard, *Hotel Amerika,* Fall.
RACHAEL HANEL
Bello Rostro de la Muerte, *New
Delta Review,* June.
NICOLE HARDY
Single, Female, Mormon, Alone,
New York Times (Modern Love),
January 9.
JOHN HASKELL
The Persistence of Muybridge, *A
Public Space,* no. 12.
SUSAN CAROL HAUSER
Measures of Loss, *Terrain: A
Journal of the Built and Natural
Environments,* Spring/Summer.
AMES HAWKINS
Optickal Allusion, *Water-Stone
Review,* no. 14.
CLARISSA HAY
Queens of Pain, *New Letters,* vol.
78, no. 1.
ROBIN HEMLEY
To the Rainforest Room, *Orion,*
May/June.
ALEKSANDAR HEMON
The Aquarium, *The New Yorker,*
June 13/20.
MICHELLE HERMAN
No Place Like Home, *River Teeth,*
Fall.
CHRISTOPHER HITCHENS
Widow of Opportunity, *Vanity
Fair,* December.
JEAN HOEFLING
Remission, *Relief,* 5/2, Winter.
RICHARD HOFFMAN
Love and Fury, *River Teeth,* Fall.
LINDA HOGAN
Snow, *Orion,* March/April.
KAREN HOLMBERG
In the Museum of the Body,
Alone, *Black Warrior Review,*
Spring/Summer.

AMY HOLWERDA
Family History, *Sycamore Review,*
Winter/Spring.
LANDON HOULE
The Plains We Cross, *Natural
Bridge,* Fall.
DANIEL WALKER HOWE
Classical Education in America,
Wilson Quarterly, Spring.
HUA HSU
Seeing Jay-Z in Taipei, *Daedalus,*
Winter.
ANDREW HUDGINS
Helen Keller Answers the Iron,
Kenyon Review, Spring.
WILLIAM HUHN
I Know You Rider, *Jabberwock,*
Summer.
T. R. HUMMER
A Length of Hemp Rope,
Crab Orchard Review, Summer/
Fall.
BARBARA HURD
Dissonance, *Sun,* May.
SIRI HUSTVEDT
The Real Story, *Salmagundi,*
Spring/Summer.

MICHAEL IDOV
The Movie Set That Ate Itself,
GQ, November.
PICO IYER
The Terminal Check, *Granta,* no.
116.

LAWRENCE JACKSON
Christmas in Baltimore, 2009,
n+1, no. 12.
HOLLY JACOBSON
On Other Shores, *Memoir (and),*
no. 8.
PAT JORDAN
The Haircut, *Southern Review,*
Spring.

DONALD KAGEN
On Patriotism, *Yale Review,*
October.

KITTY KELLEY
Unauthorized, but Not Untrue, *American Scholar,* Winter.

RALPH KEYES
Euphemania: Show Me the Liquidity, *Antioch Review,* Winter.

JUDITH KITCHEN
Night Piece, *Georgia Review,* Fall.

PAUL A. KRAMER
The Importance of Being Turbaned, *Antioch Review,* Spring.

CAROLYN KREMERS
John Haines and the Dream Place, *Permafrost.*

KIM DANA KUPPERMAN
Attraction Next Exit, *River Teeth,* Fall.

MATT LABASH
Eyewitness to History!, *Weekly Standard,* October 17.

ROBERT LACY
Four of a Kind, *Sewanee Review,* Spring.

LINDA LANCIONE
The Currency of Love, *New Letters,* vol. 77, no. 2.

BERYL LANG
Replenishing the World, *Michigan Quarterly Review,* Winter.

LEWIS LAPHAM
Democracy 101, *Harper's Magazine,* April.

SYDNEY LEA
Now, Look, *River Teeth,* Fall.

AMY LEACH
The Safari, *Massachusetts Review,* vol. 52, no. 1.

JOHN PATRICK LEARY
Detroitism, *Guernica,* January.

BARBARA F. LEFCOWITZ
Memory and Photography, *Southwest Review,* vol. 96, no. 2.

DAVID LEHMAN
Why I Love *You, American Scholar,* Summer.

NATON LESLIE
Odd Jobs, *Florida Review,* vol. 36, no. 1–2.

LEILA LEVINSON
Cracking Open the Silence,*War, Literature, and the Arts,* no. 23.

AIMEE LEVITT
Little House in the Present, *Riverfront Times* (St. Louis), November 24–30.

E. J. LEVY
To Cèpe, with Love (or, The Alchemy of Longing), *Salmagundi,* Spring/Summer.

CHARLIE LEWIS
Apartment No. 9, *Ten Spurs,* no. 5.

MICHAEL LEWIS
The King of Human Error, *Vanity Fair,* December.

K. N. LIAO
Bodies in Motion, *Fourth River,* Autumn.

MARK LIEBENOW
Hiking over the Edge, *Chautauqua,* no. 8.

MEL LIVATINO
The Perfect Raincoat, *Under the Sun,* no. 20.

SUSAN LOHAFER
In the Bullring, *Iowa Review,* Spring.

PHILLIP LOPATE
Between Insanity and Fat Dullness: How I Became an Emersonian, *Harper's Magazine,* January.

BRETT LOTT
Writing with So Great a Cloud of Witnesses, *Image,* no. 69.

TRACY LYNCH
Inappropriate, *Brain, Child,* Fall.

PAT MacENULTY
Fixing the Deck, *Apalachee Review,* no. 61.

STEVE MACONE
Standup Comity, *Morning News,* November 28.

JANE MAHER
Raw Material, *Hudson Review,* Winter.

THOMAS MALLON
Never Happened, *The New Yorker,*
November 21.

TED MANN
Magnificent Visions, *Vanity Fair,*
December.

HARVEY MANSFIELD
The Wisdom of "The Federalist,"
New Criterion, February.

CLANCY MARTIN
The Drunk's Club, *Harper's
Magazine,* January.

MICHAEL MARTONE
Against the Beloved, *Upstreet,*
no. 7.

DAVID MASELLO
The Empress's New Clothes,
Memoir (and), no. 8.

WYATT MASON
The Danger Artist, *GQ,*
December.

DESIRAE MATHERLY
Flashbacks and Proliferations,
Hotel Amerika, Fall.

NANCY MCCABE
Threads, *Prairie Schooner,*
Fall.

TYLER MCCABE
Something Carries Through,
Ruminate, Autumn.

MAC MCCLELLAND
Goodbye, Columbus, *Mother Jones,*
November/December.

HEATHER A. MCDONALD
How to Fix Everything, *Creative
Nonfiction,* Spring.

BILL MCKIBBEN
A Little Leeway, *Orion,* July/
August.

JAMES MCMANUS
Full Tilt Boogie: The UIGEA
and You, *Grantland.com,*
December 8.

JOHN MCPHEE
Progression, *The New Yorker,*
November 17.

REBECCA MEAD
Middlemarch and Me, *The New
Yorker,* February 14/21.

KAT MEADS
Neighbor Trim, Also Awake, *Crab
Orchard Review,* Summer/Fall.

GILBERT MEILAENDER
Transitional Humanity, *New
Atlantis,* Spring.

DAPHNE MERKIN
Between Love and Madness, *Elle,*
July.

KENT MEYERS
The Makings, *Georgia Review,* Fall.

MEGAN MICHELSON
In a House by the River, *Outside,*
February.

DEBRA MONROE
The Sex Trade in Northwest
Wisconsin, *Morning News,*
July 13.

BARRY MOSER
A Bookwright's Tale, *Image,*
no. 71.

KERMIT MOYER
A Stranger to Himself,
Washingtonian, August.

ALAN NASLUND
What I Saw in the Country,
Minnetonka Review, Spring.

DEBORAH NELSON
The Cruelest Show on Earth,
Mother Jones, November/
December.

JESSICA HENDRY NELSON
The Whitest Winter Light,
Alligator Juniper, 2011.

JOHN NELSON
Parting Words, *Massachusetts
Review,* vol. 52, no. 1.

MARC NIESON
In the Basement, *Green Mountains
Review,* vol. 24, no. 1.

NANCY J. NORDENSON
Metrics, *Indiana Review,* Winter.

MARY NORRIS
It Hurt to Hum, *Epiphany,*
Spring/Summer.

JOSIP NOVAKOVICH
Shopping for a Better Country,
Witness, vol. 24, no. 1.

SARAH WELLS
  Those Summers, These Days,
  Ascent, December 11.
SEAN WILENTZ
  The Mirage, *New Republic,*
  November 17.
CHRYSTAL WILLIAMS
  Mirror, Mirror: A Guide to
  Pathos, *Tin House,* no. 50.
MELORA WOLFE
  Hearing Voices, *Gettysburg Review,*
  Autumn.
LAURA ESTHER WOLFSON
  Haunting Synagogues, *Bellingham
  Review,* Spring.

JAMES WOOD
  Shelf Life, *The New Yorker,*
  November 7.
SAINT JAMES HARRIS WOOD
  The Wild Courtroom Speech,
  Inkwell, Fall.

ROB ZARETSKY
  Plunging to Earth, *American
  Scholar,* Summer.

Notable Special Issues of 2011

Antioch Review, ed. Robert S. Fogarty,
  Illuminated Manuscripts and
  Other Enlightenments, Spring.
Asian American Literary Review, guest
  eds. Rajini Srikanth and Parag
  Khandhar, Commemorating the
  Tenth Anniversary of September
  11, Fall 2011.
Bellevue Literary Review, ed. Danielle
  Ofri, Tenth Anniversary Issue, Fall.
California, ed. Wendy Miller, Articles
  of Faith, Spring.
Chautauqua, eds. Jill Gerard and
  Philip Gerard, Nature and the
  Natural World, no. 8.
Cimarron Review, eds. E. P. Walkiewicz
  and Toni Graham, Work, Spring/
  Summer.
Columbia Journalism Review, ed. Mike
  Hoyt, Fiftieth Anniversary Issue,
  November/December.
Conjunctions, ed. Bradford Morrow,
  Kin, no. 57.
Daedalus, guest ed. Gerald Early, Race
  in the Age of Obama, Winter;
  guest ed. Lawrence D. Bobo, Race,
  Inequality, and Culture, Spring.
Fugue, ed. Mary Morgan, The Play
  Issue, Winter/Spring.
Hotel Amerika, ed. David Lazar,
  Aphorisms, Spring.

Manoa, ed. Frank Stewart, Almost
  Heaven: On the Human and
  Divine, Winter.
Massachusetts Review, eds. Jim Hicks
  and Kevin Bowen, Casualty, vol.
  52, no. 3–4.
Michigan Quarterly Review, ed. Keith
  Taylor, The Great Lakes: Love
  Song and Lament, Spring.
New Atlantis, ed. Adam Keiper, Place
  and Placelessness in America,
  Spring.
New Letters, ed. Robert Stewart,
  Connected, vol. 77, no. 3–4.
New Literary History, eds. Rita Felski
  and Herbert F. Tucker, Context?,
  Autumn.
North Dakota Quarterly, ed. Robert W.
  Lewis, Hemingway in His and Our
  Time, Winter/Spring.
Oxford American, ed. Marc Smirnoff,
  The Education Issue, no. 74.
Slake, eds. Laurie Ochoa and Joseph
  Donnelly, Crossing Over, no. 2.
Think, ed. Christine Yurick, The
  Symposium on Form, Spring.
Tin House, ed. Rob Spillman, Beauty,
  no. 50.
Witness, ed. Amber Withycombe,
  Blurring Borders, vol. 24, no. 1.